Desert Strike

Desert Strike

Sundown Apocalypse Book 4

Leo Nix

Contact the author, Leo Nix: http://www.leo-nix.com/

Facebook - https://www.facebook.com/LeoNixSundown/

Web: http://www.wingtipdesign.com.au/

A special 'thank you' to Marja and Terrie for your generous support and the difficult task of proof reading; to Peter, for his ongoing technical assistance in all things military. I am especially indebted to Danny for his awesome editing and US military insights without which this book would be far less readable and enjoyable.

I would like to take this opportunity to acknowledge and show respect, to the first Australians, our land's traditional custodians, the Australian aboriginal people.

Dedication: To my brothers, James and Mark, who supported my every hair-brained idea.

AUSTRALIA

Statute Miles

Dominion Capitals   Colony Capitals
Size of type indicates relative importance of places
Copyright, J. W. CLEMENT CO.,
Matthews-Northrup Works, Buffalo, N. Y.

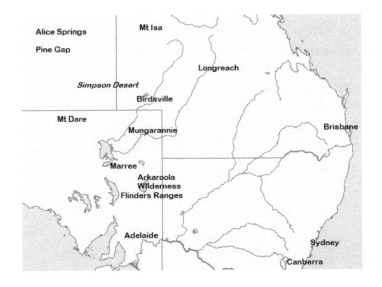

Use anger to throw them into disarray, use humility to make them haughty.
Tire them by flight, cause division among them.
Attack when they are unprepared, make your move when they least expect it.
Be extremely subtle, even to the point of formlessness.
Be extremely mysterious, even to the point of soundlessness.
This way you become the director of your opponent's fate.
Sun Tzu, The Art of War (circa 5th Century BC)

Contents

Chapter 1

Of Horses, Camels and Donkeys

"Hey, watch out there!" yelled Nulla instructing the Alice Springs boys working with one of the wild horses. "These brumbies can kick backwards so don't walk around his tail 'til he knows you a bit better."

Nulla's leading horse-breaker was Kristofer, he loved horses, always had. In Darwin he would go riding when he was off duty. It was a good opportunity to pick up girls but right now he wasn't so keen on horses or girls. They'd been at it all week and he'd lost count of how many horses and camels they'd rounded up and broken in.

"Nulla, it's got to be knock-off time, mate. Come on, we're all stuffed," cried the lean, suntanned horseman coughing up a lungful of dust and sand.

"Not until we finish this mob. Only three more to go then we'll call it a day," said Nulla, wiping the sweat from his eyes for the umpteenth time.

"That should only be an hour or so, beauty." Kris cracked a smiled for the first time that day.

"That's three each, mate," Nulla managed to grin back at him. With the constant heat, scorching sun and choking dust they were all simply exhausted.

Sundown had taken Chan off patrol to help them. The young ex-Revelationist was doing way too many back-to-back patrols trying to get payback for losing his best friend, John. It was good to see him laughing as he helped along with the bike patrol boys and a dozen of the Alice Springs troops experienced in working with horses and camels.

Some were kangaroo, dingo and pig shooters; some were stockmen from the cattle stations; and some just loved animals. Together they'd broken in over two hundred horses and camels.

"Nulla, what sort of horses are these anyway?" asked Simon. The dark-haired, lanky teenager, leaned heavily on the stockyard rails. His chest still heaving with the effort of lifting the bar for the wranglers as each horse or camel entered for training.

"Most of these are Walers. They're what's left over from the Australian Light Horse. They had the last successful cavalry charge in the history of warfare. That was at Beersheba, in the deserts of Palestine during World War One," Nulla called over his shoulder as he was about to head over to see if Fat Boy had arrived with their lunch. "They bred Walers for the British soldiers of the East India Company a few centuries ago. They're tough, courageous and have a gentle nature." But catching them in the wild and breaking them in was time consuming and hard work.

Arthur was seated just above Simon on the timber railings of the yard. His face was covered in fine, red desert dust, and there were rivulets of dirt running from his scalp to his chin. "Hey Nulla, where did camels come from? Are they Australian too?"

Nulla turned and trotted his horse over to the boys. "Arty, both horses and camels were brought to Australia. Horses arrived with the convicts and the camels came later, to carry supplies to the stations and homesteads out in the desert." Nulla shook his head and wondered what on earth kids learned at school these days. "They carried wool, minerals and farm produce to be sold in the cities. With the arrival of the railways and trucks they were left to run wild."

Simon was deep in thought and looked up as Nulla finished explaining. "So, if camels came from England, how come they can live in the hot desert? Shouldn't they die from heatstroke?" he asked.

Again Nulla shook his head in disbelief. "Camels came from Arabia and the horses came from India," he paused and thought for a moment, "at least I think so anyway." He tipped his hat back off his forehead and considered how to extract himself. He'd only had a few years of schooling himself, just enough to read and write.

"You'd better ask Heidi or Tricia… or someone who finished school. I'm not really sure where horses or camels come from."

Simon winked at Arthur who grinned back, the tracks of mud on his face made him look like a zombie.

"Does that mean you don't know, boss?" he asked, his mischievous grin caught Nulla's eye and he knew Simon was back to his old tricks.

"I tell you what, boys. If Luke knows where horses and camels come from, I'll shout you all a beer." Nulla knew this would shut them up.

"Boss, what if Luke doesn't know? Do we still get a beer then?" Simon was always willing to push Nulla every chance he got.

"Well, let me just say, if Luke doesn't know then you all owe me a beer."

"Hey boss, we're under age and you're not allowed to give us alcohol. So if we win then we still don't win do we?"

Nulla grinned, his eyes crinkled into slits and he laughed. "I think you grow smarter by the day, Simon. I can't give you alcohol but I can give you a kick up the rear-end if you don't open the gate for Kris here."

Kris was waiting patiently to enter the training yard with his camel while Simon jumped down off the fence. With the help of his friend, Arthur, they lifted the solid timber gate open for what was probably the hundredth time that day.

"Come on boys, slowly, just let them get use to you. You're their friend, their protector not their dominatrix," called Kris, teaching the boys how to break in the sensitive camels the 'Nulla way'. "Remember, camels are like horses, they're herd animals, they like company. They form friendships and they like to follow. Herd animals like to belong to a group. We're their herd and you're their leader so do it gently and calmly." It became his mantra: 'gentle, calm, slow'.

"Boys, all my life I've broken horses the old way, but this sure beats a jarred spine and a broken head. Where I came from horse breaking was a trial of manhood. For Nulla it's a game of out-psyching them. I'd rather this way." Kris eased his muscled, raw-boned frame onto the stock yard railing.

"Nulla said he learned it from his uncle. They trained horses on the properties they worked together. He said his uncle could talk to horses and they listened," said Simon as he jumped nimbly from the raw timber rails when he heard Fat Boy's raucous call. Together they headed over to the food truck for a late lunch prior to heading back to their Christian Palace home.

Sergeant Nulla made sure everyone had a full plate in front of them before he helped himself to Fat Boy's food. When he saw Luke sit down he walked over to join his boys.

"Hey Luke, I've got a quiz for you. Can you tell us where horses and camels come from? Your mates wanted to know and I said if anyone knew, it was you."

Luke looked up at him and considered the request. "Well boss, seems to me that camels came here with the Afghans so they must have come from Afghanistan. And horses came with the British back in 1788 with Captain Phillip and the first fleet from England. So, horses came from England and camels from Afghanistan. Did I get it right?"

Some of the stockmen were listening and gladly pitched in their opinion. "Luke, horses came from England? Nah, mate, they're from Asia. The Mongols introduced them to the rest of the world. Genghis Khan conquered India and Asia and right up into Europe at one time, all on the backs of their horses. Did you know the Mongols had twenty remounts each?" said one beefy cattleman through a mouthful of stew.

"I read it was from America. They had little horses growing there millions of years ago. They had camels too, I think, before they migrated around the world across that land bridge in the Arctic. Those little camels turned into big camels in Asia and into lamas in South

America," offered another cattleman considered to be a bit of an intellectual.

"The Spanish brought them to America you dumb-arse, they weren't already there. That Columbian guy, Christopher someone, he invaded America with his horses and killed all the indians with them," said another who always offered everyone the benefit of his opinion.

Simon piped up, "Nulla, which is it? You have to choose the answer."

Nulla held up his hand, he knew he was screwed no matter which opinion he chose. "Well boys," Nulla pulled his hat off and scratched his head in exasperation. "I have no bloody idea which is the right answer. I'm going to ask Tricia and Andy tonight, I reckon they can decide. For someone who never finished high school, let alone primary school, I haven't got a damn clue."

"Does that mean we win?" Arthur had taken to speaking freely with Nulla since their time on the Arkaroola wilderness to Birdsville trip. After Luke told everyone how Arthur had been blown up and shot twice he'd become a bit of a legend in the commando.

For once Nulla didn't have an answer. "Well, Arty..." he paused, thinking, he knew he was cornered but he wasn't in the habit of backing down or giving up either. "I tell you what, let's raise the stakes. If Andy or Tricia don't know I'll make you boys a special drink of herbs and spices, it might even contain some contraband. How's that?"

The three teenagers looked at each other suspiciously. "Herbs and spices? Contraband? Nulla, if it's curry powdered then the answer is yes!" said Simon. His two mates weren't as keen on curry so they decided to take the initiative themselves.

"Nulla, Arty and I'll settle on a glass of Andy's home brew beer, cut in half and you can add the other half from Fatima and Mel's lemonade – a shandy. We don't trust your contraband, it's probably that stinky desert tobacco." Luke looked up at his friends who nodded excitedly, they loved Andy's shandies.

The men around the camp fire had been listening intently to the conversation. They were interested now they knew the boys were in a competition with their sergeant.

"So this is a competition is it?" called one cattleman. The boys nodded in response. "Well in that case we need to discuss it as unionists and decide on the proper rules for such an important competition." The others sitting around the camp fire called out in agreement.

"I propose that if Andy and Tricia come up with the same answer, an agreement that is, then let that be the official answer," proposed the cattleman who said horses came from Asia. The men replied, "hear hear".

The bloke who said the Columbian named Christopher defeated the indians with horses then said, "and let the reward be a shandy, one glass of Andy's brew mixed fifty fifty with lemonade for the boys to share. And Simon can get a curry drink if he wants," he added to a chuckle or two and more "hear hears".

Nulla was a union man from way-back as well and joined in. "Yep, that's fair, I'll agree to that. Now what's my reward if Andy and Tricia don't agree where horses and camels come from?"

The horsemen started to argue over Nulla's reward. "I would ask as to why Nulla should get a reward in the first place?" called a red haired giant finishing his second helping of Fat Boy's stew. "Why don't we all get a reward then if that's the case?"

"That's right," came the union view.

The intellectual added, "If Tricia and Andy can't agree, and if Luke got it wrong, I propose Nulla gets a day off nagging everyone."

To that everyone roared with laughter and Nulla was forced to accept a surrender.

"Righto fella's, I give in. History was never my best subject anyway. In fact none of them were." He joined in the genial laughter. It was a perfect ending to another day in the bush where they could all enjoy just being alive and free.

"Hey, Fat Boy!" called one of the sunburned stockmen as he stood to get another serving of stew. "Has Andrew finished brewing that beer he promised us thirsty horsemen? We haven't had a beer in two weeks and I'm about jack of it." He looked around at the nodding heads.

"We've run out," replied Fat Boy. "Andy said it's gonna take a few more weeks for the current brew to mature ready to drink." Fat Boy had lost weight but not an ounce of muscle. He was still the biggest bloke in the commando. "Come on, fella's, even Halo wouldn't drink it." He laughed and his roar echoed through the dust-flecked shafts of the setting sun.

Halo called out from somewhere among the cattlemen, "I heard that, Fat Boy!"

"Andy said," Fat Boy paused for emphasis, "we even have to preserve the wine and spirits at the palace because we're running out of that too."

"That's just bullshit, Fat Boy," called another one of the men. "I think it's time some of us brewers made our own and challenged you and Andy's monopoly. I reckon we could out-brew you pair hand's down," he added, "and I reckon we can make better whiskey too."

The boys had scoured the countryside for miles to bring in saddles, bridles and all kinds of horse and camel gear. They found some food and other goodies like four wheel drives, trucks and trail bikes but sadly, what beer they did find went in the first week. Sometimes it was 'finders-keepers' and many didn't return until their hangovers had cleared. Although this did happen, most of the commando shared what they found, but it wasn't enough to go around.

Since the apocalypse, alcohol had become an important defense mechanism for everybody in the commando - perhaps for everybody in the world.

"Tomorrow we start bringing the camels and horses in to the house paddocks and start training them to handle people, rifle fire and then patrolling as a group. We all need to learn how to handle them. We'll each need a dozen remounts so that means you'll work with your own mounts, horses and camels, every day. They're your mounts and if you treat them properly, they'll stand by you through thick and thin." Nulla lifted his eyes to gaze into the red sky of the afternoon remembering his uncle and their times together.

"My uncle knew some of the Light Horse fellas who were at the Beersheba cavalry charge in 1917. I told you that already, but you know what?" The broad shouldered aboriginal looked at his attentive troops. "He said that when they came home many of them went straight out to the bush to find a replacement for their neddys. Sadly some blokes never recovered after they found out their horse was shot and sold for meat at the end of the war."

Simon tipped some of Fatima's precious home-made curry powder onto the remains of his beef stew. As insensitive as ever to the sentiment of the conversation he said, "Hey boss, I'd rather ride my bike than a camel or a horse."

Nulla turned to look at Simon and screwed up his face, he was always amazed by his teenage protégé's simplistic approach to the complexities of life. He watched Simon massacre his food with his never-ending supply of curry.

"When your bike runs out of fuel, then what?"

"Get some more. We've got trucks and fuel drums," replied Simon speaking through a mouthful of food.

"Arty, would you please tell Simon what's wrong with that?" said Nulla now sitting with his own plate of Fat Boy's delicious stew and Mel's fresh baked 'desert bread'.

Arthur spoke up clearly, he did that more often these days. It seemed the more time he spent with the men of the commando the more his confidence grew.

"Well, Simon. Nulla is saying that horses and camels can eat the grass and stuff in the bush but bikes need caches of fuel everywhere. They use the same fuel as cars and four wheel drives. Don't forget that the Bushmasters and ASLAV's burn diesel. So any cars and trucks that use diesel have been grounded, except for emergency use. We need to conserve what we have and not waste it. Horses and camels can help us do that." Arty smiled and looked around at the nodding heads as the men grabbed their cups of black tea and sat back to enjoy the boy's banter.

"But what about speed and what about water? Deserts don't have water bottles growing on trees you know," came Simon's somewhat tortured reply, even he smiled at the silliness of his argument. But, being Simon, he just wouldn't let Nulla have the last say. Not that he ever won that competition, not against Nulla, only Heidi had ever done that.

"Simon, you are a dick," said Luke as he finished his stew then tapped his plate on Fat Boy's food truck for another serving.

"Simon," said Nulla in the voice he sometimes used to make a point with his boys. "I'm going to put you on the camel patrol with the rest of the bike boys. If you don't like it after a month I'll give you back your bike. How's that for a deal?"

Simon looked up from his empty plate and licked his spoon one more time to get at the last traces of curry. "Boss, you're on." He considered himself lucky to have won that small concession from Nulla. Simon knew that two almost-wins in the one day was the best he'd ever get against the 'Boss'.

Kris was perhaps the quietest of the men in the patrol. He worked solidly and was proud of his ability to handle a horse. "Nulla, let me help these cameleer bike boys when we get back to the palace. Anything that can go nearly two weeks without water and eat anything that grows is pretty impressive, I reckon."

Major Lewis, or 'Louie' as he was now known, had earlier spoken to Nulla and Kris announcing that Sundown wanted camels for their future desert patrols. While everyone wanted horses the argument for camels came from the experienced cattlemen and desert hunters. Horses would be best suited to manage their large cattle herds and to help short range patrols around the house paddocks. Camels would best be used for the long range patrols into the deep desert itself.

"I want you to make sure every bloke who touches a horse or camel knows how to ride and care for them," Major Lewis told them.

When they arrived back at the Christian Palace that evening the Girl Guards were there to greet them. They fussed over the horses like they were Red Dog's puppies.

"What is it with girls and horses?" asked Halo. "Can't you girls see these are working animals and they deserve respect not cuddles." He turned to Heidi, "One day they'll be going into battle and cuddles just won't cut it then will it." Halo led his horse into the fenced home paddock with the other tired horses. The girls followed and helped the men rub their horses down.

Halo wasn't finished though. "But if any of you lovely girls want to help then you are most welcome." His boyish smile meant he would prefer if they did the work.

Nulla decided he'd better take control as he spied Heidi about to jump down Halo's throat.

"Girls, you can help any time you're off duty, but please, ask permission from the boys." When he saw Heidi about to open her mouth again he quickly continued. "I'm sure none of us will say no, but it's just a sign of respect to the animals and their riders. Ask Kris if no one else is around." Heidi now closed her mouth and watched Nulla suspiciously. "Righto, everyone, finish grooming your horses then shower and supper on the rooftop. I heard Andy say his new beer is ready."

"Nulla?" called that familiar voice and Nulla could feel the hackles rise at the back of his neck.

"Yes, Heidi?" he said politely, knowing she was going to speak even though she knew he'd probably say no.

"Well, so... girls like horses and I think the Girl Guards should get horses too." As she spoke he lifted his eyes to the heavens. Heidi noticed and then said a little more firmly. "Come on, Nulla, don't be so blasted stubborn. Girls are better at riding and caring for horses than men, it's a known fact." That last bit was louder than the rest. Nulla was well aware that this teenager with the body and smile most men would die for was just starting to wind up.

"Kris, Simon, Luke, come over here, boys. Arthur, you'd better stay well back." Kris knew from first hand experience that what the girls wanted they always got. Not by bullying but because they were so darn cute that everyone gave in to them. Simon and Luke just stood by smiling. They knew what was coming and wouldn't miss it for the end of the world.

"Yes boss?" said Simon and Luke together. Kris reluctantly loped his tall, lean body over.

"You boys heard the boss-girl, what do you think?" he asked, his face was now a blank space.

"Simon, if you don't support us..." Heidi left the sentence unfinished.

"Simon, if you want to live... I suggest you be on our side," said Lulu giggling behind her hand. Lulu was keen on Simon, they had sat together every chance they could before they'd left for the muster.

"Boss, I think the Girl Guards are right on the ball with this," grinned Simon. "If we can just find a few donkeys for them that should make them happy."

"Simon! I'm going to beat you for that!" cried Lulu. The teenagers spent most of their spare time together now, usually sitting by the lagoon talking - as teenagers do in every society. "Bloody donkeys!"

Halo over-heard the conversation and wandered over. "Donkeys?" he asked curiously. "I love donkeys, Lulu. I'll capture one for you." He was actually quite sincere. Nulla felt a laugh struggling to burst from his chest.

"Nulla, can we take the girls out-bush and get some donkeys? Donkeys are very intelligent and gentle, I think they'd be perfect for our Girl Guards." Halo, at five foot ten and almost as wide across the shoulders was completely unaware of Heidi's stare.

She smiled to herself as she saw a crack in the door and quickly jammed her foot in. "Nulla," she started, but seeing his look she quickly changed tack, adding in a seductive voice, "Boss, can I suggest Halo and these lovely, handsome boys, go back and catch some mounts for us? I don't care much for donkeys though." Her voice was soft, sexy and her face was turned slightly upwards. The fading afternoon sunlight caught her sensual throat and cleevage. She'd seen Glenda do it when she wanted something from Nulla and was now doing it herself every chance she got. She found it worked with the other males, except Captain Johnny Walker. Nothing worked on their Girl Guards captain.

"Kris, what do you think?" called Nulla still chuckling inside. He silently admired how Heidi would do anything to get her way.

"Yeah, we could do that. We know where the donkeys hang out. They really are beautiful creatures once they trust you. They take a bit more care than horses but I think they would be well suited to the Girl Guards needs." Kris' comment made the boys laugh out loud.

"I mean, no, I didn't mean to be rude when I said that, Heidi. I mean, donkeys are special creatures, they're not like horses. They think differently, more like humans. Yeah, I'll take you out in the morning, if Nulla lets us." He looked sheepishly at Nulla.

"OK, I'll give you five days to bring back enough donkeys to train as pack animals for our patrols. If they work out OK we'll keep them." Nulla had never worked with donkeys but he was willing to try if Kris thought he could make it work.

Heidi smiled at Danni and Lulu, turned and grinned at the boys. Lulu went up and hugged Kris. "While you're out there I think you should round up some horses for our house patrols. What do you think, Kris? If you do that for us we'll make you something special for supper tonight, something just for you." She giggled as she winked at Danni and Heidi. "You're our saviour against this mean, wicked man."

Nulla laughed softly to himself. He knew he'd been manipulated into saying exactly what he was planning on doing anyway, though not with donkeys.

"If you girls join our 'animal management team' then you'll have to do a lot of the work, you know that, don't you?" he said seriously. "Our boys'll be out on patrol for weeks at a time and they'll need their remounts cared for while they're away. Can you promise me you'll do that? Every day up at the crack of dawn, feeding, grooming and caring for the animals?" He saw their faces melt with joy.

Danni spoke first. "Nulla, boss, if you let us have our own patrol animals we'll do anything for them." The girls had quickly learned that if they used the term 'boss' the way Luke and Simon did, Nulla was a lot more agreeable.

"Righto, it's now up to you lot. Let's get cleaned up and you can plan how you're going to bring back that herd of donkeys… and maybe a horse or two." Nulla chuckled to himself as he walked off to talk with Andy and Captain Walker - there was always so much to be done.

———◆———

The entire community at the Christian Palace became animated when Sundown announced that their troops would soon be mounted and sent out on training patrols. The commando soon began to organise itself into horse and cameleer cavalry from the many volunteers both men and women.

Every day some of the soldiers and their families came out to watch the boys training and handling their mounts in the stockyards behind the palace. It turned out that although they looked cute, the stubborn donkeys were more of a damn nuisance than anything. Both Kris and Halo agreed that they would train them as pack animals – or just keep them as pets.

Jaina was still getting a feel for her new found friends in the commando. As she had been with the Revelationist Intelligence some of the community treated her somewhat diffidently, some outright rudely. Jaina wasn't one to hold back though. She easily won friends and just as easily made enemies. Fortunately Donata, Chan, Blondie, Fat Boy and even Poolie, her former prisoner, stood up for her.

Private Jason Little, her genius but awkward boyfriend, had become a welcome addition. His boyish enthusiasm for anything anti-Revelationist won everyone over. It wasn't too long before he was accepted as a member of Sundown's Commando.

"Hey, Jason! Hey, Jaina! Want to come with us to see the donkeys?" called Assassin leaning out of his truck window. "Kris and the boys are going to spend the day training them. It should be fun." The lovers had just arrived from the Birdsville outpost and were taking their breakfast outside.

Jason Little, the small young man with the wide girth, suddenly stopped eating his plate of beef and bean porridge, as if he'd been shot. Jaina looked at him curiously, so did some of the others.

Assassin looked at Jason and asked, "Are you OK, Jason?"

Jason had a mouthful of bean porridge in his mouth and it began to dribble onto his shirt front as he said in a small voice, "Donkeys? You mean real donkeys? Are we allowed to touch them?"

"Yeah, you like donkeys then, Jason?" Assassin laughed.

"Yes, I love donkeys. I've loved donkeys since Shrek." He turned to Jaina excitedly. "Jaina can we go. Please, can we go with the boys?"

His well-developed girlfriend took the plate from him and set it down on the bench. He'd spilled most of it anyway.

"We'll go with the big boys." She smiled then asked affectionately. "But since when have you liked Shrek's Donkey? You've never said anything about it before."

"I never told anyone because they'd laugh at me. But Sundown wouldn't let anyone laugh at me here and neither would you or Blondie." He giggled like a kid as he ran and tried to get into the back of the truck, but it was too high for his short legs. Everyone else was now settled in for the ride except Jason and Jaina.

"Assassin, can you please come and help Jason get in the truck?" called Jaina. Jason tried again and again but he was so clumsy that, despite the well-meaning hands grabbing at him, he stayed firmly on the ground.

"Mate, hold still and I'll help you up," said Assassin as he grabbed him by the waist and lifted. The boys in the truck heaved too sending Jason over the back board to fall in a heap on the floor.

Assassin then helped Jaina into the truck although she really didn't need help - but she was female after all. All the ladies considered Assassin Creed one of the most adorable men of the commando. At just on six foot tall, blond haired, broad shouldered and a surfer's muscles that put everyone else to shame, he was constantly teased by Halo and Beamy for being the 'best looking bloke in the commando'. They reminded him of it every chance they got. Assassin had no idea what they were talking about which made the girls gush even more.

"There you go, Jaina. Just make sure young Shrek here doesn't fall out. It's a bumpy ride." Assassin then climbed into the truck cabin to begin their journey to see the donkeys.

Chapter 2

Post-Apocalypse Newcomer

It was their weekly management meeting and an impatient Tricia had matters she needed to discuss. Pinkie brought in some of Fatima's home-made cheese for everyone to try as they settled down to their meeting.

"Sundown, before we begin we've got some news for you but we need to invite someone in to tell it," said Tricia as she looked outside to see if her special visitor was ready. Nulla sat there grinning as he struggled to keep his mouth closed, he didn't want to spoil the girl's fun.

"What special visitor? Did someone just drop out of the sky?" Sundown asked absently as he enjoyed this new type of 'Fatima cheese' made from their small but growing herd of milking cows. It was the best he'd tasted so far.

Pinkie led Glenda into the room by the hand and the men stopped eating to look up. This was something they hadn't expected.

"Hi Glenda, so how's things? Ah, so what's so special? Has Nulla been a boofhead again or something?" asked Pedro. He was just as perplexed as the others.

"Nulla already knows, Pedro, but the big news is… we're going to have a baby." Glenda had picked her nails to the bone worrying over this moment but, despite rehearsing her lines, it came out in one rushed sentence.

There was a moment of stunned silence until Sundown stood up and slapped Nulla on the back. Then he walked around to gather Glenda in a bear hug.

"I didn't know, you can't tell. You're so slim. Congratulations to you both. This is the best damn news we've had since, well, since the apocalypse. We now have hope for the future, a brighter future," he said, struggling to find the right words for such an occasion. He wiped absently at his eyes which had suddenly grown moist. Then everyone was up and hugging. Even Pedro had a tear in the corners of his eyes as he wheeled himself across to hug Nulla now standing proudly beside Glenda.

"Hey, all of you, shoosh. I'd like to make a toast," said Andy lifting his glass of communion sherry which the palace seemed to have an abundance of. "To the happy parents-to-be and to our first post-apocalypse baby."

Everyone grabbed the nearest glass of wine, water or tea and repeated, "To the parents and our first post-apocalypse baby!"

Glenda smiled making her face glow with joy. "Thank you, but nothing much has changed except we're going to add another member to this wonderful Commando." She stopped and became somewhat serious. "Nulla and I, and our group, we lived in fear waiting to be discovered by the terrorists every single day. That was before we crossed the deserts to be here, our sanctuary. When we arrived you so generously took us into your hearts, sight unseen. We're so glad we made the choice to come here to start our family." Glenda started to cry and Pinkie came to her aid. Together they left to get more supplies for their little celebration.

Tricia brought everyone back on track as they began to sit back down. "I'll personally be taking care of Glenda and the other women who need obstetrics. Lorraine and Gail have experience in midwifery too." The commando's head nurse paused before announcing, "I've got a few updates. After our last meeting we've begun physiotherapy and rehabilitation work with Katie and Lorraine in charge. We've some injured men and women who need therapy but they've been neglected.

My fault, but now we have some respite from the fighting, we can start seeing to Charlene's shoulder. Bongo's leg needs therapy but he is up and walking on it so that is good news. We've got Roo's arm but that seems to be coming along fine. Then we've got Arthur's arm and leg which, I'm afraid..." she stopped and turned to Nulla and Sundown. "I'm taking him off all fighting patrols because he pushes himself too hard. He has such a strong ethic to give everything he has, such a courageous young man. Lorraine wants to get him in for some physio work before he goes back to patrolling. Beamy, well he's been shot up too many times and his breathing... it sounds awful. It's going to take some time before we allow him to go on any fighting patrols too."

Sundown nodded. "Yep, take Arthur and Beamy off the patrol rosters and anyone else you consider needs a break. Tricia, how about Slimmy, how's he doing? Last I saw he was sitting outside sipping a beer with some of his mates in Birdsville. Is he going to be OK?"

"Slimmy wins the 'You Lucky Bastard Award', Sundown," said Pedro. "He's looking good. It must be them bullets whizzed past his tubing and just left a few holes in him."

"Yes, Slimmy's doing well, Sundown, but it was a close call. We really need to look into alternatives for antibiotics. The Alice Springs hospital has next to nothing in the way of antibacterials now. Pedro was just lucky, he was given their last infusion," said Tricia.

"I studied biochemistry, antibiotics was one area I worked on in the food industry. We used the older class of drugs which worked a treat, but my knowledge of biologicals is limited and very dated these days. What about natural medicines, aboriginal remedies?" asked Sundown, looking at both Tricia and Nulla.

"My mother was our tribal healer back in the old days and her favourite remedy was Castor Oil," offered Nulla. "I think it stopped Arty and Glenda's wounds going septic. We might consider it for inflammation as well as constipation. I know Katie used acacia bark and clay for Bongo's blood poisoning in Arkaroola when he and Roo were shot up. It's an old aboriginal remedy we used when I was a kid too. We could get Katie and maybe Jeda and Jenny too, to teach us a bit more. Katie learned a lot from her father, he learned it during his time working with the desert aboriginals."

Major 'Louie' Lewis wasn't so easily convinced. "I'm not so sure we should trust dirt and oil, it might kill more than it heals. Isn't there someone in Alice Springs who studied this sort of thing? What about Darwin or Pine Gap?"

Captain 'Johnny' Walker spoke up. "Forget Pine Gap, Louie, we've tried all year to get them to join us - you know that. They'll never share anything they've got. That yank bitch they've got in charge has busted more balls than our entire commando have dangling between their legs." He stopped talking and his face turned bright red as he realised what he'd just said.

"Ooops, sorry girls, that's army talk. I promise to watch my manners in the future," he said awkwardly.

"Cut the bullshit, Johnny, these girls here were knocking out terrorists while you were playing soldier in Alice Springs. I doubt there's a swear word they haven't heard. Besides," Pedro winked, saying in a mock British voice, "we've got proper British nurses and British nurses bust balls too." He chuckled softly to himself when he saw Glenda and Pinkie giggling with him.

Tricia patiently continued. "Louie, we're backs to the wall here. In the middle of the desert in the middle of the apocalypse and we have nothing. I don't see a choice really. I've been talking to your medics and they said they'd like to set up a unit to study medicine, natural and modern. Their thoughts are the same as mine, we need to set up a university-style course to continue training our field medics and our hospital staff. I'd like to go to Alice Springs and talk to the hospital heads there and find out who knows what and get this training program happening."

Pinkie was half listening, lost in thought about Glenda's pregnancy. She picked up on the Alice Springs comment. "Hey, Sundown, that's a great idea. Why not send Tricia in Bill's plane? It's only a day trip. The sooner we get our medical supplies and trained staff the sooner I can stop worrying about Glenda."

Sundown looked around and saw heads nod in agreement. "OK, Shadow, can you grab Bill for me some time today, please? I'll need to chat with him and organise a flight out. Tricia, are you up for a trip in the next few days? I've got to see Colonel Thompson anyway."

"You bet, Sundown. Glenda has plenty of time and I'm confident the girls and I can handle her birth, but it's the wounded I'm worried about. We've been lucky so far. Slimmy was too close, so was Pedro." Tricia turned to look at her dear friend and frowned. "Pedro, I was going to ask later but, how's your legs these days? I notice you've not been using your prosthetic legs very often."

"Well girlie, one thing I can tell you is my butt no longer fountains when I fart." He enjoyed the chuckle around the table. "Actually, the truth is me legs still hurt if I put weight on 'em too much. I'm not sixty years old anymore and I've decided I'll let the younger lads do the hard work from now on. I'm just easing into retirement and I don't need legs for that." He looked wistfully at Tricia then at his friend Sundown.

"That's fine, Pedro, but no retirement for you. Major Louie here said he and Johnny want to set up an NCO and officer training program at the palace. Seems Fat Boy disobeyed my orders to stay out of the tunnels. He found a room full of paintball equipment and crossbows, archery things, swords and all sorts of ancient weapons. Johnny Walker's been down there with him and a few of his lads are still sorting it out. Johnny said you might want to use the gear as part of your training program." Sundown scratched at a mosquito bite on his arm. "Paintballs and swords... can you imagine what those idiots got up to here? There are other things down there that I'm too embarrassed to talk about."

"You mean the sex rooms?" offered Pinkie with a cheeky smile at her husband.

"Yes Pinkie, thanks for reminding me, sex rooms," he said drily. "And what about the room filled with gold and silver bars? Or the cash room and that room full of pistols and silencers? What were they planning I wonder?" Sundown took another piece of Fatima's cheese and popped it into his mouth.

McFly had been silent all this time but the talk of hidden treasure in the tunnels forced a question to form in his mind and it just popped out.

"They didn't find any fishing gear by any chance did they, Sundown?" His eyes twitched with anticipation.

"Damn it, McFly," said his wife, Shadow, sitting beside him. "You've got that big lagoon out front to play in. Sergeant Ahmet said he saw some huge fish in there, he thought it might be barramundi. He said he wants you to run a course on fly fishing for the boys when you get a chance." Shadow hid her smile from her husband.

"Bullcrap! Did he really said that? Ahmet really did say he wants me to run fly fishing classes? Did he? Sweet!" came Matty McFly's ecstatic reply. The rabid fly fisherman's eyes popped and he stood up to leave.

"Captain, are you going somewhere special?" asked Major Lewis flatly.

"What? Aw shoot, um, may I leave the table?" he asked then realised what he'd said when everyone laughed. "I mean, is this meeting over yet?"

"McFly, sit back down. We haven't finished yet and I have a feeling your misses is just teasing," said Sundown.

McFly looked at his wife and his face changed from disappointment to one of, '*damn, you got me that time.*'

"Sorry McFly, I just couldn't help it. You left yourself wide open my man," chuckled Shadow.

"OK, back to order," called Andrew, keen to get to his book work. "I'd like to report on the progress of our vegetable gardens and general food situation." He waited while everyone stopped laughing and settled down.

"Thanks. We've had two months of fine weather and the gardens have flourished. We'll have fresh herbs and Fat Boy's hydroponics system is producing a growing supply of fresh vegetables. The cow herd is producing a surplus of milk and we're making yoghurt and cheese, as you can see here on our table. Unfortunately we've just about run out of wheat flour so grains are a problem. That means we're struggling to get enough beer brewed for the soldiers and drinkers and we've no bread, sorry Sundown."

Sundown, the ex-baker and bread scientist, nodded. He already knew the situation was bad and despite he and Fat Boy's best efforts, along with Mel and Fatima's creativity, basic bread was no longer on the menu. They still had some wild bush grains along with some rye and wheat growing in their hydroponics system but it was a long way from harvest and simply not enough to go around.

Tricia looked at Andy and quickly jumped in before he started talking again. "Andy, I've spoken to the pharmacist in Alice Springs, he's wanting to set up an opium and cannabis garden there. The pharmacist said we might be able to produce a decent painkiller with some luck."

Andrew stared at her for a moment. "Are you saying they want to grow heroin?"

"Yes, it's what our most effective painkillers are derived from. Opium's been cultivated for at least 5,000 years." She stared at him for a moment. "Andy, it's for medication only, and no bastard's getting their hands on it," she replied heatedly in her proper British nurse's voice.

"OK, as Sundown says, '*you outrank me in the medical department*'. We've got nothing else and narcotics is something I know nothing about. I'll just butt out of the conversation then, won't I." Andy paused, shook his head in bewilderment then came back to life. "If anyone wants to object you'd better do it now."

Sundown looked at Tricia and saw she meant business so stepped in to support her. "I see no reason to object as long as it's managed by the Alice Springs medical staff and no one else gets their hands on it. We need every form of medicine we can get and if it saves one life or eases the suffering of one of my Commando, I say we go for it." Sundown looked at the last piece of cheese but hesitated. "Um, Tricia, when you get to the Alice, make sure you have a good chat with this pharmacist fellow. If we do this we do it properly or not at all."

With a look of annoyance on her face Tricia couldn't help herself snapping at him. "Properly? I'm a damn professional, Sundown!" She abruptly stopped fuming and calmed down when she saw the hurt look on his face. "I'm sorry… well, I take that as a yes vote." She turned to Pedro. "Pedro, can you please tell Fat Boy to call by my office tonight? He might know where to get some plants."

"I don't care for it myself but if it helps our wounded then let's give it a try." Major Louie Lewis paused and looked around. "But can we now get back to our meeting? What about our fuel situation, Andy? Captain Walker said he's optimistic we'll have enough fuel for ongoing armoured patrols for the next two years if we can keep the underground fuel tanks clean and dry."

"We're on track, Louie. By introducing horse and camel patrols we should cut our fuel demands down dramatically. Petroleum absorbs moisture and deteriorates over time so we'll eventually need some sort of method to clean it." Andy looked around at his friends seated at the table. "Two years we've got but we really need an engineer, know of any?"

The major nodded. "As a matter of fact we've got a few. Some of the men from the oil industry were in Darwin when the apocalypse hit. They've joined our command, I think some are here at the palace. I'll get them in to speak with you."

"Thanks, Louie," Sundown said and turned to Nulla. "How long do you think before the boys will be out on camel patrol?"

"We have some dab hands at horsemanship and cameleering. Kris is a natural and we've not had a single injury. I think you can give us two weeks to settle the animals in and get everyone up to speed. We've now got enough camels for our long range patrols and a surplus of horses for the cattleman and the house guards." He saw the questioning glances among the group. "Did you know that Genghis Khan's Mongols had at least twenty remounts each? No? Well that's the sort of numbers we need, that plus fodder."

"I didn't know you read the encyclopaedia of Mongol conquests, Sergeant Nulla," said Major Lewis looking at Nulla with squinty-eyed suspicion, followed by a deliberate grin. "So, Andy, how do we do that?"

"I've spoken to Nulla and Kris about that very problem." Andrew took his glasses off and rubbed vigorously at the lenses with a cloth. "The desert has enough feed for now and we can easily move the mobs around from paddock to paddock. We add new animals as we lose them or they become injured. Those horses are just what we need to look after our cattle. This property was a cattle station and all the adjoining properties ran cattle too. The fences, water troughs and paddocks with the best pastures are all set up for us. We've enough cattle to feed an army plus a hungry Commando. We won't starve." His face broke into a smile as he put his glasses back on. "I heard Halo's been taking the girls out to train with their own mounts, donkeys."

"Yeah," laughed Nulla. "The Girl Guards wanted in on the act. I knew they would. They just love their horses and I'm confident they'll do a great job caring for them. But them donkeys, well, even Kris hasn't been able to train them into mounted cavalry. Kris and Halo have some of the boys trying to train them as pack animals but for the most part they're pretty darn stubborn, and smart." He turned to look at Sundown. "The Girl Guards have their own horses and camels now so I expect that they will be too preoccupied to annoy Captain Walker, for a while at least."

"Johnny, you should be pleased with that I should imagine," said Sundown with a light chuckle. Captain Johnny Walker gave a lopsided smile that showed he wasn't convinced. "So, what about the guard dogs, I hear they're doing well too. And Red Dog, when is she due to drop her litter?"

"Should be soon. Kris said we've got a few dog handlers in the Commando who can train the pups as guard dogs. Captain Walker said he wanted to keep at least two for the palace. The others could be trained to go on patrol with the cavalry," replied Nulla.

Andy squirmed in his seat. He was restless and ready to get back to his work. "Louie and I have saved this for last." He paused thinking how best to present this last piece of news. "Colonel Thompson called and said he had a visit from the Pine Gap people. He said their commander wants to speak with you, Sundown. Seems they have a lot of staff, men, women and children, inside their facility. It's only a few kilometres from Alice Springs. What do you think?"

Everyone at the table stopped what they were doing for the second time.

"Pine Gap? So they've finally decided to talk to us?" said Nulla. "I wonder what's wrong. Maybe they've run out of water, or they're sick of playing dungeons and dragons?"

Sundown ran his fingers through his hair as he thought. "Louie, can you please tell the Colonel I'll be flying in tomorrow or the day after? This should prove very useful. A thousand or so staff, skilled soldiers, trained and qualified technicians and medical personnel..." Sundown nodded to himself then called the meeting to a close. "Shadow, you'd better get Bill here right now, thanks."

Chapter 3

By Snake Or By Arms

Corporal Normy arrived at Longreach with his band of exhausted Stosstruppen and comfort lady, Nancy, after their escape from the Sundown's Commando outpost at Birdsville. It was a gruelling eighteen hour drive, complete with two punctures and a scorpion sting to one of the mechanics while changing tyres.

They were met with the warmth and camaraderie he was expecting as conquering heroes. But as the days passed a coldness settled over the township. Where the Stosstruppen once walked boldly down the streets and were greeted as heroes they were now shunned and avoided as though they were infected with a disease.

It was while drinking with the locals that the Stosstruppen platoon members learned that the elite Mount Isa Claws had a new commander. Colonel Bartlett liked to run things his own way and found any reference to his battalions brethren, the Ravens Claws, distasteful.

The head of the Mount Isa Revelationists, Reverend Thomas, insisted the new name reflect the theme of his original battalion, the Ravens Claws. After some blustering and posturing he got what he wanted, just as Colonel Bartlett got what he wanted, a new and distinguished name - the Mount Isa elite Claws were named the 'Talons'.

Longreach was an unusual township, it was run by a woman, the Abbess Leonie. In Longreach no one was ordered to become a member of the church nor were they treated as slaves. The townsfolk ran the community basically as church employees. Some Crusader wits called them 'serfs'. It was modelled on the feudal system of medieval times. Although the Revelationist Church owned everything the church ensured that their workers were properly supported and their needs provided for – no one appeared to have any complaints.

Their control extended south and east towards the Queensland coast which included the region's extensive wheat and grain fields and farmlands. The Longreach Revelationists ran protection for the farmers keeping raiders and looters at bay. They were respected for their genuine compassion for those they were responsible for.

At one time the Longreach farmers had a problem with the Brisbane Revelationist Battalion raiding their supplies. It suddenly stopped the moment the Longreach battalions hit their headquarters. The Longreach Revelationist all-girl, Warrior Sisterhood Battalion, threatened the Brisbane general at gunpoint and they'd had no trouble since. The Warrior Sisterhood officer in charge of the operation, Captain Martene, was sharp, driven and as hard as nails – like her girls.

A few days after the Stosstruppen had arrived the Abbess Leonie called Corporal Normy to her office. In one corner he noticed several enclosed glass terrariums – they contained snakes which looked very much alive. There were several Taipans, the deadliest snake on the planet, and another three contained fat, evil looking Death Adders. Both species will kill; the first within minutes, the other a slow, painful death within a few hours.

As he entered, Normy saw his Stosstruppen company's 'comfort woman', Nancy, seated at the table next to the Abbess. He scowled to himself, *'What the hell is she doing here?'*

The Abbess Leonie, Longreach's charismatic preacher, was one of the founders of the International Revelationist Church in Zurich. As such Abbess Leonie was entitled to call her Longreach battalion the 'Crusaders of Light'. A tribute to her leadership skills and the genuine compassion she held for her flock. The Abbess had returned from her missionary work in the South Pacific islands to be with her family in

Longreach for the glorious Apocalypse. She loved her family, she loved her flock and they loved her in return.

More than her flock she loved her little sister, Nancy. When she learned that her beloved sister was being used as a comfort slave, she was outraged.

'*How dare anyone treat my sister as a slave,*' she thought. What was more upsetting was that it was the Adelaide church who were using her - as a sex slave.

Throughout their difficult childhood, Leonie had looked out for Nancy at school and on church outings. Her little sister was one of those kids who had so few life-skills that she was the perfect victim. The Abbess wanted revenge for the Stosstruppen's disrespect, but distance and Sundown's Commando prevented her sending anyone to rescue her. She would have her revenge now that the Stosstruppen had so conveniently arrived on her doorstep.

With the Adelaide Stosstruppen's arrival, and with Nancy among them, she was going to make sure they paid for abusing her sweet sister. Abbess Leonie knew that revenge is best served cold and to her delight none of the newcomers knew what they were in for. Once her outrage had cooled she called for the corporal of her most loathed military unit in the Revelationist Church.

"Corporal Normy, I believe you know my little sister, Nancy?" began the Abbess. Just like the snakes in her collection she held her prey dumb-struck with her eyes.

For a moment the corporal stood speechless but quickly found his voice.

"Yes, Abbess, I do know your God-blessed sister quite well but I didn't know that she was a relative of yours. Nancy was part of our company for this past year and she's held an esteemed position as comforter for our men and women. I have a great deal of respect for her," he answered carefully. His eyes now shifted from the Abbess' noticing for the first time that there were others in the room.

"I would like to draw your attention to the words you spoke a few days ago. May I quote what you said?" She turned towards the sweating corporal as she waved to her sergeant-at-arms to close the large office doors.

"I can't say I remember much of what's said in every conversation I've had, Abbess. But please, if you wish, go ahead." His eyes shifted from the closed doors to the terrariums and then to the men and women surrounding him. They sat silently in comfortable ornate chairs lining the walls of the Abbess' office. He felt like a naked gladiator in a Roman arena.

"You said, '*Get the fuck down, bitch. Do what you do best and hurry it up this time.*' I believe that may have been in reference to a head job from my sister?" The Abbess turned to Nancy who nodded affirmatively.

"I don't believe I actually said anything of the sort, Abbess. I recall I ordered one of our overly excited privates to leave her alone when she protested he was hurting her." His lie flowed so smoothly from his lips even he believed it – no one else in the room did.

"Liar!" screamed Nancy. "You treated me and the other girls like filth!" She stood up, leaned forward and spat in his face. The members surrounding Normy watched, no one moved or spoke. The tension grew as Abbess Leonie waited for Normy to break. She'd played this game many times and knew that it was only moments away.

"You lying bitch!" Normy exploded with indignation wiping the spittle from his cheek. "You've set me up, haven't you! I knew it the day I saw you. You're no God-fearing crusader at all, you're just heathen scum wishing to drag our church into the gutter like the rest of them." Normy had the sense to stand up for himself, he dared not show any sign of weakness. He too had played this game and knew how to bully and dominate a subordinate.

"Corporal Normy," Abbess Leonie interrupted him with her soft voice. "I've interviewed every member of your platoon and they all said much the same thing. That's interesting, don't you think?" She paused long enough to see a bead of sweat break from his forehead and roll down his face. "This little interview today was just to confirm that my decision to excommunicate you and your men is the correct one."

"What?" yelled Normy. "You're not my fucking commanding officer! You're just some dumb slut from Longreach who thinks she's head of us Crusaders. You have zero jurisdiction over me." Normy looked around and saw the hardened faces and quickly changed tact. "If you would just let me have my vehicle back I'll take my people home to Marree where we belong and get out of your hair." He was just starting his usual game of confuse and confound but stopped when the Abbess stood up behind her desk. The twelve Apostles, the elders of her church, followed suit standing as one, surrounding him.

"It has been decided that you will be allowed to return to Marree," came the Abbess' soft voice. She'd won again. "The Apostles have agreed that you and your Stosstruppen don't belong here. You should return to your own congregation, your own people. I shall have my Prior explain this to you." Abbess Leonie noticed his lips part in a smile and thought to herself, '*he thinks he's won, I might enjoy this after all.*'

One of the elders took a step forward and announced formally. "You are most fortunate, Corporal Normy. You have been offered the traditional Longreach Crusader's choice of punishment."

Normy's face seemed to turn green as his head swung around the room once more. "And what choice is that?" he snarled.

"It's a tradition of the Church of Revelations, Crusaders of Light Battalion, that when a member fails to show respect to the church or fellow church members his choice is trial by snake or by arms," replied the Prior lifting his hand and waving it towards the glass terrariums.

Abbess Leonie smiled to herself. When she heard her sister's story over dinner the night of her arrival the Abbess had begun to plan this very moment.

"Well, Corporal, what will it be?" the Abbess walked over to the nearest terrarium and moved her hand towards the curled snake inside. An enormous Northern Taipan immediately struck out slamming its fangs into the transparent barricade. It left a smear of poison to drip down the inside panel of glass.

The lone man seated in the centre of the room shuffled his feet nervously for a moment then stood up. He didn't need further demonstration.

Decisively he snapped his feet together and gave the stiff-armed salute of his battalion.

"Abbess Leonie, it is my honour, as leader of my platoon of the illustrious Stosstruppen Battalion, to accept your trial by arms." Inside he knew he'd won. These yokels had no idea what they were up against. His platoon were ranked the best of the Stosstruppen Battalion and the Stosstruppen were the best of the best. Hadn't he and his platoon beaten the famed Sundown's Commando and easily escaped from their prison?

"Then you accept trial by arms over trial by snake?" asked the Prior as he lifted the eyebrow over his right eye.

"On behalf of my platoon, I accept." Normy's voice was clear and prideful.

"Be it on your head then," said the Abbess as she walked from the room with her sister. The circle remained unbroken except for the Prior who spoke next.

"Corporal Normy, Stosstruppen Battalion, Army Corps Alpha of the Revelationist Church, Adelaide. You and your platoon have acted without respect for the tenets of the law of the church. Your punishment is trial by arms." He paused waiting for Normy to acknowledge then continued. "You and your platoon members will be issued one weapon apiece and driven to a location in the desert where upon you will be matched one to one with the Crusaders of Light, the Mount Isa Ravens Claws and the Talons. As has been practised by our church since the Apocalypse, each force shall meet with and defeat the others. The winning team is the platoon that survives the confrontation."

The corporal frowned, he was confused. "What is this shit? We have to face a platoon from each of the battalions? That's, what, sixty soldiers against my eighteen? In a pig's arse! That's bullshit!"

The Prior calmly spoke again. "Corporal, you fail to understand. Each battalion is evenly matched to your numbers, eighteen apiece.

Each battalion is pitted against the other. You will all be dropped off in separate locations in the desert. Whichever battalion holds out and defeats the others by the following morning, wins. You will go home to Marree if you win."

The Prior paused to let this news sink in then spoke again. "It's an honour for your platoon to be the first Stosstruppen to participate in the Cup. We've only competed against each other, now we have you. Wonderful!" As his face lit up, Normy noticed the other elders smiling at him. *'This is odd. Something's going on here, I've been deliberately left out of the loop.'*

A voice came from the surrounding elders, a woman's high pitched voice, weak from age. "Corporal, if you win you gain your freedom and the Cup. We will be waiting for the outcome with high expectations of your success. Your Stosstruppen have quite a reputation against Sundown's Commando you know."

Again Normy snapped in anger. "What cup is that? The bloody Holy Grail? This is plain bullshit! That's not trial by arms that's a game of paintball, a game of capture-the-flag!"

The same frail voice spoke again. "Young man, you're lucky we're even giving you assault rifles. The last time we ran the competition for the 'Thunderdome Cup' the contestants were given knives."

Normy went cold inside and slumped down into his chair. The elders filed out leaving him alone while his guards waited for him to stand. In a daze he was quietly escorted to his dormitory.

'So that's why those other battalions are here,' he thought to himself as he watched four proud Talons, wearing red beret's and red stripped beading worked into their breast pockets, proudly walk down the footpath.

By the end of the week the four teams had been assembled but only the Stosstruppen remained weaponless until the day of the competition.

On the day of the Thunderdome Cup it was hot, dry and the sunshine was so bright it was disorienting.

"Hey, Dory, look up there. They've got a flamin' drone filming us," cried one of the Stosstruppen. "Wave, everybody. Let them know we're not afraid."

But they were. The reputation of the battalions they faced preceded them. Within each heart rested the fear of facing the best of the northern churches - the Mount Isa Talons.

Chapter 4

Thunderdome Cup

The Diamantina lakes region was once a national park complete with billabongs and creeks. It was lush with life in the wet season but just a dusty hole in the dry. Corporal Normy and his platoon of eighteen were dropped off with supplies for two days, weapons and ammunition. They stood together quietly as the armed lieutenant spoke, his automatic raised just high enough to show he was in command.

"You Stosstruppen can unpack your gear and set up over there on the edge of the creek." He pointed his chin at a line of trees marking the creek bed. "If you're careful and very lucky you'll eventually be able to make your way to the park headquarters. Unfortunately your enemy have already started their hunt so I wouldn't bother trying to get there now. If I were you lot I'd set my ambushes here and wait for them to arrive."

"What direction is the park headquarters, Lieutenant?" asked Dory, a tall man of forty odd years with a bushy black beard streaked with gray.

"Across the creek, mate. Just cross it and keep walking for about six hours," replied the lieutenant. "If you survive the fire-fights you can win your freedom by making it to the park headquarters. But... take a gander at the last platoon who tried that, they're lying out there." He pointed towards the creek itself.

"So you bastards have done this before, hey?" said Dory, curious to know exactly what he was in for.

"We do this regularly, mate. We have a special competition. We call it the 'Thunderdome Cup'." The officer's smile broadened. "Once a month we gather a handful of civilians, give them a rifle or two and if they make it to the park headquarters they get to go home. No one's ever gone home."

Corporal Normy pushed to the front of his platoon. "That's because you blokes have never faced the Stosstruppen. We'll eat your Talons and Crusaders for breakfast," he said his face dark with suppressed rage.

"Bravado doesn't win a competition like this, Corporal. Skill, discipline and good luck might." He paused for a moment. "Anyway, I'm off to enjoy watching the fun with a few beers in the cool of the Diamantina Park headquarters. You've got a few hours of sunlight left so use it wisely and set yourselves up around the creek. The competition starts tomorrow morning. And don't forget, without water you'll be easy prey for our boys."

Normy looked at the lieutenant and asked, "so who will be coming at us first?"

"You've got all three battalions against you. The Ravens Claws, the elite Talons and the Crusaders. But this time we've added a catch." He grinned broadly. "Each battalion will compete to take you out but they also have to compete and take each other out at the same time. No one's allowed to band together either, it's each battalion for themselves." His eyes sparkled. "I'll be filming it with my quadcopter drones. You can see one of them above us now." He pointed at the tiny speck flying high above them.

Dory called out to his platoon members as the lieutenant climbed back into the truck with his two guards. "Hey, fella's! He must be thinking of making a Mad Max movie. Don't worry, it won't be a flop. We'll take out those battalions of theirs and we'll be movie stars."

The truck drove off leaving behind a cloud of choking dust. Corporal Normy called his platoon together. "We've got a shit-storm coming and I bet they've only given us enough ammunition for a single fire-fight. Grab your gear and hump it, we've got no time to spare. I don't trust that prick when he says we've got till tomorrow, so double-time it." He reached down and lifted the first of a dozen packs containing their ammunition, food and water. "We've got to prepare our defense and plan our counter attack in case they come early. So let's get moving."

They ran to the tree line where Normy sent his men off to reconnoitre the area while he unpacked and sorted out their gear. Within the half hour he'd enough information to decide their best course of action. The smell of decaying human bodies helped with his decision.

"They've set us up. This is no ambush position. There's no way we can defend it. We collect as much water as possible then head up onto that hill over there. If we gain the high ground first we might survive an assault or two before we give our lives to the glory of our Lord. Come on." He led his men to the creek edge away from the horrific smell of death.

They filled their water bottles but not one of them showed concern that there may be bodies in the shrinking water hole. These men had other things on their minds. The Stosstruppen reached down with determination and discipline to collect their kit and jogged behind Corporal Normy across the salt-pan.

As they marched across the flats the drone followed them. Even though several of their marksmen tried to shoot it down the drone remained untouched. It was a tormenting reminder of their predicament as it floated high up in the darkening sky.

It was late afternoon before they climbed to the top of the hill. Normy carefully placed listening posts overlooking the creek approach which was the most vulnerable to attack.

"Come on, fella's. Build them rock shelters strong and deep - they just might save our miserable lives."

Normy walked from post to post making sure his men were properly prepared. Each position was strategically placed to fight any invaders climbing up the escarpment or storming across its broad top. This was a defensible position and certainly a better prospect for their survival than the creek.

"Dory, I'll sort out some food. As I call them in can you keep an eye on the approaches? We don't know if what that officer said was true or not, we'd better be prepared for anything." Normy set about feeding his exhausted men section by section.

Their church comrades came for them at first light as the lieutenant said they would. Among their equipment they'd found a set of binoculars and now they watched a platoon of eighteen Longreach Crusaders walking towards their hilltop position from the north. A call from the south side made Normy and Dory scurry over to investigate. When they arrived at the lookout's position they saw another platoon approaching. These were probably Ravens Claws from Mount Isa.

"And where the hell are the Talons then? I thought they'd want to be the first to get stuck into us," mumbled Dory through his beard. "Unless they've sent them as back-up in case this lot fails."

"Corp, I can see something to the right of the Ravens Claws. It looks like a dust cloud," called one of the lookouts.

Normy pointed his binoculars in the direction the private was pointing. In the pale dawn light he saw another smudge on the horizon.

"I see what they've done. They've dropped each battalion at three points of the compass, North, South and West. The only way we can escape is to recross that salt-pan. Then we'll be sitting ducks if we do." Normy stood thinking quietly. The dagger tattoo on his neck pulsed with each heart beat. "All we've got to do is hold them off for a few hours. Single shot only, no automatics. We have to last just a few hours then they'll start shooting each other. I guarantee it." He sounded confident enough for some of the heads around him to nod in agreement.

"I hope you're right, Corp. If you're not then I'll say goodbye to you now," offered Private Elias as he put his hand out to his mate, Tim, for a cigarette. So waited Charlie Platoon, Stosstruppen Battalion, recently of Marree, Revelationist Army Alpha.

As the enemy came closer the platoon members became nervous. Normy called them to gather in front of him. They still had time before they would need to defend their position.

Corporal Normy stood tall and strong. In the desperate eyes of his platoon he looked the sort of leader they needed right then - confident and in control.

"We're Stosstruppen! We kill soldiers like these dick-heads every day!" He spoke with a conviction they'd not heard from him before. "The Stosstruppen are the elite of the Revelationists. We're Army Alpha, the military arm of the church. We carry the sacred tradition of all Christian Knights of the Crusades in our hearts. We were trained by the best to be the best." He looked at his men and his chest filled with a pride he'd not felt before. "Colonel Rommel served with the Australian army for thirty years. He's a veteran of four war zones with the SAS and before that with the British Commandos. Us lot, we were hand-picked by Captain Burgess, hero of Afghanistan, East Timor and Bougainville. We are the best of the best boys. It was us what they called in to show the Deaths Heads how it's done. We're the ones who took Sundown's Commando down at Mungerannie." He spoke with passion and his men responded in kind. "Remember your training and let's show these desert yokels how the Stosstruppen fight!" His short but powerful speech lifted the misery that tried to congeal deep in their hearts.

Corporal Normy may have been an obnoxious, narcissistic son-of-a-bitch at times, but right now, he was like Archangel Michael leading his troops like the Horsemen of the Apocalypse.

Bullets spattered against the stone wall that Tim and Elias built the night before. Their job was to stop the enemy storming up their side of the hill. It had an escarpment or lip of about a metre high that would prevent a charge but a determined assault would simply rise over it like the ocean tide.

"Tim, these bloody rocks won't hold up for much longer," said Elias softly. "Look, they're falling apart." He shrugged as he pushed several of the rocks back into place then crawled across to a pile of rocks bringing back enough to replace the broken ones. He leaned against the rock wall as Tim raised his rifle and fired twice down the hill at the enemy.

"Got one!" shouted Tim excitedly as he ducked down. "That should slow them down a bit."

They could hear more rifle fire coming up from below and from each side of the escarpment. They were surrounded by at least two platoons of their fellow Revelationists. One was assaulting from the right flank where Elias and Tim were and the other from the front and left flank.

Normy placed most of his men to hold the front where several dingo and kangaroo tracks led all the way to the hill top. A gentle slope which fit, well-trained soldiers could easily run up to assault their position. The right flank was held by just these two, Elias and Tim. They knew they probably wouldn't have any support when the shit hit the fan.

"I reckon you'd better hit a few more heads, Tim. I heard Dory shout out that Allan's down and you can hear the front positions are under heavy fire." Elias winced as bullets hit the rock wall again and a blast of rock shards cut into his face.

"Bastards!" he said as he wiped a trickle of blood out of his eyes. Elias pulled out his tobacco pouch and rolled two cigarettes. Tim fired downhill a few more times while waiting for his smoke. He leaned back against the rock wall and pulled out his lighter. He had to flick it a dozen times before it lit. They both drew on their cigarettes inhaling deeply.

"Hey look, Elias, the drone's filming us. Wave!" Tim raised his AK to fire a single precious bullet at the drone. It missed.

"Tim, mate, leave the damn thing alone, don't waste any more ammo on it. Just keep these bastards back while I build a wall across the side in case they break through the front and rear positions," ordered Elias, flicking his cigarette butt over the wall. It was hot and it was exhausting, his breath came in rasping gasps. To make matters worse they had already run out of water.

After a few minutes rest Tim said, "Elias, have you finished with the rock wall?" When his mate nodded, Tim continued. "I'll try to get around behind them. Cover my back, will ya, mate."

Tim crawled a few metres away from his friend and lifted his rifle ready to fire down at the enemy below.

"Tim, go a bit further across, mate. They'll probably be ready for you to show yourself from there. You're too close," called Elias softly. Tim crawled another few metres struggling in the heat of the morning sun. Leaning on his blistered elbows he raised himself into a firing position and fired two more rounds.

"How'd yer go?" asked Elias when Tim crawled back to their position.

"No good, missed. I think there's about three left down there but they're well hidden. I'm going to have to crawl out of our position and down the hill to get behind them properly," he said licking his cracked, dry lips.

"Just give me a moment to get this rock into place and I'll give you some covering fire." He paused then said, "How many magazines do you have left Tim?"

"I've got three. How many do you have?"

"I've got four, here." He threw a magazine to his mate. "Grab this, you'll need it." Tim stuffed it into his chest pouch and began crawling to the end of their hill top position. As the bush cover ended he slowly snaked another ten metres before easing his head to look down the slope of the hill.

"SHIT!" he screamed as a head appeared right in front of him. The Crusaders had the same idea and a bullet cracked past Tim's ear as he swung his own rifle around and towards his enemy.

'Crack! Crack!' Tim saw the Crusader of Light's head shatter. The man's body and rifle were flung down the hill to lie at its base.

Tim breathed heavily and his dry lungs made a horrid rasping noise as he tried to calm his breathing. There were more enemy down there so he decided to crawl a little further.

'Crack! Crack! Crack!' He heard the firing from Elias' position.

"Got him!" came his mate's roaring voice. "Come on you gutless Crusader dicks! I've got more where that came from!" He picked up a large rock and hurled it down the slope. Tim could hear Elias' satisfying grunt as it landed on someone below.

"Fuck you, Stormtroopers! You mongrel arse-wipes!" came a pained voice.

Tim had to smile, Elias was a good mate but he was as subtle as a meat axe. That one rock would bring every damn soldier of Christendom towards their position, damn him. With bruised and blistered elbows from crawling on the hot rocks, Tim edged further away from Elias, determined to find a way to get behind their enemy. If all else failed at least he'd die doing his best to defend his mates.

There came the sounds of heavy fighting from behind him. The staccato 'brrrrip' of automatic rifle fire increased in volume and he knew his mates on the front line were copping it.

'*Poor sods, I bet the front post is done for. Better get this over with.*'

He slid stomach first down an incline and landed softly on a patch of red sand several metres below the top of the escarpment. He looked across to where he expected the enemy to be. There weren't two as he'd expected, there were nine. Fortunately, they were still watching out for Elias' rock bombardment.

"Oh, shit," he sighed.

As he was trained to do he silently checked his AK, switched to a full magazine and selected it to fire three round bursts. With luck he'd take out most of them before he'd have to change magazines. If he didn't then he'd just back away and keep retreating until he came across a defensible position. Then he'll fight it out until he ran out of ammunition. Tim knew he was dead, but at least he'd go down fighting, and on film too. He smiled at that thought, then pulled the trigger.

Chapter 5

Diamantina Massacre

Tim's initial burst of fire took out two of the enemy, the others fell to the ground screaming their surrender. He stood and saw two Crusaders of Light squirming in agony while the other five, their hands held high, were clearly freaked out.

"Elias!" cried Tim at the top of his voice. "Elias! Get your arse here. I've got prisoners!"

A few seconds later he saw his mate's head peep suspiciously over the rock wall.

"Well I'll be hot dogged! You bloody beauty, Timothy! You've captured their whole damn army!" he yelled. Waving his rifle at them he called for the Longreach Crusaders to climb up to his position and sit on their hands. In the meantime, Tim collected every weapon he could find and stripped the dead bodies of ammunition.

The two wounded soldiers were in a bad way, both were now unconscious. He had no time to care for them so he did what he considered the right thing to do. After a short prayer he dispatched them to Revelationist heaven.

"I'll get Normy, he's busy but he'll like this," said Elias. Tim kept his weapon on the five prisoners and told them to empty their pockets.

"Hey, mate," said one of the Crusaders turning his face to keep his mouth off the dusty ground. "What the hell are we fighting you heroes for? We should join up and beat them Ravens Claws and their blood brothers, them bastard Talons."

Tim looked at him, he'd had exactly the same thought. Just then, Normy scampered over and flung himself behind cover just as a burst of rifle fire came at them from across the flat top of the hill.

"Shit! They've come up from behind, bloody mongrels!" Normy wiped sand from his rifle as he looked at his prisoners. "We had them pinned for a while at least." Before he could say anything else, a startled Elias opened fire at the approaching Ravens Claws not thirty metres away now.

Tim repeated what the Crusader said, they wanted to join up with the Stosstruppen to fight the Ravens Claws and the elite Talons.

"If you boys want to join us…" Normy started to speak but didn't finish as a burst of machine gun fire hit their position.

"Holy shit!" cried Elias as he pulled his hand away from his rifle. He saw that his little finger was missing. Blood dripped down his arm, leaving a red trail on his shirt. "Bastards shot my finger off," he said in bewilderment.

"Hold on a bit mate, I'll fix it," said Tim as he looked at the wound. He pulled a bandage from Elias's webbing and wrapped it around his mate's shaking hand to stop the bleeding.

"Now grab your rifle and get back to work," said Tim gently as more bullets hit their position sending shards of rock among the Stosstruppen and their Crusader prisoners.

"Hey mates! I've got our last grenade here in my pouch. Let me pass it to you so you can shut that fuckin' machine gun up," said the Crusader sergeant.

Normy took the grenade, primed it and waited for the machine gunner to pause. He saw a squad of three Ravens Claws race forward and knew he had a tiny window of time to throw the grenade. He stood and lobbed it to land at the base of the machine gun tripod. The explosion not only killed the gun team but destroyed the weapon as well.

Elias, his face screwed into a grimace as he tried to control the pain in his hand said thickly, "Nice throw, Corporal, can you finish that mob with the AK's off as well?"

The incoming fire from the three Ravens Claws that accompanied the machine gunners hit the wall like hail. The flying rock fragments forced Tim and Normy to duck down lower.

"You blokes interested in joining the fight on our side then?" asked Normy, trying to catch a glimpse of the Ravens Claws through the cracks in the rock wall.

The sergeant sat up, leaning low against the rocks. "You bet, mate. We've been competing against these pricks all year and they've won ninety percent of our contacts. They're proper mongrels and they don't play fair, they kill their prisoners." The sergeant turned to his squad. "What do you boys reckon? We join these heroes who've knocked over the Sundown Commando or would you rather die here when this position gets overrun by the Talons?"

One of the Crusaders rolled onto his back pulling out a pack of cigarettes, he offered them around. "Mate, just give us our weapons and we'll join your mob. We'll gladly help you kill these Mount Isa bastards."

Corporal Normy ducked once more but this time the fire was coming from the other side. Their front line was folding and his position was close to being overrun. He had to make up his mind quickly.

"Shit! Tim, give the Crusaders their weapons. You blokes need to share your ammo with us though. We're just about out." Normy turned his back on the Crusaders and fired at the three Ravens Claws trying to crawl forward towards their position.

There were noises behind him as the men cocked their weapons and waited for the corporal to direct them. Normy turned around and saw them waiting expectantly for his command.

"Right, you lot, on the count of three, we're going over the top and rush these three bastards shooting at us. Anyone who holds back I'll personally kill. Got it?" He stared at them, but not a face showed anything but solid determination.

The sergeant spoke up just as another volley hit their weakening rock wall. "Corp, don't worry, we know how to fight and we know how to kill Ravens Claws. Just give us the count and we'll follow you."

"Right! One, Two, Three!" They rose to leap forward, firing from the hip. It was over in seconds. The three Ravens Claws lay riddled with bullets.

Without waiting Normy turned and yelled, "Quickly, follow me! We're gonna push these shits off our hill!"

Normy knew he had to maintain the momentum against the enemy swarming over their frontal positions. He glanced at the carnage of his front line and saw men fighting hand to hand, wrestling each other like a swarm of bull ants. His front had collapsed and they were at risk of being rolled right off the hilltop and exterminated.

With a roar loud enough to instil fear even in the most hardened of warriors, Corporal Normy led his squad towards the fighting. Two of the Crusaders squatted, took careful aim and began providing covering fire. They'd done this so many times it was automatic. Within moments they'd pushed the assault back over the edge of the escarpment. The small force quickly dispatched the remaining Ravens Claws caught in the open.

Normy looked around at the bodies. He had just seven of his Stosstruppen left and that included himself, Tim and Elias. These plus the five Crusader prisoners made twelve. He watched as they squatted together on their haunches and passed their water bottles around as though they were all old mates.

"Sergeant, do you have any idea where the rest of your boys are?" he asked quickly, mindful that the battle could swing against them at any moment.

The sergeant cupped his hand to his mouth and yodelled loudly. They heard a similar yodel coming from the side where Tim and Elias had been fighting.

"Can you bring your boys up and put them here, here and here?" Normy pointed out the defensive positions that had been overrun. The sergeant jogged to the escarpment and called for the rest of his platoon to climb up to the hilltop with him.

Tim noticed that the Crusaders weren't at all fussed at joining them. It was then that he realised the Stosstruppen really were heroes to the Crusader soldiers who had never faced an enemy other than their own Revelationists - the Talons and Ravens Claws of Mount Isa.

Each new arrival nodded to the three Stosstruppen and squatted among their mates as they went to their appointed positions. They reverently dragged the bodies out of the pits and repaired the rock walls.

Tim took his tobacco pouch out of his pocket and rolled himself and Elias a cigarette. He lit them handing one to Elias who held it in his shaking hand.

"There ya go, mate, sit down over there and rest up a bit. I'll grab some food and water from our visitors and share it around," Tim said.

The sounds of activity down in the gully below heralded the arrival of the elite Talons. There came shouts and loud yells of frustration as the Talons realised what had happened.

"Bastards!" came a voice from below. "That's cheating! You're not suppose to join your platoons."

Tim walked to the edge and called back. "Go fuck yerselves! We're up here so come and get us!"

There came a few chuckles from the survivors on the hill. But they all knew things would soon change. The Ravens Claws were good, the survivors on the hilltop had just seen what they could do. But the Talons, the elite of the Mount Isa battalions, had yet to prove themselves against the Stosstruppen. Everyone knew that it was just a matter of time before one side or the other perished.

The Crusaders passed their water bottles to their parched Stosstruppen mates and tended their wounds as best they could. Combined there were now fourteen defenders against eighteen Talons plus the remaining Ravens Claws.

"You're all going to die you know! We're going to give you the bayonet treatment when we get up there!" came the same voice from below.

Tim called back once more, "Up yours mate! One Stosstruppen can beat a dozen of you dick-head Talons!" He added as an afterthought, "With plastic spades!"

"Mate, ignore them, they're deliberately distracting us from what they're really up to," said the Crusader sergeant. He rubbed absently at a bloody wound on his arm and turned to Normy. "Corporal, you'd better strengthen the defenders back where you took out the machine gunners. I'll look after this end if you like."

Normy looked at the sergeant and then the defenders. They looked tired but he noticed that there was also hope. The two battalions had developed a camaraderie he hadn't expected. He saw soldiers sharing ammunition, cigarettes, food from their kits and water from their bottles - it looked like a gathering of close friends.

The drone passed over them again. High up they could barely discern the buzz of its engines. One of the Crusaders waved to it.

"They sell this film to the other battalions you know. All over Australia it goes, bastards. They're sick pricks filming blokes dying like this," said a gray-haired man as he leaned across one of the wounded to help him drink from his water bottle.

Just as they were settling into their positions, there came a voice from among the Crusaders. Everyone stopped to listen. A powerful baritone voice begun to sing the '*Hymn For The Dead*'. One by one the troops from both battalions joined in to sing the popular tune often sung at the end of a church service. It wasn't a funeral song but rather a song to rejoice a life lived to glorify their Lord. It was a popular song which inspired even the most hardened non-Revelationist.

The men picked it up, singing loudly with a passion knowing they were soon going to die. The song peaked just as the Talons sprung forward up the slope and onto the crest of the hill. They were among the survivors before they knew it. The Ravens Claws and their elite brothers, the Talons, had attacked each weakened position simultaneously.

The incoming fire was tremendous. Each squad raced forward under fierce covering fire from the squad behind and within moments they were into the defenders positions fighting hand to hand with knife, rifle butt and fist. Each terrorist in the Diamantina reserve was now in a vicious fight to the death. Not a single soldier was under the illusion they would survive so they fought with a passion and desperate savagery to die as they lived, for their Lord.

Elias leaped up swearing as he furiously swung his empty rifle like an axe at three Talons. His voice was hoarse from screaming their war song a moment earlier. He tripped one and smashed the man's head with a blow from his rifle butt. As he stood to face the others he felt a knife slide between his ribs and rip into his lungs. He tried to call for his mate, Tim, but blood gushed from his mouth. Gagging, he collapsed to the ground on top of the body of his dead enemy. The other Talon smashed the pummel of his knife into the side of Elias' head killing him instantly. The two Talons turned to rush towards the fighting, milling crowd only a few metres away.

Corporal Normy held off two Talons, their bayonets drawn and already dripping blood. They each knew no quarter would be granted so no quarter was asked. Normy raised his head for a split second to watch the drone dip down to film his death.

In that second he resolved himself to die gloriously for a God he didn't believe in, a religion he'd paid lip service to but which had given him a power and pleasure that he'd never known in his former life. In that moment his heart filled with an enormous joyfulness. He jumped at his two assailants catching them by surprise. His fist smashed one in the face. The man went down as his nasal bone punctured his brain. The other tripped as he fell over a body trying to escape this madman.

Normy had his hands around the Talon's throat screaming with joy. He was no longer Normy the poolroom hustler, he was a Knight Crusader in the Holy Lands of Palestine. He could clearly remember the heat, the sun and the glare of the Holy Land. He could smell the stale sweat of men and horses and he felt the camaraderie of his fellow warriors of a thousand years ago. He was there right now, a warrior of Christendom, a soldier of Christ.

Only ten metres away Tim was on the ground caught in a crushing headlock by one of the Talons. His head felt like it was going to explode as he desperately swung his foot behind his opponent's leg and flipped him over. They both landed heavily on the dry earth. The solidly built Stosstruppen tried to stand but another Talon dived onto him and stabbed his knife blade into his arm. The blade stuck in the ground and pinned Tim allowing his enemy to grab at his exposed throat.

In desperate pain Tim reefed his arm upwards and the knife sliced through muscle rendering his arm useless. Weakened and losing blood he clutched at the man's face managing to shove a finger into his assailant's eye. As the Talon let go Tim pushed himself away with his good arm.

He didn't realise he was on the very edge of the hill top and as he rolled he fell over the cliff edge. His head smacked into a rock and his limp body slid down the slope to lie unconscious at the base of the hill. There he lay beneath a patch of spiked desert spinifex. In the panic of the fight no one noticed that he had disappeared.

The fight continued its fury unabated. The Crusader sergeant, veteran of Afghanistan and Iraq, formed a circle of his troops as the Talons hit them with rifle fire followed by a vicious rush with bayonet and knife. They slipped in the blood of their mates but still they fought with a savage instinct for survival. The Talons may have been an elite battalion but the desperation and ferocity of the Crusaders after a year of humiliation met them at every thrust of their blades.

They fought each other to a standstill until not one was left standing. Neither Talon, Ravens Claw, Stosstruppen nor Crusader remained unscathed. The appalling sounds of men killing and dying persisted as each furiously fought to squeeze the life force from the other.

Normy tried to rally his men but he had no voice, a Talon had his hand at his neck and was throttling the life from him. He felt a panic rising as his throat was forced closed. With an animal's instinct for survival a burst of adrenaline shot into his blood stream.

His arm was pinned beneath the enemy's buttocks. In that moment of panic he managed to wrest it free to jam his thumb into his assailant's anus. The hand around his throat at first slackened then quickly let go. The Talon was horrified at the ignominy of his enemy's act. He roared with outrage, absolutely furious at the underhanded jab. With an evil, spiteful smile on his lips he reached to his belt and pulled his bayonet free. Normy pulled the Stosstruppen blade from his scabbard matching his enemy's knife fighting stance.

They circled each other slowly, not for a second did they take their eyes from the other. As one lunged forward, the other would deflect and counter thrust. They fought not just each other but their own exhaustion - their sweat dried as fast as it flowed in the dry desert heat.

Neither realised that all fighting had ceased, not a single attacker or defender remained on their feet except themselves. The sound of dying men was the only sound that could match the bone-weary grunts and heaving, laboured breaths of the two fighters.

The elite Talon soldier knew he was the superior of the two. Not once but twice his knife drew blood. He smiled again knowing he would kill this cowardly bastard. What sort of Revelationist would use such dishonourable means to escape death? The kind who died at the end of his blade he decided.

The young Talon was an experienced knife fighter and he saw it clearly, an opening. With a flick of his wrist he twisted his knife into Normy's stomach driving it deep slicing into his liver and stomach. But in his weakened state he slipped in the blood pooled at their feet.

Normy had also used a knife before, in the old days, before he found the church had better means to control people. Instinctively he thrust his knife into the groin of his opponent. It happened so quickly that neither had a chance to avoid the other's blade. They fell forward entangled together.

Normy dropped his knife to clutch at his stomach and groaned. "You bastard, you've done for me." He keeled over vomiting blood and bile. His enemy was already dead, Normy's knife had sliced clean through the Talon's femoral artery.

The drone buzzed overhead like a dragon fly looking for survivors, there were none. It continued filming the scene for the next few minutes before the bored controller brought it back in.

It was dark when Tim woke to the sound of dingoes howling and he shivered. The moon shone brightly as he looked around wondering where he was and why he felt so much pain, then he remembered the battle.

The sound of movement came to him and he sensed a pack of dingoes, wild dogs, forming a circle to surround him. Tim knew the dogs were starved having had two seasons of heavy breeding and now their population had outgrown the available food in this region. It happened in every area he'd been posted to, they'd become a real menace since the apocalypse.

"*Just what I need,*" he groaned to himself, "*starving dingoes and here I am, lame in one arm and no weapon in the other.*' He heard a growling whine as the dingoes tightened their circle, their red eyes glowing in the moonlight. The pack of wild dogs closed upon him.

Chapter 6

Wiram's Worry

Within a day of Colonel Vic Thompson's message, Sundown, McFly and Tricia were in Bill's Cessna bound for Alice Springs and the Pine Gap Intelligence Facility.

Things were now quite settled at the palace and so Major Lewis pulled the rest of the original Sundown's Commando from the front line for a break. Most of them were already working with the horses and camels anyway so it didn't interrupt the usual proceedings at the palace.

When Pedro had returned from Alice Springs he and Fat Boy took to spending their free time together. Fat Boy idealised his father who died when he was just a boy, and now Pedro became the father he'd lost.

From the time their father died until they met Sundown's Commando, Fat Boy and his sister Blondie lived life on the edge. When their father was killed they were sent to live with their cousins, the Wilsons. The community workers who sent them there had no idea the Wilsons were sadistic predators who repeatedly brutalised and assaulted the two children. Things changed the day Fat Boy turned fourteen and nearly killed Brad, the leader of the Wilson pack.

Pedro's one complaint in life now was the tobacco. Supplies had run out and everyone was forced to use wild tobacco. It just wasn't the same. One drunken night, Fat Boy went down into the tunnels below the Christian Palace whereupon he discovered a secret room.

The room was packed to the roof with cured tobacco leaf, no doubt meant for sale on the black market.

Fat Boy wasn't quite sure what to do with it but he'd lived a life where a secret as valuable as this was worth keeping. He gave some to Pedro while he thought about how he could use this new-found treasure. He managed to keep his find a secret until Nulla noticed Pedro's special tobacco.

"Pedro, you can't hide that leaf from me, mate. I smuggled contraband for years and that, my friend, is just what I need for my own tobacco pouch." Pedro, in his wisdom, handed Nulla a bag the very next day. Together the three men sat and laughed as they swapped stories of their past criminal activities.

Each evening the Commando spent a lot of their free time sitting, drinking and talking. Pretty soon Blondie was drawn into their private group. Then along came Cambra, Jenny, Jeda, Shadow and McFly. It was a mixed group of unusual individuals but they soon became known as Pedro's mob. The teenage girls were always dropping in with Cambra to chat with Pedro and for some reason Simon and Luke were usually with them - when they weren't on bike patrol or with the horses and camels.

Jaina and her boyfriend, Jason, who now sported the nick-name of 'Shrek', enjoyed hanging around the riggers and the soldiers. Halo, in particular, was one of the ringleaders of the military set. His stories of the Commando battles always drew a crowd no matter what time of day. He would set up camp just at dusk on the top floor landing overlooking the lagoon. Somehow he'd convinced the girls to keep them supplied with food and drink so everyone could party while he held court.

Pedro and his mob were often called over to join them. Together they competed to tell the biggest lies. The Alice Springs boys loved to ask about Sundown's berserker demon. Even though the very few who saw him in action didn't like talking about it, Halo sure did.

One night Luke mentioned how Arthur had been shot and blown up twice in Adelaide while fighting the terrorists. For a while, the attention shifted away from Halo.

"Arty, why didn't you guys use rifles? Surely there were plenty out there in the shops and from dead Revelationists?" asked Halo.

Arthur and Heidi didn't like talking about those times, they were times of paralysing fear. It was a terror that couldn't be shared with another, not even each other.

"Halo, we had to hide, like rats, in the houses where they couldn't find us. They ran patrols, they ruled the city completely. There were thousands of them right on our door step. Me and my mates blew up some trucks once, that's how I met Heidi and Charlene and nearly got them killed. Two of my friends were killed when we escaped." He was visibly upset but continued. He wanted to tell this story, at last.

"We had a close friend, his name was Tony. He was Lucy's husband. Tony and I went to rescue some of the prisoners the terrorists held captive. The terrorists found us and I was chased into a chemistry room. I was shot through the leg and bleeding. I left a trail of blood a blind man could follow so I had to hide somehow." He paused while someone called out a question.

"What sort of rifles did they have, Arty?" came a young voice from the middle of the group.

"What? Rifles? They had AK47's like wot all the other terrorists have, ya bloody boofhead." Pedro looked to Arthur who nodded in thanks before continuing with his story.

"I found a hole in the floor. It must have been for chemical waste or something so I climbed down and started crawling along a tunnel. It smelled of sewerage and I nearly passed out. That's when they threw a grenade down into the tunnel. I was blown out the end of it and into a creek. It burned all my hair off, even the hair in the crack of my butt." He smiled at last and the others joined him understanding just how much this story took out of him – except one young soldier who was always asking questions.

That same disembodied voice called out again. "Arty, did it hurt getting blown up and all?"

"Yes, it knocked me out and I woke up nearly drowning in the creek. When I crawled out I saw the building on fire and terrorists running around in flames. The stupid bastards blew the whole building up and themselves with it." He stopped when he saw Heidi cover her face with her hands and she began to cry.

"I'm sorry guys, I can't tell you any more because that was a bad time for us. It led to Tony getting killed, he was my best mate. I'm sorry, maybe some other time." Everyone went quiet as he led Heidi away to their room.

"See wot ya done, ya damn boofhead," said Pedro as he tried to make out who it was that asked all the questions, but he couldn't find him. "Next time ya see Arthur you make sure you boys show respect. He's seen more action and shown more bravery than any of you lot. That young fella is the sort of hero Sundown's Commando need, real heroes that aren't afraid to face the enemy." Pedro paused as he looked from face to face and started to tear up. Most of those in front of him were in their late teens and early twenties, new recruits, refugees from Darwin.

Halo stepped in to help his mate. "And don't forget, Arthur tried to rescue his friends without a weapon. He had nothing to fight with but sheer guts. How many of you have the courage to do that?"

It was at one of these top floor parties that Cambra asked Blondie to sit with him. Everyone knew Cambra had been badly hurt by his ex-wife and how he now steered clear of women. Lorraine once tried to get close to him. Even Donna tried way before the apocalypse but Cambra was too badly burned to consider another relationship.

Blondie though, she was different, very different. The memory of her running towards him during the fight at Mount Isa kept sneaking its way into his mind – it aroused something within him that he recognised as more than just sexual desire. Her image kept him awake at might and he knew that he needed to find out if she felt the same way about him. Perhaps, maybe he had a future with her?

"You want me to sit with you? Why?" the blond model asked sweetly in her best '*yeah right*' voice, but when she saw Cambra wasn't flirting she stopped. "Sure," she said. Blondie sat down with him spilling some of the drink in her hand. She had taken to drinking a lot lately. It seemed at times she couldn't get drunk enough.

"I like you, Blondie," Cambra said looking into her eyes. "I'm not someone who plays games, you know that. It's just that sometimes I'd like to talk, you know, with you." Blondie saw this was not the Cambra people knew. Cambra was always the strong one, always in control.

"Cambra, I like you. You're strong and you know who you are. I like that in people. But I don't like men, plain and simple. I don't foreplay and I don't fuck. I just kill," she said flatly and finished her drink clinking her glass on the spirits bottle for Cambra to fill again.

"Yeah, I know that, but you're different to people, different to everyone here. I like that in you but it bothers me to see you slowly destroying yourself. I want to know you better and I don't mean the sharing body juices thing. I care for my friends, for Lulu and Danni and I care for you." He finished pouring her drink and filled his own glass.

Blondie swirled the liquid in the glass in her hand. "You know what, Cambra? I like gin and this tastes surprisingly like gin. It's not real gin, it just tastes like it. I can see you as an old man one day, still playing at liking something that's not real. I'm not real. I'm poison and you really shouldn't get too close to me."

Cambra's brows arched upwards and his voice became harsh. "I know who I am and I think you may have once known who you were. I also know what I like and what I don't. I haven't met a girl I wanted to sleep with in ten years, maybe even longer if I think about it. I don't trust women. But I trust you." Blondie looked at him for a second then lazily took another gulp of her drink.

Cambra saw her look and baulked. "And that's the last I'm ever going to speak about this subject, Blondie. I promise you I'll never come on to you and I'll never speak my mind again." Cambra stood up, slammed his empty glass on the table and walked away. He didn't look back.

Jaina was watching from across several groups of happy commandos and ambled slowly over to her old friend and mentor of the Tajna Sluzba. The two had worked together for several years in the Revelationist Church's secret service unit. They were now together on the other side of the fence, fighting against their former institution.

"What the hell did you say to him, old girl? Did you tell him his dick was hanging out or something?" she asked sitting in Cambra's vacant chair helping herself to the bottle of spirits.

Blondie didn't answer straight away, she was thinking. "Well, I didn't actually say anything but the truth and sometimes that's the wrong thing to say."

"Tajna Sluzba never tell the truth about anything, especially themselves," explained Jaina, as though she were addressing a student.

"Jaina, you're wrong," Blondie said looking down and picking at her thumbnail. "When we come home from work we should step out of our role and into our lives again. I've lived this life for so long I no longer know who I am. I'm lost, girl." She downed the rest of her drink and clinked her glass on the bottle for Jaina to refill.

That same night Major Lewis called Wiram on their secure line from the Birdsville outpost. The major, Captain Walker and Wiram swapped shifts every few weeks between the palace and Birdsville where they continued to run reconnaissance and fighting patrols. They made the Marree terrorists' lives hell.

With the fire-power of the Bushmasters and the ASLAV 25mm cannons the commando strength was now superior to the terrorists. Sundown, Colonel Thompson, Wiram and Major Lewis all agreed that they were still not in a position to push them out of Marree. The commando had their enemy where they wanted them, contained in a region they themselves controlled. Each week there was a contact and it was their policy that every soldier be blooded in action.

"Wiram, I've got a bloke here and I need Riley and Roo to talk to him. He's a cattleman from the Flinders region. Bloke by the name of Jarl Horsely. He says the Wilsons are on a rampage, with the Revelationists imprisoning the farmers they think helped Riley and Roo kill those Wilson boys," Major Lewis said.

"OK, I've got that, Louie. Do you want them now or in the morning?"

"The bloke's a mess, I don't know if he'll last till the morning. He mentioned Riley by name. I really need them here now," replied the major, the stress in his voice was clear.

"Right, give them two hours to get there. Is Lorraine on or Gail?"

Major Louie Lewis rubbed his face then noticed the dried blood on his hands. He'd helped their medical team undress the cattleman when he was brought into the first aid room. "It's Gail tonight, Lorraine's been busy with Beamy and Slimmy. She's been working them hard on their physio exercises. Why?"

"Just thinking, Gail's the best I've seen treating gunshot wounds, besides Tricia, of course. Was he shot?" asked Wiram.

"Not sure, I think it's a knife wound. It looks like he was stabbed and left to die. He's suffering dehydration and starvation. He crossed the Strzelecki Desert on horseback and the boys found him at the Coopers Creek patrol station. He's an old bloke and in a very bad way. Better tell the boys to hurry." Major Lewis signed off and went back to sit with the brave old man.

Wiram had the boys ready and gone within fifteen minutes. Bongo said he was going too, Wiram didn't stop him. The three scouts raced against time to be with one of Riley's old friends.

This new development of the Wilson's escalated violence needed to be conveyed to Sundown. Wiram called in their comms specialist and together they coded a message and sent it off straight away.

While this was going on, Halo held his audience, a new group of soldiers from Alice Springs, in an ecstatic trance as he told stories of glory to his young audience.

"These Revelationists are absolute arse-holes. I tell you, they believe in a God but practice heathenism. They kill everyone, kids, women and they particularly hate other religions. When we were at the mines fight we saw a pit filled with the people they'd killed. There was a little kid down there, the bastards." He rambled on finishing his glass of home brew that one of the soldiers had running in competition with Andy's.

"Halo, my boofheaded mate, what the hell do you know about how the Revelationists live?" said a half-tanked Fat Boy. He noticed Halo was holding on to his chair so it wouldn't fall out from under him.

"Fat Boy, I've killed more terrorists than anyone else on this station. Each soul I send to paradise I get to read their mind before they go. I know because Sundown blessed me with a demon of me own," Halo rambled on. He'd just had his beer renewed but had no memory of how it got into his hand.

"You're a first-class boofhead if ever there was one, Halo," Fat Boy said. He loved these commandos and even though he stirred them at every opportunity he would rather die himself than see them hurt. But Halo's talk of what the Revelationists were capable of riled him up. He knew far and beyond anyone else at the palace just how evil these 'God Botherers' really were. Fat Boy was drunker than a skunk and he desperately needed to bash a few heads to ease his own guilt.

"So... best buddy of mine... how many terrorists have... have you sent to paradise? Huh?" taunted Halo, trying to steady himself before he fell out of his chair.

Fat Boy, ex-Tajna Sluzba like his sister, went silent. There was a line he kept and this was it. There were two things his father drummed into his beloved son's head; a real man never boasts of the men he's beaten or the women he's had. A simple rule and Fat Boy kept it reverently in honour of his father.

"Well my beautiful man?... how... many of... those bastards... have you sent to hell...?" said Halo again but he was way past the point of no return and he keeled over unconscious. The party was over, once Halo went so did the entertainment.

"OK boys, time for bed," called Pellino who'd been watching to make sure the troops stayed within the bounds of good behaviour. It was an old habit from his many years working in the Northern Territory prison service. He couldn't get it out of his system; always be ready to step in to settle things down and to rescue a mate. As one of the original Sundown's Commandos, Pellino, a solid man in his mid sixties, was a gruff authoritarian when he needed to be. He was always conscious of how important it was for the older crew to help mentor and manage the young lads.

He helped Fat Boy carry Halo down the stairs and placed him in his bed. It wasn't the first time he'd done this and he was thinking he might mention the boy's drinking at the next committee meeting. He'd spoken to Tricia, or rather, she'd spoken to him before she left for Alice Springs and it might be time they set a curfew and a drink limit.

They understood it was the apocalypse and all but still, drinking oneself to oblivion when you might be called upon to fight off a hoard of terrorists the next morning just wasn't on.

Pellino called a committee meeting the next day. Halo and some of the other soldiers were up and about bleary-eyed and moody. It didn't sit well with a lot of the Commando and Pellino was keen to do something to stop the binge drinking.

"I think there's a few strategies we can put in place, Pellino," said Jenny. "We could set up a bar and that's the only place they get a drink from; a curfew so that the drinking only starts after sunset, except for special occasions. Then we make everyone responsible for their mates - if your mate's drunk you stop giving him alcohol and send him to bed."

"I think they'll argue that they work hard and deserve a drink. I'd like to see them kept better occupied though. More training patrols, alcohol-free days, that sort of thing," piped up Pinkie. "When they have nothing to do they just get drunk."

Andrew shifted uncomfortably in his seat then finally spoke. "It's not just the boys, has anyone noticed Blondie lately? She's been hitting the bottle real hard and I'm worried about her."

"Yes, I've seen that too," said Captain Johnny Walker. "Interesting woman that one, can't say I can get very close to her. She's like a brick wall with me."

"She's had a hell of a life, Johnny." Pedro turned to Pinkie. "Pinkie, darl, do you think you and the girls can pick it up a bit with her. You know, get her involved with running the place."

Pinkie thought for a moment. "Fat Boy likes cooking but I've never seen Blondie show any interest in cooking at all. I don't think I've even seen her in the kitchen. But yes, I'll talk to Mel and Jeda, they might have an idea or two. They all get along pretty well."

Pellino was listening keenly, waiting for his opportunity to speak. He did now. "What you've said is what I've been thinking. A curfew and a set bar with bar staff to police it. I like that idea. We start a habit of drinking in one set place at one set time and everyone watches out for everyone else." He looked across at Captain Johnny Walker and asked, "Do you have a sergeant major type who can organise it? I know Hassam did that before the Mount Isa battle knocked him around, but is there someone else you can appoint? We need a few strong reliable types who can manage the boys without getting their backs up."

Johnny nodded and looked at Pellino. "Yeah, Louie and I have already been thinking about this. We had civilians in Alice Springs running the military police but you heard what Sundown did to them." Everyone nodded, recalling the news of John and the knife fight on the Todd River. That was the night Sundown was made second in command of the Australian Defense Force and Pinkie saved the day by finding Sergeant Tobi to help sort out the mess for them.

"Consider it done, Pellino," said Johnny. "I'll pull the boys in and give them a talking to. Nulla and Wiram are my choice to take on discipline, the boys all respect them. I'll up the training and perhaps,

Pellino, you'd like to run the bar?" Pellino looked up in surprise then nodded his acceptance.

"The home brew situation has been interesting. Your thoughts, Andy, since you're our expert?" Captain Johnny Walker winked at the old administrator.

"Ha ha, yeah right Johnny. All they ever do is drink the damn stuff. No one really appreciates the hard work and skill that goes into that brew of mine. Hours of toiling to collect the freshest wild herbs from the bush and testing each brew to make sure it's acceptable. Scrounging sugar, malt and starch of any kind is almost impossible these days. But now there's another brewer and there's talk that each armoured crew have started their own brewery. They're even talking of a beer competition," said Andrew flatly. "But yeah, competition is good and we'll just need to make it hard for the brewers to get their sugar and starches. I'll just let Fat Boy know and he'll bop a few heads if they try to steal his kitchen supplies."

Jenny was restless and waited for Andrew to finish, then said, "I'm worried about Halo. In fact most of the boys who've been fighting since the apocalypse are showing signs of stress. We all are. Sundown took McFly off active duty because he was breaking. I'd like to see Halo off patrols and on to full time training." She turned to Captain Johnny Walker. "He was once our weapons master. Can you reinstate him, Johnny?"

"Halo's our hero, Jenny. We all love him so that's probably a great idea. I'll put him back training up the new boys. He'll like that." Johnny looked around at the faces of the management team. "What about you lot, how are you doing?"

Before anyone could answer, Wiram walked in. His shoulders stooped and his face fatigued. He saw everyone looking at him.

"Hi, I'm sorry to tell you this but the boys got there too late. The poor old fella died before Riley and the scouts made it to Birdsville." He sat down heavily and reached for the tea pot, poured a cup of warm tea and drank it down.

"What's the news Wiram? What's Louie thinking of doing about the Flinders Ranges situation?" Captain Johnny Walker shifted his weight and eased himself onto his elbows waiting for a reply.

Wiram refilled his cup. "Louie said the old man was one of Riley's neighbours. Before he passed away he said the Wilsons were burning down every homestead they could find and grabbing people for their prison farms. Apparently the Revelationists are up to their old tricks too. The Deaths Heads have been resurrected and doing most of the dirty work and they've started recruiting more soldiers to make up another few battalions."

Pedro looked up quickly. "Wiram, you're not letting our scouts go back to the Flinders, are you? That'd be suicide."

"No way and they know it. Riley's upset but Louie spoke to him and explained we're not in a position to take on the Stosstruppen plus the Deaths Heads right now. They're on their way back as we speak. They want to talk to Sundown when he gets back."

Pedro nodded, satisfied. "I think we really need to put our boys on a horse or a camel's back and send them away for a while. I know Sundown's been thinking about it. Our originals are just worn out."

"And worn out soldiers make mistakes. I'll speak to Halo and Assassin and get them to talk to the scouts. I'd like Nulla to talk to the boys too, all of them. He's got a special bond with them," added a tired Wiram.

"I'll get onto Sundown and find out what's cooking. If this means we have to run long distance patrols deep into enemy territory, we might come unstuck. We're still not ready for extending ourselves in that direction. Especially if they've resurrected the Deaths Heads." Captain Walker stood and pushed his chair in. "Right, I'd better run. Thanks everyone, we'll catch up same time tomorrow."

Chapter 7

The Conundrum

Colonel Vic Thompson was in a muddle. He'd sent his staff to the Pine Gap intelligence facility every week for a year offering to join forces and share resources. Each time he was told to '*bugger off*'. Now, only a few months after Sundown took command of the Australian Third Army, their commanding officer, US Navy Commander Sue-Ellen Cullen, wanted to talk. Vic was stumped. Why now? Was it because Sundown was in command?

Before he flew out for Alice Springs, Sundown's last word to his management team was to get the troops up to speed with their camel training. Just simple training exercises, that's all he wanted, training and no contacts, not until he was back. He'd spoken to Captain Walker separately asking him to get his Girl Guards up to speed. He wanted to start them patrolling the house paddocks and palace grounds on their horses. They'd given up trying to train the donkeys but Halo and Shrek insisted they be kept as pets.

Sundown had then called Nulla to join them.

"Sergeant Nulla, I know you love those girls of yours but I need them as part of our camel and horse patrols. Not long range patrolling, just around the house and yards will do for now. Can you and Johnny here work on that while I'm gone?"

Nulla frowned. He knew Sundown was up to something but he wasn't quite sure what it was. "Yeah, of course, but that's just a couple of guards. What about the rest? I've already given Johnny a hand to sort out another dozen troops to train as home guards… so what's brewing inside that head of yours Sundown?" he asked bluntly.

Sundown scratched at the stubble on his chin. "Smart bastard, aren't you, Nulla. You and Andy would make a good team. Both of you read my mind like a book. OK, I want this kept secret, got it?" Both Captain Johnny Walker and Sergeant Nulla nodded in assent.

"I've asked Blondie to get some of the girls up to speed because they're going to cross the desert and slip into Darwin. I've a feeling we might be able to upset the terrorist network there. Vic's intelligence says the Revelationists in Darwin are fractured and back to terrorising the civilians and now they've turned on each other. We might be able to organise a resistance in preparation for our push up north. I need intelligence and Blondie is the girl for that."

Nulla nodded, he suspected as such. Johnny Walker looked into Sundown's eyes and said, "Sundown, if we send the girls in, they might, you know, get hurt. If any of them get hurt I'll be more than pissed off." His face was drawn and he looked pissed off already.

"Johnny, this is war and people get hurt, you know that. Blondie assures me that she has a lot of support in Darwin, as have we. She and Fat Boy lived there for quite a few years and know a lot of survivors. She said the bikers up there will support and protect them. We need this, the people we are sworn to protect need this – it's our duty."

He stopped and scratched at his whiskers again. "In particular I want Blondie, Lucy, Heidi and Jaina trained up and patrolling on the camels and horses. They've got to be able to manage on their own if they have to. We'll send Fat Boy by bike up to Darwin before we send the girls in. He'll set things up and do some work behind the scenes, like he and Blondie did at Mount Isa." He stopped because he could see Nulla wanted to ask a question.

"Sundown, there's more to this isn't there. What is it?" he said quietly.

"Damn it, Nulla! I didn't want to tell you everything right now but I guess I'll have to finish it. You'll be training them, you, Shadow and

Johnny. This has to be kept 'top secret'." He paused long enough to gather his courage. "I'm sending them in to do an assassination... or three." Sundown then grabbed the bag Pinkie packed for his flight to Alice Springs and left the room.

Johnny Walker looked at Nulla nodding his head slowly. "War is hell, ain't it," he murmured.

Nulla seemed to be in a trance. "If I'd known what he was going to say I wouldn't have come to this damn meeting."

The captain slapped Nulla on the shoulder lightly as he stood up. "Sergeant, if Sundown thinks it can be done then we need to support him. I've watched our boys sitting on their arses for most of the year, biting their nails in frustration while those terrorists drove our world to hell. I'll not stand by another second afraid to act against them. You teach the girls how to ride, I'll teach them how to kill." Together they walked out into the midday sun. Their minds reeling with both elation and dread.

Bill flew into Alice Springs in the late afternoon and taxied over to the hangers. Colonel Vic Thompson was there to greet the small group. Tricia was whisked away to the hospital while Sundown, with McFly in tow, went with Vic to his headquarters.

As they settled down to a whiskey to wash the dust from their throats they discussed local events and how to approach this request by Commander Cullen.

"Colonel, first off, what's the news from Darwin? I've told Nulla and Johnny about our plan and they've expressed their fears for the girls. I need to be sure we're doing the right thing." Sundown sat heavily in the previous general's chair. He wrestled with the lever trying to adjust its height but didn't succeed.

Colonel Vic Thompson flicked through the papers on his desk. "McFly, can you ask the duty girl to find my spreadsheets? The ones on the refugees for the past month. Thanks."

The Colonel waited for McFly to return before continuing. "We've settled another hundred or so refugees from up north, mostly from around Darwin. The news is not bright. The terrorists have gone wild killing more civilians, it's like nothing we've seen since the days of the apocalypse." He pulled out another sheaf of papers from inside his desk.

"These reports came from civilians who worked in the terrorist headquarters. They say there's a power struggle happening and each side is executing members of the other factions. There's three factions up north: Reverend Albert, who's head of the southern hemisphere Revelationists, he's at the top. Then there's Reverend Thomas and Reverend Mark. These two are locals who've been pushing for control of the church since the apocalypse. They're each as nasty as the other. So far it has remained reasonably tame and covert but when it breaks out into a full scale fight they'll no doubt halve their numbers. We hope so anyway, we need to speed that up a bit."

Vic looked up from his papers. "From our intelligence reports we expect things to go to pieces just before or around the time of their annual conference. That's in a few months. We'll have enough time to get Blondie's team trained and into place but a camel ride from here to Darwin is going to be hell on earth and would take about four months. It's a long walk but there's a few station helicopters around that we can use as transport."

McFly was looking blankly at the Colonel so he explained further. "Them little things they use to chase cattle with, helicopters, we might use them to transport the team to Darwin. But getting home might mean they come back by other means, camel or horse or even walk if they have to. We could go in through their front door but Reverend Albert knows Blondie and tried to kill her once so that's probably out."

Vic looked outside at the swirling willy-willys kicking up spiralling clouds of dust. "I'm thinking either helicopter or even Bill's plane could get them there fast. But that trip home is not so simple. There's still the logistics to sort out."

"So that's our plan, McFly," Sundown said to his adjutant. "I've asked Blondie to take some of our girls into Darwin. She'll make contact with her friends in the bike gang and from there into the halls of power. She was once Reverend Albert's consort but that's between us three here." Captain McFly wasn't taking notes like he usually did, he just sat with his mouth open. This was all new to him. "McFly, your mouth is open, behaviour unbecoming of an officer, I believe," said Sundown.

Vic smiled, he enjoyed his new-found friends, they were so un-military.

"Oh, sorry. Um, you're not going to send Shadow, are you?" His left cheek twitched nervously.

"No, not at all. I need her to help train the volunteers though. Shadow's already started the girls training and she's kept it quiet, even from her husband." Sundown stood up and began pacing the room while he continued to talk.

"I've worked on this for the past month. I've spoken with Vic and Louie. I've brought in Fat Boy and Blondie and talked at length about which is the best way to go about setting each faction on fire. I've spoken to the volunteers, Heidi, Lucy and Jaina. They're brave girls. They've each had their share of hardship and want to strike back. Make no mistake, they are our best weapons for this task." Sundown stopped pacing. "We've left no stone unturned, mate. I'm even going to make sure everyone has a holiday before we begin."

"Holiday? Soldiers don't take holidays in the middle of a war, do they, Vic?" asked McFly, his face was brighter than it was a moment ago and his joy was evident now that he knew his wife wasn't part of this suicide mission.

"I think Sundown means he's taking a few of his old commando into the bush to get everyone together again. It's a bonding exercise before we begin the big push. This excursion into Darwin is an assassination, covert and dangerous. The girls know that. Sundown wants to make the most of the time we have before they leave on their mission." Vic stopped and eased himself back into his chair. He hadn't realised how tense he was. Talking about a mission as sensitive as this and where the lives of some of his friends were at stake put him on edge.

"You know, McFly, we might lose some of our friends on this stunt but we can't stand by and let more civilians die because we were too afraid to act. General Hughes is paying the price for that right now." Vic looked at Sundown. McFly saw it and lifted his eyebrow asking the obvious question.

"McFly, you won't be needed to defend the general now. He's a broken man." Sundown had resumed his pacing but stopped momentarily. "He's under the care of the hospital staff. They have a room for him and a few others. I'm sorry it had to end that way but at least the decisions are no longer in his hands. He can now rest without worrying about people's lives and those damn armoured carriers."

"Sundown, there's something else before we get to Commander Cullen." Colonel Thompson sat up straight as he prepared to tell of the latest developments.

"What is it, Vic?"

"The boys have noticed an AW119 Koala helicopter flying regularly from south to north and back again, probably from Adelaide to Darwin. It crosses the West McDonald Ranges almost every Saturday but it's too high for us to fire on from the ground." Vic shifted some of the papers on his desk and pulled out a map.

"How high is it, Vic? Is it too high for our Bill and his Cessna?" asked Sundown.

Vic nodded and continued. "You've read my mind. Our pilots have been observing it. They reckon one of our planes should be able to get above and into the sun. They believe that they could shoot it down if given the opportunity."

"McFly, you'd better have a chat with Bill. Call a meeting for tonight and ask the pilots along too. And include Sergeant Tobi, he knows a bit about aircraft weapons I believe." Sundown was still pacing back and forth his hands shoved into his pockets.

"Yes sir, consider it done." McFly left the room.

Sundown stopped his pacing and tried to sit down but got back up again. The Colonel was becoming a little anxious just watching him and decided to say something.

"What is it, Sundown? You look edgy. What are you worried about?"

Sundown stopped and swung around to look at him. It was as though he'd not noticed he was even in the room.

"Sorry, Vic. I'm feeling really jumpy and I don't know why. I've got this meeting with the commander of Pine Gap, maybe that's what's making me nervous." He went back to his pacing then stopped and sat down. It was deliberate and he forced himself to sit still.

"That's the part I think we need to talk about next." Vic paused while he waited for Sundown to stop wriggling as he tried to set his chair at the right height – and failed again.

"Thanks Vic, please fill me in. I think the berserker inside me is restless and it's getting to me."

The colonel continued smoothly as though he was telling a fairy tale. "Commander Sue-Ellen Cullen is an experienced American navy intelligence commander. She's smashed more balls than Steve Waugh or Babe Ruth. I don't know what she wants to talk about but be careful. She's smart, attractive and always gets her way. We've had next to nothing to do with her or Pine Gap since the day of the apocalypse. They're US intelligence and so outside our jurisdiction. They've never shared a damn thing, no news, no information, nothing. Those Pine Gap spooks are close mouthed and they've never even visited the Alice for a feed or a drink since the apocalypse. The only contact we've had is when my boys have gone knocking on their door each week to see if they'll come out and play. Each time we were told to go away." Vic looked at Sundown to see if he wanted to say something. He didn't so he continued.

"I have no idea what Commander Cullen wants. I bet she even has a bug in this room and she's listening to us right now." Vic looked at the walls and ceiling to emphasise his point. "I've got a jeep ready to take you there in an hour. Here's the little information I have on Pine Gap, the sort of supplies I think they have and their personnel."

Sundown took the handful of papers and stared at them. "OK Vic, I'm off to freshen up." He paused for a fraction of a second. "Hm, attractive, did you say?" He smiled in spite of his obvious agitation.

"Sundown, that's exactly what the young Praying Mantis boys ask before their wedding day. You do know male Praying Mantis' never live to marry a second time?" Together they chuckled as Sundown walked to the door.

"See you in an hour, Sundown. I'll send McFly to get you."

Chapter 8

The Saviour

To his surprise Tim's hand fell on the stock of an AK47. Just as the dingoes rushed forward he found the trigger and fired. The sound of gunfire frightened the skittish dogs sending them howling into the desert night. He sat wondering how the rifle came to be there. Then he remembered, this was the same place he'd shot the Crusader in the head, this must be his rifle. His own head hurt like hell and he closed his eyes to dull the throbbing pain.

Tim woke at dawn having fallen unconscious not long after the dingoes had disappeared. He threw the strap of his rifle over his good shoulder and looked around.

'How did I survive this? It must be God's doing. I must be blessed,' he thought to himself.

A voice spoke inside his head. "*I am here, and yes, you truly are blessed, my son.*"

Tim flinched and sat back down, his head spun from the pain of movement and he put his good arm to his face.

'Blimey, I don't believe it. I survive a massacre and the dingoes, now I hear voices.'

"*I'm no voice, Timothy, my beloved. I deliberately placed you down here out of sight of the enemy. I placed the AK47 under your hand to fight off the wild dogs and now I shall guide you to complete the mission I've set you,*" came the voice once more.

Tim felt a buzzing in his ears and his head swayed but he distinctly heard that voice, the voice of his God.

He must have fallen asleep again because the next thing he knew he was climbing the hill to find his mates. The voice came to him again.

"Timothy, it is not a pretty sight up there. Your friends have all joined me in paradise. Your mission is to stay on earth and finish what I've planned for you."

Tim paused as he rested his injured arm against his side, then wrapped his shirt around it like a sling. It hurt and he grimaced as he tried to clench his left hand into a fist, he couldn't even move it. Slowly, putting one foot in front of the other the Stosstruppen survivor climbed the hill and up over the lip of the escarpment.

Once on the hilltop he could see that what his God had said was true. He saw bodies piled atop of each other where they'd died. Some were torn apart by the starved wild dogs. He had to step carefully over entrails and patches of dried blood. It looked like the inside of a slaughterhouse that Tim had once worked in.

The cawing cry of the gathered crows came to his ears. As he looked up he realised just how sore he was. There was blood in his hair and his ear was smashed and swollen where his head had hit the rocks. His head swam in a misty haze and he wondered if he'd been shot in the head.

Thirsty, he was so thirsty his tongue was swollen. He struggled to open his mouth and his lips started to bleed.

The first thing he did was take a water bottle strapped to one of the dead Talons. With only the one useful hand he pulled it out of its pouch, opened the top and poured the refreshing liquid into his mouth. He groaned in relief as he poured some over his face.

"Slowly now, Timothy. I suggest you go back down the hill where you came up, there are others, dangerous others," came his God's soothing voice.

Tim looked around at every body on the hilltop, not one showed any sign of life. Those who survived must have either bled to death or were torn apart by the dingoes.

'There must have been a dozen or more dingoes up here last night. What a disaster, poor beggars,' he thought, noticing some of the bodies were wet with blood, these had their throats ripped out. He walked over to one of the Talon officers, the body was stiff. The morning sun was already blazing down upon his back, it was going to be a hot day. Pulling the Talon's Luger from its holster he tucked it into his pocket along with a spare magazine.

Tim stood straight and bent his back to the sides and felt it crack as the vertebrate shifted back into place. Still thinking of how strange it was to hear God's voice he returned to the base of the hill. For the past half hour he could smell something pleasant in the morning air but couldn't quite place it in his disturbed mind.

"Go around the base of the hill and you'll find food and water at the Talon's camp site. Check your weapon and have it ready, the Talons are your enemy."

The young Stosstruppen stopped and checked the Luger's magazine, it had one round in it's magazine.

"Yes," came the voice, *"it's just as well you checked."*

Tim's training took over as he moved into stealth mode and he crept around the hill the pistol held in front of him. He heard voices, not the one inside his head but other voices. Tim didn't recognise any of them. They weren't the voices of his friends. Flicking the safety off his pistol he silently crept forward.

On a dead tree branch he saw two Talons. They were sitting together having their breakfast. Their red embroidered shirt pockets stood out in the morning sunlight despite the many blood stains on their clothing. There was a billy of water on the fire. They appeared to be waiting for it to boil for their morning cup of tea.

Tim walked straight up to them, his pistol in front of him.

"Hey, mate, you can put your pistol down, it's all over," said a startled Talon, a distinct tone of fatigue and sadness in his voice.

The other leaned forward and began to stand up. 'He's going for his rifle,' thought Tim as he noticed that neither of them had a weapon near at hand.

"The shows over so put the pistol away," said the bloke who was now standing, moving towards his weapon.

"So you're the elite Talons, hey? I don't think you guys are really that good at all. Like I said yesterday, 'one Stosstruppen is worth a dozen of you bastards.' " Tim giggled as he pulled the trigger.

There was grim satisfaction in finishing what they'd started the day before. The Stosstruppen were superior. The fact he was now under the eye of his Lord on high made this shameless act righteous.

"They would have killed you, Timothy. Now they have provided you with a hot meal and a resting place while you await the arrival of the lieutenant. He'll return you to Marree as your reward for surviving and winning the battle."

Tim ate the remaining bacon and eggs in the men's mess tins and drank their hot tea. He'd never before eaten a meal that tasted so good.

"My gift to you, my loyal, beloved child."

As the blessed of all Stosstruppen finished his meal he suddenly felt dizzy. His head buzzed with a loud whistling sound then he collapsed. Tim awoke to the sound of a truck approaching. Looking up he saw the lieutenant climb out of his truck followed by the two guardsmen.

"I don't believe it! You survived that massacre? It was bloody brilliant! We watched it again this morning that's why we're running late. A damn fine blood bath it was too. The best so far. That knife and bayonet charge? Wow, that was the most vicious hand to hand fighting we've seen," said the excited lieutenant.

The young officer stopped talking when he noticed the two dead Talons around the camp fire, his face darkened. It was then that Timothy noticed the red insignia on the officers front pocket, the lieutenant was a Talon. He looked at the two guardsmen, they too had red embroidery on their shirt pockets.

"What's your battalion soldier?" asked the lieutenant holding his rage in check.

"I'm Stosstruppen, Lieutenant, the finest of the finest," replied Tim. His head still hurt and he didn't quite understand the change in the officer's manner. He reached for his cold cup of tea while nursing his inflamed and throbbing arm.

"What about these dead soldiers here? It looks like you killed them this morning. Did you?"

"I woke up and came around the hill and found them here. My Lord told me to be prepared for them and I did. They would have killed me so I shot them, dead. I won, they lost," said Tim looking confused as he noticed the lieutenant's tone was now quite different to that of a moment ago.

"I believe your Stosstruppen joined up with the Crusader platoon. Don't bother answering because we saw it on the video. I'm sorry private but you've broken all the rules. No one's allowed to kill after first light the following morning and no battalion is allowed to join and support another." The Talon lieutenant pulled his Luger from its holster at his waist and chambered a round with a loud click.

Tim looked up in bewilderment. "But I'm the blessed son of the Lord on high. I've a mission from God. I was rescued from this hell-hole to complete the mission my Lord planned for me," he stammered looking into the barrel of the pistol. His eyes widened as the realisation struck him. "You can't kill me! Not me lieutenant, not me!" he yelled as he started to rise to his feet.

The voice of his God spoke clearly inside his head. In a resigned voice it said, "*Oh, shit.*"

"Son, your fucked that's what you are. You, the Crusaders and your Stosstruppen." Then he pulled the trigger - but his pistol jammed. In frustration the lieutenant threw it to the ground and looked impatiently at his guards. They opened fire with their assault rifles.

"Mate, your mission from God will have to wait until your next incarnation."

As the lieutenant picked up his jammed Luger he looked at his guards and his face brightened. He said with a bright smile, "Wouldn't it be great to run this competition against Sundown's Commando?"

Chapter 9

Girls Train to Kill

Sundown and Colonel Vic Thompson, in consultation with Major Louie Lewis and Wiram knew that they weren't in a strong enough position to assist the Flinders Ranges community. Even though Riley argued strongly for some sort of involvement he was ordered to sit tight and wait. The fighting patrols on the Birdsville Track reported that the Revelationists had tightened their control of the region causing the flow of refugees into Birdsville and Alice Springs to become a mere trickle.

With news that the Deaths Heads were back in Marree everyone was nervous. It was now possible that by combining their two elite battalions the Revelationists could push them out of Birdsville. The ASLAV's and Bushmasters were the only things stopping them.

The day Riley, Roo and Bongo arrived at the palace from Birdsville, Nulla sat down and spoke with them. "Boys, I'm sorry but it's a no go. We're expecting resistance to increase from the Marree terrorists and you fellas aren't fully recovered yet. We can continue to put pressure on them but as for a rescue in the Flinders that's a no-go from the top."

After their talk they reluctantly went back to their horse and camel training in readiness for the newly announced holiday patrol.

As Bongo said, "Sometimes we just have to wait. I guess this is one of those times."

Nulla liked and respected the three scouts. He was there after they took down Joey Wilson in the Arkaroola wilderness. It was during their desert trek to Birdsville that he learned how much Riley and Katie loved the Flinders Ranges and their community. Katie had nursed many of them back to life in their one-room home. Nulla was satisfied the boys wouldn't do anything silly but just in case he spoke to Katie and Charlene knowing they would keep an eye on their men.

He worried about Bongo though. It was obvious that the young scout liked Lucy but Lucy had ignored every hint and opportunity Bongo presented to her. Glenda had spoken about it quite a lot. They both liked Bongo and were keen for him to find happiness but it seemed he would never find what he sought with Lucy. Glenda told Nulla not to worry, sometimes love just happens.

"You're a smart one, me girlie," he chuckled trying to sound like Pedro. "Maybe Bongo will just knock his future true love off her feet one day. They'll fall in love through an act of bravery like Shrek and Princess Fiona."

Glenda looked lovingly at her man. "Or maybe it will be on the battlefield like Nulla and Glenda."

The girls were on a mission to get up to speed on managing the camels under Kris and Nulla's tutoring. When they weren't riding they were learning the art of killing with Shadow and Captain Johnny Walker.

Lucy and Heidi complained that they preferred Nulla because Johnny was tough, tougher then Nulla ever was.

"NO! How many times have I got to show you, Jaina. Get them tits of yours out of the way, strap them down or something! You've got to put your knee in there, harder! Then your arm goes here, then the knife!" He was clearly frustrated. Even Blondie, who'd participated in self defense courses for many years, was fed up with him.

He stopped when he saw Jaina tearing up. Johnny's hardened face changed when he realised what a bastard he'd become. He was pushing the girls too hard.

"I'm sorry, Jaina, I didn't mean that." He walked her over to the bench where the other girls were sitting. Jaina saw Heidi crying then broke into tears herself.

"I think we might grab some water and take five, what do you think, Johnny?" Shadow said throwing water bottles to everyone. Her pulse was pounding and her face was red. "Johnny, I'm taking over the self defense classes as of now. I want you to grab Pedro and Halo and ask them to bring the weapons and pistols. You can start weapons training and skirmishing this afternoon. Go take a break, it looks like you need it." She didn't stay to notice his stunned reaction. Instead she turned to the girls.

"Right girls. In pairs, follow my moves." Then she went back to the kung fu kata they were learning.

Behind her Johnny's voice was soft, seductively venomous. Shadow knew a fight was coming and she was prepared for it.

"I do believe I outrank you, Lieutenant," the captain said coldly.

In a whirling blur of fury she spun on the balls of her feet and Shadow was in his face. She stood right up on her tip-toes in a fighting stance that needed just that split second to decapitate the captain.

"You may outrank me, Johnny boy, but I'm a Sundown's Commando, an original. And you're confusing your rank with my authority." Shadow stood in his face for just long enough to see his eyes shift away from hers. She then coolly turned back to the girls and resumed her lesson.

Nulla was watching the lesson held inside the enormous sheering shed. He wandered over to Captain Walker and tapped him lightly on the shoulder.

"War is hell ain't it?" he chuckled. Walker put his arm around Nulla's shoulder and together they walked across to the newly erected tent city – this was their new meal venue to cater for the influx of refugees and soldiers from Alice Springs. They went over to Halo and Pedro who were surrounded by a group of admiring off-duty soldiers.

"… then he spun around and kicked the bloke in the stomach. He continued his spin, a full circle, then he sliced the bloke's neck with his knife, like this," said Halo who was demonstrating the move standing above everyone on the table. Halo looked up to see the two older men approaching and stopped.

Pedro didn't notice and continued with the tale. "He's not human I tell yous. When that berserker takes over, he's a demon. He dances among them terrorists and just cuts 'em up like a samurai, then throws his knife like a circus performer." He moved his hands to show how Sundown held his knife and performed a perfect re-enactment of throwing. "He threw Shamus' commando knife and it went into his eye socket and right into his evil brain. The boofhead just stopped dead in his tracks and then dropped into the creek bed."

A young voice called from the middle of the group of soldiers. "Hey Pedro, what sort of knife was it?"

Pedro suddenly stopped talking as though shot. He peered through a gap in the group of soldiers below him trying to locate the voice. "It's you ain't it! That bloody boofhead wot asks all them damn questions!" He didn't have time to finish because Captain Walker had called for their attention.

"Pedro, we've got a job for you and Halo after lunch." He lifted the tea pot, felt that it was still hot then reached for a spare mug and poured himself a cup. He looked to Nulla who nodded and poured one for him as well.

"What's this about then?" asked Halo rubbing the itchy bullet scar on his scalp.

"Special training session for the Girl Guards, mate. I need six AK's, pistols and knives. You've still got that Deaths Head knife collection of yours?" Nulla had Halo pegged and wouldn't let him look away.

"Aw gee, Nulla, that's my private victory knife collection," he whined. "Damn it, I earned them. Each one tells a story of death and destruction." The boys around him laughed. They'd heard the story many times of the Marree Hotel battle and how Halo had collected every Deaths Head knife before they escaped to Birdsville.

"Halo, sorry, mate, we only need six, just six. I'll let you officially award each girl their own knife and they can kiss your cheek, the one on your face that is." Captain Johnny Walker chuckled and turned to Pedro. "Pedro, I need you and your sniper rifle, and can you grab a Blaser with ammo as well?"

Pedro nodded, he already knew this was on the agenda. Sundown had spoken to him before he left for Alice Springs. "I need you both at the sheering shed to walk the girls through their weapons and then onto the range."

A voice called out from among the troops. "Can we help? Them girls are... cute."

Johnny reached across several bodies and from the very middle of the pack pulled up a young soldier, pimply faced and just out of short pants.

"Ah ha! Bob, my boy! So, you like these young girls so much you want to help them out do you?" he said smooth as silk.

The young man smiled with delight. "Thanks, Captain Walker, I'd really like that."

"While the girls are busy with weapons training they'll need some-one to shovel the manure from the camel sheds. I want those three sheds of theirs cleaned of every scrap of camel shit before 3 pm. Got it?" The captain finally released the frustration that had built up inside him all morning.

"That's what you get for being a boofhead and asking questions all the damn time!" added Pedro. "'Koala Bob' is it? Matey, I'm going to kick your butt with me tin legs if you don't have those yards shining by three o'clock. Johnny here can relieve me when I gets tired of it."

Koala Bob, turned and grinned at his mates. Any attention from the legendary originals was worth even the worst punishment. Besides, he knew he'd get to meet the girls when they came back from training so this wasn't punishment at all. He immediately began thinking of what he would say to Heidi and Jaina.

After weapons training with Pedro and Halo, the girls were back in the sheering shed their heads hung down from exhaustion and the heat.

They had started the day working with their camels. Each had their own mounts and were now expected to sleep next to them each night to help speed the bonding. After their camel work they did physical exercises followed by self defense with Shadow and then they discussed possible assassination scenarios with Captain Walker. Next was their lunch break followed by weapons training and learning how to move like a sniper through the desert scrub. Right now Nulla and Johnny were introducing them to strategy and tactics.

Much like Blondie, Jaina had been through basic terrorist training followed by specialist training for the Tajna Sluzba.

"Nulla?" called Jaina. "Why did you choose us four? Shouldn't it just be Blondie and me? Lucy and Heidi shouldn't have to be put through this intensity of training in such a short space of time. How will they remember anything?"

Both Lucy and Heidi were lying on the floor of the sheds massaging their feet just like Nulla had taught them on their desert trek from Adelaide. Their life in Adelaide seemed so long ago now.

"Jaina, we're all fond of you girls, you know that. Even Johnny here is." Captain Walker smiled sheepishly. "I wanted you two on this mission and so did everyone else Sundown spoke to. But what I've seen of these two Adelaide beauties was so impressive I thought four was better than two."

Heidi's head slowly rose from staring at her feet to look up at Nulla. This was followed by a cautious Lucy.

"Nulla, did I hear that correctly? You said we were... 'beauties'?" asked an amazed Heidi.

Walker chuckled lightly and Nulla grinned. "I'm sure I said that you impressed me with your courage and loyalty. I saw how both of you handled yourselves when Arty was shot. I heard from Simon and Luke how Lucy stayed to help them when that mongrel Wilson bloke fired at you. Both of you are hero's in my eyes."

The girls were silent for a few moments then Lucy spoke. "Nulla, do you really mean that?"

"I sure do, Lucy. Didn't I want you to take command of our group if I was killed on our way here, to Birdsville?"

"And the boys stood up for me too?" she continued, her eyes bright with unshed tears.

"Those boys think the world of you two. If it wasn't for what they told me you wouldn't have been invited to join this elite group." Nulla reached down and lifted her to a standing position beside him. "Lucy, you showed your true worth on our way here, to sanctuary. You helped Simon take out those terrorists at the motel. You helped cover Luke at Arkaroola. You've not skimped a dirty job here at the palace. Even helping Fatima and Pinkie clean those sex rooms in the tunnels wasn't too much for you. So that's why you're here, because I trust you." Nulla stopped then added, "No, that's not true. It's because we all trust and respect you."

Of course Heidi wasn't going to let Lucy take all of Nulla's attention and perhaps she also wanted the ruggedly handsome Johnny to take notice. "Nulla, when you said we were 'beauties' you did mean 'pretty' didn't you?" Heidi had her chin lifted slightly, again, just like Glenda did when she wanted something from Nulla. Her throat was pale, she was young and at that moment she was simply gorgeous. It had no effect on Nulla though.

"Heidi, if you ask me one more time if I think you're beautiful, guess what I'm going to do." Nulla said firmly knowing exactly what she was up to. Behind him he heard Captain Walker grunt as he tried to suppress a laugh.

Heidi dropped her chin and said into her chest. "I know, you'll take my AK off me." Under her breath she whispered loud enough to be heard. "Glenda gets away with it all the time, why not me?"

Captain Johnny Walker couldn't stop himself adding, "You girls are all beautiful, that's why we chose you. But don't forget, this is an assassination and it might end up a suicide mission. If you get caught you'll be executed." A chill air entered the shed and the girls, except Blondie, sat down, the smiles slipping from their faces. There was no more fun it was serious again.

"Not only will you be killed but being pretty carries its own dangers. Beauty is a myth isn't it Blondie?" Captain Johnny Walker deliberately asked the prettiest and the toughest of them all.

Blondie had been quiet throughout their training. It wasn't just a case of her ongoing hangover from the nightly binges but because she was bored with life. This was all so meaningless to her.

"Heidi," she said turning to the girls sitting beside her, "look at me," she commanded, "look at me and tell me what you see."

The girls knew her story, of how she had escaped the entire Mount Isa Revelationist army without the help of her brother, Fat Boy. Blondie, the ex-Revelationist secret agent, intrigued the entire commando. They all fell silent waiting to hear what she was going to say.

"Well?" She waited another few seconds before continuing. "Beauty is a myth. It's not the key to happiness like they told you on TV. Beauty is a commodity, others want it and they'll do anything to get it. People will deliberately hurt you to take what they want from you. Men use you and women are jealous of you. Being beautiful is a curse." She wanted to have that cigarette she saw Nulla rolling but she put it off until she'd made her point. "Beneath this so-called beauty I'm just a boring person. I'm not even a woman any more, I'm just a chattel, something to be used up and thrown out." She spat the last sentence into the air.

Jaina looked at her mentor, her face betrayed her concern. "Blondie, we're Tajna Sluzba. I'll always look after you, you know that."

"Yes, I'm Tajna Sluzba, I can survive anything. I'm a protected species." Blondie replied wiping at her eyes which had mysteriously grown moist.

Nulla saw what was happening and stepped in. "Righto, I think Johnny is about to begin the tactics lesson. Blondie, would you please walk with me." He reached across and took her arm gently. Blondie walked meekly with him towards the back door of the sheering shed. They sat quietly watching the sun easing its way towards the horizon.

"Blondie, what's going on with you? I've been watching you slowly drift away from us. You've gone somewhere in your head and I'm worried that we now have to worry about the greatest asset we have against the terrorists, you," he said looking directly at her.

Blondie sat silently watching the reds and orange streaks against the high clouds on the western horizon. They sat without talking for some minutes, then she began.

"Nulla, between you and me, I just want out. Cambra noticed too and tried to help but I threw it back in his face. I've just stopped wanting things, life is meaningless." Her legs swung back and forth over the wooden sheering shed platform much like a lost school girl. Nulla waited noticing the tears running down her cheeks.

"You've got Glenda and a baby on the way and that's meaningful." Blondie lifted her legs up and rested her chin on her knees. "Everyone else has family and friends and they have meaning. But I've got nothing, not even pleasant memories. I've just got emptiness. All I have inside is revenge."

Nulla knew there was something coming so he reached into his pocket and pulled out his tobacco pouch. "Want one?" he asked as he began to roll two cigarettes, one for each of them.

Blondie waited for her cigarette to light before drawing the smoke deeply into her lungs and resting her chin back on her knees.

"Reverend Albert organised for the gang to rape me, Nulla. Fat Boy found out the truth off the Iceman. We weren't wanted any more." Blondie paused as she drew on the cigarette and waited for the head spin. Their supplies of cigarettes and tobacco was now gone. Everyone, including Blondie, smoked the smelly bush herbs, dried tea leaves and something people called 'bush tobacco' but tasted like camel manure. Pedro and Nulla appeared to be the only ones to have real tobacco.

"That's what I've been craving, a proper smoke, thanks," she said and continued as she waved at the flies darting in to land on her face. "I know where he is and I know Reverend Thomas and Reverend Mark have him in their sights. They all have their own special mansions in Darwin. When we get there I'll hunt them down, in my own way and in my own time. I'll kill them, all of them." Nulla could hear the venom in her voice and he looked carefully at her.

"Blondie?" Nulla said quietly. "Do you mind if I ask Charlene to talk with you? She's helping Tricia and Katie in the first aid team and she's good to talk to. I've had a few chats with her myself, so have Halo and McFly. I'd like you to as well. What do you say?"

Blondie just nodded as she drew on her cigarette again. "Yeah, I like that girl, she's quiet and peaceful. She's a good find, Nulla. It won't do any good but I promise to have a chat with her."

With the training day over, Captain Johnny Walker and Shadow walked with the three girls to their camp near the camels while Nulla and Blondie stayed behind to talk. They now cooked their meals around the camels so they would get use to the smells and flickering of the camp fire. The camels made noises of complaint but the group got on with their evening preparations regardless.

"Shadow, look! Spooky's coming over to see what we're eating!" Spooky was Jaina's camel. Gently and slowly Jaina handed the young camel a piece of flat bread made from what wheat they had left and other edible seeds Fatima and Fat Boy had grown, harvested and baked.

"Amazing!" whispered Captain Walker. He and Shadow now had a truce of sorts, they simply ignored each other.

"Captain?" asked Jaina, after Spooky returned to his camel friends, satisfied. "When did you say Sundown would be back?"

Captain Walker wiped the food from the corners of his mouth before he spoke. "Andy said they should be on their way back tomorrow or the day after. There's more to this than we know, Jaina. Sorry I just can't tell you more because I don't know."

Lucy watched from beside the fire. "What's it with Blondie? Does anyone know why she's acting so strange lately?"

"She's angry at the world these days," said Jaina, cleaning up her mess gear. "The church people up north treated her bad and she wants revenge. I think it's eating her up so bad that she can't get there fast enough. If we travel by camel it's going to take us months to get there.

Then we have to find the targets and execute the assassinations… it's gonna take ages to do the job."

Lucy sat thinking for a while. "Didn't Nulla say Fat Boy's going to do some prep with his friends in the biker gangs before we get there? Aren't we suppose to just turn up, charm the churchy's and then kill them?"

"You make that sound so easy, Lucy," said Heidi. "We have to survive the trip first. Don't forget Wiram and Nulla will probably come with us. They're needed to arrange our escape. If we don't get the local aborigines on-side we're going to have trouble hiding the camels and gear. Then we'll be at the mercy of the bikers. You know what wankers they can be."

"I worry about Donna and Glenda, Heidi, they'll miss their partners. It's going to be dangerous you know." Lucy was helping Jaina set up their swags for the sleep-out. It was a simple rug on the ground and two sticks to support a cover for their head.

"Huh," said Captain Walker, "dangerous for the boys? Give me a break, it's you lot we're worried about. Why the hell do you think we've been pushing you so hard?"

Shadow was about to say something when Lucy spoke up. "Johnny, you can share my bed if you like and then we won't be scared." Her impish face creased into a smile and she winked at him.

"Lucy, I'm not like that you know," he hurried on. "Not that I don't like you or find you unattractive." Captain Johnny Walker's face turned red. This was dangerous territory, a single male with a group of intelligent females.

"The best looking fella in the camp and he's gay!" cried Heidi as she put more wood on the fire and set the billy to boil water for their cup of tea.

"Well, young lady, I quite like who I am," he said teasing the girls. He was back in control and on safe ground. The group had this conversation at almost every meal and he was getting used to their rough and tough, girlie way of teasing him. He reached down and grabbed at his crotch. "You know I could still entertain you if you wanted."

Jaina burst out laughing. "Johnny! Put your meat mallet back into your trousers before one of the dogs thinks it's a sausage!" She was holding a length of rope in one hand and a stick in the other but right now she couldn't remember what she was supposed to do with either of them.

"I hear your Shrek man is, ah, well-hung my dear. I guess you just don't need me anyway," he called to Jaina as he got up to walk towards the shed. He called back to them over his shoulder. "I'll get Blondie and Nulla. Final lesson in half an hour." It was back to business and time was running out for everyone.

He met Blondie on his way there. She told him that Nulla had gone back to see his wife and wouldn't be back for another few hours.

Johnny thanked her and smiled. "Did he now? I think he forgot it was his turn to walk you girls through night stalking. I'll send someone to get him."

"Nulla?" Glenda was pulling her top on while Nulla showered ready to go back to help with the girl's training.

"Yes, love?" he called as he towelled himself dry.

"Come back here for a minute," she said coyly.

"Why? What do you want now?" he asked absently, pulling on his trousers.

"I just want, you know, I want to..." she let her voice trail off.

"Oh, that again. Righto, I'm on my way." Nulla came out of the bathroom, threw his towel and trousers into the corner and eased his muscled body beside her. Glenda was lying on the bed with just her t-shirt on. She reached up and took it off as he pulled her body in close and snuggled his face into her swelling breasts.

"Nulla, I'm worried about this holiday patrol Sundown wants you to go on," she said softly, enjoying his firm body pressed tightly against hers.

"I told you darling, Wiram and I are just there to entertain the camels. Sundown wants the originals plus the cameleers, to go on a short training patrol, that's all. It's safe and it's going to be a quiet holiday. I promise we'll be back even if I have to kill every terrorist in the territory to get back to my lover." He held her close as he rolled her over, she now lay on top of him.

She was strong at first but then she began to cry again, a soft moan that hit every nerve in his heart. "I know you'll be safe, but I worry so much. You're so damn brave and heroic. You'll charge in there and shoot everyone and then every damn idiot Revelationist in the territory will want to shoot you."

"Glenda, darling, look at me," he cupped her face in his hands then kissed her. A long slow kiss that might have gone further if there wasn't a knock on the door.

"What is it?" Glenda called out impatiently. She liked it when Nulla kissed her like that, she didn't want it to stop.

"Nulla? Are you in there? Sergeant, Captain Walker wants you pronto," came the messenger's voice.

The powerfully built aboriginal warrior lay back in resignation, his arms loosely wrapped around his wife. "Tell Johnny I'll be there in a minute," he called through the closed door.

"Sergeant, Captain Walker said now. He said it's important," came the youthful voice again.

'Damn!' Nulla muttered to himself. He kissed Glenda on the lips and let his hands slide down her naked body revelling in the sensual softness of her pale skin. He eased himself off the bed and quickly pulled his trousers on.

"OK, tell the captain I'm on my way," he called.

Chapter 10

Secrets of Pine Gap

It was dusk when Sundown arrived at the Pine Gap Intelligence Facility with McFly. The two desert fighters were transfixed by the domes and defences set up for the facility's protection. There were trenches, barbed wire entanglements and they drove past two heavy bulldozers working to extend the earthen barricades around the perimeter.

McFly pointed out what appeared to be a robot-like weapon outside the main entrance. They could just see it's mini-gun turret. He told Sundown he thought it would have laser sights too.

"That is a Robocop for sure. It probably has radar or some sort of thing to pick up movement and then it'll fire if it looks human. It's probably totally automatic, just arm it at night and go to bed," said McFly confidently.

Sundown smiled at his adjutant's enthusiasm. If he were to join forces with these people this was what he wanted to see: preparation, professionalism and people, lots of trained personnel he can call upon to fight.

Four special forces guards searched the two men before leading them through the entrance gate. They guaranteed no one would touch Sundown's commando knife as he reluctantly handed it over. The two visitors were escorted into the lift which took them deep into the bowels of the earth to Commander Sue-Ellen Cullen's quarters.

McFly tried to engage the guards in conversation but failed. Sundown observed and noted it accordingly.

'*Well trained and serious, good. I need boys like these. Commander Cullen must be one heck of a leader to maintain discipline like this through the apocalypse,*' he thought.

Soon the doors opened and they were led into an antechamber with comfortable seating. They were directed to sit and wait for further instructions.

"I bet they're watching us. See that picture, Sundown, I bet that's got a camera inside it. See those beady eyes? They look like camera lenses." McFly stood up and walked over to check the colourful oil painting. He picked at one of the eyes and grunted, shook his head and sat back down. "Maybe it's in those specks on the wall there?"

Before Sundown had time to reply the door opened and in walked three women with refreshments. They were soon joined by a forth who was clearly their leader. Her face appeared to be sunburned but that only added to her light blond hair and bright, curious eyes.

"My name is Commander Sue-Ellen Cullen, I gather you are Commander Sundown, and this is your adjutant, Captain McFly?" She took a plate of biscuits and cheese from one of the girls and offered it to the two men.

Both Sundown and McFly were slightly taken aback. They hadn't expected the commander to address them as fellow human beings. Everything they had read in Vic's papers was to the contrary.

"Welcome to the Pine Gap Intelligence Facility, please come with me, my office is just down the corridor." The group walked only a few metres before entering a small but comfortable room. They noticed a makeshift bed against the wall. "Please ignore my mess, I often sleep here when I'm working."

Commander Cullen asked her girls to show McFly around the base, she wanted time to speak with Sundown, alone.

Sundown was delighted to be asked if he would like a private tour of the base. Unfortunately he became distracted each time Commander Cullen brushed up against his arm and shoulder. The contact disturbed him as it caused the blood to rush to his head, it was something he had no control over. The honeycomb of tunnels and wide open rooms populated with the busy Pine Gap staff just added to his sense of disorientation.

Without realising the impact she was having on Sundown, Commander Cullen continued to explain that there were secrets inside the facility which would be revealed when the time was right. The thing Sundown remembered most about the tour was that the base was in touch with other such facilities around the world.

"Fortunately, none of those bases have been handed over intact. There are weapons in the sky that we don't want in terrorist hands. At the moment we have the means to ensure there is no unauthorised access to them." Sundown noticed that Commander Cullen didn't smile as she spoke.

"Don't worry, Commander, I have no interest whatsoever in seeking to take control of your base. But I'd like to talk to you about sharing information for our mutual benefit." Sundown shifted his weight from one foot to the other. "What you know will certainly come in handy for our patrols."

When he saw the massive screen or 'big board', as she called it, it took his breath away. It was just like he'd seen on TV. The commander casually asked the operator to zoom in on the enemy patrol that they were currently observing. Sundown could clearly see the individual features of each terrorist soldier and the effect was immediate. It threw him back to his childhood reliving the thrill of waking on Christmas morning to unwrap Santa Claus' gifts.

When they returned to Sue-Ellen's office Sundown's demon was fully aroused and alert. His instincts lay scattered as he floundered trying to comprehend the incredible asset this woman controlled. In this confused state he tried to pigeon hole exactly what Commander Sue-Ellen Cullen triggered within his unconscious to make him feel so... he couldn't even form a single word in his head.

"Commander Sundown, or perhaps just Sundown?" Sue-Ellen's voice drifted into Sundown's consciousness. "Considering the current state of the world we can do without formalities I think."

Sundown found himself sitting on the lounge as the commander poured herself a drink. He blinked himself back into consciousness just as she offered to fill his glass. Looking at his hand he wondered how the glass got there.

"Thank you, Commander." He took a mouthful of whiskey on ice to calm his befuddled mind. Fortunately the alcohol had the effect of clearing his head and he remembered why he was there. "I don't quite know why you've called me here today, particularly since you've given Alice Springs Command the cold shoulder since the apocalypse."

Sue-Ellen gave a light laugh and Sundown's skin tingled as though she had stroked it lightly with her finger nails.

"Sundown, that was simply because we couldn't trust their leader. General Hughes was a political appointment not a strategic or military one, and Thompson, well, I wasn't sure of his capabilities either. Besides, the world as we knew it is gone. I'm now in command of this asset and I no longer answer to anyone. Between you and I the US administration is no longer, there's only a few facilities like this left intact in the world." She paused to watch his expression – Sundown stared at her, he didn't know what to say.

"As far as I am concerned I am whatever I wish to be. I'll never return to the states. None of my staff will ever see their homes or loved ones again. It's over. I have accepted that if I want I can run my own war in my own way. Fortunately I am a reasonable and intelligent woman and that's why I've contacted you," Sue-Ellen said as she casually moved a strand of hair from her face with the back of her hand.

The demon inside Sundown groaned with desire and he knew right then that he was in big trouble. *I've just met this woman and already she's got me in an absolute dither. Damn it demon, get down!'* he said to himself.

The commander continued as though she hadn't noticed his momentary distraction. "I've been watching you Sundown." She paused to let that sink in and Sundown didn't miss it. "We're Intelligence with a capital 'I' and I think you already know we've intercepted every conversation you have ever had since the apocalypse. We're quite impressed with what you've done I might add."

"Ah, right, thank you." Sundown took another gulp of his drink as he felt the temperature in the room rise by several degrees. He had to say something to gain some level of control over himself.

"Commander, can I ask what you know about the Revelationist intentions, both Marree and Darwin. I'd like to shift our discussion in that direction. I'd also like your opinion on a few things we're planning." Sundown forced his mind to stay on track and it did, to a point.

"Sundown, I know what you're planning and that's why I've invited you here today." For a moment Sue-Ellen looked vulnerable but her mask shifted and she was back in control. "I've got interests in the situation in Darwin. Personal interests and I need your help, I'm proposing that we join forces." She stopped and took a long look at Sundown before continuing.

"I've been a widow for fourteen years. I loved my husband, he was my hero. Reece died doing what he loved, flying navy planes." Sue-Ellen looked at the table and placed her empty glass on it. "We had a son, an only child, the apple of our eye. Sadly his father died before he really got to know him. But it didn't stop Tanner joining the navy when he was old enough. I've always worked for navy intelligence and, naturally, Tanner gravitated towards intelligence too."

Sundown nodded for her to go on. He realised that she was as attractive as the reports had stated. She was in her forties with straight blond hair, sharp, lively eyes and a well formed womanly body. Sue-Ellen looked fit and was clearly intelligent. He hadn't yet witnessed her power but he knew she had it in her, her presence was almost overwhelming. Sundown lifted his drink, it was already empty. He asked if Sue-Ellen wanted a top-up of her drink too. She nodded as she continued speaking.

"Tanner has a natural talent for covert operations so we sent him to investigate the upper echelons of the Revelationist church. He ended up in Darwin to keep an eye on Reverend Albert. Up till recently he worked as Albert's secretary. He's performed outstandingly, leaking information to us for the past two years. But this week it stopped, suddenly and without explanation. We have two other operatives in Darwin, they operate out of Mount Isa and Longreach. They've stopped communications too." Sue-Ellen paused to look directly into Sundown's eyes. "Sundown, I know you and Thompson are planning a trip to Darwin, I want to go along."

Sundown's mouth opened and closed. His demon went silent and he didn't quite know what to say, so he didn't.

The navy commander giggled nervously. "Sundown, please, don't do that, you make me feel like a school girl. I haven't given in to temptation in all my years of marriage, not even as a widow." She lifted her glass and drank half of it before putting it down to look again at this handsome man with the smouldering dark eyes.

"I'm sorry commander but I don't know what to say. You want to go through the desert, with Blondie and the girls? To Darwin? That's going to be dangerous."

Sue-Ellen stopped her flirting and flared. "Don't be condescending to me, Commander! I know it's going to be damned dangerous why the hell do you think I called you here!"

Immediately Sundown's demon shifted forward into his mind and body, ready. Sundown stood up but instead of releasing his berserker demon he breathed deeply and settled back down into the lounge chair. His demon, under control for the moment, permitted him to continue.

"Commander Cullen, you are most welcome to join my patrol but you will then be under my command. I want you to understand that before we take this conversation any further."

"You bastard!" she said softly, almost breathlessly. "I… Sundown… damn it, call me Sue-Ellen please, it's uncomfortable being so formal with you sitting so close to me like this."

The tension in the room dissipated. Sundown leaned back on the lounge and unconsciously put his arm over the back of the chair – his fingers almost touched her shoulder. It appeared to be a deliberate manouvre. Sue-Ellen noticed and moved a fraction of an inch closer, they were now physically in contact with each other.

"Friends?" she asked, her face a mixture of joy, longing and fear. Even she didn't realise how vulnerable she would be with a man, a man who was so like her husband it sent her head into a spin.

"Yes, I'd like that, Sue-Ellen. Friends." Sundown lifted a finger and caressed her cheek which appeared to have willed itself towards his hand. There was a groan from inside his mind and Sundown recognised his demon was awake and restless again. Its urgency pushed but he forced it back down quickly. *'I can't go there today, mate, back off.'* He quickly pulled his hand away as if he had been slapped.

"Sue-Ellen, I've just met you and I like you. You're attractive and intelligent, everything a man could want. There's something I can't do with you that I'd like to do. Like you were with your late husband, I'm faithful to my wife. No matter how strongly I'm attracted to you, that's a bond I could never break." Sundown stood and began pacing the room as he tried to assemble his thoughts.

"Sundown, for crying out loud sit down will you. I had to put up with watching you pacing in Thompson's office today. It's making me sea-sick." She giggled again and Sundown, his mouth opening and closing involuntarily once again, sat back down.

"Vic and McFly were right, you do have your spy camera's everywhere."

"I know you're married. I've seen Pinkie several times and she seems like a lovely woman. Please don't think that I am trying to seduce you, Sundown, I just can't help admiring what I can't have." She shook the wandering strands of hair out of her face and regained control of herself. "When you leave here this evening it will be with myself and four of my people. I want to meet with and find out more about your commando. If I like what I see, and I'm sure I will, then you will have gained eight hundred personnel who will come under our joint command." She knew she had him hooked now. It seemed a game was needed and she excelled at playing games.

Sundown thought for a moment. "Yes, I can do that, I think. You'll need transport and I've got just the one Cessna. It'll seat four, five at a pinch." Sundown mused, his mind making rapid calculations.

"It's fine, I've got a helicopter. A stealth MH-X Black Hawk. We've had a few problems with the electrical system but it's a great chopper. It's looked after us since the apocalypse. We'll all travel together in that." Sue-Ellen smiled a smile that took his breath away. Sundown was smitten with just how perfect she looked right then.

Without thinking he moved across the gap between them and they were so close they could have kissed. Sue-Ellen breathed deeply and brushed her lips across the stubble of his cheek and broke the spell.

"If I knew I'd get this close to a man I'd have put on some perfume. Damn, I wish you weren't married," she said and pulled back.

"You don't need perfume, Sue-Ellen, you smell just fine right now." His eyes were closed and he seemed to be in a semi-trance.

When Sundown opened his eyes he saw tears on her cheeks. "I'm sorry, I don't know what's happening here. I never do things like this. I really don't want to do the wrong thing by you or by my wife." He stopped speaking when she placed her fingers on his lips.

"Don't talk. I know, me too. It's just that you remind me of my beautiful husband. He was just like you and I can't stop liking you."

For a single awkward second they stared into each others eyes across the chasm of rules, morals and common sense. Sundown reached for his drink.

"Strewth, I sure need a drink."

"Me too." They smiled recognising just how close they had come to crossing the line - and liking it.

"Sundown, my friend, and I would like you to be my friend, I don't have many. I want you to know that I won't let this go any further. I have a son to rescue and you have a patrol to organise. Finish your drink and we'll get started."

Sue-Ellen stood up and held out her hand. Sundown took it and she helped him out of his chair. Her breast brushed against his chest and she leaned into him. "Damn it man, I just made a promise I don't think I can keep."

With his suntanned arms around her Sundown chuckled. "Sue-Ellen, if you don't behave yourself I'm going to put you over my knee and spank you."

"You would too I bet and I might enjoy it." She teased then led him to the door only dropping his hand when she was ready to open it.

"Sundown, we're back in the real world, are you ready?" asked Commander Sue-Ellen Cullen softly. As she opened the door she called to the girl seated at the desk in the corridor, "Inform my team that I'll meet them at the helipad in fifteen minutes."

McFly was fascinated by the special forces team's equipment. They had bags of everything. From radios and grenades to secret spying equipment which, no matter how hard he tried, they wouldn't talk about.

Tricia was too busy going over the notes she had taken from her visit with the Alice Springs medical team to notice the four handsome American special forces men sitting beside her. When she did look up she became a little too flustered to speak so she buried her head back into her papers until they arrived at the palace.

The stealth MH-X Black Hawk helicopter arrived at the Christian Palace around midnight. Captain Walker met them and formally welcomed the commander of the Pine Gap facility and her team.

"Commander Cullen, welcome to the Christian Palace which will be your home while you are here with us. If you need anything just ask any of our people." He was very proper and formal but his smile belied how his time with Sundown's Commando had spoiled him.

As he walked the new arrivals towards their accommodation Sue-Ellen took the opportunity to embed herself with the commando.

"Thank you, Captain Walker," she said. "I believe you led the retreat to Alice Springs? We heard about that and were very impressed. I'd like to see you, Nulla and Wiram in the morning to discuss certain plans we have for a joint operation. Can you do that for me please?" Sue-Ellen had taken command and even Captain Johnny Walker was impressed.

"Um, commander, wasn't I supposed to manage this outfit?" asked Sundown now wearing a worried frown.

"Sundown, you're too slow for me. If you don't get up to speed I'll leave you behind." She looked at Sundown in such a way that Captain Walker did a double check.

'*If I'm not mistaken,*' he thought, '*Commander Cullen is flirting with Sundown.*'

"Commander, I've put you and your team in the quarters just here." Captain Walker politely cut in. He left Sundown and Sue-Ellen alone in the unit while he returned to show the four special forces soldiers and helicopter crew to their rooms. These were right next to Roo and Charlene's.

When he had finished, Captain Walker returned to Sue-Ellen's room where Sundown was just leaving.

"I'll come and get you for breakfast first thing in the morning, Commander." Captain Walker saluted and with a subdued Sundown they left Sue-Ellen to ponder her next move.

Chapter 11

Special Operatives

Sundown was usually first up each morning. Sitting outside with him were Pedro, Liam and the dogs while Cat was asleep on Roo and Charlene's bed. The dogs went crazy on mornings like this. Sundown threw sticks while Liam or one of the other children chased the dogs.

"Sundown, what's this?' asked five year old Liam bringing over a piece of canvas strapping left behind in the dark last night.

"Let me see… that's a piece of belt that the soldiers used to tie things down in their helicopter," he answered, handing the canvas webbing back to his little mate. A minute later Liam was back with more bits and pieces.

"That's a piece of webbing one of the soldiers dropped. You might want to hold on to it in case he needs it." He threw another stick and the three dogs raced after it. Red Dog was missing, probably preparing to birth her litter of pups, Sundown thought.

'Sundown, matie, you'll stuff your shoulder throwing sticks like that, just relax a little," said Pedro rolling a cigarette with real tobacco. Sundown looked at him and then at the cigarette enviously.

"I picked a great time to give up smoking but if I didn't, Pinkie would have kicked me out of her bed." His eyes crinkled at the edges. "She said I smelled like an old chimney. I was flattered by the chimney but it was the 'old' that made me stop."

"Matie, them girlies are always trying to control us wild men of the desert." The old man licked the shred of newspaper he used to roll his tobacco and lit up. It flared brightly and Liam watched in fascination.

"Pedro, what's that?" asked the youngster reaching to touch the glowing cigarette Pedro held between his fingers.

"Be careful little laddie, that'll burn ya like a fire." Pedro pulled his hand upwards, out of the child's reach. Pedro liked to get up early so he could be with Sundown for an early morning cuppa and smoke. He enjoyed the company of the commando's children but he was never quite sure how to handle a child's curiosity.

"Them kids, matie, they amaze me. They have no fear and they have no sense of danger. How the hell did the human race survive?" he muttered to Sundown as Liam wandered off to chase Roo's dog.

"Damned if I know, Pedro," said Sundown as Liam came back with more bits and pieces of lost equipment and rubbish, some of it too sharp for little fingers. Pedro and Sundown were about to go and clean up the enormous paddock of dangerous looking objects when their rescuers arrived.

It was Roo and Charlene.

"Hi, Sundown," called Charlene. Roo smiled and the two older men nodded in greeting.

"Roo, you know how to say 'Hi' to Pedro and Sundown, so go on," she prompted the silent kangaroo shooter.

"Hi, Sundown. Hi, Pedro," he said clearly but in a gentle nine year old voice. Roo had lost his grandfather at that age and stopped talking, completely. Now his speech was back at that same age. Charlene was surprised he could talk so clearly but she was a little dismayed his voice was somewhat, immature.

"Hi Roo, hi Charlene, and a nice job you're doing there too," said Sundown admiringly. He'd not had much time to talk with the new comers, especially Charlene. Every time he saw her she was chatting with someone.

Since she and Katie arrived the two were inseparable as they plied their healing skills. Charlene was the counsellor and Katie the hands-on healer. The two worked together a lot of the time and the Commando enjoyed chatting with the two attractive young ladies at meal times.

"I don't get much opportunity to talk with friends or newcomers these days. Even playing with Liam in the mornings is a rare treat." Sundown rubbed at cat's ears as it jumped into his lap. "Roo, do you think you, Riley and Bongo would like to go on a camel patrol with us and the bike patrol boys? You and Bongo haven't had much chance to get out since your trip to the Flinders Ranges and I'd like Riley to spend more time with the rest of the boys. What do you think?"

Sundown had decided that most of the patrolling should now be done by the army boys from Alice Springs. Nulla's 'house rats' from Adelaide, and his own commando, were exhausted from almost a whole year of fighting and living on the edge.

The soldiers of Alice Springs Command loved it. They were keen to finally have a crack at the enemy and spent their free time talking with anyone they could get their hands on who had seen action. Sundown knew that he had to keep his team up to speed but a few months rest would make them sharper and tougher.

Riley, Katie and their two children were also bunked down in the servants quarters a few doors down from Roo. The rugged cattleman was a favourite with the soldiers but he kept a smouldering anger inside. It sometimes forced him to avoid company which upset Katie.

Charlene looked at Roo prompting him to reply to Sundown's question.

"I think, yes. Bongo's good and Riley's good," he said and smiled when Charlene hugged him with her good arm.

"Beauty!" said Sundown, "and how is the counselling going, Charlene, do you enjoy being here and helping out?"

"I love it here, Sundown," she said as she leaned forward to lift Liam into her lap with her good arm. He was busy trying to tie the broken webbing around his tiny waist. "I've met the man I love and I've made so many great friends." She was all smiles as she leaned across and kissed an embarrassed Roo. "Living the way we did, hiding in houses, afraid the terrorists would trap us or grenade us. It was hell, Sundown, every day was just hell. Here you've got the expanse of the desert plains. You can see anyone sneaking up on you for miles. Give me the desert any day."

Sundown nodded in agreement. "And how's the arm going, any progress with your elbow or shoulder, any movement yet?"

Charlene eased her skinny arm out of its sling and moved it a few inches back and forth. It looked more claw than hand. "It's coming along slowly but it's painful. Lorraine's given me exercises and Roo helps me. I have more movement than I've ever had. Lorraine said that because I've had it immobile for so long it's going to take a long time to get movement back into it. She said I'll probably not get my shoulder to move because the bones were smashed and fused together, like a knot."

Sundown realised that Charlene was happy here in the safety of the Christian Palace, much like every one else these days. The morning sun suddenly shone on her golden hair, and with the light in her eyes it matched the early morning sunrise. No wonder everyone loved her, he thought. Not only was she nice to look at but her manner and attitude to life was something special, something he rarely saw in people. In fact, he realised, Charlene was one of a kind.

"Charlene, Nulla told me you've been talking to Blondie. I don't need to know anything about what you talk about, that's your job not mine. He said that Blondie's responding well. He said she's coming out of that dark place she was in. I'd just like to say that the work you've been doing has been noticed. You're becoming one of the commando's greatest assets and you've only been here a few months." Sundown looked back at Roo. He had a question he'd wanted to ask for a while now. "But what I'm really curious to know is how you have managed to help get Roo's speech up to speed so quickly."

The young lady was a little overwhelmed. Sure, she'd been doing what came naturally to her but for someone like Sundown to notice? She thought he would have been too busy running the commando to notice someone as insignificant as her.

"Thank you, Sundown, I appreciate you saying those nice things. I just want to help, that's all. As for Roo, well I had access to all those books on psychology from the city and the university when we went there." She paused, that was why Tony was killed and Arthur wounded. It was a horrible time she would rather forget. "I... I tried some hypnosis with Roo and took him back to nine years of age, when he lost his grandfather. It worked. I'm amazed as much as everyone else. That was a miracle."

Roo put his arm around her, something he hadn't done in public before. "I like you Charlene, you're good to me," he said in his funny voice.

"Roo?" Sundown looked at him strangely. "I don't think I've ever heard so many words come out of you in all the time I've known you. Not only is your girlfriend an angel but she's also a miracle worker. I think we need Pedro to find a suitable name for you, Charlene, something that describes angels doing miracles perhaps?"

Pedro quietly smiled and eased back into his wheel chair puffing away at his mangled cigarette. He watched curiously as Roo bent to whisper in Lenny's ear. Lenny dashed into their room and came back with Kimberly, the pink Power Ranger doll. Charlene kept it as a reminder of her power to face and overcome her personal grief and loss.

"Look, Sundown," said Roo smiling broadly. "Charlene's angel." His arm was still around Charlene and she was snuggled into his shoulder.

As the kids ran off with the dogs Sundown wondered why he was so lucky to have such wonderful people around him.

By now there were others up and walking around. The four early risers watched as Katie told the kids they had to wait before getting Annie out of bed. Riley now stepped out of their room. The tall, suntaned cattleman walked over and asked if anyone wanted a cup of tea.

"I was just asking Roo if he'd like to bring you and Bongo along on our camel patrol. What do you think, Riley? It'll be the bike patrol boys, some of the Girl Guards and most of the old commando crew, the originals," said Sundown nodding for that cup of tea.

"I'll get the tea, Riles, you sit and talk for a while," called Katie winking at Charlene as she sent the kids off to play with the dogs somewhere else. She reminded Liam and Elle to be careful with Red Dog because she had babies inside her.

Just then Danielle arrived with Annie. Lucy was half asleep and carried a mug of Mel's coffee in her free hand while the other held onto little Harry's hand.

"Look what I found, Katie. He was looking for Annie. He wanted to take her to see if Red Dog had any puppies." Lucy sat down with the rest and sipped her coffee.

"Hi, Lucy," said Sundown, it was becoming a busy morning and yet he relished this opportunity to touch base with his commando. "How's training going? Didn't you get to sleep out with the camels last night?"

"Morning, Sundown. Annie's been sick these past few days but she seems to be better this morning. I had to sleep in the unit to keep an eye on her." Lucy knew what was coming next. "But I want you to know that Katie said she'll look after Annie for me if I have to be away for anything, ah, special." She continued, "I volunteered for this job and by hell or high water I'll see it to its end. Them bastards killed my husband and I'm prepared to do anything I can to pay them back, bullet by bullet."

"Hi all, hi Lucy," announced a cheery but tired Bongo. He smiled at Lucy but she wasn't looking. Charlene noticed it though. She had watched Bongo trying to get Lucy's attention ever since they met on the desert crossing from Arkaroola.

"Hi Bongo. How's the leg going?" Charlene asked sweetly. "I saw you chasing the kids yesterday. It seemed to be holding up well."

"Yeah, I can run now. That's better than last month when all I could do was limp about and crawl on my butt. Lorraine said I'm ready for patrol but only local. She said I was allowed to join the Girl Guards." He laughed and there were smiles from the others. Most of the commando knew he was keen on Lucy but she just didn't appear to be interested.

"Bongo, you've been invited to join the camel patrol with Sundown and the originals. Did you want to go?" asked Charlene. Lucy's ears pricked up and she looked around at everyone as though she had been left out of something.

"What? Me? Sure, I'd love to," Bongo said and picked up a smooching Cat at his feet to sit him on his lap. Cat thought he was in heaven with so many of his human slaves spoiling him.

"You, Roo and Riles will be joining us. I'd like Chan to come along but he won't leave. He said Doff's Bushmaster patrol might need his specialist knowledge of the re-formed Deaths Head Battalion. That might be a job for you, Charlene. When you get a chance see if he'll talk to you." Charlene nodded, she'd already been asked to speak with him.

Sundown was pleased that Roo's cousin, Riley, agreed to go along with the camel patrol. The tall, handsome cattleman was popular because of his quiet, reliable manner.

"We have some training to do before we go on a proper patrol and that's better than sitting around getting bored."

"What about us girls Sundown, you've not said anything to us about a holiday patrol. Can we come too?" asked Lucy brightly. Her face looked younger and brighter in the morning light than he'd noticed before.

"Yes, the Girl Guards are coming too, I believe, but I've got to talk with Captain Walker and the Pine Gap commander first. There's a lot of planning to get through today and I have a feeling a short desert patrol on camels would provide a good break for all of us." Before he could elaborate the Pine Gap special forces boys came across from the kitchen with plates of food and mugs of coffee to join them.

"Hi guys!" said one of the tall Americans with a plate piled high with Fatima's minced meat pie and some sort of bush herb sauce. "Mind if we join you?"

Sue-Ellen was just behind them. Her hand rested on her hips like a school principal as she introduced everyone. "This is Soldier of Fortune, biggest Delta gun-slinger you'll ever see. That blond-haired surfer over there is a Ranger, our staff sergeant and crypto-analyst at Pine Gap. We call him Obi-Wan but he looks like Yoda when the light hits him at the right angle. These two trying to hide behind me are SEALs. That one's Murphy, the only fellow to get left behind and survive a day by himself with no one to talk to but Taliban terrorists." Murphy shyly shrugged his broad shoulders nearly spilling his mug of coffee.

"And his fellow Seal is Pipeline. He's long, he's slippery and he goes on and on and on. Just ask anyone who's had to share a flight with him." The heavily built Afro-American smiled broadly but his mouth was full of breakfast and he didn't get the chance to prove his nickname.

Sue-Ellen charmed everyone. She relished being outside in the morning sunshine with the people she so dearly wanted to meet.

"This lady, my dear friends, is Commander Sue-Ellen Cullen, of the US Navy. Sue-Ellen is in charge of the Pine Gap facility." Sundown paused and looked with a mischievous light in his eye. "Sue-Ellen is a spook, so be careful what you say," he grinned at his audience. "Seriously, welcome aboard Commander, Deltas, SEALs and Rangers and our Black Hawk boys over there." The flight crew had been working hard overhauling their aircraft since first light. There was an electrical glitch somewhere that had played up on their flight from Alice Springs. "We enjoy having new faces and especially those who know how to kill Revelationists." Turning to Sue-Ellen and the special forces, Sundown added, "I know you've been watching the apocalypse from a distance but if you hang around Sundown's Commando long enough you'll get the chance to see it up close and personal."

When she heard that last comment Sue-Ellen's face went red. She wasn't going to let Sundown get away with this 'spectator' dig.

"And who told you we haven't been up close and personal with the terrorists, Sundown?" Commander Cullen said in what was almost a snarl.

Sundown stopped grinning and looked at her clearly confused. "I gathered that, being holed up inside your compound for a year in the middle of the desert, probably meant you had observed but not made contact..." He almost stuttered then stopped talking. He realised that he was on very unsafe ground. This woman had a reputation for busting balls and he knew he was stupid enough to stand with his legs wide apart. "Um, Commander, maybe you'd better educate me on what you have been up to?"

Everyone was watching the interplay between the two commanders. One was their beloved Sundown who always had time and a kind word for everyone. A leader who led from the front and put his own life on the line for his people, his family. The other was an unknown. A tough bitch by the look on her face. She appeared about to explode, ready to launch an attack at the very one who held their commando together.

"Commander Cullen?" said Charlene stepping in to calm the waters. "We would all like to welcome you, and your men, to our Commando at the Christian Palace. I don't think you've met any of us so I'll introduce you." Before Sue-Ellen had time to speak Charlene began introducing everyone. Immediately the soldiers and their families stepped across the emotional divide to become friends. Even Sue-Ellen had to change tack and join in.

When the introductions were made Sue-Ellen took control of the situation before Charlene had a chance to move away.

"Thank you, Charlene," she said in her lovely American accent. "I admire how you rescued your leader just then. Sundown should learn not to step into the lioness' den because that's how people get their heads bitten off."

Everyone went quiet and the chatter stopped as they waited for Sue-Ellen to play her next card.

"But you know what, the lioness has decided she isn't hungry today. But she has one paw on his chest and won't let him up until he promises to take me and my boys with him on this holiday patrol. The one I just heard him talking about. Perhaps I'll tell him what my boys have really been up to, if he behaves himself." There came a collective sigh as everyone released their breath.

Sundown's lips parted as he was about to speak but he closed them again, wisely. Instead he nodded. "Sure, I'd like that. You are more than welcome to come on our inaugural long range camel patrol. I even have an acronym for it, LRCP. But be warned our young American heroes, Sundown's Commando are rough, tough and uncompromising. If we meet the enemy on patrol, we'll wipe them out..."

"With the assistance of my special forces here no doubt." Sue-Ellen said drily.

"Why yes, of course, that's what I was going to say next." Sundown stopped speaking knowing full well he was back to digging a deeper hole. "It's time for breakfast. I see you boys have already begun. Sue-Ellen, please join us and meet everyone. The entire commando are curious to see these mysterious Pine Gap special operatives. They think you're all aliens and spooks."

The four aircrew ate where they were, busily going over their Black Hawk with a fine-toothed comb. They were trying to find bugs in the electrical system that had developed on the flight over. They were determined to fix it before they were called on to fly again. The crew chief said that it meant that they will have to strip the entire electrical system to find the fault.

Pedro rolled his wheel chair up close beside Sundown. "Hey, Sundown, what's this about our patrol? I thought we agreed it was just going to be a small group? Looks like you've invited every man and his dog to a party."

Sundown looked at his dear friend. "I decided to expand it, Pedro. Plus we are going to take dogs. There's Roo's Dog and Black Dog; Blue and Red are staying behind." A slight smile crept across his lips. "And if you want to come along you know that you will have to get back into those tin legs of yours. Tricia said if you don't then you can't go. As you know, Tricia outranks me on things medical."

"You're a funny bugger ain't ya. How long have I got?" Pedro's jaw tightened.

"I think you've got a few days, better get them legs on today and start walking." Sundown looked at Pedro's cigarette and continued.

"And everyone wants to know how come you're the only one with real tobacco? Where the hell did you find it?"

"Promise you won't tell anyone?" Pedro leaned close to Sundown's ear. "The tunnels. Beneath the palace there's a secret room full of raw leaf tobacco. I think it's contraband, illegal tobacco grown somewhere around here. Fat Boy found it and since I'm his mini-me, I got first batch. I did give a pile to Nulla, I owe him for a few tricks, but it's still a bit of a secret. I'm not sure what Fat Boy plans to do with it but maybe you'd better have a word with him. I'm too close, he might get upset, you know how touchy he is with things." He gave a snort and a laugh then pushed his chair into the dining room ready for breakfast with the rest of the commando.

Shortly afterwards Fat Boy and Sundown had a chat about following orders and sharing things that didn't belong to him. They decided that as head of victuals, Fat Boy should manage distribution of said tobacco leaves as part of the commando's daily rations. Fat Boy would need to get used to the idea of sharing, Sundown thought.

Major Lewis had returned to the palace that morning to meet Sue-Ellen and her staff. Captain Walker was now filling in for him at Birdsville. There were over two hundred people now living at the Christian Palace. They included many of the soldier's families from Alice Springs and refugees they had picked up over the past few months. It kept Andrew on his toes and he now relied more on Pinkie, Wilma, Mel, Harry, Jeda and Jenny to help him administer to the needs of the growing community.

The visitors were introduced as Pine Gap Special Forces personnel who wished to learn how to patrol in the Australian desert. For most of the Commando this was enough and they were satisfied. But for the Alice Springs Command it was a case of '*wink wink nod nod*'. They knew something was in the air but the real reason remained with only those who needed to know. An enormous stealth Black Hawk sitting in their back yard clearly announced something was afoot.

"It's been a few months since we've had a meeting like this and I'd like to announce a few things," the major began. "First of all Sundown is taking his original company out on a training patrol. We've decided, as you all know, to introduce long range camel patrols and this is a perfect opportunity to see how it works. We have a few days to prepare and we'll need everyone to pitch in and help. I've got Harry and Jenny here," and he got them to stand up. "If you haven't already got a job then please talk to them." He paused as the two sat back down.

"Some of us will need to step up and take on extra duties," and he nodded to his own uniformed soldiers. "So if you see someone sitting on their hands when there's work to be done it's your responsibility to find them something to do. There is some good news, direct from Sundown himself. We now have a proper tobacco supply. So if you're a smoker you can go and see Fat Boy for your ration after the meeting." There immediately came a cheer from the Commando's smokers.

Sundown got up to speak. "I can see that Fat Boy will be a busy fellow in a few minutes. OK, you've all seen the Black Hawk parked behind the sheds. That's what I came home in last night with our visitors." He waved across the table to where the Pine Gap special forces sat with a few of his own commandos. "These experienced fighters are joining us to learn about desert patrolling and how we've managed to fight off the entire terrorist army so far. Not just one army, I might add. Nulla and Charlene's group fought against the Adelaide terrorists for nearly a year as well.

"I know you'll support us with your hands and feet, we also need brains as well as brawn. If you've missed the opportunity to lodge your skill-set with Harry or Andrew now is the time. That's it for now. Have a nice day, it's going to get hot so make sure the kids are covered. When we get back from our patrol we'll have a bash-up party." He added quickly, "and for our newcomers you've probably heard that the palace parties are well worth attending. If you have any questions speak to Harry, Jenny or Andy."

Sundown sat down with the rest of his admin team while the smokers rushed to the kitchen to find Fat Boy. Sue-Ellen had watched him up there working the crowd and smiled inwardly. *'Just like my Reece, how lucky is Pinkie to have a man like that.'* With a faint flutter still tickling inside her chest she watched the couple chatting making everyone around them feel special.

"Major Lewis, can you introduce our visitors please?" asked Sundown as the Girl Guards gathered in the big sheering shed behind the palace.

"Sure, first of all we have Commander Sue-Ellen Cullen, she's head of the Pine Gap facility. Her special forces team are Soldier of Fortune, Murphy, Obi-Wan and Pipeline." He was secretly impressed by how modest the visitors were. These men were all experienced fighters, hand picked by Sue-Ellen herself. They were the pick of the best but even so they were very shy around Sundown's Commando.

"These are the girls who'll be going with you to Darwin. This is Blondie, Heidi, Lucy and Jaina." Each of the girls said 'Hi' politely as they were introduced.

Over the next three days the special forces trained with the girls and the camels. Nulla and his crew also focused their efforts in training the original commando in preparation for their LRCP - long range camel patrol. Their holiday appeared to be set in motion.

Chapter 12

Camel Patrol

Major Louie Lewis stayed at the Christian Palace while Captain Walker remained at the Birdsville outpost managing the fighting patrols. The troops were rotated on a fortnightly basis so those who had family now living at the palace experienced a semblance of normality. It also meant they could have a decent break from patrolling and it allowed ongoing skills training.

Colonel Vic Thompson remained in Alice Springs and was apparently wooing one of his secretaries. For all intents and purposes life was beginning to settle into a pleasant routine for the commando in Australia's red centre.

Sundown, Sue-Ellen, her special forces staff along with the original Sundown's Commando, had left early that morning on their camel patrol holiday. It wasn't a fighting patrol as such but they went fully armed with pistols, assault rifles and several magazines of their now very precious ammunition. There was a lot of laughter which made this training patrol feel like a holiday.

The older members of the original commando decided it was too hot to go on a camel ride. Mel stayed back with Andrew and Wilma while Jenny and Harry asked if Katie and Charlene would look after their kids. Annie didn't want to go either. She and Danielle were like sisters and did everything together.

Sundown looked back over his shoulder where he could see a string of almost sixty camels. The majority had riders, while the rest were loaded with food, water and gear. The patrol planned on heading north east for a few days then they would take a break at a secret hot spring that Roo and Pedro used on their hunting trips. After that they would return home.

The mild weather was over and the days were getting hotter but the nights remained pleasant. They rode until it got too hot to continue then they would stop and put up their shade tarpaulins to rest until it cooled in the afternoon. After their break they would walk until it was dark. Most of the Commando were experienced at desert living and this was something they could do with their eyes closed.

"I'd love to explore beyond the Diamentina lakes area. It's just a relaxed ten day ride." Sundown said while laughing at the silliness of patrolling all that way on a whim. "This little stroll to your hot spring will give everyone some camel riding experience and we might even have some fun. God knows we all need a break."

"Sundown, matey, you do realise this is our first holiday in a year? It was this time last year when the apocalypse happened, ya know," said Pedro, as his camel stood up under the careful eye of Kris.

"A whole year ago? In that case I think a trip along the edge of the Simpson Desert before it gets too hot is a good opportunity for everyone to relax a bit." He turned around awkwardly to watch Halo and Shrek bringing up the rear with the pack camels.

"Those two are funny aren't they?" called Sundown to his old mate strapped to his camel seat. "They get along like a house on fire. That Private Little, Shrek, he's a natural with the animals isn't he."

"He might not be one of our originals but he's a hard worker, I'll give him that. Did you know that Kris begged for us to bring him? He says the camels love him." Pedro had trouble staying seated on the lurching camel with just his stumps to hang on with but there was no way Sundown was going to leave the palace without his mate Pedro, legs or no legs.

"You know, I miss me ol' mate, Shamus. He'd love to go on a trek like this," mused Pedro.

"Yeah, me too. I have a lot of wishes, Pedro, and that's one I put up behind an end to this madness," replied Sundown as he willed his mind to turn away from the sadness which came with thinking of his mentor's death.

By midday the camel train was ready for lunch and a siesta. Everyone lent a hand to unpack the animals, set up the shade tarpaulins and prepare the midday meal. Black Dog was their official guard dog and he alternated between riding with the Girl Guards and walking.

Roo usually had his dog with him on his camel's saddle to keep his paws from burning on the hot sand. Every now and then he'd let Dog run along beside the camels, sniffing in ecstasy at everything in his path.

It was quite a crowd and Sundown went from group to group with Wiram and Nulla. He made sure to walk them through their drill so that everyone knew what to do if there was a terrorist contact. Anything that could go wrong just might and they well knew it.

That first night was magic. The sunset spread right across the western horizon. It flushed soft pinks to oranges and deep reds ending with purples and a violet blue. The colour show then pulled itself over the horizon to disappear only to reveal a mass of stars so bright the Commandos felt they could reach out and touch them.

Wiram, McFly and Sundown took out their guitars and began their camp fire sing-along while Jenny and Jeda passed the precious bottles of Andy's Palace Port around the circle. Pellino and Nulla kept an eye on the youngsters who were of age to kill but not yet of age to drink.

Sue-Ellen found that she thoroughly enjoyed the camaraderie and good humour of these desert warriors and their womenfolk. The Pine Gap visitors sang along when they recognised a song. They sang bush ballads and pop songs from the seventies and eighties but were content to just hum along to the songs they didn't recognise.

When she heard Wiram start to strum the first few bars of '*The Pub With No Beer*' Heidi called out loudly: "I don't believe it! I thought I'd listened to the last Slim Dusty track when we pulled into Birdsville. Now we're in the middle of the Simpson Desert and Wiram tortures us all over again."

Simon called out, "That's why we stayed on our bikes, Heidi, so we wouldn't have to listen to Nulla's CD's any more. Don't forget that we had to live with him for almost a whole year listening to his mournful music."

It was Luke's turn. "How much did Nulla pay you to sing Slim Dusty, Wiram?"

"That's not fair," called Nulla in defense from the other side of the fire. "I let you girls pick your own songs."

"Yeah right, Nulla. We had a choice? '*Which Slim Dusty CD do you girls want to listen to next?*' was the only choice you gave us. That's all you had in the car, Slim Dusty CD's," cried Heidi.

"I bet if Glenda was here you'd be in trouble Wiram, she'd throw something at you. That poor lady spent a whole month stuck in the car with Nulla's country music. Can you imagine? A whole month!" laughed Luke as he noticed Danni's bright eyes staring at him in the firelight.

After the sing-along Halo was called on to recite the speech he gave at the Birdsville Hotel after the Mount Isa battle. But before he began Cambra had to tell the story of the battle itself to the visitors. He told how he and Halo witnessed Blondie taking out the Raven's Claw officer with her Heckler and Koch pistol then driving full speed into the stockade. It knocked the whole stockade over preventing the machine gunner decimating the Alice Springs Command assault.

Everyone was quiet as he spoke of the bravery of the Alice Springs soldiers who courageously went forward into the enemy fire. Their selfless action allowed Blondie and Fat Boy to get the vital aeroplane parts and Pedro's antibiotics into the Bushmaster and ASLAV. He finished with a description of the brutality of their 25 mm cannon as it ripped apart the trench system and wiped out most of the enemy.

Wiram then spoke of Halo's presentation of the Sundown's Commando battle flag to Colonel Thompson. He then called the girls, Lulu and Danni, to stand up so their Pine Gap guests could see them.

"These girls made the flags and I know for a fact that Vic Thompson has the replica inside his ASLAV and the original flag now hangs inside his office in Alice Springs. He's the proudest officer in this entire post-apocalypse universe," said Wiram. "Thanks girls, you sure did us proud."

After everyone stopped laughing following Halo's speech, Assassin was called on to tell the story of how he managed to survive the Mines battle. His description of when Halo had his head wound treated by Tricia caused everyone to erupt into laughter again.

It was while Assassin was talking that Cambra realised the anniversary of their first battle was coming up. An idea entered his fertile mind. He decided right then that he wanted to present the Commando with something special to celebrate its anniversary.

He elbowed Halo in the ribs to get his attention and whispered, "I've got a secret stash of Irish whiskey in my pub at Marree, wanna help me get it?" Cambra winked and Halo caught on immediately. "It's almost the anniversary of the Marree pub fight and Shamus' death. We need something to commemorate that, it's important mate." Again Halo nodded in agreement.

"We'll organise something on the trek tomorrow, Cambra. It should be an interesting visit given the Revelationists just resurrected their Deaths Head Battalion and posted them back to Marree. We'll have to fight our way through the Stosstruppen and the Deaths Heads to get that one bottle of whiskey," whispered Halo thinking he might change Cambra's mind.

"Who said it's a bottle? There's two cases of Jameson Gold and some bottles of 18 year old single malt, plus some vintage port hidden in the cellar. There's no way the Revelationists would find it," replied Cambra with a Shamus-like lilt in his voice. Halo's smile broadened. A whiskey rescue mission should prove to be very interesting indeed.

Chapter 13

Camel Camp Fire Show

On their second day out Roo took his shirt off after his camel decided he'd had enough walking and spat on him. He used it to wipe the spittle off his face. None in the Commando had seen him bare-chested before.

Danni walked over to him and stared. "Roo, you're an initiate? Why didn't you say something?" She stepped back a few paces in respect and lowered her gaze. Then she realised what she'd said and even against her dark aboriginal skin she blushed bright red. "I'm sorry Roo, I didn't mean to be rude."

"I... couldn't talk, Danni. When I was little kids laughed. I've got scars..." he said slowly finding the right words just as Charlene had taught him. His voice had retained his nine year old inflections but every day it matured a little more.

Bongo was watching and came over. "You could have told us, Roo. We're your family, you know that."

"I know, Bongo," said Roo watching everyone's reactions, not quite sure if he should put his shirt on or leave it off. Should he hide like he did since his grandfather died or should he let the world see who he really was, an initiated warrior of the Gangardi people? For a few seconds he felt vulnerable and exposed but when Danni reacted so respectfully he realised that he should be proud and not ashamed.

Nulla came over to see what everyone was so excited about. When he saw the scars he stopped a few paces from Roo.

"Brother, we need to talk. Tonight we'll sit - you, me, Harry and Wiram." Roo nodded and smiled. This was so different to the treatment he'd experienced as a child. At the mission school he was whipped when they found out he'd gone off into the desert with his uncles and grandfather to undergo his manhood initiations.

On their third day out they arrived at Roo's hot spring in the Diamantina flood plains. This particular spring, an oasis, was hidden deep among a jumble of enormous sandstone rocks. Roo knew of its existence from his mother's aboriginal father and uncle, his mentors. He had only ever shown it to his friends Shamus and Pedro. It welled up from the depths, from how far down no one really knew. Hot, fresh water three hundred million years old had given life to the desert aborigines for thousands of years.

Those ancient nomads had excavated the sand down to a depth of a metre, then build several rock enclosures where they could sit to ease their aches and pains. Roo was told by his aboriginal grandfather that this particular spring was used by the old people for healing. It was a sacred spring and not to be approached without due respect and ceremony. In his mother's culture Roo knew that those who abused the spirits of the desert suffered the severest of consequences.

Jeda, Jenny and Roo spent a few days before their trip discussing whether they would use that particular spring or not. These women were of the Gangardi people, just like Billy and Roo. This was their people's spring and therefore the decision was theirs.

On their arrival it was agreed that the men would perform a ceremony asking permission to use the spring. If the signs were good it would become their home for the next three days before turning back for home.

They also made everyone camp well away from the waterhole and the animal pads leading to it. This ensured the thirsty animals and birds, which relied on the water for survival, wouldn't be frightened away to die in the parched desert.

At first the aboriginal members were very nervous and wouldn't go near the sacred spring. Even the daring teenagers, Lulu and Danni, stayed well away. So as soon as practical the warriors, Harry, Roo, Nulla and Wiram sat around the spring and sang the song Roo was taught by his grandfather and uncle.

When the song was finished the four looked at each other and smiled. They were each men of high degree within their own tribe. Wiram was nangarri which the whites would call a sorcerer or 'medicine man' but he never spoke of it. His status was only known among his people.

Roo had never told anyone of his initiations, only those closest to him knew. Like Harry, Nulla and Wiram his chest and back showed the thick scars indicating his initiation into secrets he was not allowed to speak of, even to tribal men not of his degree or totem.

Charlene knew of the scars but from the little she knew of his time in the mission school she thought they might have been torture marks. She didn't want to open that can of worms before he could talk properly and she had the skills to manage it.

Now the secret was out Roo spoke of certain things to Harry, Nulla and Wiram, things he was permitted to speak of. The girls already admired his lithe, good looks but now they were in awe of his manhood and warrior status. Though of different tribes Sundown's aboriginal community closed their protective screen around Roo.

By the time Kris and Shrek watered their sixty camels the spring water had splashed and spread to form a massive mud puddle. The superfine desert mud was slippery and coated everyone who helped. Nearly everyone slipped over ending up covered in mud.

It was late that afternoon when Luke and Simon called for Shrek and Arthur to go with them to have a 'dip in the pool'.

"Come on Shrek, you need to wash that camel manure off you," called Luke as the teenagers gathered on the edge of the mud puddle. To get to the rock pools they had to somehow walk across without slipping over.

Simon looked at his friend and Luke smiled back. "Are you thinking what I'm thinking?" he giggled.

"Yeah! Let's do it!" cried Luke as he stripped off his clothes and dived stomach first onto the mud. He slid for a good ten metres before stopping. Simon was right behind him. They both squealed in teenage glee.

Shrek looked at Arthur hesitantly. He wasn't sure if he should strip buck naked like his new friends.

"Arty, can we do that? I mean, are we allowed to take off all our clothes in the Commando?"

Arthur looked at him sideways as he hurriedly pulled his own trousers and shirt off. "Shrek, from what I've heard being buck naked in the desert is nothing to what you and Jaina get up to." He leaped with a screech of pleasure into the mud sliding almost as far as Luke and Simon who were now slinging mud at each other.

Terrified of doing the wrong thing and upsetting his mates, Shrek took off his shirt and then his trousers. He lay them carefully on a rock so they wouldn't get wet, not like the other three who just threw theirs on the ground.

His enormous penis hung almost to his knees in the heat and when Simon saw it he let out a gasp.

"Crikey, Shrek! Don't let that slug get anywhere near us virgins!" The other two looked up and collapsed in laughter when they saw what Simon was referring to.

"Now we know why they call you 'Shrek'," yelled Arty, "because you've got an ogre between your legs." The boys cracked up laughing. They shrieked even louder when Shrek looked down trying to find the ogre.

"Come on Shrek! Get into the damn mud before the dingos see your one-eyed trouser snake and think it's dinner time," cried Luke throwing a handful of mud at him.

Simon and Luke had invited the girls to join them for a dip in the spring and as expected they took their time. When they did arrive the girls looked at each other trying to work out why the boys were laughing so much. They couldn't see past a large rock and thought the boys were just having fun in the spring. But as they rounded the rock Heidi took one look at the four naked boys and screamed. The other three girls joined in, their squeals caused the boys to turn and stare at them.

Shrek was still undecided. He'd not yet made the plunge into the mud but the girl's screams and laughter made the decision easy. With a wild up-country yell he dived forward sliding beyond the three before stopping. He spun in circles with delight laughing and yelling like a child.

Jaina looked at her three friends and shrugged, pulled her top off followed by her trousers and leaped forward. Sliding up to her boyfriend. Jaina playfully wrestled with Shrek until both were covered in mud. Seeing their friend's nakedness covered by the clinging mud the two modest aboriginal teenagers and Heidi decided that if Jaina could do it then so could they.

With much giggling and laughter the girls quickly stripped naked and dived in among the boys. They spent the next half hour sliding, spinning in circles and throwing mud at each other, completely oblivious to the dangers of the world around them.

Danni whispered to Lulu that she and Luke had kissed on the first night of their patrol. The two were giggling so much that Jaina, Heidi and Donna decided to wander over with their camp oven. Heidi dropped the heavy cast-iron pot by her side as she asked Lulu and Danni what they were giggling about. As they sat together preparing the vegetables for dinner they listened excitedly as Danni related her adventure all over again for their friend's benefit.

"You gotta believe it." Her breathing was deep with emotion. "He said poetry to me, he did!" She giggled when she saw the look of amazement on her friend's faces. "He said I was his coy mistress! He sure did. Luke's cute isn't he? His kiss was so soft..." Her voice drifted off as her eyes closed, recalling the sensation of that special moment.

"Oh, come on girl!" laughed Heidi. "There's no way that dumb ass knows poetry! I should know, he never said a word of poetry all the way across the Strzelecki Desert. Not to me or anyone."

Donna, a few years older than Heidi, decided she needed to say something. "Heidi, don't forget you have Arty. Why would Luke speak love poetry to you?"

Heidi paused and was thoughtful for a moment. "Huh? Oh yeah, I guess you're right..." She was silent for but a second then bounced back in. "Why don't we ask him to recite poetry at tonight's camp-fire? We could do with some culture out here in the desert." The girl's giggling grew louder causing some of the commandos to look, enjoying the teenager's happy abandon.

"You ain't gonna let him kiss you in front of everyone are you, Danni? Not when he says that poem?" For Lulu, love was serious business especially since their time as the terrorist's sex slaves.

"NO WAY! That'd be so embarrassing! But I might afterwards." Danni said and the girls conspiratorially giggled together behind their hands.

As it happened a lot of things had to be organised before meal time that evening. Wiram and Harry gave their reports of security and supplies. Sundown listened with his team gathered around one side of the camp fire. No one interrupted or came near them, these meetings were administrative and very boring to the younger set anyway.

"OK, thanks, Harry. How's the stomach going mate, that camel ride causing you pain?" asked Sundown.

"One day, when I'm brave enough, I'll tell you my story Sundown. But yeah, I've got the shits with me gut pain but I've lived with it for years so it's just part of me existence these days," replied Harry as he stood and went off to help organise the camels with Kris, Halo and Shrek.

"Wiram, do you and Nulla have that roster for patrols? And who's got tonight's watch? I'll take the last one if you want." Sundown was always keen to be first up in the mornings and didn't mind the final hours before dawn. Even though named 'Dimas' for his birth time, sunset, it was the sunrise that gave him the most pleasure. For some reason he became melancholy towards evening, he'd rather go to bed early than face a late night.

"You've got the dawn watch then Sundown, thank you," said Wiram. "I'll get the rest of the orders to you presently. What I wanted to talk about was how much ammunition to issue our patrols. We're low on ammo, as you know. We've trained everyone to conserve ammunition and police their cartridges but the problem is that we've been running through it fast on the front line against the terrorists at Marree. Harry's been on to us to find other means to fight the terrorists. The tunnels under the palace have a room filled with archery equipment and swords and things. I spoke with Johnny and Louie and I've been mulling it over with Nulla this week. I reckon we need to seriously explore alternatives."

"Yeah, Louie spoke to me too. I think it's a goer but I don't think going up against the Stosstruppen or Deaths Heads with bows and arrows is going to cut it. We have to first bleed their supplies down to that level and there's only one way to do that," said Sundown. He closed his eyes as he considered several pathways that formed as he spoke. "I need to consider this some more during my meditations with Shamus."

Sue-Ellen was sitting beside Pedro, she now leaned forward to speak. "I want my boys on duty as well Wiram, have you found a job for them yet?"

"Ma'am, I wanted to get your permission first. Sundown told me to keep them busy but as you two are joint commanders and all, I ah..." he hadn't finished speaking when Sundown spoke.

"I know I know, I'm a bossy bastard at times and I don't know when to back off. I need to learn to let others take responsibility but I can't make that sacrifice. I fear that if I do I'll fail everybody." Sundown's eyes went red and Pinkie saw he was wrestling with emotions he usually kept hidden. "When we lost Shamus I swore to look after everyone. Then we lost John and Sergeant Doff's boys because I wasn't there to lead. I can't, I mean I struggle... Sue-Ellen, I hope you understand what I'm trying to say." He had to stop. The memory of Shamus and their time together nearly a year ago always hit him hard.

Sue-Ellen watched curiously at first then her expression changed, she got it. "Sundown, it's all right. I'll just kick you under the table when I need you to shut up and let go." That broke the tension. She called the meeting to an end not waiting for Sundown to come back from where he'd escaped to. She stayed a little longer as did Pedro, Wiram and Pinkie.

"Wiram, send my boys on patrol when you're ready will you please?" She smiled evilly. "Any dirty job you've got, get them to pitch in and help. Maybe send them on a midday run to the homestead and back as well?"

Wiram smiled, he understood what she wanted him to do. "Got that ma'am. I was thinking much the same thing. If you don't mind I need a hard hitting experienced crew who know how to break an assault. Your boys asked if they could go with the scout patrols at dawn but I want to consolidate here first. I've been talking to Nulla and he has the same plans for them as well. Assault training Nulla style. I promise they'll get a work out and I'm sure they'll teach young Nulla a trick or two."

Just outside the light of the camp fire Luke recited the poem over and over in his mind so that he would get it just right. A natural performer he was confident he could pull it off. He'd watched how Halo and Cambra managed to tell their stories and engage everyone the previous few nights and was visualising his performance just like Nulla had taught him. Luke rehearsed a few jokes he wanted to throw in as well.

As Pinkie and Jenny handed the bottles of Palace Port around to those who enjoyed it, and tea and coffee for the rest, Heidi stood up to introduce the evenings entertainment.

"Everyone, I would like to introduce you to our youngest member, Luke." There was a round of polite applause. The Commando were uncertain what to expect as the youngsters took control of the camp fire entertainment. "Luke, it turns out, is a poet, and not just any poet, but a love poet." Now she had their attention.

Shrek seemed to have found himself on this trip. He and Jaina continued their physical relationship and were very much in love. They pitched their swag away from everyone after Blondie quietly suggested their lovemaking was keeping people awake.

"Hey, Luke," Shrek called loudly across the camp fire sparks rising to the stars above. "Can you teach me some of your love poems?"

Jaina glowed with joy but at the same time was a little embarrassed. She pulled at the shirt tails hanging out of his trousers and told him to '*shush up*'.

"Shrek, our giant green ogre and master cameleer, tonight I dedicate this poem to you and your beloved, Jaina." He glanced at Danni and caught her smile. She'd told him not to embarrass her and he didn't want to spoil their blossoming relationship.

"Ladies and gentlemen, Sundown's Cameleers, tonight we celebrate something special which goes way back, like a thread stitched through the tapestry of human existence. The sun is setting and the moon is rising - it is a night for love." The commando were now entranced by this amazing word craftsman standing in the flickering firelight.

"The poem I am about to recite was written by an ancient poet, Andrew Marvel, who lived in England about four hundred years ago. Life in those times was just as troublesome as it is today." He looked around to make sure that he was engaging his audience. He needn't have worried, he had them mesmerised. "Time's winged chariot will always hurry for young lovers, and old lovers alike... it goes like this: '*To a Coy Mistress*', by Andrew Marvell.

"*Had we but world enough and time - this coyness, lady, would be no crime.*

"*We would sit down, and think which way - to walk and pass our long love's day...*"

Just as Luke was finishing the last few lines Simon prepared to enter into the light of the camp fire. He was dressed in a skirt, long grassy hair, his cheeks rouged from clay ochres and mascara from crushed charcoal. He looked hilarious but was amazingly female-like thanks to Danni and Lulu's costuming and make-up.

Off stage Luke hurriedly pulled on a cloak, a slouch hat and his holstered pistol worn on the outside. In his hand he held a stick sword. He took centre stage once more.

"Fair folks, tonight my partner, Simon, and I, would like to present our remembered fragments of a famous love scene." He stopped as he tried to find the right words. "Some would say 'butchered' fragments from Shakespeare's *'Romeo and Juliet'*." There was excited applause from the girls then everyone else enthusiastically joined in.

Turning to his now rapt audience, Luke spoke loudly and clearly, his hand to his mouth as though speaking to co-conspirators.

"Simon and I learned all about love-making from our mentor, Nulla. We learned how to make love as we watched him woo the fair Glenda." Nulla shook his head and laughed softly. "However, tonight's Romeo and Juliet is not for Nulla and his lady love, Glenda. It is dedicated to our fair heroes, the newly weds, Wiram, now known as Romeo, and his fair maiden, Donna, now known as Juliet."

Wiram almost choked on his port and Donna went red in the face.

"But soft!" Luke moved as though he was Leo DiCaprio on the stage. *"What light through yonder window breaks? ... "*

Time stood still as the two flawlessly performed the window scene of Shakespeare's *'Romeo and Juliet'*. There was laughter, lots of laughter but there was also an air of stunned fascination. Everyone wondered: where did these two scallywag teenagers get this incredible talent?

At the end of their performance Luke threw a handful of leaves onto the fire. The leaves roared into flame and the scene brightened. Then, as the shadows returned the performers exited the stage - 'twas the end of their play.

No one spoke, no one moved. All the audience could hear was the sound of the camp fire crackling in the still desert air. The only entertainment they experienced all year was a story or a song, but poetry and Shakespeare was, to the Commando, as refreshing as water is to the parched desert sands.

The boys returned and bowed deeply. The audience stood as one and clapped while their girlfriends cheered and helped them back to their seats.

"If I could stand up right now boys, I'd leap over and give you all a hug. But alas, my Juliet here will have to do it for me," called Wiram sitting comfortably beside his partner.

Donna shyly stood and embraced the boys. "Thank you for embarrassing us. I'm going to ask Sundown to make you our Court Jesters, then you can entertain us on all our patrols," she said brightly. "But I confess, I have but one question dear Jesters. Where did you learn to recite poetry and Shakespeare like that?"

Luke answered for them both. "We ran the drama group in high school. We performed, produced, wrote, directed and set the scenery, we did everything. We booked the hall and practised every morning and lunch time. Simon and I produced a new play every term. We were even in the newspaper."

"Well how about a bush play about Sundown's Commando? But make it a comedy, not a drama, we get enough drama as it is courtesy of the Revelationists," Donna suggested.

"Consider it done fair Juliet!" Luke replied. To Simon he called, "our next show will be an adaptation of 'All's Well That End's Well', 'Hamlet', 'Macbeth' and 'A Midsummer Night's Dream' rolled into a desert survival comedy thriller."

Throughout Luke and Simon's performance Pinkie couldn't help but observe the lovers among the commando. The boy's voices cast a spell over the entire camp, not a single person had looked away from the performers faces or their expressive movements. She felt Sundown's head drop onto her shoulder and his hand curled into hers. It was a moment in her life that felt just right as she closed her eyes the better to experience this special moment.

Sue-Ellen was also mesmerised by the show but in her heart she felt confused and sad. There were images of her husband, Reece, now long dead, all but a memory that faded with each passing year. But what hit her hard was recalling the thrill she felt at Sundown's warm breath on her neck. She knew this fantasy of love was just that, a fantasy, and the tears that coursed down her cheeks were left to water the dry desert sand.

"OK everyone, time for bed." Turning to the young lovers Nulla said, "and no hanky-panky while on patrol." He looked at everyone now alert and waiting for their orders for the morrow. "I want all patrols out an hour before dawn. Stand-to is false dawn, anyone I find in bed after that becomes my personal toilet."

"Don't try it on him, guys," called Luke still in entertainer mode. "He really will pee on you if he catches you asleep. One time I woke up staring at the most frightening sight a teenager could ever witness." He paused as everyone waited expectantly for what this might be. "You guessed it, Nulla's hairy apples and hose pipe!" He roared in laughter along with everyone else.

Nulla nodded in agreement. "He's right of course, it's hairy and scary down there. Righto, serious now please. Here are tomorrows orders: Cambra, Halo and Assassin patrol south; Wiram and McFly you're up north; Roo, Riley and Bongo you fellas head out east and you might want to check out that homestead nearby; Arty, Simon and Luke you go west. Our Pine Gap specialists will stay with Sundown and the Girl Guards. Staff Sergeant Obi-Wan will command the camp defences tomorrow.

"I want Kris and Shrek up before everyone else to prepare the camels and help the cameleer's get going." He looked at the nurses sitting upright and enjoying the entertainment. "Tricia, you, Heidi and Donna have breakfast to prepare for the patrols so you've got to be up with

Kris and Shrek. And Gail, you, Lorraine and Jaina have the cameleer's lunch to prepare and pack before you go to bed tonight. If you see Jenny and Jeda you'll find it ready but it needs to be put aside so the dingoes don't steal it." He watched as the commando settled and their heads nodded as he called their names.

"Lulu and Danni you get to sleep in until stand-to." He smiled when they let out a soft 'whoop!' "Each watch will need to be aware that the camels are hobbled but they'll wander in the night. You already know this but remember there's dingoes aplenty around water, they'll be curious to see what they can steal from us. They've bred like crazy since the apocalypse so just be careful because the camels will be skittish.

"Tomorrow we go out armed and prepared for contact. We're miles from anywhere so I don't expect anything but just in case, be prepared. We only have enough ammunition for one solid contact so don't drop any of your magazines while on patrol." He leaned down to pick up a stick that had fallen away from the fire. "We only have the one working radio so you're all on your lonesome, don't break a leg. I know we're getting low on ammunition but if you can, bag a kangaroo or two for dinner, that would be nice. And," he looked around the group smiling, "if you're up early enough you get to share a hot spa with Dog, Black Dog, Wiram and me." There were groans from the youngsters.

"Wiram and myself will take first watch tonight, Harry you and Sue-Ellen have mid watch while Sundown and Pellino have the final watch and will wake everyone for stand-to." Nulla stepped back from the firelight as he began to prepare for his watch.

Everyone stood up, those with jobs stayed back a little longer while the rest headed for bed.

As Sundown crawled into his swag he said to Pinkie, "Honey, I'm a bit nervous about this patrol. I woke up this morning with that same feeling I had on the day of the apocalypse." He pulled the swag over them both. It was getting cold and they snuggled together for the warmth, and for the nice cuddle. "Pinkie, I want you up early too. In fact I want everyone up early. If anything happens I want Black Dog to stay with you, to protect you."

Pinkie just grunted. She was exhausted, it had been a hell of a day. Three days on a camel's back was a daunting trek for anyone. Sure, they'd had time to soak out their aches and pains in the hot spring but tonight was their first full night's sleep. The opportunity to sleep in was dashed by Nulla's announcement that stand-to was false dawn. It was the promise of another three days camped by the spring that had kept her spirits up but now Sundown had to go and drop this on her.

"Darl, go to sleep, we'll worry about it in the morning. Besides, Wiram and Nulla are warriors, they know how to run a battle better than anyone, even you. You've just got to let go sometimes." With that she rolled over and was soon asleep.

Sundown lay on his back with Pinkie's head resting on his arm. He stared at the enormous expanse of the Milky Way above him. It stretched from one horizon to the other. With both the moon and the starlight it was almost bright enough to read by.

As he did on most nights he closed his eyes and brought up an image of Shamus. Over the next half hour he discussed his concerns with his mentor who had died almost a year ago. How it seemed a lifetime since their first meeting at the Birdsville Hotel he thought.

He watched as his inner Shamus showed him the best way to prepare for a contact with the enemy in this particular location. Sundown stayed in a state of semi-consciousness going over scenario after scenario to cover every possibility. As his inner world faded Sundown heard Shamus' voice, *"Sundown, tomorrow our Commando will be blessed a hundred fold but there will be sacrifices."*

Sundown shivered unconsciously as he drifted into deep sleep.

Roo's evening ritual was to send his dream body on over-watch allowing him to sleep soundly at night. If anything threatened he was always forewarned and prepared. As the night wore on his dream body became restless, much like the night before the Arkaroola wilderness fight. He woke when he heard Sundown and Pellino noisily waking everyone for stand-to. Somewhere in his sleepy mind he knew that this was going to be a day of hardship and sadness.

Chapter 14

The Warrior Sisterhood

Riley, Roo and Bongo weren't due to finish their patrol until that afternoon. It was mid morning and there was plenty of time to go out and explore the area. Roo decided that they should investigate the homestead of a cattle family he knew nearby. The abandoned farming property was inside their patrol area and close to the spring.

Going on patrol together was a good opportunity for the three to become reacquainted. Bongo in particular was keen to relax and enjoy his time with Roo and Riley, they'd become close friends from their time in the Arkaroola wilderness.

Bongo handed his tobacco pouch and papers to Riley. They both folded their feet over their camel's saddle trying to copy Roo while they rolled their misshapen cigarettes. Roo was born to the saddle but neither of his friends had the skill to stay upright for long.

"Damn it, Roo, how do you do that Afghan thing with your legs. I keep falling over," laughed Bongo, his boyish personality was coming back now he was out patrolling with his best friend.

Roo's voice had already begun to change from his earlier nine year old voice, it was starting to mature. He called out over his shoulder, "It's practice, Bongo."

"Bullshit, Roo. There's a secret you're holding back from us. Come on, what is it?" said Riley.

"I'm not, it's practice," Roo repeated. One thing Bongo noticed was that Roo couldn't make a joke, he lacked the verbal dexterity and mindset to do that. He still thought in all five senses at once. His thoughts remained complete - sounds, pictures and sensations, not in words. So his statement was simply a statement and not bullshit. It didn't stop his friends from stirring him up though.

"Smarty pants, it's because you've got Afghan blood, that's why you don't fall off," said Bongo thinking he had the answer. Then he realised that Riley was Roo's cousin and he had Afghan ancestry too. "Bugger! So do you, Riley, so what's your excuse, mate?" he challenged Roo's part Afghan cousin.

"Me?" answered Riley. "I've got no excuses. My Afghan blood must be well diluted because I'm blowed if I can sit like that without falling off this wobbly desert tank under me."

They arrived at the homestead where they quickly settled and hobbled their camels. They had plenty of time to explore the single-roomed stone building while the rest of the commando soaked in the hot springs.

As they quietly pushed the door open they saw the table set for four people. Riley opened the oven to peer in then called out to his mates. He pointed to a petrified roast still in its baking tray. There were tools and equipment placed carefully on hooks and pegs and two double bunk beds were ready made for the owners return. It was spooky and no one spoke as they respectfully explored the homestead.

Suddenly Dog and Roo lifted their heads in unison to listen.

"What's that?" asked Roo in his peculiar young voice. "Truck!"

Bongo and Riley heard it a second later. They quickly wrestled their weapons off their shoulders and readied for a fire-fight. Was it terrorists or perhaps the owners returning? They were unsure. The three raced to the front door but just as they opened it a woman's head appeared in the doorway. Behind her they saw armed Revelationists.

Before the amazed commando's could do or say a thing the woman ordered frantically, "Get out of my way! I'm coming through and so are my girls."

The three men froze, uncertain what to do as an older woman and five Crusader women carried two of their wounded into the stone house. Bongo and Riley immediately leaped forward to help the girls ease their injured into the ancient leather chairs.

The woman turned to Roo and said calmly. "Hi Roo, how's Shamus and Pedro going?"

Riley and Bongo stopped what they were doing and looked at the two curiously.

Bongo noticed that the new-comers looked extremely fatigued and were agitated. There was also a sense of urgency, a panic swirled in the air around them. He could see that these girls had been in a fight. As he stepped back to take in the scene he saw that they were now preparing their defenses. They were clearly expecting to defend their position inside the stone homestead.

"I'm good, Martene. Shamus is dead but Pedro is good," he replied.

The woman, who must have been in her early sixties, frowned. "What did you say? Did you just speak?" she asked, completely taken aback.

"Yes," was his simple reply. Roo rarely smiled but he did then.

"How is it that after all these years you're suddenly talking now, young man?" Martene held the door open while she spoke, glancing every few seconds in the direction they'd come from.

"Charlene's nice and Bongo and Riley help me," said Roo, his smile grew larger, prouder.

"Bloody wonders never cease do they," said Martene absently as she once again checked the desert expanses outside. She then felt a horrible sharp sensation in her chest.

"Shamus is dead? Oh dear, I'm so sorry, Roo, he was a good friend, a very dear man. But Pedro's fine?" For a split second she looked confused then sad, elated and finally hopeful.

But her expression changed quickly, she visibly snapped herself from her thoughts.

"Boys, get the hell out of here," she said forcefully. The three men now noticed her face was streaked with dusty rivulets and the red around her eyes reflected the fatigue in her stance. "If you don't leave now you'll be fighting the whole Ravens Claw army with us."

Bongo noticed that this mature woman with the engaging looks had a captain's insignia of the Longreach Crusaders of Light Battalion on her shoulders.

Martene spoke to the question in Bongo's eyes. "We've been fighting off a company strength Ravens Claw patrol all night. We're now at war with the Mount Isa battalions, they and us are no longer best friends." She stopped as she directed her small band to cover the windows and continued. "You've got about ten seconds to get out of here. There's sixty or more Claws right behind us. Today me and my girls are going to paradise but we'll take some of them bastards with us."

Riley had already summed the situation up in his mind when he spoke.

"Roo, you'd better head off and get Sundown, quick. Ride like the wind, cousin!" Roo nodded and raced for the door knowing that if anyone could handle a camel in full flight it was him. Turning to Bongo, Riley continued, "I'm staying to help, this just isn't right."

Bongo looked at the girls, they were exhausted, most were bandaged and bloody. They reminded him of what the commando had looked like after the mines fight.

"I'm staying too, Riley. I'm not going to leave these girls to fight and die alone. And I'm not leaving you behind either, you're my blood too you know," he said quietly then bent to help the young lady tending one of the wounded girls.

"Boys, please don't," pleaded Martene, her face softening for just that moment. "We're already dead, but thanks for the kind offer. Now get the hell out of here. I don't want you sacrificing your lives for nothing. Damn it!" She finished with a high pitched yell as she pushed at the door and opened up with her automatic. The other girls at the front windows opened fire too.

A convoy of trucks and four wheel drives carrying the Ravens Claw company swung towards a dip in the sand dunes and poured out a stream of soldiers. They quickly skirmished onto the nearest sand dune and opened fire in return.

In seconds the incoming fire ranged accurately on the homestead. Bongo saw the bullets hitting the wall opposite, smashing glasses in the only cupboard in the room. He grabbed the nice looking girl beside him and together they crashed to the floor. The bullets smashed loudly on the stone walls outside, those inside ricocheted dangerously around the room.

Bongo had his face buried in the young woman's hair and for that fleeting moment he noticed how nice she smelled - of sweat and something else, the scent of a woman.

"Hey, lover boy," the girl twisted slightly to murmur in his ear, "we hardly know each other. Do you always knock a girl off her feet on your first date?"

"Sorry, I'm Bongo." He looked into her red rimmed eyes and introduced himself. He couldn't help but smile as he breathed her scent deep into his body again.

"I'm Denise." She pulled her face back so she could look into his eyes, she liked what she saw.

Bongo peered back at her. "Denise, I know this is a stupid question with bullets flying around and all, but, can I ask why you girls all have short red hair?" Bongo knew it was an innocuous question, especially given the circumstances. Besides, he needed an excuse to keep her gathered in his arms.

Denise shook her hair to get some of the dust out of it and Bongo's breath caught in his throat. Not only did she smell just right but now he saw that she was beautiful too.

"We're Crusaders, the Warrior Sisterhood, the personal bodyguard of the Abbess Leonie." She didn't try to get up but let her body lean into his. He made her feel safe and Denise thought that right now was a good time to have a good looking man's protective arms wrapped tightly around her.

The sounds of battle raged above them. Cries of pain, screams of rage and then Martene's voice cut through their special moment.

"You two! What the flaming hell! This is not a love nest, we're at war! Get up and fight damn it!"

Bongo released his arms from around Denise's slender body and helped her up.

"Come on, we'll take this window. You take that side and I'll take this one," he said pulling at the curtains and letting the heavy rod fall between them.

Denise saw two Ravens Claws running towards a clump of bushes right in front of them and opened fire.

"To answer your question," she spoke between bursts and ducking down as incoming fire spattered around them. "We have red hair because we're a sisterhood, we do everything the same. And because it makes us look pretty." She deliberately smiled to show she was making fun of him.

Bongo grinned and nodded in agreement. Denise then whispered so only he could hear, "and you're not bad looking yourself, handsome."

Riley held tightly to Roo's dog. Dog was usually quite comfortable with the sounds of rifle fire having lived with a kangaroo shooter all its life. But when Roo raced out of the door and the tension in the room increased, Dog started to fret.

Roo drew his knife as he raced for the door, sliced through the rope between his camel's feet and then leaped onto its back. He had the beast up and running in moments. No other member of the commando could have done that. But within a few seconds he heard the wet slap of bullets striking his camel's side. It shuddered then collapsed back to the sandy ground it had just risen from.

As he was falling Roo grabbed his Ruger American rifle from its leather pouch and jumped to the ground. With bullets zipping past his ear he threw himself behind the water trough. A burst of automatic fire smashed against its concrete side and he was soon covered in shards of cement and grey dust.

Dog must have sensed what had happened to his master because it wrenched itself free of Riley's arms. In one bound Dog jumped through the broken window and within seconds was by his master's side at the trough. Riley saw Dog disappear as Roo's arm dragged it behind cover.

"Shit! Roo!" Riley had one foot on the window sill when Martene grabbed him and pulled him to the floor. A burst of machine gun fire spattered against the wall and into the room right where he had just been.

"Get down you idiot! Do you really want to die that much?" snarled Martene, her heavy breathing made her voice harsher than she intended.

"That's my cousin out there, he's trapped, they'll kill him!" Riley screamed in panic as he wrestled with the Sisterhood captain.

"You go out there and they'll kill you deader'n road kill. Haven't you got someone you want to live for?" She forced her voice to soften as she tried to calm the wild cattleman.

A picture of his wife Katie and their two children came to him and he shuddered. How close was he to throwing his life away?

"If you're OK I'll let you up. Take position here and cover your cousin but don't try that again because next time I won't stop you." She let him stand then moved back to her own position.

She called across to Riley. "Roo's my friend too you know. He, Shamus and Pedro spent a lot of time with me and my family back in the days before this hell broke lose on the world." She paused to fire several rounds at their enemy.

"We're going to die anyway, just make sure we take a few of those traitors with us." There was a question that now popped into her mind. "So, why are you boys sacrificing your lives for us girls?"

"Martene, if we ran that would be dishonourable and disrespectful, to you and to us." He looked down at his feet for a moment. "I guess that sort of says it." Riley looked up to snap off several single rounds at a group of Ravens Claws trying to get behind Roo's position at the water trough. "Besides, Roo and Bongo almost died saving me and my family. This is the right thing to do."

Martene nodded understanding exactly what he meant. She then recognised that both Riley and Bongo were firing single shot. "Are you boys low on ammo?"

"Yep, I've got two magazines left," he replied ducking down as a burst of machine gun fire hit the wall beside him. He slipped the empty magazine from his weapon and pushed his second last magazine in to replace it.

Martene reached into her ammunition pouch and threw him one of hers. "Here, now we're even, make each bullet count."

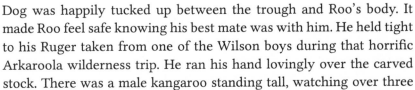

Dog was happily tucked up between the trough and Roo's body. It made Roo feel safe knowing his best mate was with him. He held tight to his Ruger taken from one of the Wilson boys during that horrific Arkaroola wilderness trip. He ran his hand lovingly over the carved stock. There was a male kangaroo standing tall, watching over three female kangaroos eating grass beside a water hole. For just that moment it made him feel like he was back in the solitude of the bush.

He pulled his AK47 from under his body and cocked it. Smiling he recalled how he and Bongo had escaped Mrs. Sow and her seven piglets on their trek back to Marree. That was so long ago, a lifetime. He traced his fingers over the AK's wooden stock where he'd carved Mrs. Sow and her babies running into the desert that night. He planned to carve a camel train on his Ruger one day. The drumming of bullets against the water trough snapped him back to reality.

He glanced across to his right flank and saw several Ravens Claws taking up position to fire on him. With practised agility he raised his AK and fired before they had time to do more than stare. Three singe shots and he scored one hit. The other two Ravens Claws moved out of his line of sight. He listened as the one he hit choked his life away. Roo grimaced at his poor marksmanship and promised to himself not to goof-off under fire again.

The sound of single shots coming from the homestead made him aware that everyone inside were low on ammunition. Stuck out in the open he had to cover both his flanks and that made him an easy target if the terrorists coordinated their assault. He considered what he might do if the fighters inside ran out of ammunition, things were grim.

A bullet zipped past his ear flicking the skin. He flinched and turned to his left flank to see four terrorists firing at him. Switching his fire mechanism to semi automatic he emptied his magazine into them. He scored several hits before they too pulled back out of his field of view. His weapon clicked empty so he reached for his Ruger. Roo then felt a sting in his foot. Swinging back around he saw three enemy firing from the right flank again. The Claws he'd missed previously must have brought a friend to join in the fun, he thought.

Roo was an experienced kangaroo shooter. Not only did he shoot kangaroos for a living he also shot wild pigs, rabbits, camels, horses and anything he was paid to kill. Automatically he sighted along the barrel instead of the awkward scope and fired. On reflex he killed the terrorist furthest from him so the other two wouldn't see it and be scared off like wild kangaroos.

He now saw the front terrorist lean across in front of his mate to get a better view of his target. Shifting his aim a fraction, Roo fired a second time. It went through the first man's throat and into the skull of the man behind. Roo knew he needn't waste another bullet.

Denise now leaned against the wall next to Bongo, they each had but a few bullets left in their rifles. The drumming of the Ravens Claw bullets against the stone wall vibrated through their backs and into their chests.

"Denise, I think this might be it." Bongo's mouth was so dry he could barely croak. He was bleeding from a cut to his cheek and Denise's laboured breathing suggested the blood seeping from her chest was more than just a broken rib.

"Yeah," she wheezed, "I'm tired of this game... time to finish I think." She sighed and put one hand on the floor as she tried to get back up, she couldn't.

"If we get out of this alive..." Bongo paused as he tried to think of how to say this, "will you be my girlfriend?" he blurted out.

More machine gun fire beat against the wall and Denise slid further down towards the floor. She chuckled softly which ended in a wet cough, it wasn't a nice sound. Bongo turned to look at her pleasant face again. What he saw made him feel as though a blade had stabbed him in the chest and his heart stopped beating for a moment. Denise's face was ashen, blood seeped from the corners of her lips.

"Sure lover boy... I'd like that... a lot..."

Bongo had tears in his eyes when he stood up to fire his last few rounds at a group of advancing Ravens Claws, he could barely see them.

"You bastards!" he heard himself screaming. His weapon clicked empty so he reached down for Denise's which now lay loosely in her lap.

Chapter 15

Sundown's Sacrifice

It was mid morning when the sounds of gunfire could be heard coming from the homestead. At first it was a single weapon but within seconds it grew to a dull roar.

"Sundown! Sundown!" cried Shadow, who had been out practising her camel commands.

The commando leader looked up from his cup of tea with Pinkie and Sue-Ellen, the sounds of gunfire had yet to register with them. They saw Shadow hurrying her camel towards them. Her face reflected her fear of both the racing camel and the now obvious roar of gunfire. Not the most experienced camel rider she clumsily fell to the ground trying to dismount.

Sundown was already standing, his hand raised to shield his eyes to see if the firefight was approaching their camp site. Other members of the commando were now doing the same. The four Pine Gap special forces soldiers didn't hesitate, the moment they heard the sound of gunfire they began to gather their weapons and ammunition. They were with Sundown and Sue-Ellen just in time to hear Shadow's report.

"Sundown!" panted Shadow. "It's Roo and Bongo's patrol! They must be in big trouble." She pointed towards an approaching camel, its legs splayed like a spider as it ran to join its mates. It was Bongo's camel, Star.

Sundown snapped alert recalling his dream with Shamus and hurriedly called his commando to form into their teams ready for action.

"Obi-Wan, it's coming from that homestead we spoke about last night. Take your boys up as far as you can and see what you can do. I'll send support as soon as I can. You'd better just hoof it, the camels are spooked and won't be of much use to us. Run and hold, wait for us to support you, got it?"

"Got it Sundown. We'll hold a defensive position and see if we can influence what's happening with Roo's patrol. You'd better hurry though, that's a lot of rounds in the air out there," said Staff Sergeant Ben Kennedy, Obi-Wan, the leader of the special forces men.

Sundown now allowed himself to relax a little knowing that these professionals were on their way. If anyone could influence a fire-fight as wild as what he was hearing it would be these four.

"Good luck. Don't take chances. I want you boys alive when this is over." Then he turned to his commando. "Nulla, I need a sniper up on that big sand dune over there. It must overlook the homestead where Roo's patrol are probably holed up."

"Sundown, what about me, I'm not useless. You'll need me too." Pedro was by his side, his tin legs in a pile beside his modified wheel chair. He began strapping his legs on while slipping the strap of his M21 sniper rifle over his arm.

"Pedro, that's almost a kilometre away! How the hell will you get there in time?" Sundown's exasperation showed right at the wrong moment.

Pedro suddenly felt tears forming in the corners of his eyes. "Don't do this to me, matie. Please, don't tell me I'm worthless."

Sue-Ellen watched as she held Black Dog by his collar. She saw what was happening and quickly spoke up.

"Sundown, I'll get Jaina and Blondie to help Pedro. I heard these girls couldn't hit the side of a barn so they might as well support someone who can." She looked at the two women and handed Black Dog over to Pinkie.

"Come on girls, if the three of us pull together we can do it." The commander saw they were each armed with pistols and considered that was good enough. She instructed the women to support Pedro in a fireman's lift and they set off walking as fast as they could behind Nulla.

"Shit!" Sundown swore in frustration and shame. "Lulu, you and Danni better go with them and provide as much support as you can. Quickly!" He knew the girls were excellent shots and seeing them race after Pedro and the three women made him feel a little less anxious. Those two girls were everyone's favourite and he knew they would die for Pedro if they had to.

'What have I just done?' he thought to himself, *'I hope I haven't made the wrong decision sending those two kids into battle.'* Sundown shook his head, everything was happening too fast. *"And where the hell are our scout patrols? By hell I hope they hear this noise and come running..."* He didn't have time to dwell on what might happen, instead he turned to the small gathering beside him.

"Harry, I know you can fire a rifle better than most but I need you here. Can you take command of the camp defences for me?"

"Yes, Sundown, I can do that." He had his kangaroo rifle in his hands, a World War II Lee-Enfield, scoped and obviously an old favourite.

"Donna can you and Beamy stay here and guard the camp with Harry. I need you as back up in case it goes wrong and I fear it might. Take the girls and hide up in the rocks. Just sit tight."

Turning to Kris and the diminutive Shrek he said, "If we lose those camels we're dead, even if we win the battle." The infantrymen turned cameleers nodded and returned to the task of securing the nervous animals.

"Jenny, can you and Jeda help Kris and Shrek with the camels please?" He had complete trust in these aboriginal women who'd lived all their lives with the animals of the desert. "Right! Pellino, Shadow, Lucy and Heidi, you're with me! We'll be going in as support to the special forces. Grab your gear, some water and let's go. Our cameleers need us." He gave them a moment to grab extra water bottles, kissed his wife then they began the kilometre jog towards the sounds of battle.

It wasn't until they were half way there that Sundown heard a wheezing sound. He turned and saw Beamy only a few metres behind him. He waved for him to catch up.

"Damn it, Beamy, you're still recovering. You should have stayed behind." He knew he was sounding like a proper bastard but he didn't want a single unnecessary death on his conscience.

"Sundown, if you leave me behind I swear I'll kick your arse all the way to Birdsville. I'm a Sundown Commando, I'm an original and I've got the scars to prove I'm staunch. I'm coming with you, like it or not." Sundown looked at Beamy, his breathing sounded like he was having an asthma attack.

Between his own laboured breaths Sundown croaked. "Listen to your damn breathing. Lorraine said you shouldn't be running. She'll kill me for letting you come with us."

"I'll kill you first if you don't." Was his firm reply. With an exasperated shake of his head Sundown continued jogging towards the sounds of gunfire with Beamy struggling beside him.

Sundown was pleased to see Sue-Ellen with Blondie, Jaina and the two aboriginal teenagers helping Pedro. His squad passed them as he swung his small band along the trough of a sand dune on the left flank and behind the homestead. He was impressed at how fast the girls had reacted and how not one of his commando had panicked. A plan was forming in his mind on how best to approach a flank attack - just as his party ran into the enemy.

Lucy was the first to react as a squad of Ravens Claws suddenly leaped over the top of the sand dune and among them. They were just as surprised as the Commando. Lucy's first burst hit the leader in the chest and he fell on top of Shadow. Her instinctive reaction was to chop his throat with her free hand and to fire her pistol into his chest as she fell.

Heidi went down, tangled under two terrorists who fought to get back to their feet as fast as possible. One of them fired at Lucy but Beamy knocked him back down on top of Heidi. Shadow ducked under a second terrorist soldier swinging his rifle butt as he tried to smash her skull.

It was a wild melee of arms, legs, rifles and fists. Beamy's automatic jammed so he grabbed it by the barrel and swung it wildly back and forth. He managed to keep the enemy from Shadow and Heidi for those vital few seconds of madness.

A fist collected Shadow's cheek and she spun twice before digging her feet into the soft sand. The Diamantina plains then heard a scream of defiance and rage it had never heard before as Shadow went ballistic.

With a snap kick she struck out at a crouching terrorist who was taking aim at Beamy. His head flew back and there was a sickening sound as something snapped in his neck. She ducked beneath a fist then pulled her stomach in as a bayonet lunged at her. With the athleticism of a gymnast she leaped above a second bayonet thrust at her thighs.

With her pistol in one hand she fired point-blank into her assailant's head. While still in the air her free hand drew her Deaths Head knife - gifted to her by a reluctant Halo a week earlier. As she came down she sprang forward stabbing a third enemy in the throat as he was strangling a semi-conscious Heidi.

Sundown was put out of the fight in the first few seconds. One of the Ravens Claws had king hit him from behind and knocked him out. His demon didn't have a chance to even make an appearance. Seeing stars and feeling a rising nausea from his concussion he could only watch the mayhem happening around him.

While Sundown was lost to the world of humanity, Lucy checked to ensure all enemy were accounted for then quickly placed herself on guard at the top of the dune. With trained precision she fired at three stragglers who were coming up behind the first squad.

Pellino was still jogging twenty metres behind. His sixty odd years of life on planet earth had slowed him somewhat. He arrived to see

Shadow and Beamy dispatch the last two terrorists so he helped Heidi get up from where she was lying on the ground.

"Did I miss anything?" he remarked as he held the young girl in his arms letting her cry the fright from her system.

Beamy suddenly bent over and vomited up his breakfast. He couldn't breathe and Pellino had to leave Heidi and tend to him. Sundown was holding his head in his hands rocking back and forth. He was the second to lose his breakfast. Lucy turned back to see what was happening and quickly assessed the situation. It didn't look good so she instinctively took control.

"Pellino, leave them. Get up here next to me and stand to. Heidi, pick up your weapon and go to that bush there and cover our left flank, it's exposed." The two didn't argue, they automatically followed her orders.

"Shadow." No answer. "SHADOW!" she yelled at the still figure now standing between worlds.

Shadow came back from wherever she was and answered softly, "yes?"

"I need you to come back to us, darling. Load your pistol and go with Heidi over there and cover that flank. We're vulnerable on that side. Do you understand?" she asked gently.

In a faraway voice Shadow replied, "I'm OK." She walked over to Heidi, touched her young friend on the arm and automatically reloaded her pistol magazine with the bullets in her cartridge belt.

Lucy slid down the sand dune and leaned over Beamy's crouched form. She gently rubbed his shoulder.

"Are you OK, buddy? I need you up on top of the sand dune, can you do that?"

Beamy turned and Lucy noticed his face was white, there was a blue tinge to his lips.

"I've got you covered, Lucy," he gasped tightly. "Just give me a second to get my breath back." He looked at Sundown who was now pouring some of his precious water onto his face. "And don't tell Sundown I spewed up my breakfast."

The young fighter stood from sheer will power and determination. He staggered to the bottom of the sand dune which looked as though it was a mile high. Then he began the colossal task of putting one foot in front of the other. Lucy listened to the sounds of his wheezing as he struggled not to pass out at each step.

She quickly leaped over to Sundown and crouched over him.

"Sundown? Are you OK?"

Sundown looked at her and she saw the pain in his face and how his eyes couldn't focus on hers. He grimaced as he spoke, "What's happening now Lucy? I need to know if we're safe."

"Our left flank is now secure. The front is covered by the homestead and the right flank is covered by the special forces fellas." she reported.

"Is everyone OK? Did any of us get hurt?" he asked, his eyes shut tight against the light.

"We're all good to go. Beamy has a breathing problem but no worse than you or Pellino," she said.

Sundown looked around, his eyes mere slits. There were five dead Ravens Claws strewn around the sandy ground in front of him. One had his dead hand on Sundown's shoe, he unconsciously pushed it away. He could now see Heidi and Shadow on the flank and Pellino and Beamy at the top of the sand dune. He nodded painfully in approval. As he nodded he brought up a stream of yellow bile almost fainting in the process.

Turning back to Lucy he struggled to speak. "Nice work, Ninety Nine, now I know why Nulla picked you." His breathing was rapid and he felt like shit. "Thanks, you saved us, Lucy." Lucy just nodded and stared at him knowing he was out of the fight. "Now help me get up." But instead of standing he collapsed onto his hands and knees and vomited again.

As he fell there came a 'brrrip' 'brrrip' from Beamy and Pellino's position. He knew they were still in the fight but his enthusiasm wasn't there any more. Sundown's head throbbed like he'd been kicked by a horse and he had no choice but to relinquish leadership of this patrol to Lucy.

"Lucy, I feel like shit warmed up. Grab my ammo and what's in these terrorists pouches and take command." He felt a wave of nausea but fought it down. "I'll stay here, I'm bloody useless right now." As he spoke he leaned forward on the sandy slope and brought up more yellow bile then collapsed onto his side closing his eyes as the world spun around him.

Lucy stroked his forehead as she wondered if she could do it. "Sure Sundown, I'll look after the Commando for you, don't you worry."

Sundown couldn't have cared less. He vomited again and then again, nothing but bile came up. Lucy handed him her water bottle and with a kiss on his forehead she left him to take command.

The Pine Gap specialists had managed to force their way to the rear and right flank of the homestead. With bursts of fire from Soldier of Fortune's aged M-60 their assault was so vicious that the terrorists were forced to retreat to the front and left flank of the building. But they wouldn't give up, not while their traditional foe, the Longreach Crusaders, were within their grasp.

They still had over twice as many fighters as Sundown and the Crusaders, they saw no reason to withdraw. They pulled back and reformed for an all-out assault on the building itself. They knew the Warrior Sisterhood were low on ammunition and it was just a matter of time before they would overwhelm them.

By pulling back to the front of the building, though, it gave Roo an opportunity to get himself and Dog back inside the homestead with his friends. He reasoned that one more defender would be useful.

Roo quickly checked the situation in the small room. He saw his best friend, Bongo, sitting on the floor crying over a girl cradled in his arms, she looked like she was dead. He recognised her as Martene's daughter and his friend from the many times he, Shamus and Pedro had visited while in Longreach.

Instinctively he crouched over and placed his hand on Denise's wound. Closing his eyes he sent his dream body into her chest and saw the injury. A bullet had hit a rib, the sharp edge of the broken rib had then torn through a swollen vein. The girl was bleeding internally and she was dying.

Roo was no longer in the world of the living, he was between worlds feeling the girl's life force slipping to the other side. He clearly saw her relatives watching. With his mind he pulled the pieces of damaged vein together and sealed it with a web of light. The bleeding eased but Denise was far from safe, she needed professional care now.

Having done what was needed he came back to the sounds of gunfire and screaming. Roo whispered to Bongo that the girl was going to survive. He then crawled next to Riley to help even the odds against them.

"Fortune?" called Obi-Wan. "Those people inside must be in a bad way, they're firing single shot. Can you hear that?" Fortune merely nodded. Neither moved as they watched the enemy laying down heavy fire on the stone building just in front of them. "They're trying to take the homestead where our Sundowners are. You lay down fire while I take Murphy and Pipeline forward, then you follow."

Fortune didn't speak, he just nodded and opened fire again. He had used all but a few rounds of his scant ammunition. There was maybe fifteen seconds sustained fire left in his machine gun so he relaxed and tried to make every bullet count. His ancient M-60 was now next to useless. Its aged barrel had deteriorated in the heat spitting bullets off to one side and he had no spare barrel so he decided that it was time to retire it.

The terrorists wisely kept the homestead and sand dunes between his M-60 and them. They'd already lost too many to the deadly fire of the special forces team and they didn't want to be exposed to more. The Ravens Claws desperately wanted the Crusaders dead and it seemed they didn't care how many of their own died doing it, but there were limits.

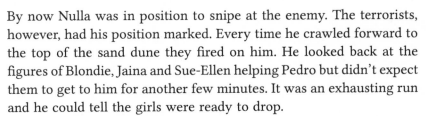

By now Nulla was in position to snipe at the enemy. The terrorists, however, had his position marked. Every time he crawled forward to the top of the sand dune they fired on him. He looked back at the figures of Blondie, Jaina and Sue-Ellen helping Pedro but didn't expect them to get to him for another few minutes. It was an exhausting run and he could tell the girls were ready to drop.

He could hear the special forces boys to his left controlling the centre of the battlefield with their accurate automatic fire. They were also picking off targets on his own flank so he felt safe from an immediate assault. Knowing these specialists, the elite of the US military, were on his flank, he relaxed a little. Looking across to the back of the battlefield he saw Sundown's squad go left and along the trough of a small sand dune.

In fascination he watched their vicious hand-to-hand melee with the Ravens Claw squad through his rifle scope. His hands shook from its ferocity. It wasn't just the savagery of the killing but Shadow, Lucy and Beamy's courageous fight back. He saw Lucy crouch down onto one knee firing at something in front of her but he couldn't see what she was firing at, his view was blocked by the curve of the sand dune. He desperately wanted to provide covering fire but everyone was too close, if he fired he'd hit one of his friends.

He noticed his scope shaking and pulled his hand from his rifle. It was he that was shaking. *'Damn,'* he thought, *'this fighting business has really got to me.'*

Trying to shift to a better position, Nulla came under accurate automatic fire again. Without warning a blast of sand smacked into his eyes. He let out a scream as he fell back down the dune rolling all the way to the bottom. Knowing not to rub at his eyes he knelt on all fours letting his eyes water so as to wash some of the sand away. He pulled his water bottle out and flushed his eyes to remove as much sand as he could. There still remained tiny traces of sand which continued to make his eyes water, his head burned and he felt dizzy.

Nulla knew he was a liability at that moment so he rolled onto his back and pulled out his tobacco pouch and papers. Keeping his tortured, watering eyes closed he rolled a cigarette by feel alone. Breathing steadily and deeply through his nose he kept his eyes watering for as long as he could to wash them of every particle. Putting the cigarette to his lips he drew deeply, then, as he released the smoke from his body, he fell into his mind palace to gain a degree of relief.

"You lazy bastard, Nulla! While our visitors are saving our arses you've gone and done a boofhead job of falling asleep." Pedro lay above him firing off round after round keeping a squad of Ravens Claws from coming up over their right flank. He had sweat dripping down his weather-beaten face and his three girls were firing frantically with their pistols. None of them had an automatic rifle.

One of the terrorists, braver than the others, had crawled right up behind their position to fire on them. Sue-Ellen reacted quickly, spinning around on her heel to fire her Glock 19 pistol almost point blank into the man's face.

Nulla shook himself awake and rubbed absently at the blister on his finger where the cigarette had burned. He blinked several times to clear his vision and was satisfied he could see well enough to fight.

Lulu and Danni were engaged in their own furious fire-fight with two Ravens Claws not ten metres away. They were hidden from the others by a sand ridge. They swapped bullets back and forth as each tried to outflank the other. Within half a minute the girls were twenty metres from Nulla's position fighting a personal war with the two terrorists opposite them.

It was two against two but the men were players. They could hear the teenage girls talking and when they popped their heads up they could see them quite clearly.

Two experienced predators versus two teenage girls. The two Claws wanted to keep these two prizes alive, for other things before they killed them. When the mad rush of fighting abated they confidently sat with their backs to the sand dune smiling knowingly to each other and planned their next move.

In the sudden silence Lulu leaned forward and spoke softly to Danni. Her hands were shaking and she dropped her magazine onto the sand. When she tried to pick it up she couldn't feel anything, her hands were numb with fear.

"Danni, I'm scared, girl. I don't want to get caught. I can't go through all that again."

Danni saw the tears running down her best friend's cheeks and began to cry too. "I want my Luke, I just want my Luke with me," she sobbed.

"Danni, If I die today I'll know what real love is. You're lucky, Luke loves you," said Lulu finally punching her magazine into place. She sobered a little and said, "This is my last magazine, I hope we do a good job. I don't want anyone to say we let everyone down when we die."

Danni wiped at the tears blurring her eyes. "Lulu, you're my best friend, I'd rather you here than Luke any day." Just as Danni spoke two powerful bodies landed on them knocking the wind from their lungs and fists smashed into the girl's faces.

Chapter 16

Desert Strike

As Nulla looked across at his squad he noticed Blondie lying face down on the sand but he couldn't work out why. Then he saw a spreading redness around her shoulder. She groaned then moved slowly as she rolled onto her back.

"Blondie, are you OK?" Nulla called.

"Someone shot me, Nulla." He could see she was in shock but he didn't have time to go to her, a second squad of Ravens Claws now reinforced the first. The incoming fire forced he and Pedro to crawl backwards, quickly.

"Jaina, help Blondie!" Nulla yelled as he pulled his pistol and fired at the heads bobbing behind the sand dune. It didn't look good for the three girls. They were in a worse position than he and Pedro. They had some cover but only five metres separated them from their enemy. If they stood up or moved they'd be fired on. He and Pedro couldn't do much because the incoming fire forced their heads down too.

Right at this point in time Nulla wished he had been more careful and not put himself in a position to be injured, even if it was just sand in his eyes. He felt responsible for letting the Ravens Claws gain ground on his flank.

'*I've let everyone down again,*' he berated himself.

Sue-Ellen snapped off rounds from her pistol, each time a head appeared she fired. '*Like hitting dummies with a mallet,*' she thought to herself. It reminded her of the old game, Whack-a-Mole, that she was so good at when the circus had come to town.

"Nulla, ya boofhead letting these bastards sneak up on ya like this. I'll crawl around the back and come up behind them. You stay here and anchor this point." Without waiting for a response Pedro began crawling but his tin legs were impossible, they caught on every bush and rock in the desert. Just like their assault on the mines outside Marree he was stuck if he kept the darn things strapped on. So he undid the laces and began crawling with his stumps. He found it easier but a damn sight more painful. Pedro knew that if he was surprised by the enemy now he was a dead man.

Halo, Cambra and Assassin moved silently towards the two enemy squads. Although Cambra was the one who heard the sounds of battle, it was Halo who had taken command of their assault. He stood on his camel's back like a dare-devil rider in a rodeo and took in the battle scene. Just as he'd learned from Shamus while training for the Mines Battle, Halo took a series of mental pictures of the battlefield and brought them together. Within a few seconds he had his plan and moved his tiny assault squad to rescue Nulla's surrounded squad.

"On three we go over the top, we empty our magazines and drop down behind the dune. Cambra, you provide covering fire. We'll need fifteen seconds, that's all we need mate, fifteen seconds. Can you do that?" asked Halo, his face flushed from the heat and the excitement of battle.

"What the hell do you take me for, Halo? You prick. I'll give you fifteen seconds if you want fifteen seconds and then I'll give you another fifteen because you're an arsehole." Cambra was stressed, this was another contact and that meant more heartache and loss.

"One, two, three!"

Yelling like idiots they raced the few metres across the top of the sand dune and into the first enemy squad. It was ugly, they had little time to aim and fire, so they just cut down what they could in the first few seconds. They smashed their way through the press of Ravens Claw bodies with their rifle butts and fists.

One Ravens Claw slashed wildly with his knife and Halo parried with his AK taking the knife blade on its barrel. The large-fisted terrorist kicked and Halo's rifle went spinning out of his hands. The man dived at him as he tried to recover. The enemy soldier clamped one hand around Halo's throat and the other held his knife ready to plunge it into his enemy's heart.

Instinctively Halo punched upwards into the man's jaw. It was a purely reflexive punch, no thought went into it nor did he feel anything right then. The man went backwards and collapsed struggling frantically to get back to his feet.

Halo pulled out his own knife but dropped it, he couldn't hold a thing in his right hand. His prized Deaths Head knife remained on the ground beside him but his hand was useless. He looked at the man now standing and shaking his groggy head.

The sounds of Assassin screaming as he wrestled a terrorist on the ground penetrated his consciousness. The pandemonium of men dying surrounded him, it was like being in the middle of a vicious dog fight. Halo realised that he was alone and vulnerable, unless he did something right now he would die.

'There's got to be something,' thought Halo, and there was. His pistol was in his left side holster, he'd forgotten about it. Drawing it awkwardly with his left hand he slipped the safety off and pulled the trigger just as the man cleared his head and dived towards him.

Halo stepped to the side and watched as his enemy dropped to the ground. He put a round into the back of the man's head then turned to see what else he needed to do. The squad of Ravens Claws were all dead. Assassin was panting and it sounded like the whining of a distressed dog.

Assassin's whole body shook as he crouched trying to wipe the bloodied blade of his knife on the dead man's body. He then turned and Halo saw a look of shocked horror on his friend's face. That's when he felt the pain.

"F... f... fuck me!" Halo stammered dropping his Ruger GP 100 .357 pistol to the sand as he tried to return it to its holster. "Assassin, I think I've broken my hand on that terrorist's head." When Cambra finally arrived the two studied Halo's hand and saw that one of his knuckles was pushed backwards into his fist.

Assassin shook his head to clear it and examined his friend's hand.

"Forget it, Halo, we've got Revelationists to kill." Quickly he grabbed Halo's hand and reefed his finger back into place before his friend knew what was happening. Halo bit down hard on his bottom lip trying his hardest not to make a sound. He now had two wounds as fresh blood poured from his bleeding lip.

"Fuck you! Assassin! That hurt, you prick!" He was bent over and grunted in pain several times holding his hand tightly.

"You deserved that, Halo. Now get back to work," said Cambra who now crouched down to fire wildly at the second enemy squad which had come around the dune to investigate. "And for Pete's sake hurry will you!" he screamed as he ducked to escape a burst of incoming bullets.

While Halo's cameleer patrol was rescuing Nulla's band, Pedro had continued to crawl slowly, but steadily, behind the enemy position. He could barely raise himself to see where he was going. When he heard voices he had to stop to get his bearings.

"Hey, looky here Ollie, nice tits!" Pedro heard the two men chuckling.

"Look how they jiggle when I shake them. Come on, we don't have much time. Fuck 'em then we'll kill them," came the second voice.

Pedro went cold inside. He knew what was going on behind the dune. He'd heard that kind of trash-talk during his time in Vietnam and with the CIA too many times not to know. There came a squeal of a female voice and Pedro saw in his mind's eye the terrorist's hand over Lulu's mouth to stop her screaming.

"You stinking bastards!" he cursed softly as he struggled to climb to the top of the sand dune as fast as he could. His every movement ripped more skin from his stumps which now bled freely.

Each muffled scream cut into Pedro's heart like a knife as he pushed himself mercilessly up the sand dune. He desperately needed to rescue his two precious friends, they were like daughters to him.

"You bitch, bite me will you!" The sound of a fist hitting flesh came to him from behind the sand dune. Pedro's blood froze with each savage sound.

"Hurry up and get into her, Ollie, I want a turn!" came the second voice again.

In desperation to get to the girls in time Pedro had ditched his rifle and pulled his pistol, a Vietnam war M1911A1, .45 calibre. One bullet would take a man's head off. As he crawled to the lip of the sand dune he saw a sight that made his heart stop. Danni was pinned to the ground by a uniformed man with his hand around her throat. The young aboriginal girl's eyes were glazed and open, her mouth formed into a silent scream. Lulu lay unconscious bleeding from a cut to her face, her pants were down and a man was leaning into her.

That man lost his head a split second later. The second Ravens Claw looked up and took a bullet in his chest followed by two more before he hit the ground. Pedro rolled down the slope of the dune then crawled across to gather the girls in his arms. He sat holding them to his chest crying his heart out.

Assassin knew Halo wouldn't be able to do much with his broken hand but knew that he would do his best. The two stormed the depleted remnant Ravens Claws squad from behind while Cambra kept them occupied from the opposite direction. Halo fired his pistol wildly with his left hand hitting everything but what he aimed at.

"Shit! Halo, cease fire! Cambra, cease fire! They're dead!" cried Assassin. Another burst of gunfire came from Cambra's position nearly hitting the two Sundowners.

"Don't you fuckin' listen, Cambra!" screamed Assassin again. "I said CEASE FUCKING FIRE!"

Cambra's face appeared sheepishly from behind the edge of the dune. He stood up when he saw his two mates standing over the dead Revelationists.

"Sorry, Assassin, I didn't hear you through all the firing," he said softly. His face was filmed in sweat and dirt, there was blood on his shirt and tear streaks ran down his face. Cambra, big tough Cambra, was human after all, thought Assassin.

"Come on mates, we'd better get to the girls and help out. We're done here." Assassin Creed put his arms around both men and walked them along the dune base to Nulla and Sue-Ellen's position.

Obi-Wan leaped forward a few metres then opened fire as soon as he hit the ground. Up jumped Pipeline who raced a few metres further and did the same. Murphy followed as they worked their way to the edge of the homestead. They covered twenty metres in a matter of seconds. Soldier of Fortune was putting in short measured bursts from his M-60 but pretty soon he'd be out of the fight. He pulled his M9 Beretta pistol and placed it by his side then fired the last few rounds of his aged machine gun.

With a roar Fortune jumped up and raced for the homestead popping off a few rounds from his pistol at the heads peering from behind one of the dog kennels. By now the Ravens Claws knew what was happening and were waiting for him. But the special forces had worked closely together for so long now that they could read each others minds. The three were positioned to provide their buddy with enough fire power to force thirty terrorists back behind cover. Only the very brave or very foolish ventured from cover to fire, they didn't last long.

"Why the hell did ya do that for?" yelled Pipeline into Fortune's ear. "I thought now you'd run out of ammo you'd want to have a rest?"

"I saw you sobbing because you missed me, so I decided to come over and comfort you." Fortune grinned at the enormous black SEAL.

"Delta's always take lunch time naps, Pipeline, we must have woken him up," called Murphy while continuing to fire short bursts of his M4A1 at the bobbing heads trying to return the special forces fire.

"Hey, Pipeline, why haven't the Ravens Claws used smoke or tear gas on the homestead?" asked Murphy pulling his head back as a burst of machine gun fire sprayed the wall he was hiding behind.

"I guess they've got none. That would've been the first thing to do. So no gas, no smoke and no grenades. It's a good sign, bud," Pipeline replied.

Staff Sergeant Obi-Wan peered inside the homestead and saw bodies lying on the floor. He called out, "Hey, you guys inside, what's you're status?"

Martene called out in answer, "We're doing fine, we don't need you to rescue us." She'd had a tough time and was in a bad mood. The Sisterhood started out with two platoons and were now down to just the two girls standing.

Riley called out to his special forces mates. "Obi-Wan, we've got wounded, serious wounded, we need help in here."

Pipeline continued firing as did Murphy. The two swapped position as each changed magazine allowing Fortune and Obi-Wan to crawl in through the window to provide first aid.

The first thing they saw was the mess on the floor. There were pools of blood, empty cartridge cases, bodies and the smell of blood and cordite was overpowering. What affected them the most was the sight of Bongo sobbing quietly as he cradled a young woman in his arms. Obi-Wan summed it up, he could tell these people were ineffective and out of the fight.

There were still rounds going in and out of the windows. Roo and Riley had positioned themselves to take turns firing through a small crack in the wall.

Just then Riley cried out, "Roo, I'm out, they're all yours, cuz!"

Fortune called to his mates outside. "We're ineffective here. We'll stick around and provide first aid, you guys will have to carry us for a while."

Obi-Wan nodded at Fortune and took one of the windows. He then became business-like, doing what he did best, protecting his buddies.

The Ravens Claws assaulted the left flank again and again only to be confronted by a staunch Lucy and her team. She held the high ground and beat the now cowed terrorists back to their sand dune cover at the front of the homestead. The Sundown Commando squad's final defense was with their pistols having run out of automatic rifle ammunition some time earlier.

The terrorists next tried to get around the right flank but an angry Nulla and his reinforced team fought them back. Reduced to only a dozen men the Ravens Claws were now sent reeling at each turn.

There came three shrill blasts from a whistle and the incoming fire from the Ravens Claws ceased. Murphy looked at his partner, he nodded and together they leaped towards the sound of vehicles starting up from behind the sand dune.

There were two, four-wheel drives, just starting to move when they arrived. While Murphy and Pipeline opened up on them with their automatics Obi-Wan raced across and popped a precious 40 mm grenade into his launch tube and fired. It exploded beside the front vehicle sending the second one accelerating into it.

The special forces poured fire into the two vehicles until all movement ceased. Satisfied that all was under control they carefully walked around the battle scene to make sure not one Ravens Claw survived.

Halo, Assassin and Cambra had raced across the sand dunes when they heard the whistle blasts and the cars revving up. They missed the opportunity to fire on the escaping vehicles, the special forces had completed the mission for them. The boys watched the precision and professionalism of the three American warriors from the top of the sand dune.

Holding his broken hand, Halo said, "Did you guys see what I just saw? Now that's better soldiering than Halo4 any day. Way better than any Assassin Creed game too. These guys are good."

Obi-Wan looked up to see his three commando friends and waved for them to join them. "Hey, how's things up there, any trouble?" he asked grimly.

"All cleaned up, Obi. We'll go back and check again but that was some shooting you did here," said Assassin taking over now that Halo was struggling and in pain. Cambra stood silent with his own thoughts.

"What about the other flank? Can one of you go and check for me, please?" Obi-Wan asked Assassin.

The cherub faced commando noticed that Cambra was not in such a good place. It was prudent to give him a job to prevent him breaking down.

"Cambra, can you go and check Sundown's squad, mate?"

Cambra looked up then nodded, he loped off while Halo squatted down and tried to wrap his hand in a bandage.

"Give me a hand will you, Obi," he called to his special forces mate. Obi-Wan took the bandage from Halo and wrapped his friend's hand for him.

"That's ugly, bud, it looks like a rattlesnake bite. How'd it swell up like that?" asked the Ranger Staff Sergeant.

"Ravens Claws have hard heads." Halo grunted between gritted teeth as Obi-Wan wrapped the bandage tight over the fast swelling hand.

"I'd get the nurses to take a look at that when we get back to camp. It might need plaster, if you guys have any that is," said the Ranger his eyes wrinkled in fatigue.

No one ventured inside the homestead until the perimeter was checked and double checked. Obi-Wan took command of the clean up.

When he was satisfied he called for Pellino to climb onto the homestead roof to keep a look out while they helped the girls inside.

"Hey! Hey, you guys! We're coming out, don't shoot us, OK?" came a fatigued but strong female voice from inside the homestead.

Bongo had just exited, his tear streaked face reflected just how exhausted they all were. Everyone looked pale, they were completely done-in.

"Come out without your weapons and your hands in the air, or we'll shoot!" called Lucy with an authority that seemed to come easily to her.

"The girls inside are Crusaders, Lucy. They could have killed us when they arrived, instead they told us to leave. We agreed to stay and help them against the Ravens Claws. They're now our friends. Don't hurt them." Bongo looked at the hard faces in front of him and continued. "If anyone has a problem with that you'll have to kill me before I let anyone harm a hair on their heads," he said, his grim face showed he was serious, deadly serious.

Riley came out at that moment and stood beside his scout mate. "As Bongo said, these girls are our friends, we stayed to help them. They're now our blood sisters, friends, and I'll die beside Bongo to defend them too." He saw the hard looks soften and some of them nodded approval. "They're badly shot up and need medical help." He waved to Assassin and Cambra. "Come on, Soldier of Fortune needs help with them."

Those gathered at the homestead looked at each other and began to move towards the entrance. Bongo took that for a yes and called into the single roomed homestead, "Martene, bring your girls out."

"You won't shoot us will you?" came the commanding female voice again.

"No, of course we won't bloody shoot you," answered Lucy in a slightly softer but gruff voice.

The door was in pieces and fell apart as the first Crusader exited the building. She carried a bloodied red haired girl gently in her arms. Captain Martene was followed by another woman who also carried one of their Sisterhood.

Obi-Wan tapped Beamy on the arm. He was dazed and drifting off somewhere in his mind but the tap brought him back to the present. The two went over to help the wounded girls.

"Would someone tell me what's going on here? Sundown's going to want a few answers," said Assassin easing a thin wounded woman onto her side as Pipeline and Obi-Wan applied aid.

Martene put her hands on her hips. She was so exhausted she could barely stand but she wouldn't let her girls down and spoke with pride, clear and strong.

"The Ravens Claws attacked us last night while we were on a training and clean up patrol. They chased us here this morning. Our sister platoon is completely wiped out and I've almost lost mine. We cut them up bad last night in a counter attack. We knocked them down from company size to what you saw here." The captain's hand was shaking as she pulled a packet of cigarettes from her shirt pocket. She tapped it vigorously but it was empty. The other Crusader, a woman of even more mature years, handed her one of her own cigarettes.

After a few seconds Martene spoke again. The Commando members noticed she wore the insignia of an officer in the Crusader's of Light Battalion and had the bearing of a formidable warrior.

"Young man," she said to Assassin, "you said 'Sundown' am I right?"

Obi-Wan and Pipeline bandaged the wounded girl's thigh. She was barely conscious and groaned as they tightened it to stop the blood flow. Assassin tried to help but was just in the way so he stood up to answer Martene's question.

"Sure did, ma'am, I mean, Captain. Sundown's just over there." He pointed towards the sand dune. Sundown was still concussed and quite incapable of greeting his guests.

"We're Sundown's Commando, ma'am. We would like to offer you our hospitality, I think you need it." Assassin nodded to Jaina who only now put her pistol into its holster. She then went over to help with the wounded. Shadow was checking on Sundown.

When Halo returned from the homestead he said, "There's not much ammunition left there, Captain. You were in luck this morning, we were thinking of heading home tomorrow."

"I don't think luck had much to do with it. We've been fighting a running retreat into this damn desert all night, sonny-boy. We would have been throwing rocks in another ten minutes. Our Lord saw we had honour and those Ravens Claws had none, so he put you here to help us," explained Martene. She looked haggard and the only thing keeping her from collapse was the cigarette in her hand.

Martene turned to Bongo. "If it had clicked that you were Sundown's Commando, I might not have allowed you to stay and play with us."

"That's what I was just thinking, Martene." He gently held Denise's hand between his own.

"Now where's Pedro, young man, did you say you knew him?" asked the captain of the Warrior Sisterhood as the rest of the Commando gathered to help where they could.

Shadow had walked over and was carefully observing Martene, she stepped forward. "Captain Martene, are you with us or against us? I need to know, you know the rules." It was apparent that Shadow was on Sundown's leadership committee for her brains as well as her talent for killing terrorists.

"So Pedro's a secret then?" Martene asked with a chuckle deep in her throat.

Just then one of the special forces soldiers came out of the homestead and walked up to Martene.

"I'm sorry, ma'am, but the others inside are dead. I wish we'd been able to get here earlier. I'm truly sorry." It was Soldier of Fortune, the special forces medic, his drawn face reflected his grief.

"You said you fought the Ravens Claws, a company? And you were just platoon strength? You're quite an officer lady," said Obi-Wan, the respect reflected in his eyes.

The other aged Crusader survivor answered. "Captain Martene's one of our best. The Ravens Claws ambushed us on the Diamantina nature reserve while we were cleaning up after the Thunderdome Cup. They didn't win this time so they declared war on us, without even telling us either. Captain Martene led the withdrawal and ambushes all the way here. Those Ravens Claws really wanted to get their hands on her. She's the one that led the assault on the Brisbane church head-quarters and stopped them harassing our farmers. Yes, she's one of our very best."

Martene offered more information as Sue-Ellen and Nulla came over to join them. "We're the Warrior Sisterhood, personal bodyguards to the Abbess Leonie, of Longreach. I'd like to extend the hand of friend-ship to whoever runs this outfit. I see Sundown's unwell but I still can't see Pedro. So who's going to shake my hand?"

"Pedro?" said Halo looking directly at Nulla. "Where's Pedro, Nulla?"

Cambra was standing beside Halo and his face turned white. He did a quick head count then said hurriedly. "And where's my girls? Where's Lulu and Danni? We've got to find them, Nulla!" His face ceased in fear and he started to fret.

"Oh, shit!" exclaimed Nulla. As he turned he grabbed at Jaina's arm and ran back to where they'd been fighting. He called over his shoul-der, "I'll shake your hand madam but right now I'm busy."

Sue-Ellen felt plain exhausted. The race from their campsite with Pedro and the fight had taken it out of her. She was no longer a tanned and toned twenty year old she'd decided.

"Captain Martene is it? I'm Commander Sue-Ellen Cullen. It is my pleasure to meet you and I would like to welcome you to Sundown's Commando. Sadly I hear that Sundown is unwell, he received a blow to the head and is currently throwing up his intestines. Best we leave him to it for a while, we don't want to embarrass him."

Martene couldn't help but like this woman. She looked tough as nails but she had a nice smile and manner. With a loud sigh she said, "I'd like a cup of tea if you don't mind - thick, dark and strong, just how I like my men." She paused then looked down on Bongo sitting beside Denise at their feet. He held the girl's head gently in his arms and was speaking softly to her. Denise's eyes were open and she had a wan smile on her face.

Martene could see what was happening and it warmed her heart. In the midst of this madness her daughter just might have found herself a hero who truly deserved her.

"But first I'd like my daughter here and her wounded cousins taken to your camp. They're not doing too well and I don't want to lose them."

Sue-Ellen heard the tight strain in her voice and knew that Martene was fighting exhaustion.

"Sure, my boys will organise that," she said gently then turned and called to her special forces troops. "Let's get these stretchered and out of here."

Fortune looked up and nodded to Murphy who loped off to find a couple of stretchers from among the terrorist vehicles.

Turning, Sue-Ellen noticed Blondie lying on the front porch of the homestead. Her shoulder was bandaged and she appeared to be sleeping.

Looking around at the wounded commandos she said, "Halo, you, Blondie and Roo better go with the wounded Sisterhood girls."

A moment later there came the roar of a four wheel truck from behind the sand dune where the Ravens Claws had parked their vehicles.

"It seems Murphy's found us our transport. I think he might want to drive us all back to our camp site for that cup of tea."

Lucy wasn't quite finished with her mission that day. She leaned down to pull a fresh magazine from one of the dead terrorists as she walked over to Sue-Ellen.

"Sue-Ellen, I need to check for wounded Raven's Claws."

The Pine Gap commander was still recovering from the long run and the vicious fire-fight, she absently nodded her exhausted head.

Through his nausea, Sundown knew they had won the battle but he could still hear gunfire. It was a single shot AK47 and he wondered who it was and what they were doing. There was movement to his left and he turned his head painfully to see.

It was Lucy. He watched as she carelessly walked over to a wounded terrorist squirming on the ground. Putting her booted foot on his chest to hold him still she raised her weapon. With his mind screaming for her to stop she fired a single shot into the terrorist's forehead.

Chapter 17

Treaty

Nulla directed Jaina to stand on the top of the sand dune they had defended to watch for movement. Cambra checked once more to make sure there were no terrorists before walking along its top looking for Pedro and his girls. The aboriginal sergeant now examined the ground until he cut Pedro's crawl marks. It was easy then. He followed the tracks and noted first the tin legs then his M21 sniper rifle lying at the base of the sand dune. Surely that was where Pedro would be, on the other side.

He felt a sinking feeling in his chest as he climbed to the top of the dune. Even though he didn't want to he looked down. There he saw Pedro with the two girls. They appeared to be snuggled up and asleep, like small children in his arms.

"Pedro, are the girls OK?" he called tentatively, quite uncertain of what he was seeing. Nulla shivered fearfully at what Pedro might answer.

"Yes, matie, they're safe as houses," came Pedro's very tired reply.

Nulla heaved a huge sigh of relief as he waved for Jaina and Cambra to join him. The two ran over as fast as they could in the deep sand. They slid straight down the dune and hugged the three survivors tightly. The old man began to cry again.

"Damn it, I feel like a right boofhead I do. If I hadn't thrown me legs off when I did this might not be so..." he stopped talking and swallowed a choked sob.

Cambra now began to cry too. His deep, heart-wrenching sobs upset Jaina. She fought not to show her tears of relief. Just then Danni opened her eyes and looked around.

Sitting up with a start, she asked, "What's happening? Where's Lulu?"

When she realised she was in Pedro's arms and lying next to her best friend she relaxed a little.

"Is Lulu going to be all right, Pedro?" she asked in a small voice.

"Yes Danni, she's fine," he said smoothing her black hair with his hand. "I've checked her over. Those bastards didn't do anything unseemly but she's going to have a sore head." Pedro absently wiped the tears from Danni's cheeks. "How's your throat, me little darlin'?"

Danni reached her hand to the bruising on her neck and winced. "It's sore but I'm all right. I'm just worried about Lulu. I heard her screaming and it... it... it upset me." Nulla decided it was time to move them back to their camp site before they all started crying again and he with them.

He looked at the two dead bodies beside the commandos on the sand. "Pedro, we'd better get some help over here and head back. We're pretty knocked about but we survived." He smiled as he added, "and Pedro old fella, we're mighty proud of you."

Cambra was next to useless. All he could do was hold on to the girls and sob. The tension of the past twelve months had finally hit and broken him. Nulla put his arm around Cambra's shoulders and sat with them while Jaina sought help to carry Pedro. She wasn't in the mood to carry him back to the camp site so when she heard Murphy start the truck she knew she was saved.

Murphy found three vehicles left behind by the Ravens Claws and all were in serviceable condition. Martene's vehicle was trashed beyond any hope of repair. The engine and every panel had been ripped to shreds in the vicious fire-fight. The four special forces took turns to transport the wounded and exhausted troops to the main camp.

Roo sat with Riley and Dog beside their two dead camels. They didn't speak, there were no words to describe their loss. It had been weeks of hard work to get to know these beautiful and sensitive beasts and now they were dead. Even Dog sensed their sadness and went from one to the other licking their hands.

Roo grabbed Riley's proffered hand and pulled himself upright. "Come on Roo, we'd better head back. I'm sure the girls will have some food and drink for us. We've still got our spare mounts back at the palace, they need us too you know."

Roo's injured foot left a small trail of blood as they shouldered their weapons and kit. With his arm over Riley's shoulder the cousins limped back to the camp site together.

When Murphy brought Pedro and his little band into camp they received a special reception. Cambra embraced his two girls once more and hugged them to him. Usually it was the girls who wouldn't let go of him but this time he couldn't let go of them.

"Pedro!" came a loud, commanding voice from somewhere in the middle of the gathered soldiers and supporters. Pedro's head popped up and he looked around, he knew that voice from somewhere.

"Pedro! Front and centre. Now!" ordered Martene and Pedro's face cracked into a smile.

"Martene! You ol' flirt! What on earth are you doing here me gorgeous girlie?" he called through the crowd.

He wasn't able to do much. His wheel chair bogged in the soft sand and his tin legs needed a good clean before he'd be able to wear them. Besides, his stumps were red raw from the long and painful crawl over salt bush, spinifex and wicked desert thorns. Martene walked over and bent down to hug her old friend.

"Pedro, you old buzzard, you stood me up the last time you were in Longreach and now you owe me." She smiled brightly holding on to his hand as she chastised him.

"Ah, me darling lass, I was young and stupid in those far off days. If I knew then what I know now I would never have left you." He was as charming as he always was.

"Pedro, that was only a year ago. You were old then like you're old now," she said firmly as though reminding a school boy he should know better than try to teach an old hand to suck eggs.

"And you grow more beautiful the older I get. Come on, Martene, sit with me girlie and tell me what the hell you were doing squattin' in old man Hives' homestead. I heard you were ambushed by a company of Ravens Claws and beat them the hell off." They chatted warmly while Jeda and Lorraine finished dressing his stumps.

Sundown lay on his swag in the shade of their tarpaulin. Pinkie had given him a wet cloth and another water bottle. He tried to sleep but his head throbbed and his mind was all over the place. Shamus' words continued to echo in his mind, '*there will be sacrifices.*'

So who was the sacrifice? No one had died. Sure the girls had a horrific experience, Halo broke his hand and Roo had a nick in his foot but otherwise everyone was fine. There was Blondie's shoulder wound but it was a flesh wound which should heal quickly... it was a real puzzle.

Then it occurred to Sundown that it must be him. Shamus meant he was the one to make a personal sacrifice. With a sore head and stomach muscles screaming from over-use he thought it through. He'd taken no part in a decisive battle which could have swung either way and he was forced to sacrifice his leadership and trust his instincts.

The uptake of this was that Lucy showed she clearly had leadership skills and a calm head for fighting, just like all of his originals. He could see her massaging the scar tissue in Beamy's aching biceps and back. She looked content and peaceful, not bad after holding the flank against seven assaults. Pellino told him afterwards that they counted fifteen dead terrorists in front of their position.

'*And my head stopped me welcoming the new people or leading the special forces assault...*' and a million other things he should have done himself.

As he drifted off into a pained sleep he replayed Shamus' conversation. Images came to Sundown of the three cameleers sacrificing their safety to stay with the Crusader girls in the homestead; Lucy and her squad fighting to hold the left flank; Sue-Ellen and her group carrying Pedro; Nulla's worrying over his pregnant wife Glenda; the special forces boys so far from their loved ones in the US; Pedro and Cambra's girls... the images flashed back and forth across his mind as every member sacrificed a part of themselves with each day of this wretched war.

While the commando was winding down and patching their wounds the forth patrol, Simon, Luke and Arthur, finally turned up. They had four kangaroo carcasses across their camel's backs for dinner. But instead of a calm holiday atmosphere there was something wrong, very wrong. As they climbed down they saw only half the number of camels and there were exhausted and tear-streaked faces everywhere. Only Heidi came out to greet them. Even Kris and Shrek were too busy to help with their fresh killed meat.

"What happened here?" asked Arthur as he 'kooshed' his camel to sit so he could climb off. "It looks like someone's been in a fight." His face didn't have its usual smile and he held onto his Steyr firmly.

Heidi put her hand on his shoulder. There was dirt all over her; dirt, blood and sweat stains... everyone still had their weapons at hand. It all suggested a contact with the enemy. He'd not lived nearly a year in Adelaide hiding from the Revelationists not to recognise the signs of battle - and the smell of fear.

"Heidi, tell me, what's happening?" he said again looking around at the exhausted commando.

"Looks like they've been in a fight, Arty. Come on, Heidi, what happened?" badgered Luke as his eyes darted from group to group trying to figure out what was going on.

While they unloaded and hobbled their camels, Heidi told her story. She described the many assaults on her position. Of how Lucy took command and stood up to fight the last one with her pistol almost single handed when everyone's ammunition ran out. How Shadow leaped into the air and fired her pistol and stabbed with her knife. She said it so fast and furiously that the three boys were completely engrossed.

"What did you do?" asked Arthur.

Heidi coughed. "I got squashed. I had three Ravens Claws jump on me and Sundown tried to fight them off, so did the others. That's how it started. We were walking behind the sand dune and the Ravens Claws ran straight into us. None of us had much chance to fire so it was hand to hand combat. Lucky that Shadow and Johnny had been training us to fight but it's not easy when you've got three big boofheads on top of you."

The boys weren't sure what to do, so while Arthur stayed with Heidi, Simon and Luke dumped their kangaroos at the meal tent and went to find Nulla to report in. From him they learned of what happened to Lulu and Danni. As soon as they heard they raced over to where their girlfriends were, sitting beside Pedro, Martene and Cambra. They rushed over to crush the girls to their chests. They were so close to losing their new found loves and it terrified them.

After a few hours rest Harry sat down with the committee and gave his ordnance report. "With the terrorist's weapons and ammunition now in our possession we have enough for the first time in quite a while. Still no grenades and it looks like no one has them. If the Crusaders have none, the Stosstruppen have none and the Ravens Claws have none then grenades must be too difficult to manufacture or too expensive to trade."

"What about our camels, how many did we lose?" asked Nulla.

"We lost half. There's still McFly and Wiram to arrive back in camp, but of the cameleers all returned with their camels bar Roo and Riley's. Bongo's Star escaped back to us. Of those that were kept back here, Kris and Shrek tried their hardest to prevent them running. We've lost half so that means we have less than one camel per person," Harry replied. "Our food supply is safe and all our gear is just as you left it. If we count the three vehicles the special forces brought back we'll have enough fuel to get the wounded back to Birdsville. Once home we'll get Louie or Johnny to send a few Bushmasters and some troops to help clean up here and bring the rest of us back to camp. They'll also need to bury the dead."

Pinkie asked a very subdued Sundown about the guests and what they were going to do with them. Jenny and Jeda in particular wanted assurances they weren't going to bring the enemy down on them. Sundown still nursed a headache but was otherwise much improved after having a few hours sleep.

"I've only had a quick chat with Captain Martene, but it seems they remain loyal to their Abbess Leonie, which is what we would expect. We value loyalty and we respect Martene and her girl's loyalty to their leader." Sundown was now able to sip some cold tea after he'd had some of Jeda's desert herbs to settle his stomach, it helped. "She's agreed to a truce and according to Roo, Bongo and Riley we're now blood brothers and sisters. Martene's going to be our contact officer to the Longreach Crusaders." His staff nodded their approval.

Sue-Ellen spoke next. "An update from our side. We lost communications with the world when one of the camels stepped on our radio equipment in the madness of this morning's fight. The Ravens Claw vehicles don't carry any radios either so we're alone. We should be safe here for tonight. My boys have reconnoitred the battle site again and report no Ravens Claws escaped alive." She stopped to address Lucy who had been invited to the meeting by Sundown. "We don't normally execute prisoners but today I've decided to make an exception. When Pedro told me what those skunks were doing to your girls I would have sliced their balls off before I shot them," she said coldly noticing that Lucy looked up at her with less resentment.

"I've got my boys patrolling out beyond the homestead. I really don't want to stay here any longer than we need given the enemy may come looking for their missing company. But we've got those three wounded girls. Tricia said we need to get them back to the palace for proper treatment. I think they should go as soon as possible." As Sue-Ellen finished she grasped at her aching calves and began to massage the cramps that kept stabbing at her.

"McFly and Wiram aren't back yet. I'm worried they may have run into another terrorist patrol." Everyone turned to Nulla, they all had the same fear. "I've just got this feeling, Roo has too. If what Martene says is true the Mount Isa battalions have gone on the offensive against the Longreach church. I'm fearful our boys may have ventured into one of their forward fighting patrols."

"We've a few hours before sunset... what say you and Jeda go with a few camels and track them. You might need to stay out overnight and continue in the morning but I want you back by tomorrow evening. We need to be packed and heading back by then," said Sundown. "One more thing, we all need to be careful what we say around our guests. We don't know exactly where we stand with them just yet."

As it turned out Donna went with Roo, Riley and Nulla to track the lost patrol. Jeda was as good a tracker as any in the commando having spent her first twenty years in the desert before marrying Bill.

Tricia ruled Jeda out though. She wanted her on-call for her knowledge of bush herbs. They'd already planned to go out together and collect desert herbs to stock-up for their medical needs and to tend the wounded Sisterhood warriors.

The meeting was interrupted by Jenny calling everyone for an early dinner. The girls had decided to cook up all four of the kangaroos for the exhausted commando and get everyone rested and in bed early. It was likely the wounded would be heading out first thing in the morning.

Jeda explained to an inquiring Pipeline who just couldn't seem to fit enough food into his massive frame. "A deep pit, bush herbs, hot stones and cover with a blanket and dirt. Leave it for a few hours then bingo. That's how you cook kangaroo, Mr Pipeline."

"Where I come from, Jeda, they just throw it in a pan and fry it, straight from the tin." He laughed when he saw her frown. "Everything we eat at Pine Gap either comes in a tin or a packet. I just hate the thought of going back there, I've sure been spoiled by you ladies."

The cameleer search party left with a single pack-camel straight after dinner to look for Wiram and McFly. The special forces boys went back on patrol of the perimeter sharing their watches with the capable Girl Guards and the bikers.

It was decided Pellino and Bongo would drive the wounded back to Birdsville. Soon after their evening meal two trucks prepared to leave with the three wounded Sisterhood girls and Blondie. Gail and Lorraine went with them. It was expected to take all night and perhaps longer at low speed. Beamy was flagged to go with the wounded but he refused. He said he didn't want to miss anything that might be fun, like fighting more Revelationists.

As they were preparing the vehicles for departure Cambra wandered over and leaned into the cab.

"Hey Blondie, I hope you have a good trip back," he said politely.

"Thanks, but I am feeling a bit sore and a bit lost, Cambra. Umm..." she paused and looked up at him, her eyes questioning his. "When we get back I'd like to talk... to you." Despite trying to sound relaxed and friendly it just came out rushed and awkward.

Cambra's face softened then immediately his walls went up. She was playing with him, he thought. The last time they spoke he swore he'd never let himself be vulnerable to a woman again. He stopped what he was about to say and pulled back from the window.

"Yeah, sure." He turned his back and walked over to the group bringing the camels in for their drink at the spring. He missed seeing Blondie's face turn pale as she dropped her head so no one could see the lost look on her face. Right now she felt lonelier than she had ever felt in her life.

The next morning Sundown decided he needed to spend some time alone with Martene but Pedro wouldn't leave her side. He understood they had been lovers at one time and the way they looked at each other one would think they still were. He couldn't put it off any longer, they were planning to leave for Birdsville that day.

"Martene, when you're ready I'd like to have that conference with you. Sue-Ellen will attend as will Pedro and Pinkie who'll act as our mediator." He thought that sounded a bit too formal but the situation called for it he thought.

Martene looked radiant after a dip in the hot springs with Pedro. Pedro wanted to spend his precious last hours before returning to Birdsville soaking in its healing waters. They had it all to themselves and her face was still flushed despite the fatigue that remained with each of the commando and their visitors. Sundown wasn't sure if that was the hot water or from Pedro's charismatic presence. He knew that Pedro was a charmer and could turn it on when he wanted. Right now he was charm itself and spoiled rotten by Simon, Luke and their girlfriends.

Pinkie opened the negotiations which went smoothly and proceeded straight to signing the treaty between the Australian Third Army acting for the Australian Government and the Longreach Crusaders of Light. Captain Martene swore the preliminary treaty would be approved by the Abbess and their Twelve Apostles, the church elders.

"Gentlemen and ladies of Sundown's Commando and the Third Australian Army." Commander Sue-Ellen Cullen and her Pine Gap facility was now considered part of Sundown's Commando and Third

Army. "As spokeswoman for Abbess Leonie I shall return to Longreach and report to my leader with your ambassadors and formalise our negotiations. I see this as a step in the right direction and look forward to working with you all in the future."

Martene's voice now softened. "I need to say thank you for stepping in when you did. Your commando saved us, saved my wounded daughter and my nieces. I take the selfless act of Riley, Roo and Bongo's staying and possibly dying with us, very very seriously. Your entire commando stepped in to help us even though we were your enemy. I'll not forget that for as long as I live."

The commandos clearly recognised why Martene was revered by her colleagues at that moment.

"Thank you, Martene, those boys did the right thing for the right people. We're proud of them. It was lucky we were camped so close and Roo wanted to check out old man Hive's homestead." Sundown added as an afterthought, "Pinkie, darling, can you please call Shadow over?" Sundown deliberately used the endearment 'darling' and saw Sue-Ellen flinch slightly. He felt like a proper bastard for hurting her but he had a job to do and he continued with the negotiations regardless of how pathetic he now felt.

"Pedro, I've appointed you and Shadow as our ambassadors. You're permitted to answer any questions within reason of course. You're authorised to make decisions in my name. When McFly gets back I'll send him along. That'll make a team of three and the Crusaders can have the same number attend our palace as ambassadors. You'd better take the last of the Ravens Claw's vehicles for your trip back to Longreach."

Sue-Ellen sat patiently through Sundown's earlier slights but that 'darling' slap in the face made her angry and resentful.

"Sundown, I do believe I'm joint commander of this commando? Is that correct?"

Sundown felt embarrassed at hurting his brave and supremely competent comrade-in-arms. Sue-Ellen was a formidable and honourable warrior in her own right. And, as he reminded himself, '*Hell knowth no fury like a woman scorned'* or something like that. He looked at her and nodded in acknowledgement.

"Of course Commander Cullen. Please contribute as co-commander."

Martene and Pedro saw something pass between the two and they wondered the same question, *'what is it with these two?'*

Pinkie finally arrived with Shadow. As they sat down Sue-Ellen said, "That's fine Sundown, I concur, McFly, Shadow and Pedro would have been my choice too." Taking the initiative she turned to Shadow. "My dear, I heard of your courage and skill in the fighting. I know Sundown gets to witness these amazing feats-of-arms every day but I'm a newcomer and I need to say that I am impressed. No, I am blown away at how yourself and your commando took on a superior enemy and defeated them."

Shadow's face creased into a smile, she didn't know what to expect from this hard woman. She'd heard Sue-Ellen was a ball-breaker but nothing she'd seen over the past week even hinted at that.

"Madam Commander, thank you. We all try to pull our weight in any way we can. I'm too small to carry an assault rifle so I have to rely on my body and my pistol." She tapped the M1911 at her hip. "But your boys did the hard work holding the centre and then finishing the job."

Sue-Ellen nodded as she brushed several stray blond hairs from her face. "If you're going to be liaison officer to the Crusaders battalion with Pedro and your husband, I'm comforted to know you can handle yourself against all comers." She stopped as she considered just how much she enjoyed being with the commando. They just weren't what she expected either. Like a school girl she'd fallen in love with Sundown and now she was gaining enormous respect for them all.

"You will look after my daughter and nieces won't you?" Martene spoke filling the silence, "and return them to us when they're well?"

Sundown saw Pedro squeeze her hand and noted that she squeezed back.

"Captain Martene, we are at peace now. Our shared blood in battle is our bond. If Bongo, Roo and Riley say you lot are all right, then I'll not say otherwise. You'll have them as soon as they can travel. Or," he paused for effect, "or Bongo marries Denise."

"Only if he comes to Longreach with her," said Martene chuckling lightly. "I didn't go through nine months of pregnancy and thirty hours of delivery to hand her over just like that. Tell that hero of yours he can have her hand but only if he escorts her home for the ceremony."

Sue-Ellen grinned as she brought the conversation back on track. "Pedro, do you or Shadow have anything to bring to our negotiations at this stage?"

"Yes, I do," said Pedro with one of his ever present grins. "I might take a holiday in Longreach when I gets there. I'm not sixty five years old any more and I think I might like to spend time with an old but rekindled flame." He turned to look at Martene by his side.

"Pedro, you deserve a break, go for it... that is with Captain Martene's permission?" said Sundown.

Martene patted Pedro's hand. "That's a 'yes' Commander Sundown. We now have a pact with the famous Sundown's Commando and it might come as a surprise to some but for the rest of my people you'll be welcomed as our saviours. We're out numbered and out gunned by the Mount Isa battalions, that's no secret. By the time I get back home, Abbess Leonie would have armed the populace, every man, woman and child in the region. It would be an ugly thing if the Raven's Claw Battalion tried to cleanse us like they did to the Mount Isa townsfolk on Apocalypse Day." Martene looked up as she recalled something she'd forgotten to mention earlier. "Oh yes, I forgot to tell you, our long range radio is usually down but we'll try to get a signal to you on a regular basis. Otherwise we'll meet here in two weeks and continue discussions of our various joint operations."

Sundown stood up and stretched but soon sat back down feeling dizzy from the exertion. "That's a done deal, Martene. Shadow, as soon as we find McFly we'll send him to Longreach to be with you." To the three going to Longreach he said, "You'll all be travelling in the spare four wheel drive. Murphy and Pipeline are working on it now. Shadow, will you be fine by yourself while Pedro is honeymooning?"

"Yes, I'll be fine but please be quick and find McFly," replied Shadow.

Pedro man-handled his wheel chair to lean across to his old flame Martene. "I'm seeing Lorraine for a stump-rub and then another soak in the spring, care to join me young lady?" Turning to Shadow he said, "And Shadow, we'll be heading off this evening, me lassie." The young woman nodded as the group broke up leaving Sue-Ellen, Pinkie and Sundown sitting beneath the shade of their tarpaulin.

"I'm getting a cup of tea. Sue-Ellen, would you prefer coffee or tea?" asked Pinkie, mindful of the tension between the two leaders. She was savvy enough to let them fight it out now before it festered. There was something else between these two besides the obvious power play. She couldn't put her finger on it and refused to consider other possibilities. As far as she was concerned if Sundown wanted another woman he was welcome to leave. Pinkie had left one relationship because of the other woman and she wasn't going to hang around, not even for Sundown.

While Pinkie was getting their tea and coffee the two commanders watched the teenagers walk hand-in-hand towards the hot spring. To Sue-Ellen that image seemed right, teenagers in love. What a crazy environment for them to forge their identity, she thought, surrounded by friendship and death. She noticed how the two aboriginal girl's heads were rested on their boyfriend's shoulders.

The moment wasn't lost on the two older members of the commando. As one they turned to look at each other self consciously, then at Pinkie as she walked towards them with a tray of food and drinks.

'What the hell am I going to do about you, Sue-Ellen?' Sundown thought as Pinkie smiled at him over her cup of tea. It was eerie, as though she could read his thoughts. *'I can't dump her, I can't have her. My demon wants her but I need Pinkie. I think I am just well and truly screwed no matter what I do.'*

"Sundown?" called Sue-Ellen breaking the silence. "What would you want my boys to do when we get back to the palace?"

Sundown hadn't thought too much about that, he wasn't really sure they were his to direct anyway even if they were joint commanders.

He didn't expect Sue-Ellen to interfere with his work and he had no desire to interfere with hers.

"I'm not sure, Sue-Ellen. I was kind of thinking you would want them with you. There's still the Darwin job and you've got the Pine Gap facility to protect. What would you like to do with them?" he asked.

Sue-Ellen had Sundown on the back foot again. She liked games on her terms but she really didn't want to play games with her Sundown. *'My Sundown?'* She remembered how she felt watching the boys entertainment a few nights ago. That was when a deep longing had erupted inside her. Sue-Ellen quickly stopped herself going down that path.

"I was thinking I might loan them to you until we return to Pine Gap. These boys are specialists and I know you don't have any like them. Captain Walker said he'd like them to help with the officer and NCO program which Pedro started. They can also help train your hit and run patrols. I spoke to Sergeant Ahmet and he was keen to have them on board too."

"I think they're both great ideas. In fact, they might want to help bring our Girl Guards up to speed before you head to Darwin?" suggested Sundown.

Pinkie was listening and added, "Blondie has a wound and won't be going anywhere till its healed, Sundown. That sort of puts the Darwin thing on hold doesn't it?"

"Yes, that's right." Sue-Ellen paused. "I'm very sorry, Sundown, but I forgot to tell you. I spoke to my intelligence before we lost our radio. Tanner has reported back in. They had to go underground for a while. There was a hit on their headquarters. One of the other church leaders tried to assassinate Reverend Albert and they all went into hiding. It's settled down for now but the tension is mounting and Tanner said Albert is frightened. He's organising hit squads for the other two leaders and when that happens it'll be open warfare."

Sue-Ellen had one of Pedro's cigarettes in her hand and blew smoke up in the air. Sundown watched, he couldn't take his eyes off her at that moment, it wasn't lost on Pinkie.

"So what do you plan on doing?" he asked politely making an effort to break the spell she had over him.

"I'm going to wait until my pins are all lined up then I'll move," she said and stood up. "Well, I'm going for a dip in the pool before it gets too late."

Chapter 18

Snakes, Sand Dunes and Salt Bush

McFly struggled to control his camel as it suddenly bucked under him. The next thing he knew he felt himself flying through the air landing flat on his face.

"Son of a bitch!" he yelled, spitting out sand and saltbush leaves. "What happened?" He turned to look at his camel, Matilda, what he saw terrified him. She was flinging her head about, spittle flew from her frothing mouth. Matilda soon collapsed to her knees and sat down, her head dropped to the sand.

"Don't move McFly, there's a snake right near you," yelled Wiram.

McFly felt his anal sphincter tighten as he slowly turned to see a massive Death Adder slithering towards him. Its body was easily as thick as his arm. There came a loud crack of a rifle and the snake flew into the air to land between his legs. McFly squealed and leaped high as though he himself was shot.

"Bloody thing must have bitten my camel, Wiram. Matilda and I were just getting used to each other too." He kicked at the snake carcass and it flew into the bushes. It continued to contort as though it was still alive. "Damn snakes, I hate them." He reached down to pat his camel's head and affectionately buried his face in her soft hair.

Wiram 'kooshed' his skittish camel, Hiram, to sit and climbed off. He rubbed its neck and crooned softly to calm the young male. Wiram had put weeks of hard work to win the trust of this beautiful beast. He named him after a cousin back home. Hiram gurgled in his throat, pleased to be rubbed so fondly and closed his eyes in ecstasy.

Wiram walked over to Matilda and placed his hand on its shoulder. "Poor old girl, she stepped right on that snake. I didn't have time to warn you, it was over in a moment. Sorry McFly, I'm really sorry. Matilda was such a placid camel too. She was a rare one, gentle and affectionate." McFly saw something he'd not seen before, Wiram had tears forming in the corners of his eyes. Copying Wiram he wiped at his own eyes.

"Why does life have to dish out a shit sandwich like this when all we ever wanted was a piece of cake?" asked McFly.

"Life is damn shit sometimes isn't it. Come on, you'd better get your gear off and we'll pack it onto Hiram here. He's strong and can carry us both if we swap around and walk with him." Wiram began to untie the straps around the dead camel's rib cage.

"Sh! Wiram! There's people!" McFly waved his hand at Wiram and they both crouched, listening. The sounds of movement and the rattle of metal on metal from the other side of the sand dune came to their ears. "It sounds like someone heard that rifle shot."

Wiram flicked into warrior mode as soon as he recognised the sounds. He reached and pulled his weapons from their camel-mounted leather pouches, grabbed his spare cartridge belt and slipped his sniper rifle over his broad shoulders. His hands were now free to use the AK as it was designed, for an assault. He saw McFly copy and nodded for him to follow. The men left the two camels where they were.

Crouching down in the low desert scrub they slowly made their way towards a slight dip in the sane dune above them. There came voices, raised voices, right where they'd been standing not a minute earlier. They were found out but not discovered.

Wiram had yet to determine enemy numbers, there was no question that they were the enemy. The cat-calls and swear words coming from where the camels sat was evidence enough. He knew that if he and McFly could ambush them they would take them out but if there were others then they really had no option but to run. They each had a single water bottle at their hips and their weapons but nothing else. Everything they needed to survive in the desert was securely strapped to their camel's backs.

The sounds of Hiram struggling and grunting came to their ears and Wiram tensed. Next there was a rifle shot and the grunting ceased abruptly.

"You stinking, rotten bastards!" Wiram said under his breath. He sucked air deep into his lungs to stop himself leaping up to kill every last terrorist on the planet. His head roared with rage but he fought it down... down. The sound of what was probably half a dozen vehicles brought him back to the moment.

"McFly?" He tapped McFly on the shoulder to get his attention. "Follow me. Be quiet and stay alert."

Leaving everything they needed for survival behind the two quietly crept along the edge of the sand dune. They then crept down onto the flat plain leading nearly a kilometre to the next one. Wiram determined that there were probably thirty or more enemy, a full platoon strength patrol, opposing them. There was no way they could take on that many so they ran.

He continued to whisper even though they were perhaps two hundred metres from the terrorist's position on the other side of the sand dune.

"We'll try to get to the top of the next dune but the ground's soft and I'm afraid they'll track us. We need speed and strategy. If they catch us out here in the open desert we'll die."

It was nearing midday before McFly heard Wiram tell him to sit down and rest. The past hour was a mess of crawling, lying and waiting for vehicles to pass. The thorns of the desert shrubs dug into the palms of his hands, his elbows and his knees. He felt hot, sore, miserable and frightened.

The whine of an engine came to their ears again but it was some distance away. Wiram pulled out his water bottle and tipped it up to drink some of the precious liquid. McFly did the same.

"Wiram, I've got a tribal connection out here you know." McFly was a little light headed and spoke to calm his fear.

"Yeah, the boys told me you went off and met some desert warriors who came to bury Billy."

"They smoked me they said. We sat around their camp fire and they made smoke. They said I'd be back to the desert, I guess that's now."

Wiram was thinking, he nodded for McFly to lie back and pull his hat over his eyes. The flies weren't too bad for this time of year and he was soon asleep. While his mate slept, Wiram dreamed. He deliberately put his mind out like a blanket searching the area around them. His dream body, like Roo's, rose above the sand dune and he saw the desert going on and on in all directions. There was one section of desert that remained brighter than the others. He was drawn to it.

He saw a rocky outcrop where he knew they would find water but he also felt a spirit presence there. He asked the spirits for permission to drink their water and received confirmation, yes, it was permitted. He wasn't of these people, the Gangardi. Wiram only knew a few of the local aborigines in the regions around the mines and Marree. Even when he had been boxing in the red centre he generally stayed away from them. They were a wild mob and he'd had a gut-full of fighting by then.

Willing his breath to slow down to one breath every thirty seconds, he gained a depth and clarity taught only to the nangarri. He slowed his breath further and stepped across the divide. He saw the spirit father of this country and gave the secret sign, it was returned. He saw his uncles, his beloved mentors who also nodded approvingly. Together they showed him the mikiri where he could find water and then he saw the cave hidden in a split between the rocks. The climb would be difficult but McFly could do it, he was young.

The aboriginal warrior felt danger approach so eased back to consciousness. There were sticks breaking and two voices floated towards them. Wiram prodded McFly who groaned softly.

"Quiet, enemy, close," he whispered and drew his knife. Wiram's eyes pointed McFly towards the sounds and he lifted his knife for him to see. McFly drew his own knife and followed Wiram in taking off his weapon belt and webbing. They quickly removed anything that might entangle them in a fight. The sounds indicated the enemy were coming straight towards them from the other side of the sand dune.

Wiram raised two fingers, two men. His first finger he pointed to himself, his second finger he pointed at McFly. McFly understood and nodded. The noises increased as two armed teenage boys appeared right in front of them as they climbed to the top of the sand dune. McFly saw they had a red shirt pocket insignia sewn on. These were the dreaded Talons of Mount Isa.

The first didn't see the giant aboriginal leap from the low salt bush at his feet. Wiram's knife entered under his jaw and into his skull, he was dead before he hit the ground. McFly was hesitant, he'd not killed like this before and he was frightened. Frightened he'd stuff it up and make a sound bringing the entire Talon army down on them.

He leaped to his feet and thrust his knife at his enemy's throat just as Wiram had done. The teenager caught sight a fraction of a second before the knife flashed towards him. He caught McFly's knife arm in his and spun McFly around and off his feet to crash onto the ground. The young Talon had his pistol in his hand and was about to flick the safety when Wiram's knife went in one ear and almost out the other. The youth froze for what appeared to be several seconds while McFly, mesmerised by the grim picture, looked up from the ground watching him topple forward.

"We're lucky he didn't call out," Wiram panted in the heat. "Quick, strip their bodies, we take what we can."

Each Talon carried an AK47, full cartridge belt and a backpack with two full bottles of water; some food, mostly bread and dried meat, and the Talon signature knife; a large folding knife in a pouch at their belt.

The two put everything they could fit into the Talon's packs. Once Wiram had hidden the bodies as best he could they crept further from their enemy towards the rocky hillock still many kilometres away.

The scouts heard the sound of a vehicle tooting its horn followed by loud whistles. It seemed the terrorists were packing up to leave. Wiram carefully wove branches from a desert bush into his felt hat. He was indistinguishable from the bushes on the side of the sand dune as he scanned the desert.

"It looks like they're going back to the camels." He kept the camouflage in his hat and made a hand gesture for McFly to follow him. They crept parallel to the top of the sand dune not wanting to go over the top and break the skyline until they were well out of sight.

They travelled like this for another thirty minutes before Wiram decided it was safe to climb to the top of the dune. Looking around he noticed smoke coming from the region where their camels lay. The sun was now dipping towards the western horizon. The rocky outcrop was illuminated by the sun and he decided it was time to head in that direction.

"McFly, we're going to have a break. Drink some more of that water, eat some of the bread and meat and close your eyes." He sat down and opened his pack to pull out some of the food and began to eat. McFly copied him. Neither spoke as they watched the smoke column wondering what their enemy was up to.

McFly was asleep when the sound of rifle shots woke him. "What the hell is that, what's happening?" he said as he struggled to come back from the depths of deep sleep.

"They must be signalling for those two blokes we killed back there. They must think they'd gone and got lost." Wiram was thinking, '*I have a feeling this lot won't walk away. When they find the bodies they'll be wanting our blood. We'd better get moving.*' He began weaving a leafy vine around McFly's cloth hat then he fixed his own camouflage.

"Hold still while I rub this charcoal into your face and hands." A second set of rifle shots came to their ears as they crawled over the lip of the sand dune. They quickly slid down its side to begin jogging towards the next a kilometre away.

It went on like this for three more sand dunes. The Talons would drive two of their four-wheel drives up onto the sand dune ridges, there they would scour the desert scrub with their binoculars. Each time Wiram sensed the terrorists were on their way up the sand dune he and McFly would hide. So far the Talons hadn't found the bodies and it was almost dark so the two felt they would be safe until morning.

"When they find the bodies they'll find our tracks. There's bound to be at least one bushman with them and on this soft ground they'll not have much trouble following us." Despite the fact Wiram disguised their tracks as they escaped a good tracker could still follow in the soft sand. "They know we have no transport, our range is limited and we have next to no food and water. They'll sleep on the tracks and at first light they'll be on to us. We'll have about half a day head start before they catch us. We've got to get to those rocks before they do." With that he hefted his pack and rifles then, crouching over, he began to jog, confident the distance and tall sand dunes would hide them.

The sound of rifles shots came to them from a distance now. Four rounds followed by another four - they guessed what that meant. It was right on dusk and the sun was hovering just on the horizon, its lower edge beginning to dip over the rim of the world.

Wiram smiled at an exhausted McFly. "I've done this desert walk twice already. Once with Bongo and once with Cambra, you're my lucky third, McFly," he said as he bent his six foot four frame backwards feeling the satisfaction of his bones cracking loudly. He felt the relief of easing his tired spine back to where it should be, upright.

"Cambra told me he watched a movie once where the hero's crossed a mighty desert on camels. We called ourselves the 'Tirari Desert Wanderers'. Cambra and I walked almost a hundred kilometres, in summer and in the dark too. It was hell. This is the Simpson Desert and it goes on forever. See where the sun is setting now? That's where we're heading. See that rocky hill way out there? That's our destination. We need to get there by morning. We run all night and we sleep while we run. My tribesmen could do it in an emergency. I did it with Cambra and it looks like you'll be doing it too." Again he stretched and bent to the sides twisting left and right to produce more loud cracking sounds. McFly decided he'd do the same but nothing cracked, it did help ease the tension in his back though.

"We're desert commandos now, Wiram. We'll be qualified to ask Lulu and Danni to sew us a special flag. It can say 'Sundown's Desert Wanderers'. You'll get three stars, Bongo two and Roo, Cambra and I can have one each. We'll get patches for our shirts and we'll celebrate with some of Andy and Fat Boy's home-made whiskey every year. It's quite an exclusive club," said McFly trying to cheer himself up. He had an image of Shadow in his mind and he fought back tears of exhaustion and fear. Their chances of survival were narrowing each minute and he felt it in the pit of his stomach.

"I'm worried about Donna," said Wiram as though he could read McFly's mind. "She'll be wondering what's happened to us about now. Sundown will send out a party to track us and they'll walk right into the Talons camp." He heaved his pack onto his back, put the water bottle into its pouch at his waist and picked up his AK to sling over his shoulder. In his right hand he held the Blaser sniper rifle in case they came across a kangaroo for food - or for survival if they met a wild boar - or Revelationists. "I've tried to contact Nulla and Roo by mind-talk all day but they're busy for some reason, distracted. I can't get through to them. I'll try again when we have a break later."

He looked at McFly. "Come on you one-star Sundown's Desert Wanderer, we've got a desert to cross."

Chapter 19

Rescue Patrol

McFly and Wiram heard rifle shots all through the night. The Talons were trying to direct their lost scouts back to their campsite. Their trucks revved and horns tooted, they also wanted the escapees to know that they were dead men. It had the effect of wearing the Sundowner's morale down but as the desert commandos continued jogging from one sand dune followed by another eventually they could no longer hear the terrorist's clamour.

Wiram spent most of the trip in his spirit world. He had Nulla and Roo's face in his mind's eye and pressed them with his spiritual 'intention'. The nangarri knew both his aboriginal brothers-in-arms sensed his presence but he wasn't sure they picked up on his message – '*we're in need of help but we're safe and there's danger, be careful*'.

McFly stumbled and often woke to find Wiram's arm around his waist holding him upright. His legs felt like swollen lumps of lead. It was like being trapped in a living purgatory. When he was awake shapes moved, sounds hit him like rocks flung at his body and every sense jumbled with the next. He hallucinated water, food, hot chips, he once dreamed he was eating a huge bowl of spaghetti bolognaise. Every now and then he tripped over roots, stumbled into holes and startled at nothing.

"McFly, sit down, take a break and I'll get some food and water into us," came Wiram's comforting voice but McFly was sound asleep.

Wiram still fed and watered him knowing if he didn't things would get worse for them both. He recalled how much trouble he had keeping Cambra upright on their trek back to the Marree township. This was a lot worse because they had to make it to the rocky hillock before sunrise.

"Come on, McFly, wake up, we've got an army to run away from!" he yelled and had to slap McFly's face to waken him.

"Sure, got it, Wiram, I'm right now." McFly stood and swayed struggling to open his swollen eyes in the darkness. "Where are we?"

"Close, another hour or two and we'll be at the hill. Now come on, we don't stop until we're there. It'll be sunrise in another hour and we can't be on the plain after that." He held McFly upright, pushed him in the right direction then continued their unrelenting dog-trot.

Exhaustion and sleep deprivation can cause bizarre psychological phenomenon and McFly was ripe for multiple hallucinations. He leaped over striking snakes; dodged past snapping crocodiles and he spoke lucidly with friends and family long dead.

Eventually he slept. Wiram lay beside him and closed his eyes. He'd set his dream body to wake him at full light.

The rescue party picked up the tracks of McFly and Wiram leading away from their camp. From the backs of their swaying camels it wasn't easy but once they had the fresh tracks in sight all they needed to do was follow. As night began to fall they pulled out their head-band torches and walked leading the camels behind them.

Roo was puzzled. Normally Dog was lively and enjoyed running about in the desert but now he was acting strangely. Then he realised the poor thing was simply exhausted from the adrenaline rush of their fight with the Ravens Claws that morning. So he put Dog on the back of Bongo's camel, Star, and continued on foot with his torch.

"I'm struggling to see anything, it's too dark and my eyes are starting to burn," said Nulla. "We'd better make camp and start again in the morning."

They pitched camp on Matilda and Hiram's camel tracks. They lit their fire in a pit to prevent the light showing and made a billy of tea. The patrol were exhausted from the day's fighting and were still coming back to reality. They had killed and each felt its burden on their shoulders - even if it was someone who tried to kill them and their loved ones.

Roo's foot was sore and Nulla looked at it again. "Righto, let's have a peekaboo," he said as he peeled off Gail's bandage and grunted. "Hmm, it looks clean enough, Roo. It's not a deep wound but it'll hurt for a while. You just have to keep it clean, mate, and air it tonight. Let it dry out a bit. If it becomes inflamed then tell me, got that?"

Roo was about to simply nod as he'd done for twenty years in response to a question but he remembered Charlene and Bongo's lessons. *'It's polite to answer when someone asks you a question.'* So he said, "Yes, I will, Nulla," in his maturing voice.

Donna grinned in the firelight at her old friend. "Roo, you've come on so well with Charlene teaching you. Every time I hear you talk I have to look to make sure I'm not imagining it."

Roo just smiled, then he wrinkled his face. "Donna, do I have to talk when other people talk?"

"Yes, Roo, it's polite to speak and be part of the conversation. If you have something to say you wait until there's a break, then you say it. Do you have something to say now? We'll wait if you want," she said.

Roo politely waited a moment then asked his question. "I want to track early but my foot's sore, I can't walk much. You can track, your mum said you tracked a possum across the caravan park and up a tree when you were a child." He paused thinking of how to say the next thing. Putting words into his mind was hard work but getting easier. "I need you to track at the front when my foot gets sore."

Roo's cousin, Riley, had known Roo and his family all his life. They both had Afghan blood but his own mother was white, one of the locals in the Flinders Ranges.

"Donna, you've known Roo since you were a kid, better than me. I only saw him at family reunions, you know, 'births, deaths and marriages'. He stayed with us once when we were both about five or six years old. He could track a beetle crawling on sandstone, even at that age. I can track, I know Nulla can but it sounds like you're our specialist tracker on this trip," he said.

Donna was flattered. She knew she had good eyesight and when she had gone bush with Billy she was the one who did most of the tracking. In fact her mother would often boast of how good she was.

"Yes, of course I can do the tracking, it's in my blood." She took one of the sticks next to the fire and placed it carefully on the flames so it wouldn't accidentally flare up or send sparks into the air. It was quiet in the desert evening and the stars made a blanket of sparkles waiting for the moon to rise.

It was times like this that the desert people would sit around the camp fire to tells stories of love, adventure, tribal lore and their dreamtime legends. The people loved this time of bonding and sharing. The three men could tell Donna was about to tell a story so they sat back on their swags to listen as the night settled upon the earth.

"My Uncle Wardiri, worked for the Northern Territory Police as one of their trackers. He loved telling us kids his stories. He told us that once they had to bring back a man who'd escaped into the wild lands up near the MacDonald Ranges. Uncle Wardiri told his police boss he would go out by himself and track him to his hideout. Then he would come back and lead them there. He had his weapons with him: three war spears, two war boomerangs, woomera, fighting shield and a tomahawk." The fire crackled loudly as a lump of resin ignited. Nulla put another log on then leaned back to enjoy Donna's story.

"My uncle found the man's tracks, his name was Dancer Charlie. Charlie was a corroboree dancer and could perform like no one else. He was admired for his dancing but feared because he had a bad temper and killed when he lost it. Uncle tracked him through some of the wildest country he'd ever been in. Uncle Wardiri said Charlie tried every trick in the book to hide his tracks and at one time he completely lost them. So my uncle walked in circles, moving out wider each time he made a full circle trying to cut Charlie's tracks. Uncle said he turned his eyes to see the sunlight shine on the stones and leaves, to see if they lit up his foot prints. But it was a toe nail scratch in a tree root that gave Dancer Charlie away. My uncle saw the tiny scratch then kept looking until the shape of Charlie's foot showed up in the light."

"Did he catch Charlie in the ranges? That's wild country up there." Riley sat up and asked with interest.

"Yes, it's wild country all right. Uncle found him drinking from a pool of water. It was deep in the ranges, a gully with a sandy creek bed and small billabongs filled with tortoises, yabbies, water lilies and fish. Charlie was living in a cave above the creek where there was plenty of food. He was a great warrior who'd come from the wild lands bordering the desert country. My uncle said he was afraid of him because he wasn't a homestead aboriginal, he was a nangarri, a sorcerer. But Uncle Wardiri was a young man, a warrior himself. He'd killed his tribal enemies in single combat as well so he knew he had a chance against Charlie."

Donna stood up at this moment and the boys watched in fascination as she spoke and pantomimed the rest of the story. It was like watching a live play as the firelight caught her movements, the flickering shadows of her moving body mesmerised her audience.

"Uncle Wardiri liked to show us kids how he fought Charlie. We'd all sit around the camp fire, late at night, like we're doing now and then he'd stand up and act it out. He was a great actor too. He said Dancer Charlie stood up straight when he recognised him. Charlie breathed in deeply so his chest grew big and powerful. He recognised my uncle and laughed at him. He yelled that he would kill Uncle Wardiri and while he died he could watch him eat his kidney fat. But my uncle was a brave man and while Charlie was boasting he threw his first war spear.

"Dancer Charlie easily dodged that first spear trying to knock it down next to him so he could reuse it. Uncle said he made sure that if he missed his spears would skid out of Charlie's reach. Then Charlie threw his first war spear and my uncle easily flicked it away with his war shield. My uncle now threw his first boomerang so that it would land behind Charlie and flip backwards breaking his legs. But Charlie knew that trick and leaped high in the air and the boomerang spun underneath him.

"Uncle then jumped to the side and threw his second war spear but Charlie saw the move and again easily flicked it away as he now started to run towards my uncle. Charlie then flipped his second war spear into his hands and sent it flying towards Uncle Wardiri before he was ready." Donna was ducking and weaving her body about, Roo, Nulla and Riley sat spellbound.

"Charlie's spear flicked up and down in flight, a deliberate throw to confuse his enemy. It cut my uncle's leg and he fell down, but only for a second. That's when Charlie threw his boomerang, right after he'd thrown his spear. My uncle said this was a heavy war boomerang that went up into the air then turned to fly straight at his head. Charlie was trying to chop Uncle Wardiri's head off.

"My uncle was hurt and off balance, all he could do was collapse onto the ground as flat as he could. The boomerang went flying over his head giving him a hair cut." Donna showed the flight of the war boomerang with her hands and her body collapsed flat to the ground beside the fire. The boys watching could imagine the heavy war boomerang just passing over Donna's head.

"Charlie thought he'd seriously wounded my uncle so he started to run even faster straight towards him. He threw his last war spear which twisted and flicked upwards then downwards just as it reached my uncle. Again Uncle Wardiri fell flat to the ground and the war spear left a scar on his shoulder. Uncle would always stop the story there to show us kids the scar where the spear sliced his skin. We'd all gather around to look and touch it.

"Now Dancer Charlie was dangerously close, he lifted his tomahawk high in the air ready to leap in for the killing blow. That's when Uncle Wardiri jumped up and threw his last war boomerang to give himself time to recover. He said that Charlie flicked his boomerang away with his war shield like it was a fly."

Donna was panting and completely lost in the telling of the story. Her audience watched and listened with rapt attention, completely lost in this life and death drama.

"But my uncle had one last war spear that he'd hidden in the sand when he first saw Charlie. Charlie hadn't seen it and thought he had my uncle without any spears or war boomerangs. They both still had their tomahawks, that's all. Uncle Wardiri used his toes to flick his spear into his hands and before Charlie had a chance to twist away Uncle threw his last spear and it went deep into his enemy's chest." Donna pantomimed Uncle Wardiri flicking the spear into his hands with his toes and then throwing it with all his force. She then became Charlie, the spear in his chest, flung backwards with the force of the blow.

"Uncle Wardiri went back to his patrol officer and took them to the scene of the fight where they buried Charlie with proper ceremony. But because of that fight my uncle was now blood enemy to Charlie's clan. He'd spilled blood and Charlie's family were duty bound to seek vengeance. From that day on Uncle Wardiri had to watch his back. He defended himself against three of Charlie's totem brothers who tried to killed him. Each time he defeated them but he received many wounds and had to give up his police tracking. He lived with us at the caravan park until he died.

"Uncle Wardiri and Billy spent a lot of time together, he taught me his tracking skills too. Mum was close to the two old timers too, he was mum's uncle and already old when I was growing up. But us kids loved it when he told stories of his days as a police tracker."

Roo spoke first, something he'd not done before. "I knew Uncle Wardiri. He and Billy went walkabout in the desert to be with their brothers, to do spirit work."

The group were keenly interested in this. "Roo, what do you mean 'spirit work'? Do you mean walkabout?" asked Riley.

"Yes, walkabout but not just a holiday, they taught warriors their spirit work," Roo replied.

"Riley, Roo's one of them who was taught that spirit work but he can't tell you much, it's secret. That's right isn't it Roo?" said Nulla.

"Yes, I'm not allowed, it's secret," Roo replied.

Donna had finished telling her story and sat sipping at Nulla's brew of bush tea. "Riley, you ain't one of our tribe. You've got Afghan in you, like Roo, so you have sand in your blood. But there are things we're not allowed to talk about with you."

Riley nodded. "So you did training, like Roo and Nulla, with your mother's people?"

"Yes, I did my woman's initiations like for my 'coming of age' at puberty. I had to do special things to marry Wiram too. That's all secret women's business," she replied politely.

Nulla shifted his body to ease the growing ache in his shoulders and back. He was sure he'd pulled a muscle in his shoulder earlier that day and it ached along with his old football injuries. Fortunately his eyes were fine and his vision had cleared since the fight in the sand dunes.

"Roo," Nulla said quietly to his friend. "I'm getting a feeling from Wiram, he's trying to mind-talk us. Are you getting that too?"

Roo nodded affirmative. Donna said, "Me too, Nulla, he's restless and angry, they're running. I'm not sure but it must be terrorists."

"Yes, it's enemy. They killed Matilda and Hiram. Wiram's sad about that," said Roo.

"Thanks, I needed confirmation. When we head out in the morning we need to scout out for the enemy as well. I'd say the Talons or the Ravens Claws were on their way to get around the back of Longreach when they ran into Wiram and McFly."

"McFly's good," said Roo. "He's got spirit work to do."

Three sets of eyes turned quizzically to stare at Roo.

"I know he spent time with Billy in the desert. I wonder if that has anything to do with it?" wondered Nulla out loud.

Roo nodded. "Billy's with McFly now."

Chapter 20

McFly's Initiation

On their all-night desert trek McFly hallucinated of water, drinking as much as he could but he was never quite satisfied. Then it was a peanut butter sandwich. It had a crunchy crust all over that made him salivate in his sleep-walking state. He ate that sandwich over and over like a video clip stuck in a loop. Next it was succulent white meat, juicy, sweet and refreshing… but then something happened and he felt strangely calm and relaxed.

McFly found himself floating above his body looking down to watch Wiram's huge frame with his arm under a smaller person, it was himself. Wiram was virtually carrying him along through the sparse scrub of the desert plain.

McFly saw himself, he was asleep. He was upright and walking but his eyes were closed. Wiram's eyes were orbs of phosphorescent light glowing inside his head. But he knew that Wiram wasn't there, he was in a trance, a walking being with eyes like headlights.

There was someone else there too, holding his other arm. As he focused his attention he saw it was Billy. Billy was at his other arm supporting him. McFly accepted this calmly, *'this is how things should be - we care for those we love'*, came a voice somewhere inside his mind, it was Billy's voice.

He now lifted higher and higher until he was touched by the beams of sunlight from the far eastern horizon and he felt alive. It was an ecstasy as though he had been plugged into the power point at his home in Sydney. The power surge sent him flying high above the wanderers below. He felt drawn to a strange glow not far from the struggling figures among the sand dunes. There he saw a spider web of light energy disguising a rocky outcrop. It made his stomach tighten as a fresh surge of energy rippled into his belly and chest.

McFly found himself standing in a cave inside the hillock. Before him were the spirit father and mother. This time they were not frightening, he remained in awe but not afraid. Automatically he extended his hands and felt the warmth of the spirit father's hands grasp his. Sunlight flooded his being as he absorbed the father's power. A force filled his body making him feel as strong as any warrior in the land.

The spirit mother then took his hands in hers to gently flow her energy into his body. It felt like a spring breeze with the scent of flowers and the silky feel of moonlight.

The father spoke. "You are welcome here."

"You're now safe, so is your friend. He is a man of power and respect, his reward is coming," spoke the spirit mother.

As McFly slowly came back to consciousness he heard her say, "But your trial has just begun."

McFly woke to the smell of wood smoke, the crackle of a camp fire and the movement of his mate, Wiram. He sat up and looked around.

"Where are we?" he asked.

"Good morning squire, decided to join me for breakfast did you?" came Wiram's weary voice. "I've got a delicious rock python on the barbecue and the last of our water for refreshments."

"Didn't we have snake yesterday?" said McFly feeling strangely buoyant and energised.

"No, the snake almost had us, I believe."

"We must be at that rocky hill you saw." McFly stared into the dancing flames for a moment. "I had the weirdest dream, Wiram. I saw Billy and the spirit father and mother again and I've got a trial or something. I've got to find a cave but you can't come with me..."

"Hey, McFly, slow down. I know, I've got to stay away from the cave. This is a place of spirit, sacred land for the local tribesmen only. I'm not of this land, this isn't my blood country. I tread here with the spirit's permission. If I betray their trust I'll be killed. If not by the local warriors then by the land itself."

McFly looked at Wiram curiously. "That's what the spirit father said. How'd you know all that?"

"Ha! That's my question to you, how'd you know all that? I'm nangarri, I live and breathe my tribal spirits but you're white. You're not of this land and yet they not only let you freely walk here, they give you something others will never experience. I'm a warrior of high degree in my tribe. I've earned the secrets of my people since time birthed us and yet I have to tread carefully even here. You don't. Why is that I wonder?" he mused as he turned the snake on a stick to cook evenly.

"I saw you walking Wirrie, you were almost carrying me. I saw Billy on my other side holding me up."

Wiram look up at McFly curiously. "You slept through the trek of a lifetime my friend and yet you saw? You amaze me. Yes, I had no choice but to carry you but I didn't know who was on the other side. I thought maybe Shamus, but Billy, yes that makes sense. You and he were close weren't you."

"Yeah, we were, I loved that old man. So how did you walk all this way without resting?" asked McFly. "You basically carried me all night and there's no way anyone can do that without a break. I saw your eyes were open but you were some place else. How did you do that?"

"That's part of my nangarri training, it's a secret technique we sometimes use. I imagine Nulla and Roo might know it, they're full initiates too..." Wiram thought for a moment as he disappeared inside his special place. When he came back he said, "OK, I'll tell you a little bit since this has now become your land and the spirits like you. When we train for our initiations we have a teacher, a mentor, usually an uncle, rarely is it our father unless everyone else is gone." He pushed the log further into the fire to ensure it didn't smoke and give their position away.

"My two uncles were nangarri, sorcerers, they taught me to walk. It's an energy walk which is why I can stay awake all night on patrol and these desert walks I seem to find myself doing. It involves special breathing, I guess you'd call it and moving energy along lines like acupuncture. I had to practice it until I could walk all day and all night. It took a long time. I can only do it now because my uncles never let up on me. They pushed me hard because I was so lazy."

He stopped talking to pull the snake off its stick and then broke it into pieces with his fingers. Half went to himself and the other half to McFly. They sat in the silence of early morning eating the succulent white flesh. When they were finished McFly searched around in his back pack taken from the Talon soldier. He pulled out a paper bag and inside was a stale peanut butter sandwich. He shared half with Wiram. It crunched like fresh crusty bread, he ate it in a state of sheer ecstasy.

Wiram broke the silence. "I'm going to have a nap, wake me at midday or if you see or hear any sign of the terrorists. After that I think you have a cave to find." He pulled his hat over his eyes and fell into a deep sleep.

McFly found he was charged with energy. He busied himself checking and cleaning their weapons. They both had AK47's, M9 Beretta pistols from Simon's personal collection; commando knives taken from the Deaths Head commandos at Marree; the two Talon's fold-away knives; a rifle, a Blaser which Wiram took as a souvenir from the Stosstruppen and a scoped .303 Lee Enfield kangaroo rifle McFly fell in love with from one of the abandoned farms near Birdsville.

His 303 was in excellent condition. Lovingly looked after with a cushioned stock which didn't hurt as much as the one he used in Marree and the mines battles which bruised his shoulder. He'd asked Roo to carve a trout on one side and a river bass on the other. Joining both sides ran a fishing line and a series of small flies and bugs that Roo created for him. They danced on his stock as though they were alive. In return McFly took him fishing in the lagoon and tried to teach him fly fishing. Roo liked to just sit and watch him flick his line to land on the water surface like an insect.

As he was daydreaming McFly saw movement several sand dunes away, it was approaching from the east. He put his binoculars to his eyes and confirmed that it was those same Talons they'd been running from.

"Wiram, wake up, we've got company."

Wiram came awake immediately. He sat up and looked through the binoculars.

"Looks like three of their four wheel drives. They're not following our tracks at all, they're lazy and sticking to some old tracks. If they continue they'll miss us by a long shot. The spirit father has disguised the hill so they might not even see it." He lay back down and pulled his hat over his eyes. "There may be more vehicles so just keep an eye out. If they head this way wake me."

The vehicles were loaded with men but they weren't too interested in what they were doing. It looked like they were on a holiday or heading to a party. They stayed on the top of the sand dune and lit a fire for their meal. Music blared from their vehicles. After a few hours they headed back the way they'd come. McFly didn't wake Wiram, he deserved to sleep a bit longer, he decided.

By now the sun was overhead and a bored McFly went off to explore. The hill was a jumble of rocks and crevasses that appeared then closed up again, it was more a rocky labyrinth. When he went to investigate one such crevasse he got stuck and had to climb higher to find a way around it.

That was when he found the cave. Actually, that's when the giant carpet snake found him. McFly freaked and climbed where no white man had climbed before. With a loud shriek he fell through the crack in the rock wall and onto soft sand.

Wiram woke up soon after McFly left to go exploring. The heat and his thirst drove him to seek out the mikiri the spirit father had shown him, it wasn't far from their camp fire. The mikiri was a well that contained more than enough water for Wiram and McFly's survival if they needed to stay for any length of time. It was hand carved into the sandstone rock and just large enough for a single person to pass up bark containers of water to those above. The local tribesmen had left a large flat stone covering it to keep the birds and animals from falling in and fouling the water. Wiram filled his belly first then their empty water bottles. Satisfied he made his way back to the camp fire and went back to sleep.

There was enough light coming through the crack for McFly to see the paintings on the cave walls. Strange clay painting of hands and figures of animals and people. He recalled his anthropology studies and recognised some of the figures but the others were alien. In fact they could have been painted by real aliens, he thought.

The cave was small and womb-like so he quickly scanned for dingo and snake droppings, but the sand was clean. It was almost shrine-like, becoming shallower after only a few metres in. Every face of the cave and the ceiling was covered in paintings.

Now he felt frightened. He was in a sacred cave, forbidden to all but initiated warriors and those of specific totems - and he wasn't even of their blood. In this fearful state he abruptly stood up hitting his head on the low ceiling. Reeling backwards he tripped on something and crashed to the floor cracking his head on the stone wall on his way down. With his head spinning he dropped into a strange state of awareness, much like what happened when he was smoked by Billy.

There was someone standing before him, a powerfully built, naked warrior, a spear in one hand and a boomerang in the other. He had fierce eyes and glared intently at McFly. Mesmerised like a mouse under the glare of a snake McFly entered a deeper state of trance.

"Son, welcome," came a now familiar voice. He was standing on the top of the hillock watching the sun rising and setting. Before him stood the spirit father, the fierce warrior and Billy.

"Don't do anything, just watch. This will explain why you chose to help my people," said Billy.

McFly saw an aboriginal family, a proud man with his beautiful wife and happy children. They were sitting with their meal, beside a camp fire in the desert, he recognised the region around Birdsville. The rains had cleared and the flowers were abundant, it was quiet and peaceful.

The kangaroos and marsupial mammals grew fat on the harvest of the late monsoon rains.

Theirs was a good life. His son was readying for his manhood ceremonies and he looked forward to escorting him to the men's secret initiations. His wife was still attractive to him and her ability to provide food for the family made him the envy of his tribe.

McFly was fascinated, this answered so many questions as to why he was so interested in the Australian aborigines, their way of life and why he went out of his way to help where he could. It also answered why he studied anthropology and had travelled to the red centre of Australia so many times. It was why he just loved the dry heat and the wide open plains. He was in love with this place and now he saw the beauty of the desert through different eyes. Eyes that saw the history of his people in every tree, sand dune and water hole.

Out of the corner of his eye he noticed a line of pack horses, leading them were three unkempt white men on horseback. These rough men entered the clearing where the family were cooking their midday meal. In shock no one moved. These strangers arrived without warning and appeared to be ghosts. They were even the colour of ghosts and the sticks they pointed smoked like ghosts.

The man and his family were shot dead where they sat, mouths open, paralysed by fear and dread of the unknown. McFly felt tears coursing down his cheeks and his enormous grief brought up painful sobs of despair. This was his family. The scene cleared to be replaced by another.

This time he was white, working as a farm hand mustering sheep. He loved his job and his small family felt accepted and part of the local farming community. He watched as the young man went out into the deep desert to shoot dingoes who were killing their sheep. The young man carried a rifle and led a pack horse as well as his own horse. McFly could clearly see this man was smart, sharp and knew his business, he was no fool. If he went into the desert ranges to hunt dingoes then he always succeeded at his task. In some ways McFly saw he was much like Roo, skilled, quiet and supremely competent, a crack marksman.

He watched as the young man walked his horses along a dry creek bed. He knew he'd soon find the permanent water hole used by the local aborigines. As he rounded a bend he saw the bodies. Fifteen of them, several family groups, lying beside their camp fire near the poisoned waterhole. As he got closer he saw the mess of their dying and grief exploded inside him. He roared in impotent rage at the wanton waste of those precious lives.

As he watched he saw the man's life fade into nothingness. Sadly the once competent young man turned to alcohol to cope. The horror took control of him, he never came to terms with what he saw that day. In each small black body he saw his own children and the women could as easily have been his wife. How could a man live knowing that others could so easily snatch life from another like that? Again, Matty McFly saw himself in the man before him.

"Watch, Matjuri, watch again," came the voice of the spirit father.

As he watched he saw himself meeting with Shadow, and many others he didn't know. Some were black and some were white. He was an ambassador, doing important work to bring peace to the wasted lives of the land.

"Matjuri, none of this was wasted, none of this was accidental. You sacrificed your joy and happiness over many lifetimes to bring you to this place in time and space. We need you to live to fulfil your promise to humanity from those lives." He explained that McFly had chosen this path, every one. His was a very long association with the Australian aborigines. He'd spent many lives being one with them and the earth. McFly had chosen to experience life as white, yellow, black and brown. His was a plan that was thousands of years in the making.

"So the apocalypse was also a plan of thousands of years?" he asked.

"It was planned at the dawning of time itself. There are many like you who have prepared for it with experiences just as painful as your own. We respect your sacrifice, we honour you for your time has finally come," said Billy. "Today we are here to show you why you chose this path and to give you gifts that you'll need on your journey."

"I don't need gifts, Billy. I need wisdom, skill and courage."

The spirit father spoke again. "Matjuri, McFly, you have those already in abundance. You need to undergo certain initiations to gain access to them when you need them – to awaken your wisdom and power."

The fierce man then stepped forward. He drew back his powerful spear arm and threw his shovel-nosed war spear. It pierced McFly's chest flinging him into another dimension.

Chapter 21

Dreaming

The small band of trackers were up before dawn. They started following Wiram and McFly's camel tracks as soon as the sun was up. Donna was keen to get moving, when they lost the tracks she would often range a hundred metres ahead to pick them up again.

Roo became nervous when she did that and tried to talk to her but the words wouldn't come out right for him. He found that when he was under stress he couldn't speak properly. Roo hadn't thought in words for twenty years and putting pictures and sensations into words in a hurry was difficult.

Riley picked up on his cousin's restlessness. Riley tried to explain why Roo didn't want Donna going so far forward. It was fortunate she did because she heard the vehicles and detected the smoke of their fires in time to race back and warn the scouts.

"Nulla!" she whispered flinging her hands in the air to attract him. "Terrorists, lots of them." She pointed in the direction of their enemy.

The broad-chested aboriginal sergeant reacted immediately. He indicated, waving vigorously, for the other two to stop. There was no doubting what the problem was.

"Righto, we pull back two hundred metres. Roo, you and Riley need to scout ahead to find out what's happening."

Dog was back to his old self running backwards and forwards. He was a dog on holiday and every smell was like candy to him. Roo snapped his fingers and clicked his tongue, Dog pricked up his ears and darted to his master's side.

They pulled back and prepared for combat. "Roo, find out what you can. I want you both back in ten minutes, no more. Then we'll plan what to do next."

The boys nodded and began their preparations. Roo was dark skinned but Riley was like any other white man in the bush. While Roo wound bush leaves through his hat and shirt, Donna rubbed red clay and dabs of black charcoal into Riley's face and the backs of his hands. She then helped camouflage him with bushes like Roo.

Nulla checked them both and nodded. "Get close but not too close. Donna and I are going to hobble the camels back here. We'll look after Dog and wait for you. Righto, let's do this."

With Riley a few metres behind, Roo crept to within earshot and listened. Apparently they were waiting for their mates who were searching for the escaped commandos. At this stage it appeared they didn't know if the camels belonged to Sundown's Commando or the Longreach Crusaders.

"So they're Talons. Righto, we know that Wiram and McFly are safe and haven't been discovered." Nulla looked at Roo who nodded in the affirmative. "If we stay here we can pick up Wiram's tracks and follow him, but we might also get in a fight if the Talons do anything unpredictable. All we need is someone to come this far looking for a nice place to take a dump and see us. We need to move well away and wait. I'll disguise our tracks just in case someone does come this way."

Riley had been thinking. "We need to send someone back to inform Sundown of what we've found. He told us we only had till tonight and he was heading back to Birdsville tomorrow. We might be out here for a week looking for Wiram and McFly. Besides, they need to be prepared in case this Talon patrol heads towards the hot springs or the homestead."

"Yeah, good point Riley. Righto, Donna, you and Riley go back to Sundown and report what we've found. Tell him we'll stay out here until we make contact with Wiram and McFly. We'll need him to leave a cache of food near the spring for us. Tell him they should leave as soon as they can in case the Talons are headed their way. We'll follow on behind with the camels when we find Wiram and McFly. We'll meet him in Birdsville. Riley, I want you to return here as soon as you can."

Turning to Wiram's new wife, he said, "Donna, I know you want to stay and help but I'm worried that if we have a contact they might separate us. If you're taken prisoner you know what they'll do to you." He shushed her up when she tried to argue. "We know, and yes, even you know, that Wiram is OK. They haven't got him nor do they know where he is. We know he's safe we just don't know much more than that." He waited for her to say something but she remained silent, fearing that if she did speak she'd just become more emotional.

"Righto. Riley, you take Dog with you so that when you get back here he can lead you to Roo. Good luck, we'll see you when we next meet, soon I hope." With that both Riley and Donna mounted their camels and headed back the way they'd come. They'd be hard pushed to get there before dark and Nulla knew it. He wanted Riley to start back as soon as he delivered their message. If he had to head back at twilight and spend the night sleeping in the desert with Dog for company then so be it.

"Come on Roo, we'll move back another hundred metres into that channel and wait it out."

When they heard the terrorist's vehicles Roo went to investigate. He told Nulla the terrorists were headed towards Longreach. While Nulla kept watch, Roo began the arduous task of finding Wiram and McFly's tracks before it got too dark to see.

Towards dusk Nulla left Roo to continue tracking while he made camp well away from the track and the dead camels. Roo had already found the Death Adder in the bushes where McFly had kicked it and he sadly unhitched the saddles from Matilda and Hiram.

Nulla and Roo knew both camels intimately, they were like family. The camels were inducted into Sundown's Commando as friends first and workers last. That was the way Nulla was taught and that was how he liked to work with animals.

Nulla was brought back from his sad reflections by Roo's shrill whistle, he'd found something. Checking there was no dust on the horizon to indicate enemy vehicles Nulla jogged across to where Roo pointed out a broken branch and tracks.

"McFly broke a branch, that's his footprint there, these tracks are strangers." Roo pointed to the tracks. "I'll track while there's light. My foot's sore, I'll need to rest soon," said Roo. Nulla just nodded and let him do what he did second best, track. It wasn't long before they found the Talon's graves. Their tracks showed neither Wiram nor McFly was hurt, now it was time to track in earnest.

McFly found himself beside a river flowing with fresh, life-giving water. The surrounding bushland was loaded with wildlife. The fierce man sat beside him talking, mind talk.

They shared the river bank with a friendly tribe who peacefully went about their own business. Sometimes they participated in McFly's education and at other times they ignored him. Day led to night which led to another day, it passed leaving barely a moment when McFly felt he wasn't learning something new. The fierce warrior never let up and when asked how much longer, his teacher would just say, 'soon'.

Billy would sometimes visit to sit and chat by the fire. It was at these times they talked about life, politics, human behaviour, negotiation, compromise and the many aspects of managing a community. At no time did McFly think he would be able to fulfil the task he had accepted but they insisted he'd chosen this path himself and that he would succeed.

"Billy, I can't do all this, look at the state of the world, it's hell on earth. Those Revelationists have gone berserk, they're worse than Sundown's demon," he said one day.

Billy laughed, "McFly, do you know what your name, Matty, means in our language? Matjuri, it means 'do', to do things, you are a do'er. You act when things need to be acted upon. You chose that name before you were born. Just follow the fierce man he still has a lot to teach you. Besides," the sprightly old man whispered, "you'll have help. You're not the only one on this journey."

In one meditation McFly found himself back with Shadow. He hadn't tried to do it, it just happened. He was beside her as she was driving with Pedro and some others across the desert. He tried to contact her but she was preoccupied with driving and watching for the enemy. 'Enemy', he thought the word and immediately lifted above the Mitsubishi dual cab, one of the vehicles left by the Talons. That's when he saw the enemy, clearly. They were on a dirt track that would intersect with Shadow and her small group.

In a fit of panic he didn't know what to do but then the sound of the fierce warrior's voice came to him, '*mind talk*'. That stopped his panic. He wondered how to mind-talk Shadow to stop her vehicle. McFly couldn't connect with her so he checked the car but it was in good condition, it had no weaknesses he could exploit to stop it. Maybe he could mind-talk to one of the occupants, someone receptive, someone already in a light trance, a daydream perhaps?

It turned out to be easier than he expected. Pedro was asleep, resting his head on Martene's shoulder in the back seat. McFly walked into the firelight of Pedro's dream. Pedro was sitting with someone in the desert, he was much younger, perhaps in his forty's, and that other person looked like Shamus. Pedro was relaxed and at peace.

"*Pedro! Wake up! Danger! Stop the car! Stop the car, terrorists! STOP THE CAR NOW!*" screamed McFly, in exasperation.

"Hey! What the flamin' hell! Stop the car there's terrorists!" Pedro woke with a start and flayed his arms in the air. He wasn't quite awake but he saw, through McFly's eyes, that the Talons were on a collision course with them. "Shadow, stop the car please, I have a feelin' there's something bad ahead. I think it's the Talons."

Shadow stopped the car but left the engine running. As the four of them got out she climbed onto the roof and pulled out her binoculars. Scanning the horizon she saw the dust cloud of an approaching convoy. If they stayed where they were they would avoid each other and not be seen.

"Pedro, how the hell did you know?" asked the old female warrior sitting in the front passenger seat next to Shadow.

Pedro was still trying to work it out in his head himself. "It was that boofhead McFly, he interrupted my dream. I was dreaming I was with Shamus sitting and yarning around our camp fire. Next thing McFly comes into my dream and starts yelling at me to wake up 'cause there's terrorists. It was weird me girlie, it was weird."

McFly dreamed again, he was with Roo walking along the top of the sand dune and he pointed out the rocky outcrop where the cave was.

"Hi Roo, Wiram and I are just there. Nulla can't go any closer than Wiram though, but you're welcome. This is your country, your blood," he told Roo.

"Nulla will wait and I'll go to Wiram. We'll wait for you to finish your initiations," said Roo in mind-talk. It sounded like a normal conversation to McFly, but easier.

Another dream, he was talking to Sundown, asking him about demons. "McFly, demons are just our deep unconscious urges and instincts. My demon is anyway. I've not met other demons. Maybe you can find out more about them for me?"

The fierce man wasn't keen on McFly wanting a demon of his own. "Yes, there are real demons, plenty of them out there but we don't play with them. They aren't the sort of demons who like to play. Sundown is right, demons of his kind are part of the unconscious. A spiritual warrior, a nangarri, seeks out real demons to tame and work for us. I have two and Billy has one, but there are very few warriors who know how to catch them and even fewer who survive the quest. You aren't ready so don't even think about it," he told McFly, but McFly wasn't satisfied, so he asked Billy.

"Billy, if I want a demon what do I need to do?" he asked.

"Matty, you don't want to know. I nearly died trapping mine. See that dingo over there, the one that has been watching you for all the days you have been here? He's dangerous. If I were to disappear he would kill you and take your energy. The demons of the inner planes live on energy, and that includes human energy. Desert demons kill humans who venture onto their land without protection. You only survived going into the desert with me that time because I ordered my demon to protect you from the others, the wild demons. The fierce man, who is much more powerful than all of us, died – his demons killed him. But he had such enormous power that he came back. He came back dragging his demons behind him. If he says don't do it then I'd listen to him," advised Billy.

The sky grew darker and the river faded, the tribe had disappeared. McFly found himself waking as though from a long sleep on the rocks below the cave. He tested his body for wounds and broken bones but everything seemed to be fine so he stood up. His body felt strangely light so he took a few steps to see if he could walk. That was fine too so he looked around to orient himself then walked back to find Wiram, asleep, exactly where he'd left him.

Chapter 22

Heroes Return

Roo met Wiram and McFly the next day while Nulla waited on the sand dune. He'd lit a fire and was cooking the wallaby they'd shot on their way to the rocky hillock. Nulla watched as the three walked slowly towards him noting that Wiram and McFly looked rested and showed no sign of injury. Not that he expected any. By the time they arrived Nulla had the billy boiled and their tea poured and sitting on the sand. The wallaby still had a while to cook but it's aroma permeated the air.

The group drank their tea slowly, comfortably resting their buttocks in the small sand-holes that Nulla had dug for them. Nobody spoke as they relaxed to gaze across the desert landscape waiting for their meal to cook.

"What's that?" Nulla asked into the silence. He pointed with his chin at the rocky hilltop. McFly looked then went very still and quiet for several seconds, he appeared to be listening to something inside his head. The three beside him watched and waited.

"It's the fierce man. He's saying goodbye," said McFly. He thought for a moment before continuing. "I never said goodbye to Billy or the families of the tribe either. Why didn't I say goodbye to everyone?"

"They know mate, they know," replied his friend, Wiram.

While drinking a second cup of scalding hot tea Nulla and Roo told the story of the fight at the homestead. Both Wiram and McFly listened attentively, their breathing accelerated until Nulla realised he'd missing something.

"Sorry, I forgot the most important thing. Wiram, Donna is fine, she didn't participate in the fight but she did help us find your tracks. She's with Sundown, I sent her back with Riley." Nulla turned to McFly, "and Shadow is fine too. I watched her take down a few of those Ravens Claws in a hand-to-hand fight when Sundown's squad clashed with them. She's one heck of a fighter is your Shadow."

McFly found he couldn't quite speak so Nulla continued to tell the story to ease his anxiety. "Matty, Shadow knocked a few out and shot a few then she stabbed a few." He chuckled softly as he shook his head when he realised he had failed to ease his friend's fears. "Nah, she didn't kill that many but she fought like a tigress. She helped hold off the Ravens Claws with Lucy... hang on, let me back up a bit. There was Sundown, but he got knocked out right at the start of the fight. Then there was Pellino, Beamy, Shadow, Heidi and Lucy. I think that's them all what was on the left flank." He stared up into the sky remembering, then looked back at McFly. "Yeah, she did well and is safe."

At last McFly could release the breath he'd held while Nulla butchered his story, but it got the message through – their loved ones were safe. He took a few shorter breaths then asked, "How did every-one else go? How's your boys, you know, those funny teenagers of yours?"

Nulla looked to Roo and lifted his eyebrows. Roo remembered that was a sign for him to talk.

"McFly, the bike boys didn't come home till it was all done. They brought four kangaroos for our dinner." He smiled shyly unsure if this was what he was supposed to say.

"Yeah, they missed the fun. The Pine Gap spooks held the centre, bloody magic having them on our side too, solid as a rock they were. If it wasn't for them I'm not sure how we'd have gone. It sure would have been a lot tougher, maybe we'd have had our arses kicked." Nulla said leaning forward to lift the blanket covering the roasted wallaby.

"And we've now scored a treaty with the Longreach Crusaders." He added enjoying the shocked look on Wiram and McFly's faces.

As the men prepared to eat there came a call, a long-drawn *'coo-ee'* from somewhere in the desert. Nulla stood and saw a group of four aboriginal warriors approaching. They carried their own kill: a young red kangaroo, a bearded dragon lizard and a large King Brown snake. It appeared as though they knew there was a brew of tea on the fire and food in the oven.

"Hey bro! I see you again in my dreaming," called Frank as they came within talking distance. "My brothers and I dreamed to come to this place and now we know why."

McFly stood and walked over to greet his aboriginal friends. He'd met them previously when they came to collect their grandfather, Billy, for burial.

"I see you brothers. The fierce man said I'd meet you," replied McFly cheerfully. His face expressed joy in seeing these wild men with a joy-for-life in their easy smiles.

"We don't call him by that name, Matjuri. One day you'll learn his spirit name," said the eldest, Bidgera, who then reached out to shake the hands of the others. Turning to Roo he said, "Roo, you didn't tell us you was coming here. We been waiting for news. You been busy, bro?"

Roo looked at his friends and smiled one of those rare smiles of his. "Bidgera, we been busy fighting and tracking." He embraced his cousins affectionately. "McFly's Gangardi, now."

The four newcomers simply accepted Roo's new-found ability to speak and nodded knowingly. They looked at McFly with curious glances, out of courtesy they embraced him again. It was extremely unusual for a white person to have undergone their sacred initiations and although they knew much of the story they were still confused and felt awkward.

Frank was the only one of Roo and McFly's age but he wasn't shy about it. "Hey McFly, that fella, the fierce man, he knock you into the other world?"

McFly nodded and pointed to Frank's heavy war spear. "With one of those spears." The men all chuckled knowingly.

Frank offered an answer to McFly's unasked query. "We've got no more bullets Matty, no shops, no bullets. So now we're back to our traditional weapons. Those terrorists better watch out now, eh, these big bastards hurt when they go through ya."

They decided to spend the night there so they relaxed and yarned all afternoon about their families and the events happening in the outside world.

After they'd finished eating the wallaby the newcomers skilfully cleaned and began preparations to cook the meat they'd brought with them. That evening, and after a long siesta, the meat was ready and shared according to custom for the evening meal.

McFly was exhausted and fell asleep soon after dinner, he didn't wake until morning. He dreamed of places he'd never seen and people he'd never met. He walked among the stars of the night sky and sat with his tribal friends singing songs by the camp fire in their own tongue. When he woke the sun was up and the boys were preparing to leave.

"What should I do, Wiram?" he asked as he helped pack the camels. "I think I belonged to a tribe around here once. My family died, killed by white settlers." His voice softened as he remembered.

"Ask Roo and your Gangardi mates, this is their country and their blood which spoke to you," replied Wiram as was proper for a visitor to this country.

Roo held the reins of the three camels and tried to explain. "McFly, you was initiated into my people, the Gangardi. That tribe you visit was Gangardi too, and now your family. Your uncle, he's in the dreaming, you dreamed with him, he taught you." The four aboriginal warriors nodded but didn't speak.

McFly couldn't understand how he lived with the tribe in the dreaming where he was taught by an uncle who wasn't here. Plus he met Billy who died months ago, and why did this fierce warrior, his uncle, have no name?

"That uncle of yours taught you things didn't he," said Roo.

"Yeah, he frightened the life out of me. I went into the dream world with his spear in my chest, it felt real. I thought I was dead," replied McFly and there was a pained look on his face as he recalled the fear he felt.

"He did that to drive you out of this world into the other, it worked," said Frank simply as he and his cousins walked beside the camels.

It was a long walk. Only three camels and eight men, all fit and healthy. They walked the desert in the early morning and slept through the middle of the day giving them time to talk and bond. McFly felt part of this new family and shared when asked. He soon learned what was men's business, secrets, and so punishable if he spoke of it.

That evening they settled for sleep and Wiram asked everyone to join him to send mind-talk to his wife, Donna. They came back smiling, even McFly.

"Ah fella's, that last bit, you weren't supposed to be in on it. That was just for me and the missus," Wiram chuckled. "Wait till I tell Donna she had an audience."

They met Riley the following day on their way back to the hot springs. They could see him riding his camel for some distance but it was Dog who could smell better than Riley could see. Dog raced towards them to leap into Roo's arms licking his face faster than Roo could wipe the wetness off.

Riley brought another camel at Sundown's insistence, now they all had a ride except for Roo's aboriginal cousins, who refused anyway. At lunch they relaxed around the fire as Riley explained why he couldn't get away until the next morning. Jeda and Jenny had told him that he wasn't allowed to interfere with the initiations so he had to wait.

"The girls were frightened something might happen to me if I arrived at the wrong time. Anyway, I let Dog off my camel's back and he led me here. He was pretty keen to see you, wasn't he Roo," laughed Riley. But he was still puzzled and waited for one of the boys to explain what was going on.

"I can tell you, Riley. It was McFly, he's now Gangardi, same as me and my mother's people and my cousins. He's not allowed to talk about it, if he does we can spear him." For the first time Roo smiled at a joke, his own joke.

McFly looked at him over his cup of tea. "Did you just make a joke Roo... or was that serious?"

Wiram decided to rescue him. "It's OK, McFly, Roo just made a joke. But never speak to anyone of what you did or the lessons you've learned, especially to Shadow. It's simple, women aren't allowed to know what we men get up to. The uninitiated aren't allowed to know either, especially white fella's like you." They all broke up laughing but both Riley and McFly just looked puzzled. "McFly, as we said earlier, no talking, got it?" McFly noticed the fierce looks of Roo's desert cousins. They were all dead serious.

Riley asked, "But how did Jenny and Jeda know? They're women and they knew about it."

"They only knew that it was secret men's business and nothing else. They knew because Wiram mind-talked them," said Nulla. That satisfied Riley. He'd lived long enough with the aborigines to know they often knew things associated with family and loved ones that could only be described as mental telepathy.

"There's a soak not far away," offered Roo.

"How much further? I want to get back to my wife," said Wiram looking up at the afternoon sun.

"Not far, two hours maybe." He saw the nods from his cousins. "If we start now we'll get there by dark. Frog dreaming time, for McFly." Roo looked up into the sky to check the sun's position.

Nulla stood up and began packing their camp gear straight away. They quickly distributed their loads between the camels and rode with Roo in the lead. They came across a muddy patch of ground, a small oasis in the middle of the desert. Wild animals had dug a hole in the middle of the oasis to form a puddle, it produced enough water for survival only.

"Nice work, Roo. We'll teach Matjuri frog dreaming tonight." Frank said then turned to the initiate. "Frogs dream while they wait for the monsoon rains to wake them up. Right now there's not enough water to keep their skin moist so they've buried themselves deep in the mud where they sleep and wait for the rains. We'll show you how to tap into their dreams. Sometimes we do other things which I can't talk about with Riley here." Frank helped McFly pull the saddle and gear off his camel and hobbled it so it wouldn't wander too far during the night.

Bidjera said there were dingoes in the area so they decided to keep a night watch. There was no way they wanted their camels to come to any harm or run off. With a rope around their ankles they would certainly break a leg if chased by a dingo pack. None of them wanted that for their precious beasts.

Once their gear was unpacked and their swags ready for sleep, Bidgera led the small group to the edge of the muddy soak. The mud flat spread over an area the size of a tennis court. He positioned everyone in a circle and indicated for Riley and McFly to watch and copy he and the others.

Bidgera began to sing in his tribal language. As he sang he tapped two sticks together softly which ceased as the others joined in to sing together. It had no words McFly could understand.

McFly hummed until, with his eyes closed, he was looking at a frog buried deep in the mud. He was instructed by someone to shift his focus, to put his own mind into the frog's mind. The drone of the song pushed him into the dreaming - he became the frog.

McFly felt pleasant sensations which he couldn't interpret, but then he slowly entered a state of perpetual peacefulness and timelessness. His dreaming was of an indescribable sensual beauty. McFly revelled in sensations of being in a womb of joy, love and security. It was a nurturing experience which somehow reminded him of his spirit mother.

During the night they heard the dingoes calling to each other. Riley quietly positioned himself near the camels and sang softly to calm them. He could see a dozen or more dingoes in the starlight. The dingoes were working up the courage to attack the young camel which Roo had borrowed from Bongo, Star.

The cattleman unslung his rifle and stood up. He walked slowly among the frightened camels continuously singing softly to calm them down and soothe their fears. He knew the animals now considered their human owners as their protectors, they trusted Riley to protect them. When morning came the dingoes were gone deciding that despite their hunger it wasn't worth their lives to challenge these humans.

Over breakfast it was decided that McFly would continue his training with his tribesmen. The four desert aboriginal warriors waved their goodbyes and headed back into their country escorting a curious but excited McFly. Their belly's full and their curiosity sated, they told him that they would continue his training the traditional way.

Bidgera laughed as he walked gripping his spears and war boomerangs.

"Hey, Matjuri!" he said loudly, "next time you see a spear flying your way, don't forget to duck!" The four men burst out laughing.

The patrol arrived at the hot springs a few hours later. Everyone had departed for Birdsville except Donna. She was all smiles and couldn't wait to tell Wiram her own big news.

"Well everyone do you want the good news or the bad news?" asked Donna.

Wiram was too tired to play guessing games, he'd had a long walk, so he said, "Come on love, just tell us both at once can't you?"

She looked coyly at him. "Well big boy, Tricia said you gonna be a daddy and we've got a long way to get back to Birdsville by camel." She smiled then laughed when she saw the look on her husband's face.

"Wiram!" cried Nulla before anyone could respond as he stepped forward to shake his big mate's hand. "Congratulations, daddy."

As the other men stepped forward to do the same Wiram hugged his wife. After days of exhausted patrolling he broke down and started to cry. They were all aware that, despite the enormous horrors of the apocalypse, sometimes hope made it through.

Riley looked on and said to no one in particular. "What a crazy holiday this trip turned out to be."

Chapter 23

Negotiations

The commando had more than enough cattle on the property to feed their community. With the absence of humans managing their properties the wildlife had exploded in numbers allowing the Commando access to a variety of game for the pot. The girl's vegetable gardens now provided enough food for the growing population and a barbeque every month was a welcome respite from the heat and boredom of routine.

Growing fresh vegetables wasn't easy though and required careful management. As Fatima liked to tell the teenage boys when they came back for seconds and thirds, *"Sufficient is as good as a feast."*

There was a problem though, there weren't enough starchy grains. Bread requires wheat grain and wheat needs an enormous expanse of productive land to grow. They could never grow enough wheat to make bread in this arid oasis anyway. Sundown's years as a bread scientist came in handy but without basic grains even the berserker didn't have an answer. The Australian desert produces edible grass seeds but they were tiny and few in number. These seeds were treasured as coffee substitutes though and added flavour to some of their dishes but they were useless for bread making.

Beer brewing can also use wheat grain. Although malted barley or wheat, plus starch or sugar are the most basic of ingredients for brewing, these were next to impossible to get much to the soldiers dismay.

Soon after their return to the palace, Sergeant Ahmet prepared to go to the Diamantina homestead to meet with the Longreach Crusaders delegation. He was to pass on the news to Shadow and Pedro that McFly was off in the desert undergoing initiations with his new desert brothers.

Sue-Ellen now managed their treaty arrangements with the Longreach Crusaders. As a master of the art of negotiations she knew that with the Crusaders in a full scale battle for survival against their ex-church comrades, the Mount Isa Revelationists, she could twist the Abbess Leonie's arm.

"I'm worried we've made a biscuit deal with the Crusaders - easily made but just as easily broken," said Sundown musing out loud.

"Sundown, I know what I'm doing so just back-off and let me get on with it." Sue-Ellen was polite but firm. The tension between them had grown on their return to the palace and even Pinkie kept well away from them both. Sue-Ellen snapped constantly and Sundown bit back. It was unpleasant for everyone.

Sundown missed his mate Pedro, he could talk to Pedro about anything. But his mate was in Longreach on his honeymoon. Andy was always too busy to chat while Pinkie simply avoided him. He couldn't talk to Vic Thompson because the Colonel was in Alice Springs. Sundown thought to speak with Wiram or Nulla but they were in a nice place with their partners and he didn't want to burden them now they were both going to be fathers. So he kept it all inside where it festered like a pus-filled sore.

"Sue-Ellen, I'm happy to leave it to you but if we don't get them on-side we lose our right wing and an ally. I want our boys up there working with theirs on patrol and you want access to their spy network. How you do that I don't care." He stood up and began pacing which had now become a habit of his.

"Damn it, Sundown, sit down will you," she snapped. "I once thought it cute but now it just makes me annoyed." Sue-Ellen said irritably. Sundown sat back down and a black cloud settled over his normally calm features. Sue-Ellen continued. "I'm the expert here. I've worked intelligence longer than you've baked bread. So just trust me on this, got it, Commander?"

Sundown knew she was close to cracking it with him again so he just nodded. He made to stand up but thought better of it and settled back into his chair.

"Sue-Ellen," Sundown looked at her and felt his demon's disturbed energy. "You know what? I just want us to be friends again. We've not had a nice word for each other since our trip to the Diamantina spring. What's wrong with us?"

She looked at him like he was crazy. "We didn't have a nice word back then either." She stopped what she was about to say and her face softened. "Yeah, I know, Sundown, let's call it a day. I'm bushed and I think we need to step out of this and send Ahmet off with a simpler set of demands. How about I write up our proposal and we'll finish it tonight on the rooftop over wine?" Her smile said more than he expected.

"Hm, yes?" he said slowly as he looked deep into her now bright eyes. "I'd like that but I think Pinkie mightn't." His face broke into a more pleasant version of his self than she'd seen all week.

Sue-Ellen shook her head. "Naughty fellow, I didn't mean that, I meant work. But if you've a nice quiet place maybe we could finish this conversation some other way?" she offered without even thinking of what she was saying.

"Oh boy, we are tired and fanciful aren't we." Sundown shook his head from side to side as the lines on his face formed into a lively smile. "Sue-Ellen, if I had a choice I'd..." he stopped himself going there. "I'd not be able to make that choice." He reached across the table. "Damn, you make me feel something inside that I just don't know what to do with. But let's do that wine thing tonight and get this blasted treaty proposal done. I'm sick of it and this bickering."

Sue-Ellen put her hand on his and looked at him. "Sundown, we both have decisions to make." She bit her lip and Sundown's face reddened. "OK, until tonight then." She got up and walked from the room.

Sundown was left alone, thinking.

The following day Sergeant Ahmet left with the Bushmaster patrol for the Diamantina homestead to meet with the Longreach party. Before he left Sundown called him aside.

"Ahmet, I don't want you to accept anything less than what we've planned. They'll try to negotiate for more, of course, but we've got the upper hand and they'll eventually have no choice but to accept. I'd say they're backs-to-the-wall with the Talons and Ravens Claws so we only have to let them simmer some. If it comes to the boil we'll have everything we want."

Sundown slapped him on the shoulder as he walked the sergeant to his Bushmaster. "Besides, I'd say Shadow and Pedro have been working on them for us." He nodded to the Bushmaster crew and sent them on their way to the Diamantina homestead. He was sure the Longreach delegation would be impressed to see the Bushmaster and the quality of his soldiers. It should help turn the cards in their favour.

Two days later Ahmet was back with a smile on his face and a gift the committee hadn't expected.

"Sir, firstly the fighting around Longreach has been fierce but patchy. The Mount Isa fellas don't quite have the numbers to overwhelm the Crusaders so their delegation managed to get through the blockade surrounding the town. They said the next time might not be so easy. Pedro talked them into keeping their delegates at Longreach because of the fighting so we'll meet at the homestead next fortnight." Ahmet went on but this time his dark, weathered face broke into a broad grin.

"They agreed to 90% of what we asked for this time around. I reckon they're ready to crack. We need to plan who we'll be sending across as their support, it might be soon." Ahmet's face broadened. "Plus we've got a dozen sacks of wheat grain in our wagon, two of barley and two of rice. There's a promise of more where that came from."

Tricia laughed for joy. "You did it! Sue-Ellen, you are a genius and Ahmet, you're my new hero! Now we have access to wheat so we can start baking bread again. We've got rice and barley for our soups and casseroles and I can make genuine shortbread the way my grand-mother taught me, woohoo!"

"A dozen bags of wheat grain should last two hundred people... now let me see..." Andy smiled broadly, "about one day! And Tricia, I'm very sorry but I'm going to confiscate some of that barley for our brewery, the boys need it, it's medicinal."

The news ignited some excited conversation around the table, it was their first win and it bode well for further negotiations with the Longreach Revelationists. It showed their 'goodwill' just like rescuing their girls, sending ambassadors and caring for their wounded sister-hood was Sundown's goodwill.

"We've got them in a corner and they know it. A sweetener like this is a good sign but it could also be a ploy, a game. Sue-Ellen, you're our expert negotiator, what do you think?" asked a bemused Sundown.

"Yes, it's a good sign. Shadow knew what we needed before she left and obviously pushed for them to include the bags of wheat. I would have done the same thing, it's a sweetener for sure. They want our cavalry and we want a secure flank and grains. But we've their church elders, their Apostles or whatever they call them, to deal with as well as the Abbess. I'd like to meet her myself if I could." It was more a question than a statement and she looked around at everyone.

Pinkie spoke first. "Sue-Ellen, I thought you planned to return to Pine Gap and prepare for the Darwin incursion, what's happening there?"

"I do," replied Sue-Ellen looking at Pinkie curiously. She quickly re-alised there was no malice to her question. What an incredible woman, she thought. "My Black Hawk crew found the electrical problem and they've finished repairs. I plan on heading back in a week so a trip across to Longreach is not out of the question, just highly improbable at this stage. I could fly in but I don't want the world to know our secret nor do I want to use it as a people ferry. My Black Hawk is a weapon to be used sparingly. So to answer your question, yes, I am leaving, soon. Although I'd like to go to Longreach and handle the negotiations personally but I don't think it will happen."

"It's a long drive through enemy territory," interrupted Major Lewis now back at the palace while Captain Walker was at the Birdsville outpost. "I'd not recommend it Commander. If you were caught and tortured, and we know they'll do that, we compromise everything we've worked so hard to achieve. I for one vote against a trip to Longreach for you and for any of our other committee and headquarters staff. Shadow, Pedro and McFly should be the last we put at risk."

Sue-Ellen nodded agreement as Andy continued the conversation in the same direction. "As it is we have three staff in Longreach who, if caught, well…" he didn't finish the sentence.

"They have their Priests and we've heard enough about them to know it won't be pretty," said Nulla. "A long range camel patrol can get there from the desert but it'll take a month. I still reckon they need a radio and a Bushmaster is the best thing for that. That way we control all their communications."

"We've talked about that, Nulla. We could do all this by radio but I want to put pressure on them," said Sundown. "Once they agree to our terms we'll do just that, send a squad of four Bushmasters and an ASLAV with its 25 mm cannon to support their defenses. It's going to impact on us but we've now got Sue-Ellen's force to compliment our own. The trip to Darwin may help us get our hands on more armoured cavalry as well."

Major Lewis continued where he had left off. "We need to get more grain across to our palace and I'm thinking a dozen truck loads over the next month and our Bushmaster and cameleers need to be out front patrolling to protect them. If the Mount Isa battalion get wind of what we're up to they'll certainly set up ambushes."

Nulla's head came up, he'd just thought of something. "What about a camel train. We can transport sacks of grain like they did a hundred years ago, by camel. Remember, 'ships of the desert' was what they were called back then."

The committee members nodded thoughtfully to each other.

"Hey, that's a great idea, why didn't I think of that, Nulla. I'm a darn baker so I should be the one coming up with ideas for transporting wheat." Sundown looked at his watch and stood up. "Right, it's getting late, the bar is closed, thanks everyone. Ahmet, I want you to stay back with Louie and Nulla." He thought for a moment. "Sue-Ellen, could you please stay back as well? I want to run through details for the camel patrol and this 'ships of the desert' idea." Turning to Pinkie he added, "and Pinkie, can you ask Fatima if she and Phil can start up that old stone mill they found? I'd like to start baking our first batch of bread in the morning and surprise everyone for breakfast."

Chapter 24

Whiskey Special Operations Patrol

"Cambra, I know you weren't at the Marree Hotel fight itself but Assassin remembers, don't you Assassin?" said Halo sipping one of the competition beers in the open-air lounge overlooking the lagoon.

"Yeah, I remember. Shadow knocked me over and smacked me around. I was as drunk as a skunk. I think we had more fun that day than we'd had in years." Assassin mused over his beer recording his score on the cards Andy handed out with each beer. Gail sat beside him with her own drink and scorecard. Andy and Fat Boy usually provided score cards for the drinkers, they said it was part of their quality control.

"That makes twelve months since our commando was formed, guys. It's also almost a year since we lost Shamus. I spoke to Halo about having a kind of wake for him. I think we could celebrate with a proper whiskey, a celebration whiskey of which I have two boxes in my cellar in Marree." Cambra had Lulu sitting on one side as his assistant taster. Simon and Luke sat across the table with Danni and Donna chatting among themselves.

"We need to do this properly, plan it out and get allies to help." said Beamy starting on his third beer. Lorraine looked up from her scorecard and then at Gail. They knew something was up and were undecided whether they should stay and listen, or escape now so they can say they didn't know about it.

"We've knocked them around so badly they'll run when they see us coming," said Halo leaning back with his empty glass in his hand. He was looking to see if anyone was close enough for him to con into getting another for him. Tricia was still at a meeting so he was stuck.

"Where's me gorgeous missus when I need her?" he mumbled, "anyone else want a fresh beer, there's still Ahmet's brew to get through. His boys reckon theirs has a special wild hops they found in the desert. It had better taste OK or else he'll get scored right down like last time." The group chuckled remembering the outcry when Ahmet's Bushmaster crew bottomed out in the last competition with their 'special herbs and spices' brew.

"Halo, buddy, you do know who's living there now don't you? There's two entire battalions based at Marree, the Stosstruppen and the Deaths Heads. They'll have already drunk it, every drop. Forget it," said Assassin.

Cambra put his beer down and stared at Assassin. "That's even better, we'll steal it right from under their noses." He stood up to get another drink but sat back down again to speak softly but with more passion than he'd shown in ages. "I keep my special selection of port and spirits down there. I bet they are all still there waiting for me."

"Not by yourselves you can't," said Lulu who was listening with interest. "You'll need Chan and Donata, they were both based there."

Donna piped up too, "I can talk to Donata, he rarely talks to anyone but me and Wiram. He's here somewhere, I'll go and get him."

"There's Chan sitting with the Pine Gap spooks. I'll call him over too." Danni began to stand when Cambra spoke.

"Girls, we need to keep this very hush hush. If Sundown or one of the others find out they'll stop us. I would, it's crazy. We have to do this under cover, a covert operation." Cambra looked around at the crowd of relaxed commandos. There must have been fifty or more soldiers and their families on the upper deck of the palace enjoying the beer competition.

"Yes, we'll need our two ex-Revelationists but it needs to be very covert, hidden from everyone including Wiram," he said to his fellow conspirators.

It was at this point that Donna, Gail and Lorraine began "la la la-ing." They had their hands over their ears and stood up.

"Guys, we'll be finishing our beer scores over there while you get on with your secrets." Gail grabbed Donna and Lorraine by the arm and the three started to giggle. "We did not hear this conversation."

Still giggling they joined Pinkie and Sundown's group calling to Tricia as she walked over, "Tricia, dear, you'd better come and join us. The boys are brewing up something you just don't want to know about."

"It could end in a massive fire fight you know." Halo was talking with Chan and Donata over breakfast the following morning. "Louie and Johnny have been running patrols along the Birdsville Track harassing the terrorists for the past few months, I have a feeling they'll be very upset if we just walk in and stir up a hornets nest. Any suggestions?"

Chan looked at Donata, they knew each other from their time in the South Australian Revelationist church.

"I see the Deaths Heads have been resurrected Donata, they're back on top you know." Chan wasn't smiling, he had no love for any of his previous comrades.

Donata nodded. "Yeah, I know. I've prayed the church would see the evil in its approach to enlightenment, but so far they haven't, or won't."

"We have plenty of uniforms so it won't be any trouble to get a few that fit you and Cambra. But you'll need one of us to go with you. We know the proper codes and signs, you don't. Donata and I can sort out a plan if you want." Chan was excited at the prospect of putting one over his ex-Revelationist comrades.

Halo looked at his two friends and said slowly, "If they catch you they'll hand you over to the Priests, they'll torture you," his voice was flat.

"That's life Halo, if I die I die. I'll go with you regardless. My battalion's on guard duty at Marree at the moment. I owe you Sundowners. I know I don't talk much about how I feel but working at the Birdsville outpost with your Commando has helped me put my life into perspective." Lieutenant Donata rubbed his hands over his face and felt the stubble. "I'll start growing my whiskers today."

"No Donata, I'll go," said Chan. "I know the Deaths Heads secret signs. They'll be everywhere, on guard duty or not. Besides, what if our intelligence is wrong, what if the battalions switch about?" The two appeared to want to put themselves in danger.

"Hey, slow down fella's, we'll all go. In fact both of you is better than one of you in situations like this." Halo was thinking there had to be a way to get in without causing suspicion. "We know the Marree Hotel is completely trashed. The last we heard was they pulled down part of it because it was falling on top of people. I'm just worried the secret trap door is covered by bricks 'n stuff."

Donata looked at Halo. "Hey, I've got a plan. We just might get in easier than we expect," he exclaimed.

The other two stared at him. "What are you talking about? They're edgy and trigger happy, they'll react like a kicked hornets nest. We might not even get close to their first guard post."

"I've got an idea." For one of the few times since his capture, Lieutenant Donata smiled.

Over the next few days Donata and Chan took Halo, Assassin Creed and Cambra into the desert on the pretext they were hunting kangaroos. They always came back with something for the table but while hunting they taught their commando mates everything they knew about Deaths Heads and Stosstruppen secret passwords, salutes and handshakes. They schooled them in how to talk like a church goer and how to dress properly in their uniforms.

Assassin dropped in on Major Lewis' intelligence office and got the latest update on who was on guard duty. He also found out which approach was the least guarded. With only days before the anniversary of the Marree Hotel fight the covert whiskey incursion patrol was ready.

They spoke to the originals who offered suggestions but ruled out Beamy because of his wounds.

"That's bullshit, fellas!" Beamy complained as he gingerly eased himself into the jeep on the way out to the sheering shed. "I can still shoot a matchstick at twenty metres. Ask Sundown how good I am if you don't believe me. I held those Ravens Claws back with Lucy and Pellino while you were playing with your goolies in the Diamantina."

Assassin put his arm around his mate's shoulder. "Beamy, no one doubts your courage, you and Arthur are the most decorated of us all. No one else has as many bullet holes as you two. But we can't let you go running around in the dark till Lorraine says so." He looked around as if Lorraine were watching them. "Besides, as Sundown always says, 'Lorraine outranks me'."

Beamy always had a happy disposition and couldn't help but laugh at his mate. "Damn it, I'm an original. I deserve to go. What about Halo's broken hand? He's not going to be much help."

Cambra stopped the jeep and helped Beamy out. "Mate, with your lungs you'll be a liability. We're worried that you might get us all killed or captured if you come." Cambra was good at keeping things black and white even if it hurt. Beamy tried to smile but it turned into a pained frown. His face went red and he flushed with humiliation.

"I'm a fuckin' liability now am I? Well tell Danny and John that!" He stormed off into the shed walking right through the pack of girls waiting to begin their weapons drill.

"You're a prick, Cambra," said Halo. He and Beamy had grown closer since the Mungerannie battle and he now stood up for his mate. "Why'd you have to go and say that for? Beamy's our mate, he stayed back to defend Danny. He had our backs on that fucked up patrol all by himself. He was prepared to die for his friend and you go and tell him he's a damn liability?" Halo was pissed off. "Where were you when we needed you, Cambra?" He stormed off after Beamy.

The tall hotelier had heard worse but this cut deep, deeper than Blondie's brush off. Chan, Assassin and Donata looked at him then walked into the cool of the shed and began to set up their training gear. After a few minutes Cambra walked over.

"What was I supposed to do, tell him he could come?" He was feeling both angry and embarrassed. "I like the guy too you know and that's why I told him - damn it."

"Not like that you shouldn't." Chan was upset too. "Beamy stayed back for Danny when he knew he was dying. He made sure he died with a mate beside him. He could have run but he didn't." He stood up and turned away so no one could see his face contorted with emotion, then he walked off to where he could hear Halo and Beamy talking.

Assassin shook his head at Cambra. "You're good at stirring things up aren't you, mate. Don't worry about it, that's what we like about you. You don't bullshit or pull your punches. Remember Lorraine on the night of the Marree fight? I'm still amazed she wanted to bed you."

Cambra smiled slightly. "Yeah, I am a bit of a prick aren't I."

"Halo won't be a problem, he'll have his pistol, that's all he needs. But Beamy stays home. He is a liability and he could get us killed if he went. Even he knew that. But now it's said we need to move forward and find an ally. We need a Bushmaster or two for back up." Assassin heaved a pile of weapons on his broad shoulders and called for the Girl Guards. They knew that something was up with the boys but were too polite to say anything. "Come on girls, time to do some training."

Chapter 25

Whiskey is Go-go

Their last job was to find an ally and Chan suggested that if they wanted to run a covert operation like this there was only one soldier they needed and that was Sergeant Doff.

When Chan lost his best friend, John, some months ago, he wanted revenge so badly he refused to take leave from the front line. It wasn't because he wanted to kill Revelationists, it was because he wanted to end this madness. All Chan ever wanted was peace, happiness and a reason to live. What he didn't find in the Deaths Head Commando he finally found in Sundown's. Chan was a rare find for Sundown's Commando, he had a pure heart.

It was in Chan's character to take on the most loathsome tasks, to fight harder and longer than anyone else which earned him the respect of the Alice Springs soldiers. Doff and his crew had gladly adopted him as their sniper and terrorist expert.

Sergeant Doff was as excited as the boys when he heard what they wanted to do. He could still remember how he felt when Halo and Beamy first spoke about the Commando's contacts with the Deaths Heads. At that first meeting Halo and Beamy made him feel a man again. For the first time since the apocalypse he was now doing something useful for his country.

A veteran of three war zones, Sergeant Doff thrived on the validation he gained through soldiering. Now his heroes came to him with another opportunity to contribute to his much loved community - Sundown's Commando.

Sergeant Doff immediately procured one of the Stosstruppen transport trucks from the transport pool. Then he found a selection of Longreach Crusaders of Light Battalion uniforms for the boys, bypassing Harry. His own crew enthusiastically looked forward to the coming contact with the Deaths Heads as much as Chan and Doff.

Sergeant Doff's crew were reinforcements, newcomers from Alice Springs except for Lance Corporal Poole. They all had the same burning desire to take down the enemy.

"Halo, you just let me know what you want and it's yours," Doff said at their secret meeting. "But if you'd thought for one second to leave me out of this our friendship would have been over." Halo knew he was serious. Ever since Sergeant Doff lost his Bushmaster and most of his crew to the Revelationist Stosstruppen, Doff had one goal in life, revenge, and everyone knew it.

On the night of the operation the boys drove along a little-used dirt track towards the enemy outpost. Their lights dimmed but purposefully visible to the sentries. Doff's Bushmaster was well behind and silent, waiting. The night was dark, clouds scuttled across the night sky and the wind blew cold through the terrorist-occupied township of Marree.

The boys were anxious, they were about to make contact with the enemy in the middle of nowhere on a mission not sanctioned by their superiors. If things went bad they would be banished from Sundown's Commando and sent to Alice Springs. It was a fate worse than death itself.

"HALT!" yelled a Stosstruppen soldier standing at the sandbagged barricade. He and his companion worked one of the lonely outposts deliberately left untouched, and unchallenged, by Major Lewis's hit and run patrols for a purpose just like this. If the major knew what the boys were doing right now they knew that he would really be pissed.

But Doff didn't care. After losing his crew at the Mungerannie battle he was prepared to take risks and wanted to do as much damage to the enemy as possible. He was still way and above the most experienced fighting NCO the Alice Springs Command had. Every time Lewis tried to pull him off the front line he refused to go. He and Chan worked the hit and run patrols almost non-stop since they had teamed up together.

Lieutenant Donata climbed out of the truck and stretched, his bones cracked loudly in the miserable night wind.

"Who are you? Is that Privates Taylor and Johansson? Don't you boys recognise me?" He stood tall and with his tanned face and moustache it made him quite the imposing officer. "And where's your salute?"

The two young men shone their torches at the lieutenant and then into the truck cabin where they saw more grim-faced soldiers in the Longreach Crusaders of Light Battalion uniforms.

"Is that really you, sir? We heard you were all shot up or captured," asked Taylor lowering his rifle before throwing a smart salute.

"Yes, we were captured and I've escaped now haven't I," replied Donata sarcastically.

"But who are these troops, sir? They don't look like ours," said the private raising his rifle half way up to the door of the truck. He wasn't sure what he should do.

"Jupiter's blazing bolts, private! Get your weapon back down. They're Crusaders from Longreach, show some respect! They were prisoners too and we all escaped together. For once think with your brains and not what's packed in your arse." It was good and the two privates lowered their weapons as they walked over to look inside the truck. As they did Assassin and Chan stepped quietly from out of the darkness and knocked them out.

"I bet they'll be sore and sorry in the morning," said Assassin as he tied their feet and hands then bundled them back into their post. He removed their weapons and boots then checked to make sure they had no communications. It was just as intelligence told them, they were an isolated outpost in the middle of nowhere. While Assassin was checking the post, Chan ran to the back of the truck and flashed the signal for Doff to bring his Bushmaster up.

"They'll be out for a while. If you're ready then let's get into action," Halo called to Doff as he climbed back into their truck and headed towards the Marree Hotel.

Chan guided the Bushmaster into its position just outside the town. He then deployed with the four special forces soldiers in one of the abandoned sheds to watch over the excavation party. Halo had let slip to his mate, Obi-Wan, that he had a secret rendezvous with some bottles of whiskey one night and that was it. Obi-Wan had an open order to participate in any and every operation the commando had going. So he invited himself and his boys along.

Their job was to provide cover when the whiskey team returned with their liquid spoils. Fortune was now using his SAW machine gun while the other three had their M4A1 and MK17's. Anyone who messed with these boys would only do it once.

The whiskey patrol arrived like the wind itself which blew clouds of dust into the eyes of the few drunken terrorists still out and about at the midnight hour. Donata parked the truck right beside the old Marree Hotel and climbed out. Cambra pointed out where they had to dig. The building had collapsed after the terrorists deemed it unsafe and had detonated explosives to bring it down. The hidden cellar door was under a pile of rubble.

"Hey, what are you blokes doing?" called a drunk weaving his way towards them with the wind in his face. He peered at them in the dark, his hand up to keep the dust from his eyes.

"Corporal Spears? I can see you're enjoying the night air. We've just escaped from Sundown's prison and we're excavating his private cellar. We found out he has a case of whiskey stashed in here somewhere and we're going to get it before anyone else does. Want to join us?" explained Lieutenant Donata smoothly.

"Did ya say, whiskey? Why sure, count me in. Here, let me help ya's." The drunken Stosstruppen corporal scrambled towards the boys tripping several times on the many broken bricks on the ground. Cambra and Assassin were lifting a heavy timber beam and immediately put him to work.

Twenty minutes into it they'd uncovered the secret trapdoor in the floor just as a group of female Deaths Heads came around the corner and stopped. Donata noted they had the skull and crossed bones tattooed on their bare forearms. His old animosity flared when he saw them.

"Hi girls, don't I know you?" asked Donata who quickly brightened for their benefit. "Well if it isn't Private Middleton and her friends. Been out partying again I see."

"What are you doing here, Lieutenant?" asked a suspicious and slightly less inebriated girl standing back a little from the others.

Donata didn't hesitate. "We've just escaped from Sundown's prison where we found out there's a secret stash of whiskey in his cellar. We're getting it before anyone else does. Want to join in?"

Three of the girls smiled broadly and laughingly began to help move some of the bricks the boys were still tripping over. Out of the corner of his eye Donata saw Halo put his good left hand into his coat pocket and move behind the truck out of sight of the forth girl.

"You should have reported to the duty officer. We've just come from there and he said nothing about a truck full of escaped prisoners." She backed away from the small crowd, turned then started to run.

Halo stepped from behind the truck with his silenced M9 Beretta and snapped off two rounds which smacked wetly into her back. It was quick and a gust of wind disguised the sounds as he awkwardly dragged her body and hid it under the truck. He nodded to Donata who stood frozen watching for any witnesses to make an appearance.

By now there were two commandos and four terrorists laughing with delight as they opened the trap door. Cambra ordered them to step back while he handed up the two cases of Irish whiskey to Assassin who took them and put them carefully into the back of the truck. Next came the bottles of port and even more whiskey, all very old and very expensive. Cambra handled each bottle fondly, like they were lovers.

When they were done Cambra gave each of the helpers a bottle of his expensive whiskey and told them to run and hide it before anyone saw them. With a giggle and a skip in their step the girls ran off leaving the drunk to weave his way to where-ever he was headed. No one missed the tattle-tale girl.

"Time to get out of here. Come on, into the truck. Halo, you jump in the back and cover our retreat," ordered Cambra now taking charge. They didn't see the four Deaths Heads standing not half a dozen paces away their weapons levelled at them.

"You! You little arse-wipe in the back, I know you. Come out or we'll fire," called one of the Deaths Heads.

Halo's face creased in bewilderment, *'how the hell would they know me?'* he thought.

"Hi, guys," he said as he jumped down from the back of the truck his hand in white plaster and sling. "Do I know you? No, I don't, unless you're a Talon or a Raven's Claw or a Crusader. So who the fuck are you?" He sounded rightly belligerent and resentful.

The man who called him out stood with his pistol raised but now lowered it, a little less sure of himself.

"I'm sure I saw you with the Sundown mob at the mines. Weren't you on of those bastards who planted the booby trap in the Bofors and ammunition truck?" he asked.

"What the hell are you talking about, mate? I'm from Longreach, I'm a Crusader you dickhead. Unless you've been up that way recently then you don't know me and I don't know you. And put that fucking weapon down soldier!" His voice snapped like a pine tree pushed too far in a gale.

"Then what are you doing here in Marree in the middle of the night?" came another voice. "It looks like you're stealing something."

Assassin and Cambra both had their silenced pistols just below the window sill in the truck cabin.

Donata knew he needed to calm things down quickly. "Hey, fellas, calm down. We've just escaped from Sundown's prison camp where we heard there was a stash of whiskey hidden in the cellar of the Marree Hotel. We've found it. If you want a bottle then you can have one but don't tell anyone or we'll lose the lot. We didn't spend months in his stinking prison cells to lose our reward."

Halo had his left hand in his pocket cradling the pistol. His right in the sling helped make their story of escaped prisoners more believable.

Donata added, "I don't know you lot because I've been in his prison but we're legit and if you want a bottle of $200 Irish whiskey, then come and get it." He walked to the back of the truck and pulled out four bottles then walked over to the Deaths Head commandos who lowered their weapons eagerly waiting to take a bottle each.

"Here take one, but by Thor's bare arse keep it secret," Donata said as he handed out the four expensive bottles of whiskey.

Cambra watched in extreme frustration and resentment. He whispered to Assassin beside him.

"That's my bloody whiskey he's handing out like they're bottles of lemonade. Damn it! If anyone else comes along we'll have none left for our celebration." He quickly looked up and down the street where he saw another group of soldiers wandering towards them. Elbowing Assassin in the ribs he said, "Fuck this! Let's do them before Donata gives all of my whiskey away!"

They each carried a M9 Beretta primarily because they'd found a box of them with silencers in the palace tunnels. He lifted his pistol to clear the truck window sill and fired.

Assassin was shocked by Cambra's reaction but recovered quickly and opened fire too. The muffled sounds of bullets hitting bodies and $200 bottles of Irish whiskey smashing on the roadside made Donata jump in fright.

"You bastards!" squeaked Halo trying to keep his voice down. "Donata had this under control!" A moment later there were shouts and the sounds of hurrying feet.

When Halo looked up he saw what must have been the duty officer and three of his guards running towards them.

"You idiots!" he said.

Obi-Wan had just eased his muscled six foot frame quietly into the shadows beside an old shed when he saw activity. It was the head-quarters communications office. The staff were still awake and very active. He knew he'd need to silence them eventually.

"Guys, cover the whiskey patrol, I'll deal with the duty staff," he said as the four others nodded their assent. Before they could move the sounds of movement and then yells came to their ears. Obi-Wan knew it was time for action so he pulled his three foot machete from its scabbard. It was shaped like a mini-sword with a foot-long handle. The blade itself was razor sharp and it made a whipping noise when swung with force. Obi-Wan spun it in his hand like a gunslinger.

The four guards, weapons drawn, had to run past Obi-Wan's shed to get to the whiskey patrol truck. The expert martial-arts swordsman knew he needed to silence them before they woke the whole town-ship and then all hell would break loose. He slowed his breathing and stopped his internal clock - time stood still. For that single moment, just before unleashing his power, Obi-Wan brought his life-force into his dan tien, his centre of power. His vital force then rippled back into present time as he stepped forward into the middle of the pack of run-ning soldiers.

With a flick of his wrist Obi-Wan slashed his blade across the first man's throat almost slicing his head from his shoulders. With a fluid follow-through he backhanded with a whipping stroke across the sec-ond soldiers face which brought a blood curdling scream. The terrorist went down his eyes split in half.

Obi-Wan's next movement was a two-handed chop that took the forearm and pistol from the third soldier who now stood looking at his arm lying on the ground. Obi-Wan kicked him in the chest send-ing the one-armed soldier flying backwards. His forth movement was another backhanded flick of his wrist. It would have decapitated the last Stosstruppen soldier if she hadn't pulled back a split second before the blade spilled her lifeblood onto the dry sands of Marree. The slaughter was over in seconds.

The screams of his second victim, however, woke half the township. Obi-Wan was annoyed, if the terrorist hadn't flinched his bladesmanship would have been perfect. He pulled his silenced pistol and ended the screaming. But now the special forces and Chan had something to do other than watch Obi-Wan's swordplay.

Donata jumped into the truck as Cambra gunned the engine into life. The wind momentarily died down and the sound of the truck backfiring must have woken the other half of the fifteen hundred enemy troops stationed in Marree. Halo was still standing beside the truck when he recognised the Deaths Heads uniforms of the four dead in front of him. In three quick steps he leaped forward to relieve them of their replica SS Nazi knives for his collection.

"Hey, wait for me!" he yelled as he threw his precious loot into the back of the truck. Then, struggling with one foot on the ground and the other over the tailgate, the truck took off. As Cambra accelerated Halo managed to lock the elbow of his injured arm over the backboard then wrestled the rest of his body into the back of the truck.

Assassin turned to Cambra and said drily, "You dickhead." Then he pulled his AK from behind the seat.

The four special forces and Chan opened fire as the first enemy troops came out of their tents. It reminded Chan of an angry meatant's nest as half asleep terrorists came running to find out what was happening. The volume of fire from the special forces covering force confused and terrified their enemy. All they could think of was to run for cover. Most of the terrorists were still waking up and couldn't see where the fire was coming from. A lot didn't even have weapons in their hands or boots on their feet.

"Quick, get in!" screamed Cambra pulling up beside their support squad. The special forces team ran for the back of the truck firing from the hip. Obi-Wan and Pipeline deployed flash-bangs and smoke grenades which added to the terrorist's confusion. Murphy and Fortune continued to lay down heavy fire while they all crammed into the back of the truck. Chan stood picking off any enemy who came towards them with his assault rifle.

The wind had now picked back up as Cambra jammed his foot on the accelerator. The wheels spun sending more dust into the air. The truck kangaroo-hopped struggling to gain momentum as the Bushmaster raced into the town firing its twin mounted 7.62 mm machine guns. The arrival of the armoured vehicle made the terrorists think it was a full scale night attack causing most to run away to hide in the desert scrub beyond the township.

The wind lifted the dust and mixed it with the smoke to cover their retreat. As they drove back the way they'd come Halo burst out laughing, "I don't believe we just did that!"

"You guys are crazy but we wouldn't have missed this for the world. Meeting you guys has been a whole lot of fun," said Pipeline in his deep baritone voice. Assassin, Cambra and Donata in the front cabin looked at each other wondering what their passengers in the back were laughing about.

Captain Johnny Walker was distracted by a call from Major Lewis as the whiskey patrol walked into the Birdsville HQ.

"Sir, how the hell do we get to Sydney from this bloody place?" he said loud and clear for all to hear in the HQ. "I know he's under a lot of stress, I spoke to him last night, remember?" he paused, listening. "Sorry sir, yes sir, I'll get on to it as soon as I can. Out." He looked up as Doff walked in with Chan, the three Sundown's Commandos and the special forces boys.

"And where the hell have you lot been?" Everyone froze waiting for the storm to break.

"Captain Walker," said Chan pushing Doff out of the way and taking control of the situation. He knew that Captain Walker wouldn't come down hard on him, not on one of Sundown's Commandos and definitely not someone with Chan's credentials and known record of patrols and kills. "We've rescued that Irish whiskey Shamus liked so much. You know, Shamus the original Sundown's Commander?"

Captain Walker was about to explode but stopped himself with some effort. "I heard you silly bastards were up to something but had no idea what it was. So that's it then? A bottle of whiskey?"

"Not a bottle sir, two cases and some extras. We knocked over the Marree barracks and put the fear of God into them. It was a swift and decisive action and the enemy were totally unprepared for us." Chan didn't pause for breath, he needed to get it all out before he lost his confidence. "We caused, perhaps, thirty enemy casualties and we got away without a scratch."

Captain Walker rubbed his face several times, turned and poured himself a strong, over-brewed coffee sitting on the wood stove. He needed to sort out his head before he answered. The coffee was bitter like his mood.

"Right, let me get this straight, Specialist Chan. You requisitioned Bushmaster Charlie, its crew chief and crew..." He looked at the four special forces and the commandos. "Plus this... lot... to rescue a box or two of alcohol?"

Sergeant Doff now gently eased Chan aside, it was time he stepped up. Being only a year younger than Captain Walker and his second in command he spoke clearly. "Captain, it was my idea. I talked the boys into bringing back a box of whiskey from the Marree Hotel to help Sundown's Commando celebrate the mines conflict and Shamus' death. It was my responsibility as senior NCO and crew chief."

Halo stepped in front of Doff holding his plastered hand awkwardly in front of him as he spoke.

"Sorry, Captain Walker, but it was my idea. Sergeant Doff was pressured into it because of me. I thought of it and I organised it..." but before he could finish Cambra pulled on Halo's shoulder dragging him backwards and then stepped to the front.

"That's bullshit, Halo. Johnny, I had two cases of prize Jameson Whiskey hidden in my hotel and wanted it for Shamus' Day. It was my idea, no one else's. If the axe is going to fall then it has to be on my neck. I'm also responsible for using your back door, that was my idea and I put the pressure on everyone to do it." Cambra was now pulled away by Assassin.

"Now that is bullcrap, Cambra. I'm the one who got the intelligence from comm's and I'm the one who pushed for us to use the back door," he said with a conviction that made Johnny Walker look at everyone like they were mad.

"What the hell are you all smoking? You've gone behind my back, Major Lewis' and Sundown's back. You even went behind your friend Wiram's back to drive into Marree, confront two battalions of their best, just to steal a box of whiskey? But even worse you've compromised the back door we've kept under wraps for the past three months?" He smacked his forehead with the palm of his hand.

"I've got Louie on my friggin' arse to plan a rescue mission for Sydney Charlie on the other side of the bloody continent, now you've got our yank mates here acting in an unrecognised, unorganised and unauthorised action... how the hell do I explain this to my superiors?"

Staff Sergeant Obi-Wan stepped forward from the back of the pack. "Captain Walker, Commander Cullen ordered us to participate in any covert action your boys had planned. I'm sure she would be pleased that you organised a hit and run patrol like this which sent a message to the Revelationists that they weren't safe even in their own beds, sir."

No one spoke but all heads slowly turned towards Obi-Wan.

"Well I'll be hog-tied and gagged" muttered Halo looking with admiration at Obi-Wan. "That's exactly what we had planned, wasn't it Captain Walker?"

The captain shook his head. If he thought the Girl Guards were bad this lot were a hundred times worse.

"OK, get out, all of you, piss off out of my sight. Sergeant Doff, you stay behind." Captain Walker now resigned himself to creating some sort of order out of this bloody mess.

"Sir. Johnny, it's my fault, those idiots were going in regardless. You know what Halo's like when he gets a thought in his head, which fortunately isn't too often," said the sergeant to his senior officer.

"Doff, I know you did what you thought was right but you've screwed up big time. You know that I need to inform Vic, Louie and Sundown about this. That back door was left open for a reason and now you've closed it on us. That is going to cost you, not me or Louie or Sundown, you." Walker now poured some rum in his second cup of coffee and offered the same to Doff. Doff took it in his beefy hands and downed it in one go. The drive back from Marree had taken them all night and he was exhausted.

"Johnny, I'll accept any discipline you dish out, and I'll accept all of the consequences. None of my crew had a say in this. For all they knew this was an exercise sanctioned by HQ," he said as he sat with his second rum and ruined coffee.

"Well my good friend, the only way out of a court martial that I can offer you is what Louie told me a moment ago. I've got to send a patrol to Sydney and extract Charlie. He's no longer safe. He's too old to escape by himself and they'll torture the poor old bastard if they catch him. He's an old friend of Pedro's and many of the desert lads, he's been invaluable for our intelligence. So," Captain Johnny Walker looked Doff in the eye, "it looks like you've just volunteered to lead the rescue mission."

Walker leaned forward and shook Doff's hand. "Congratulations. You'll take a squad of misfits to Sydney and bring Charlie back here. I'll talk to Louie, he'll be expecting you this afternoon. Dismissed."

Chapter 26

Shamus Day Celebrations

The first anniversary of the Marree Hotel fight started a week long celebration at the Palace. The first day was a live performance, a play, of the Commando founders meeting in Birdsville then arriving in Marree. It culminated in the fight between the burly riggers and Sundown's group.

Simon and Luke wrote, directed and even played some of the roles themselves. Shadow's part was the star of the play. The play was something that the Commando and their families looked forward to as soon as it was announced.

The beautifully muscled Assassin played himself and all the girls groaned when he took his shirt off. The three nurses were talked into playing their own parts which consisted of squealing and running away. That simple, delightful act, set the tone of the play. The audience couldn't help but laugh riotously at every scene.

Halo played Shamus holding off five drunken riggers and Beamy was a drunken John, the head rigger who started the fight in the first place. Sundown was played by Wiram, who was loudly cheered for his shadow boxing display. Even Arthur got up, he played McFly, falling over Bongo who played Pedro, complete with tin-foil legs. Every time Bongo fell over he called someone a 'boofhead'. The children thought it so funny that 'boofhead' became their favourite word.

Bongo did such a great job that Halo wanted to call him 'Mini Me', but Fat Boy argued that the name was already taken.

But it was Jaina who stole the show. She played Shadow, performing an acrobatic kung fu dance in a very tight t-shirt and very short shorts. Her slim legs and much endowed breasts received a bigger ovation than her acting.

"I wish Pedro was here to see this," said Pinkie in Sundown's ear. "And McFly and Shadow, they'd all be falling over laughing. Those boys of Nulla's have won everyone's hearts. They've done such a superb job haven't they, love?"

"They certainly have, Pinkie, we're so lucky. Lucky to have survived those damn horrific months before Nulla arrived and Vic's boys came across from Alice Springs. I'd hate to have to go back to those early days, it was bloody hell," answered Sundown softly.

Lucy was sitting with Mel and Wilma, she leaned forward and whispered, "Have you noticed that Bongo's got a girlfriend?"

The two older women looked at each other and raised an eyebrow.

"She's one of the girls we captured at the homestead, her name is Denise. I'm glad he's found someone, he was always so depressed. I sort of hoped he might ask me out, but, I guess he just wasn't attracted to me." The mousey haired Lucy shrugged her shoulders wistfully.

Mel and Wilma made polite sounds but when Lucy left to grab something to eat Mel said, "I was going to say, Wilma, *'I don't believe how blind that girl is'*. But I'm not sure if it's deliberate or that anything to do with the heart is completely over that girl's head."

"Lucy's a warrior through and through dear, and love seems to have left her behind. Poor girl. I do feel happy for Bongo though, he's given his all for the Commando, good luck to him," said Wilma, as she drifted off to lose herself in thoughts of young love and remembered days of youth.

Mel studied the small group of Warrior Sisterhood Crusaders and Bongo, watching the performance together.

"Just look at them will you, they're all so happy. Even that Minnie, Denise's cousin, she can hardly walk but she is laughing like everyone else. I think Sundown and Sue-Ellen made a good decision. If the rest of our Longreach friends are as happy to be joined to us like these girls we can rest assured our flank is secure."

Sue-Ellen and her Pine Gap specialists were easily talked into staying for the celebrations. They were now due to return to their home base the day following Shamus Day.

Sundown looked across at the commander of the Pine Gap facility and saw her watching him. He smiled and she smiled back. Seeing her reaction made his demon want to scream from deep inside, it made him extremely uncomfortable on many levels. He tried to focus on the rest of the entertainment but now he couldn't wait to get away and be by himself for a while.

Denise and her Warrior Sisterhood comrades were overwhelmed by the friendship and hospitality they received from everyone. They were treated as heroes after fighting off a company of Ravens Claws by themselves. It was now legend that Captain Martene and her severely depleted platoon successfully engaged and held a superior foe during their night-long retreat.

Blondie recovered slowly, not because of the wound but because of the state of her mind and heart. Cambra avoided her and it caused her to sink into depression. The Tajna Sluzba with the model looks had no desire of being in a proper relationship. But Blondie now felt something she'd not felt before and was now a very confused lady.

Bongo spent every spare minute he had with Denise but his new found lover's recovery was slow. At Halo's insistence Tricia took over supervision of the wounded Warrior Sisterhood girls. He wanted Bongo to get plenty of rest and they both wanted to make sure he had time with his girlfriend. Bongo had sacrificed as much if not more for the commando than anyone else, and Halo, as his friend, wanted to honour that.

Wiram and Nulla decided they needed to go walkabout after the Shamus Day celebrations. It wasn't uncommon for a tribal member, usually the sorcerer or one of the elders of high degree, to have healing abilities. For Roo to find it now with Denise, puzzled them and the two were keen to go bush and find out more.

Both Donna and Glenda were very proud mothers to be. As Glenda spread some of Mel's sauce on her vegetables and meat she said to her partner, "You are so clever aren't you darling?" she teased Nulla. "I wonder what you'll pass on to our little one here." She patted the small bulge of her belly and Nulla put his arm around her protectively.

Riley and Katie saw them and wandered over. They were soon followed by Harry, Wiram, Donna and Bill.

"Wiram, I heard you wanted to go walkabout. I'd better go with you, you'll need brains as well as brawn," Harry said as he sat down at the breakfast table helping himself to the plates of meat and vegetables.

Wiram held Donna who was sitting on his lap. It felt good to get together with his people and share these rare moments of kinship. "Harry, us men folk have a walkabout or two in us before the big push. Yeah, I think it's time we went bush and got back to our roots."

Wiram called Roo and Charlene over and then dragged one of the tables across to fit everyone in.

"Charlene, did you know about Roo's healing powers?" He directed the question to her, wanting her to feel comfortable with the aboriginal crew Roo now openly belonged to.

"I've never heard him talk about it," she replied quizzically. She looked at Roo and made a face to show he was expected to answer Wiram's question.

"I don't really know, Wiram, I never tried before 'cept with my dogs and cats," came his simple answer.

"Maybe we need you to go walkabout with us and find out more. What do you think Charlene?" asked Harry.

"Great idea. I think it would be good for Roo to practice socialising with the girls he helped rescue too." She spoke with some pride as she reached over and held Roo's hand.

"I can do that," Roo said as he started eating.

'Shamus Day' was going to be a long day of celebration.

Sundown was restless. In the early morning hours of Shamus Day he had business to attend to which only a conversation with his mentor could help him with.

"Hi Sundown, laddie 'tis me birthday t'day and I have a gift for you," said the spectral Shamus in his Irish lilt. *"You have a situation brewing my friend and there are two pathways you can go down. Both lead to dishonour and hardship for you and for everyone you love."*

In his meditative state, Sundown listened to his old friend and replied, "I know Shamus. I can't go on like this pulled in two directions. It's killing me and it's killing them."

"Laddie, choose your wife and you retain everyone's respect and honour. You keep the love of your life but you may lose a powerful ally and lover." Shamus stopped to let that sink in. *"Or choose Sue-Ellen and you win the love of an incredible woman who will fight to be everything you ever dreamed of. She will hand you the resources you need to defeat the terrorists. Sadly, you will lose the Commando and everyone will despise you."* Sundown nodded knowing Shamus was right, he was doomed to lose no matter who he chose.

"But all is not lost," continued Shamus. *"There is a third option."* As though hit by a bolt of lightening, Sundown's mind burst into light and he knew what it was.

As he came back to the present he heard Shamus' voice, *"You have excelled with Sun Tzu in arms, but now it is time to succeed with Lao Tzu in love."*

The anniversary of the mines battle, when Shamus was killed, was a more solemn affair. It began with a dawn service to honour those who lost their lives at the start of the apocalypse and those who were killed and wounded in action since.

Halo solemnly brought out the flags for each command. Sundown's Commando showed battle honours for each action: The Mines, Marree, Birdsville, Mungerannie, Coopers Creek, Diamantina and now Marree II. The two girls hand-stitched a replica of the original Alice Springs Command flag. They embroidered the battle honours for Mount Isa, Mungerannie, Coopers Creek and Marree II.

There was one other flag which the girls had spent every spare minute embroidering. It was a beautiful pine tree with sand dune waves. Embroidered were the battle honours for Diamantina and Marree II. Halo called Commander Cullen to come forward and accept their flag.

"To our comrades-in-arms, the Pine Gap special forces and Intelligence staff. Commander Cullen, I would like to present you with this flag to honour the bond between the Pine Gap Intelligence Facility and the Australian Third Army." Halo stopped and put his head down as he tried to remember what he was supposed to say next. He looked up and continued his speech. "And Sundown's Commando too. What I'd really like to say, personally, is that we all deeply appreciate your friendship, your fighting spirit and your coolness under pressure. I think our three forces combined are a fearsome force. The Revelationists are now wishing they'd never started this bloody war in the first place." He smiled broadly then stepped back to allow Lulu and Danni to hand the flag to Sue-Ellen.

"Thank you, Halo, and thank you, Lulu and Danni. What a beautiful flag. I am truly honoured to accept it on behalf of my staff and our joint command. Three flags but one command is what we truly are. United to stand against what is wrong and slowly but steadily setting it right."

Sue-Ellen looked around at the nearly three hundred people desperately listening to every word this now highly respected woman said. "I would like to add what an honour it is to serve with you all. Even though Halo did take my boys into the middle of the Stosstruppen and Deaths Head camp and tried to get them, not only killed, but drunk as well."

If the commando weren't won over already this certainly helped tip them across the divide to admire and respect this woman.

Halo next presented Major Lewis with his replica flag. "Major Lewis and members of the Alice Springs Command, we are brothers and sisters in this fight." Halo pointed towards Commander Cullen and continued. "Together with our Pine Gap siblings," and he deliberately paused to let those smart enough to understand the joke have a laugh, "the Australian Third Army is now in a position to hold their own and eventually take out the terrorists who started this damn apocalypse in the first place." He now called Lulu and Danni to hand the Alice Springs flag to the major.

"Halo, Danni and Lulu, and our growing community, this is a special moment for me and for my command. I know Vic would have loved to have been here to accept this today, but, sadly, he's busy in the Alice. I'll leave you to get on with the rest of your presentations, thanks Halo."

Halo had decided not to give another speech on presenting Sundown's flag because everyone had ribbed him the last time he did it.

Sundown accepted the flag from Lulu and Danni and spoke of the importance of unity to survive the apocalypse and the ongoing struggle against the Revelationists. He also wanted to impress upon everyone the necessity of family and community, of honour, loyalty and respect. His own recent moral struggle had forced him to come to terms with his own situation and this speech helped cement it.

"Members of our fighting forces and our families here today. We don't fight to crush the enemy, we fight to honour ourselves and to make a life for our children and their children." He coughed to clear his throat, it had suddenly gone dry. "We live in the harshest region of Australia but one day we will be leaving this place for somewhere safer. When we do we'll leave knowing we had sacrificed our all for our families and those around us today." Again he cleared his throat which was starting to choke with emotion.

"I clearly remember when Shamus, Pedro and a few of the originals sat around our camp fire at Birdsville. I think it was our first night together. Shamus said several times his goal was to find a place that had plenty of food and water. A place we could easily defend, a place where we could raise our families in safety. I'm sure he'd be pleased with what we've done here at Birdsville and the Christian Palace."

Sundown looked at the people gathered as he struggled to hold back the emotions that wanted to burst out of him. Instead he called, "Lenny! Annie!" When the two children looked up he waved for them to come over, "And bring your little friends."

Up on the make-shift stage climbed a group of kids, grubby and streaked with sweat from playing in the desert sand. They weren't shy or subdued at all but giggled as they waved delightedly to their friends and family in the crowd.

The children proudly held six wriggling puppies. Their mother, Red Dog, watched anxiously from between the children's legs making sure no one dropped her precious babies.

"Sundown's Commando!" he yelled, so everyone could hear, and he pointed to the children. "This, is what we fight for."

Sundown then quickly stepped aside for Halo as he returned to the stage. Halo had fought against it, and argued against it, but he was finally coerced into doing it by his partner, Tricia.

"Sundown's Commando! Australian Third Army! Pine Gap Intelligence Facility and everyone else gathered here today!" he yelled it out like he was Alexander the Great commanding a hundred thousand soldiers.

"Attention!" Three hundred pairs of feet snapped together.

"Dismissed!"

Of course his mates had quietly told everyone to stay where they were. Three hundred pairs of eyes now swung back to Halo who was standing very still, knowing he'd forgotten something important. Then it struck him.

"Oh, shit!" he said quietly to himself. He straightened his back and continued in a loud, proud voice. "May God bless us here today because he has certainly stopped blessing those bastard Revelationists! Now drink up, it's Shamus' Day! Have a bloody great time!"

Shamus Day was also market day for the palace community. Wilma, Fatima, Jenny and Mel ran a competition for home-made condiments and sauces while Fatima doubled up with Phil to show off their prize chickens and roosters. Those who had their own chickens competed for egg size and colour as well as chicken 'deportment', which brought gales of laughter.

There were displays of whip cracking; a rodeo with the roping of the calves from horseback; displays of horsemanship and shooting from the saddle; archery and rifle shooting plus races, games and competitions for the children. Phil and Arthur displayed their wooden furniture and anyone with a skill or talent had a stall and a story to tell. The prizes were pennants embroidered with the simple words 'Shamus Day 1'.

The soldiers held a special competition for each style of weapon: knife throwing, pistol, automatic rifle, unscoped and scoped sniper rifle. It was called 'John's 5 Shots 5 Kills Trophy'. Anyone of the serving soldiers could enter, the top score in all five categories would fight it out in the finals.

The final shoot off was between Chan, Roo, Obi-Wan, Pipeline, Riley and pimply Koala Bob, who, as Pedro would say, "*that young fella wot always asks questions.*"

Sundown was knocked out in the first round. He complained that the only way he could win was if he invoked his demon. But he agreed that would be considered cheating because demons weren't human. For the final shoot out Halo was called upon to be the Master of Ceremonies.

"Ladies and gentlemen, please bare with me, I've had a few drinks judging the beer competition, and a few whiskeys in the whiskey competition." The crowd now gathered around, twenty deep, to listen to their hero. Halo could hold an audience in the palm of his hand whenever he spoke of his beloved Sundown's Commando. He even looked the hero too with his white plastered hand held in a sling at his chest.

"I'm very proud to say that John was my mate. It was on that miserable, rotten day when I teased him about how many kills he'd made.

He said *'two shots two kills and go and get stuffed, Halo!'"* There was laughter but it quickly died down as halo continued. "Then the bastards came at us again and again and each time John fired he'd called out his score - *'three shots three kills' - 'four shots four kills'.* I know I should have stopped pushing him along but we were going to be overrun and every kill kept us alive. We'd almost run out of ammunition and the Revelationist Strosstruppen still outnumbered us twenty to one."

The crowd was quiet, even the kids listened, their eyes wide. "Beamy here, was on the sand wounded and so John handed him his pistol. He told Beamy that when we were overrun he should shoot the first two terrorists then Mugga then himself. It was that sort of situation." He paused for a second wiping at his eyes. "John said he was prepared to die," and Halo's bottom lip began to quiver. "He said that he had lived a good life and death wasn't something he was afraid of." Halo took a deep breath and steadied himself. "He was ready to be with his God and he was at peace with himself."

Beamy was standing next to Halo as his support person, but it was he that needed support as tears dripped freely down his cheeks. He clearly remembered that miserable rotten day too. Lorraine came over and pulled Beamy into her breast as he sobbed in full view of the community that he had given everything to protect.

Tricia stood beside Halo knowing this was going to be tough for him too. She'd been busy in the sick bay telling off drunken teenage soldiers and knew this was going to be but a short respite. There was no way she would let her partner make this speech alone. She knew that this was important to Halo and to their beloved community.

"Then John stood up and fired again. He called out to me," Halo paused and sniffed, his eyes had begun to water some more, "he said to me, *'five shots five kills, Halo'.*" Another pause as he sniffed and wiped his eyes with the back of his sleeve. "We were under a lot of strain. We'd run and fought all night and all day, in the pouring rain too. Our bikes were weighed down by our wounded and now we were down to our last bullets. It was just us, our pistols and if it went on any longer it would have been knives." Halo fought to regain control of his emotions. He wanted to honour his friend, John, by finishing this speech.

"John knew we were down to the wire and so killed the terrorist leaders first then whoever he could get in his sights. But when he went for his sixth kill they were waiting for him."

Halo went quiet, his Adam's Apple jerked up and down several times as he tried to calm himself. He then looked up and raised his beer high into the air and called to the crowd, "In memory of our mate, John, I declare this marksmanship finals begin."

They started with knife throwing and Obi-Wan thrashed everyone with four out of five bullseyes. Next was pistols at twenty five metres which saw Chan quickly move into first place followed by Pipeline and Obi-Wan right behind him. At the third stage shoot-out Koala Bob won the assault rifles at fifty metres but Obi-Wan and Pipeline were now only one point behind. The unscoped rifle was won by an outstanding shoot off between Chan and Roo who scored the most points right out to one thousand metres.

At this stage there were only a few points separating the five competitors. But the scoped rifle shoot had to be done a second time. The cable ties and sticky tape holding Koala Bob's scope to his much loved .303 Lee Enfield had broken.

It looked like it was going to take all afternoon so Halo declared a five round shoot out at one thousand metres. If anyone lost their bits and pieces then that was just tough luck because he had a port competition to get to.

Right at the very end a willy-willy came up blowing clouds of dust which now hid the targets. It even upset Roo's marksmanship. So the five men, all good mates by now, got together and agreed the best thing to do was to draw straws.

It turned out that not only did Koala Bob get to speak to the teenage girls he was so fond of, but he also drew the long straw and won the competition. He was a celebrity that day winning the inaugural, *'John's Five Shots Five Kills Trophy'*.

Tricia and Andy commented on how wonderful the atmosphere was. This was probably because for the first time in twelve months the commando could finally let their hair down.

Around mid afternoon Fat Boy held a 'cook-off' against all comers. By this time everyone was pretty much tanked and had been drinking and partying since dawn and the cook-off was a hoot.

Fat Boy's voice could be heard above all else, his endless stream of jokes kept everyone laughing. He called on Halo to compère the cook-off with him. Bouncing off each other they did such a great job that no one left the lagoon until the competition was done. As it got dark Fat Boy stoked up his barbecue and had it roaring once again for the Commando's evening meal.

After a hectic day of fun everyone returned for their evening entertainment beside the lagoon.

Shamus Day was kept an ordered affair with a proper bar and the drinks were served by bar staff - thanks to Pellino's splendid organisation. It included a beer and fortified wine competition, and now that Andrew was making his own spirits, called 'Palace Whiskey', there was a spirits competition as well.

By the evening meal everyone was pleasantly satiated with food and alcohol. The women who organised the food and entertainment schedules was led by Mel and Wilma. By sunset they were frazzled but so pleased with how things turned out that they gladly handed their aprons over to the younger girls. They then took the rest of the evening off.

Each armoured personnel carrier had their own beer brewers, wine makers and distillers. It seemed there were more alcohol specialists than any other occupation in the Alice Springs Command. The dozen or so Bushmasters and ASLAV's produced a variety of beers, wines, ports and spirits and the competition was fierce. Master brewers, winemakers and distillers abounded and were traded back and forth according to who had what to trade. It wasn't uncommon for a master distiller to run batches through his own still for several of the crews.

"The main problem is fermentables," explained Luke to Danni, leaning on his shoulder and staring lovingly into his eyes. "Beer needs a special yeast which makes alcohol. Every crew has their own secret strain. But the main fermentables are sugar and malt, which is almost impossible to get hold of. I've seen the crews use potato peelings, sweet potatoes, vegetable scraps, grass seeds and even desert yams."

Luke smiled at Danni's attentive gaze. He had no idea she wasn't listening, she simply revelled in his attention. "If someone let the beer spoil from wild yeasts or mould or bacteria, they'd be in big trouble. These armoured cavalry boys are serious drinkers, just look at Nulla." He finished, closed his eyes and then moved his face close to kiss her gorgeous, ruby-red lips.

The hearts of each crew would stop beating as the judges results were posted up on the brewers competition notice board. By the end of the day almost all reserves of alcohol had been consumed and Andrew was forced to bring up supplies from the palaces underground cellar.

In the end there were winners but the losers argued it was because their distiller or their brewer made the winning drop. It was decided that when they had enough grain from Longreach they would hold a proper competition using decent fermentables.

For the record, the ASLAVS won the spirits competition hands down winning 1st, 2nd and 3rd because they had the master distiller for Angoves of Renmark. He'd won multiple awards for his St Agnes Brandy and explained that his forty year old brandy was worth $750 a bottle. He stated that Cambra's Jameson Whiskey was over-rated.

The beer competition went to Ahmet's Bushmaster crew who'd recently found a sugar stash on one of their forays into the outback. They'd discovered a truck on one of the isolated cattle station miles from anywhere. It was loaded with bags of sugar. They decided it must have been on its way to Mount Isa when its axle broke. Where the owner was no one knew. Once their secret was out they were forced to hand over their supplies to Fat Boy who distributed it to all cavalry crews. It was also a useful addition to he and Andy's brewing supplies.

Andy and Fat Boy's 'Palace Port' won the fortified wine competition, probably because the competition was very thin. Only one bottle of wine was produced because they had no grapes. What sultanas and raisins the palace had went into cakes and desserts.

With the arrival of the bags of grain from Longreach not only did the bread eaters celebrate but there was even greater rejoicing from the drinkers. Wheat grains can be malted for making beer and if they could get their hands on enough barley grain then that would be an added bonus.

Throughout dinner they were entertained by Sundown and Wiram along with half dozen others playing guitar and singing the Commando's much loved songs. *'Eagle Rock'* and *'Stairway to Heaven'* being Shamus' favourites became everyone's favourites that night.

Not once did Nulla call out for a Slim Dusty song, but he was tempted. The musicians did a round-robin taking it in turns so they could all socialise and finish their meals. When one lot was ready to eat they simply passed their instruments to the next set of musicians.

The last event was the *'Shamus Whiskey Raffle'*. Cambra announced the lucky winners after everyone had finished the evening meal. Each winner would get a taste of the famous Jameson Gold Irish Whiskey. There wasn't enough for anyone to get drunk but he promised that it was going to be a lot of fun.

Cambra stood on a wooden box above the crowd and announced loudly, "Laddies and lasses, winners of the hottest contested raffle in the history of the post-apocalypse world." He paused until everyone had stopped cheering then held the Jameson Gold bottle high in the air.

"Here, before you, is the very same Irish whiskey made famous by Shamus, the master strategist of Sundown's Commando. The very same whiskey he drank on the night of the Marree Hotel fight." Cambra started to giggle but with great strength of character forced himself to resume. "It is now history that he spied my two hundred dollar bottle of whiskey, perched high on a shelf in the Marree Hotel bar room. I made sure to put it so high that only my dog could hear its song of joy. Thereupon Shamus placed his hands around the bottle and pulled its precious cork from its top."

With a flourish he pulled the cork from the bottle in his hands. "Next, he placed the contents of the bottle into his body, like so." He tipped a little into his open mouth. There came a groaned sigh from the assembled whiskey drinkers.

"Whereupon the hotel establishment's handsome owner, myself, came upon him drinking this bottle of very expensive whiskey." Cambra began laughing again. He'd been drinking Andy's spirits with the boys most of the day and was already quite plastered.

"When mine eyes fell upon the bottle in Shamus' hands those same eyes went straight to the top shelf in my hotel bar room. Seeing the gap the bottle was supposed to fill that handsome publican's blood pressure burst like a water pipe." He stopped to catch his breath, wiped the tears from his eyes and composed himself. "Despite the publican's best efforts to wrestle that very expensive bottle of Jameson whiskey from Shamus' hands of steel, not one drop remained."

Cambra now lifted the first winner's tiny crystal cup in his free hand. "And so, as Shamus would say if he were here today, '*cut the bullshit Cambra and get on with it laddie*' so I shall." Thereupon he proceeded to pour drinks for the raffle winners until the bottle was empty.

The evening ended with Beamy's recital of Shamus' last speech given on the eve of the Mines Battle. Shamus was killed in action, the first Sundown's Commando to give his life for their freedom. It was later said there was not a dry eye among the commando when he finished.

Everyone knew that the boys had gone into the Marree camp to retrieve the whiskey but not many knew the outcome of the administrative committee's inquiry.

Cambra was ordered to hand over all proceeds to the committee to be managed by Andrew. The Pine Gap crew were pardoned on account they were in support of the patrol and had been ordered to '*participate in any and every action*' by their commanding officer.

To her credit Sue-Ellen had no inkling of the patrol and was going to rip Obi-Wan another orifice until Sundown asked her not to.

"Sue-Ellen, your boys safeguarded our idiots. They aren't to blame and I'd rather let the responsibility rest on the shoulders of those who are," he said.

Cambra, Halo, Assassin, Chan and Donata were paraded before the committee by Major Lewis.

"What you lot did was beyond belief. Not only did you deliberately hide your activities but your actions placed our entire operations, and thus your community's lives, at risk. You are hereby formally reprimanded and your punishment must be shown to fit your actions.

"Specialist Chan, in light of your excellent performance you will be excused the punishment handed to the others. We understand that your continued exposure to battle stress has contributed to your recklessness. Therefore you are removed from the front line and confined to the palace and the Birdsville outpost to train the new recruits for a period of no less than six months. Dismissed." Chan, his face set and emotionless, saluted, turned on his heel and left the room.

"Lieutenant Donata, your position as a senior and experienced officer in Sundown's Commando was reckless and irresponsible. You are demoted to the rank of corporal. From tomorrow you will assume a support role in the training and management of the new recruits with Specialist Chan, the Home Guard, the Girl Guards and the guard dogs. You will be formally assessed as to whether we deem you suitable for promotion in three months. Dismissed." Corporal Donata saluted the major and marched out of the meeting room.

Major Lewis now called the three originals to stand to attention.

"I won't go into the why's and wherefores for you lot. We know your motives were pure and we also know your performance for the commando has been exemplary. But what you did was set a poor example to the troops and endangered the lives of our entire community. The committee has decided that rather than punish you with menial tasks which may cause resentment in the ranks you will be invited to volunteer in a long range rescue patrol." The three shuffled slightly, they knew what was coming.

"Sergeant Doff has volunteered to command a fighting patrol to rescue Sydney Charley. It is dangerous, it may take a whole year to pull off. It may also be a suicide mission. You will be his first volunteers." He stopped to look at the boys. "I don't need to tell you what the alternative is."

Cambra stepped forward one pace. "Sundown, Major Lewis, members of the committee, we've already decided that we'll go with Sergeant Doff. We would have volunteered regardless."

Sundown now stood up. "Thank you, Cambra. Sergeant Doff is the most experienced and respected fighting NCO in our command. He will need the best and you are our best. This decision wasn't easy for the committee but it was necessary. I believe Sergeant Doff is waiting for you right now. Dismissed."

Chapter 27

Love Rules

Sundown spent Shamus Day trying to show everyone that he was normal. He participated in everything, sharing the highs and the lows of the competitions, like a leader should. He complained when his knife throwing was so awful that he only had one knife stick in the board out of five attempts.

"For crying out loud, Sundown! Throw the bloody thing like a demon will ya!" yelled Halo from the crowd. Sundown looked around and shrugged his shoulders. He threw again but to no avail. By now everyone knew of his berserker demon and prowess with the knife, but without it, he was a mere mortal.

It was all good fun but when he sat down to eat his lunch he felt so alone. Where was Shamus and Pedro his mate and confidante? Pinkie and Andrew were too busy running things behind the scenes and they had no time to talk to him - no one was there for him.

'*Who rescues the rescuer?*' he thought sadly to himself. '*I'm just a miserable, lonely sod who doesn't know who he is sometimes.*' That was until Sue-Ellen brought her plate over to join him.

"Hi Sundown, I heard you missed out on the five by five finals." She stopped, looked at him, and tried again. "You're not in a great place are you?"

It was Sundown's turn to attempt conversation. "I'm sorry, I'm feeling a bit flat and miserable. Pedro's in Longreach with his girlfriend, my missus is working and hasn't any time for me and someone I admire very much is about to leave for her home. There's not much to be happy about."

"I don't believe I'm hearing this from the great Sundown, what's really bothering you?"

He looked up at the sky, there was some cloud cover but it was too thin and high to even suggest rain. As he closed his eyes he asked himself that very question - *'what really is bothering me?'*

He knew the answer but had yet to admit it to himself. "I guess it's life. I've seen too many dead people. I lost my mentor, Shamus, in our first action. He was calm, peaceful, in fact he read me like a book. He read everything like a book."

"I've known people like that, they do make an impression. But there's more, Sundown." She put her hand over his to make him look at her. "There is more and you just won't admit it."

"Yes, you're right, there is more. Shamus told me I had a decision to make. One path leads to honour and loss, the other path leads to dishonour and success. I asked Shamus what I should do and he gave me a glimpse into the future." Sundown stopped, he didn't want to go on, it was too painful.

Sue-Ellen made it easy for him. "Go on, I know the answer but I need to hear it from your lips."

It was difficult and he couldn't look into her eyes any more. "I've got to let you go."

Sue-Ellen bit her lip and shrugged back a tiny sob. "I, I know, Sundown. Pinkie and I had a talk - about you and us. She's an incredible woman that wife of yours. I don't know if you deserve her, but, I guess you do." Now it was Sue-Ellen's turn to look away so Sundown wouldn't see the tears forming in the corners of her eyes. "It was Pinkie who brought it up. I so wanted to talk to her about my feelings for you but I couldn't do it. I didn't want to hurt her, or you, I was frozen, frightened. I didn't want to admit to myself or anyone what I felt or feared. But she was nice, so bloody nice it made me hate myself for being such a coward."

"Pinkie spoke to you about us?" Sundown now looked fully at her, his face went red then white and he didn't quite know what to say or do.

"She told me she was prepared to let you go if I really needed you that badly. She saw what was happening, she's no fool, but she also knew I had Pine Gap and its military resources. The two of us together, well, we could save the world. Pinkie knew that, she knew she couldn't give you the military and intelligence which I have at my finger tips. I guess she also thought that being younger than her I was more attractive to you, but she didn't go there, fortunately."

Sundown felt uncomfortable but he was curious. His demon was just under the surface, listening, it didn't stir and he was grateful.

"Sue-Ellen, I need Pinkie and I need you. But I wasn't able to make a choice. It was Shamus who told me the choice wasn't mine, it was for you and Pinkie to decide my fate."

Sue-Ellen looked sideways at him. "Shamus is dead Sundown, how... no, it doesn't matter, this desert does strange things to people." She tried to smile at him as she continued. "Well, Pinkie and I have made an executive decision. I'll be leaving for Pine Gap tomorrow with my boys." Sundown baulked and was about to say something.

"No, be quiet, I'm not finished. I've had news there's activity down south. The Alpha army under General Himmler are trying to impress the Priests who seem to have taken control over the southern armies. Our spies also tell us that the Revelationist organisation is fracturing up north. The individual cells, armies, are gathering more recruits from their slave classes to protect themselves from each other. Tanner reports that Darwin is about to blow right open. I really need to get organised and I've put it off for too long."

Sundown's strategic brain kicked into life. His eyes lit up and he once again felt life flowing, pushing away the depression he'd felt all day.

"You'll want the girls up and ready? Just give me a list of what, who and when and I'll get it done." His boyish enthusiasm was palpable.

Sue-Ellen was smiling inside at Sundown's rapid change from depression to elation. It reminded her of why she was so attracted to him, he was so much like her Reece.

"I'll get Johnny to speed up the girl's training. He's already had your boys working with the patrols in close quarter assaults with the paintball equipment. Johnny and Wiram want to train all the troops this way." Sundown's face was so animated and alive that Sue-Ellen began to smile and finally she broke into a light laugh.

"What? What's so funny?" he asked, perplexed.

"You, you're so funny. One moment you're in the pits of depression and now you're planning the destruction of the enemy with paintballs." She giggled and his heart fluttered all over again.

"Don't do that, Sue-Ellen. I won't let you leave if you keep on teasing me." Sundown felt alive again. "Amazing, I've been miserable all day and five minutes with you and I'm my old, giddily arrogant self." He felt so alive right now, an enormous weight had lifted from his shoulders.

"Don't get carried away, Sundown." She brought him back to earth. "I'm going home tomorrow with my boys. We've got a war to fight and I'll probably not see you again for some time. I'll miss you, you'll probably miss me too."

"I already miss you, Sue-Ellen. But you're right, back to earth and back to planning. Will I see you tomorrow morning for a brief with our management team? I just want to run a few things past everyone before you go." He squeezed her hand gently, almost intimately. "We're still friends?"

Sue-Ellen lifted her hand from his at last. "Yes, we're still friends but that's all. I love Pinkie, she's special, like you are. Friends help each other, they back each other and they don't betray each other. I'll not betray you or Pinkie."

Sundown nodded, his face swept through several emotions before settling on a grin. "Pinkie spoke to you? Amazing." He nodded absently. "Yes, friends to the end. We'll see this apocalypse through to the end, together."

There was one person who's absence was noticed by several people, Cambra was one. Blondie had stayed inside the palace and didn't participate. She complained it was because of her shoulder but it wasn't that at all.

Her brother was not as attentive as he was when they lived in danger every day of their lives. He was always there for her in Darwin and Mount Isa, running errands for the Tajna Sluzba and the bikie gangs. When they did meet up it was usually on the roof top drinking where everyone wanted her brother's attention.

She was also depressed over her own existence. When Cambra made known his interest in her she had to confront herself, the brutal rapes and assaults throughout her childhood and the life she'd led since. Blondie survived because she didn't care. She'd become a chameleon, she changed herself to suit her environment and no longer knew which parts were hers or someone else's. She couldn't talk to anyone because no one would understand - but then Charlene had entered her life.

It was quite extraordinary she thought. This young lady would just sit and listen and if Blondie wasn't in a mood to talk Charlene would wait. They went for walks and chatted about anything. Blondie admitted she was a hard case and Charlene simply didn't know any different than to listen anyway.

"Blondie, we've both gone to hell and back and the way I see it we need to support each other. Maybe that might be enough," Charlene said on their second or third meeting. *"I'm not a therapist but I always wanted to be one. So here I am fulfilling my dream in the middle of the desert in the middle of the end of the world."*

One day Charlene brought her Kimberly, the Power Rangers doll, to a session. That was the trigger which helped Blondie drop her barriers with Charlene. She stopped dancing around the gentle prodding and probing. Blondie saw Charlene's action figure as herself, a model of perfection in other people's eyes. Did Kimberly think that she was beautiful? Did she think that she was powerful too? Did Kimberly want to be a Power Ranger, an action figure with a perfect body everyone wanted to touch, own and control?

"Charlene, isn't it amazing how you're beautiful but broken in body and I'm beautiful but broken in spirit. Is there any hope for us?" At first Charlene didn't know how to respond until Blondie started to laugh. It was Blondie's first laugh since... it felt like her first real laugh since her father was alive.

"Charlene?" she asked on that change-day. "I think I want a Kimberly of my own. I need to ask Annie if she has a spare doll."

"Let's go and do that now," offered Charlene and together they went to find Annie.

That was the start of their friendship. But today was different. Blondie didn't know Shamus but she did know of him and his influence on Sundown and the Commando. She also missed Pedro. Even though Blondie rarely showed emotion she had a soft spot for Pedro and in her own way, much like Fat Boy, she missed him. Pedro was just Pedro, he didn't want a part of anyone and Blondie respected that.

She was also confused about her feelings for Cambra and she realised that perhaps Charlene could help her. An action figure had put her in touch with her own isolation and she could now face her self-hatred. Perhaps Charlene could put her in touch with something more elusive than that - true love.

Epilogue

"General Himmler, we have our final report ready for you, sir," said Major Daniels handing over a thick folder. Beside him stood Captain Burgess. Both were sweating heavily in the general's office at Alpha Army headquarters, Adelaide.

Colonel Rommel stood up, he'd read the report and was already fuming. He pounded his fist on the table his face livid and the scar on his forehead stood out like a neon sign. "A damn case of whiskey? That's what this was all about? Alcohol?" he yelled.

"Twelve dead and twenty five wounded yet no one in your battalion put a bullet anywhere near the enemy? You are a disgrace!" screamed the general beside him. "It was your Stosstruppen, your watch, not the Deaths Heads at all. I've listened to you making pathetic excuses all blasted year. I wanted results not failure."

Rommel walked up to Major Daniels and shoved his face into that of his junior officer. "You've had one miserable win against Sundown all year, that's all you've had. I've given you command of the two best trained and most respected battalions in Australia - and a truck full of drunks sends your entire command running into the bush! Running like cowards from a bunch of drunks!"

The spittle from the colonel's lips dripped down Daniels' face and he fought the urge to wipe it off. He was a whisker away from being passed to the Priests as it was. Any sign of weakness and it would be a trip down 'torture alley' for him.

"And you, Captain Burgess, if you had been in Marree at the time I'd have you visiting our Priests for reprogramming right now." Turning back to Daniels he continued. "I'm breaking you to captain and promoting Burgess to major as of now. If I hear one more failure from you Daniels, it will be the Priests. Do you understand that?"

At mention of the Priests, Daniels couldn't stop his body's sudden urge to pee and he felt a spreading warmth in his crotch. "I'll not fail you or our Revelationist Church again, sir." He stood stiff then bent forward slightly. He hoped the wet patch at his crotch wouldn't show when he left the general's office.

General Himmler turned to address Major Burgess while dismissing Daniels with a flick of his hand. "Major Burgess, intelligence has brought us some interesting news from Alice Springs which I think we can exploit. You will take command of both the Deaths Head and Stosstruppen Battalions and initiate plans for Operation Vorschlaghammer, immediately. I'm handing extra intelligence staff over to you. I want your proposals for this assault in my office within the week."

Burgess smiled, his years of putting up with Daniels' pettiness was over and he planned to make his ex-boss' life hell every chance he got. For starters he would punish his disgusting perversions. If he acted fast he might catch Daniels in the act and have him passed to the Priests sooner than even he considered possible.

"Thank you, sir! I already have preliminary plans drawn up. I've had them for the past six months but that idiot Daniels withheld permission to pass them on to you." He put the knife in and twisted it a little while he had the chance.

"Marvellous, Burgess, with that fool out of the way I think we may have a chance against the growing threat of this united Sundown's Commando. If you need extra staff just ask. This is top priority Burgess, this is from the top, Reverend Albert himself," said the general puffing out his chest. "I saw him just last week and I'll be visiting him in Darwin in a few weeks time. I want those plans for our sledgehammer operation to take with me and I want them water tight."

The administrative staff thought it curious how Captain Daniels left their office with a wet patch at his groin and a wry smile on his face. For Daniels this was just a hiccup in his path to the top. There remained a few annoying obstacles which would very shortly disappear.

'The fools think they know everything about warfare because they've taken those stupid Nazi names,' he thought to himself. *'The day is fast approaching when they'll plead to be programmed by their own Priests, and I'll be the one to hand them over.'*

Exactly two weeks after the Shamus Day celebrations, General Himmler of the Revelationist Army Alpha, flew to meet with Reverend Albert in Darwin. He didn't know that Pine Gap intelligence had learned of this meeting some time earlier.

Bill, the commando's ace pilot, was helping the mechanics fit his Cessna 172 with twin machine guns and rockets when he heard that the Revelationist helicopter was seen flying north to Darwin – right on time. The thought of taking out the head of the terrorist's Army Alpha made his heart skip a beat. Now they needed to be ready for it's return flight south.

THE END

Dear reader,

We hope you enjoyed reading *Desert Strike*. Please take a moment to leave a review, even if it's a short one. Your opinion is important to us.

Discover more books by Leo Nix at
https://www.nextchapter.pub/authors/leo-nix

Want to know when one of our books is free or discounted? Join the newsletter at http://eepurl.com/bqqB3H

Best regards,
Leo Nix and the Next Chapter Team

The story continues in:

Special Ops

To read the first chapter for free, please head to:
https://www.nextchapter.pub/books/special-ops

Glossary of Australian words

Australian Light Horse – name given to the Australia cavalry in the 1st World War

ASLAV – Australian Light Army Vehicle, armoured cavalry troop carrier with mounted 7.62 mm machine gun and 25 mm cannon.

Billabong – water hole, a lagoon or small lake, often filled with water lilies, fish, crustaceans

Billy – tin to put on the fire to boil water in, for tea making and heating water

Blimey – crikey, strewth, darn, damn

Bloke – man, male, fellow or fella

Bloody – damn or darn

Blowed – confused, no idea, can also mean exhausted (out of breath)

Boofhead – meat head or beef head

Brumbies – wild horses

Bullcrap – bullshit, not true

Bushmaster – six-wheeled cavalry armoured personnel carrier with 7.62 mm machine gun.

Cameleer – someone who rides and cares for camels

Comms – communications, radio operator

Crikey – strewth, blimey, darn, damn

Cut – a tracking term to find tracks by coming at them on an angle

Dab hands – experts, good at what they do

Dingo – Australian wild dog

Fellas – fellows, people

Flaming – bloody, damn, darn

Football – rugby, like gridiron without a helmet

Four wheel drive – SUV's designed for travel in the desert, all four wheels engage for better traction

Fussed – bothered, worried

Gangardi – fictitious tribal group

G'day – good day, hello

Goolies – crown jewels, what hangs between a man's legs

Hot chips – hot French-fries, potato fries

Mate – friend, buddy

Men of high degree – fully initiated aboriginal men with elevated status in their tribe – some would have nangarri, sorcerer or 'medicine men' abilities and training

Mikiri – a hole in the rocks filled with water often shaped by hand to allow entry to collect water

Mob – mobs, a lot of, usually associated with a group of people and of kangaroos

Nangarri – aboriginal medicine man or sorcerer – see also 'men of high degree'

Neddys – horse

On the back foot – uncertain

Outback – the desert country

Reefed – yanked, grabbed and pulled hard and firmly

Salt-pan – salt covered plain, flat as a saucepan, also called salt-flats because it's flat – the desert has many such salt covered plains

Smoked – aboriginal method sometimes used to enter an altered state of consciousness

Soak – a shallow water hole, a spring

Spec – spot, a tiny object

Spew, spewed – vomit, vomited

Stations – property or large farm in outback Australia, some larger than Texas

Steve Waugh – famous Australian cricketer

Stockmen – cattlemen

Stockyards – stock pen or yard where cattle, horses and other animals are collected or trained

Stosstruppen – German for 'storm trooper'

Strewth – damn, darn, crikey, blimey

Stuffed – exhausted

Swags – bed roll, blanket or sleeping bag wrapped in a waterproof canvas

Tajna Sluzba – Revelationist secret service, have a reputation as ruthless killers

Tanked – drunk, also 'half-tanked' nearly drunk

Unit – apartment, small one bedroom room in a motel or hotel, also called a 'flat'

Vorschlaghammer – German for 'sledge hammer'

Walers – horses used in the 1st World War for their quiet, strong and courageous manner

Walkabout – aboriginals would 'go bush' to get back to their roots, sometimes it involved spiritual works as well as for a vacation

Wallaby – small kind of kangaroo

Whacked – hit, smacked

Willy-willy – dust devil, mini desert tornado, whirlwind

Worked a treat – worked well, great, terrific

Yabbies – fresh water crayfish

You've done for me – 'you've killed me' or 'you've got me'

Characters of Desert Strike

Revelationists – Reverends Albert, Mark, Thomas – Revelationist leaders in Darwin and regional Queensland

Revelationist Alpha Army – General Himmler, Colonel Rommel, Major Daniels, Captain Burgess

Stosstruppen Revelationists – Corporal Normy, Dory, Tim, Elias

Longreach Revelationists – Abbess Leonie, Nancy, the Prior, the Twelve Apostles,

Mount Isa Revelationists – Colonel Bartlett, Reverend Thomas

Warrior Sisterhood Battalion of the Longreach Crusaders of Light – Captain Martene, Denise, Minnie,

Pine Gap Intelligence Facility – Commander Sue-Ellen Cullen, Reece (her deceased husband), Tanner (their only son), Soldier of Fortune, Staff Sergeant Ben Kennedy (Obi-Wan), Murphy, Pipeline

Sundown's Commando – Nulla, Andrew (Andy), Pedro, Pellino, Halo, Matty McFly (Matjuri), Chan, Simon, Luke, Arthur (Arty), Assassin Creed (Assassin), Cambra, Wiram (Wirrie), Sundown, Beamy, Bongo, Jaina, Donna, Lucy, Heidi, Shadow, Blondie, Mel, Pinkie, Wilma, Jenny, Jeda, Charlene, Danni, Lulu, Fat Boy, Jason Little (Shrek)

Gangardi Aboriginals – Frank, Bidgera

Alice Springs Command – Major 'Louie' Lewis, Captain 'Johnny' Walker, Koala Bob, Sergeant Doff, Lance Corporal Poole, Slimmy, Kris, Sergeant Ahmet, Sergeant Tobi,

Bike boys – Arthur (Arty), Luke, Simon, Riley, Halo, Assassin Creed, Cambra, Halo, Nulla, Beamy and sometimes Chan

Scouts – Roo, Bongo, Riley

Girl Guards – Lulu, Danni, Heidi, Lucy, Jaina

Children – Lenny, Liam, Danielle (Harry and Jenny), Elle and Harry (Riley and Katie), Annie (Lucy),

Dogs – Dog, Blue Dog, Black Dog, Red Dog and her puppies

Extras – Uncle Wardiri (Donna's aboriginal Grand Uncle), Jarl Horsely (Arkaroola, book 2), Billy (see books 1, 2 and 3), Shamus (books 1, 2, 3),

If you enjoyed my book I would appreciate your review, thanks

To His Coy Mistress – Andrew Marvel (1621-1678)

Had we but world enough, and time,
This coyness, Lady, were no crime
We would sit down and think which way
To walk and pass our long love's day.
Thou by the Indian Ganges' side
Shouldst rubies find: I by the tide
Of Humber would complain. I would
Love you ten years before the Flood,
And you should, if you please, refuse
Till the conversion of the Jews.
My vegetable love should grow
Vaster than empires, and more slow;
A hundred years should go to praise
Thine eyes and on thy forehead gaze;
Two hundred to adore each breast,
But thirty thousand to the rest;
An age at least to every part,
And the last age should show your heart.
For, Lady, you deserve this state,
Nor would I love at lower rate.

But at my back I always hear
Time's wingèd chariot hurrying near;

And yonder all before us lie
Deserts of vast eternity.
Thy beauty shall no more be found,
Nor, in thy marble vault, shall sound
My echoing song; then worms shall try
That long preserved virginity,
And your quaint honour turn to dust,
And into ashes all my lust:
The grave's a fine and private place,
But none, I think, do there embrace.

Now therefore, while the youthful hue
Sits on thy skin like morning dew,
And while thy willing soul transpires
At every pore with instant fires,
Now let us sport us while we may,
And now, like amorous birds of prey,
Rather at once our time devour
Than languish in his slow-chapped power.
Let us roll all our strength and all
Our sweetness up into one ball,
And tear our pleasures with rough strife
Through the iron gates of life:
Thus, though we cannot make our sun
Stand still, yet we will make him run.
https://en.wikipedia.org/wiki/To_His_Coy_Mistress

Desert Strike
ISBN: 978-4-86751-828-1

Published by
Next Chapter
1-60-20 Minami-Otsuka
170-0005 Toshima-Ku, Tokyo
+818035793528
14th July 2021

Lightning Source UK Ltd.
Milton Keynes UK
UKHW010244270721
387818UK00001B/179